ZOMBIE, OHIO
A TALE OF THE UNDEAD

Scott Kenemore

TALOS PRESS

Talos Press books may be purchased in bulk at special discounts for sales promotion, corporate gifts, fund-raising, or educational purposes. Special editions can also be created to specifications. For details, contact the Special Sales Department, Talos Press, 307 West 36th Street, 11th Floor, New York, NY 10018 or info@skyhorse-publishing.com.

Talos Press is an imprint of Skyhorse Publishing, Inc.®, a Delaware corporation.

Visit our website at www.talospress.com.

10 9 8 7 6 5 4 3 2 1

Library of Congress Cataloging-in-Publication Data is available on file.

Paperback ISBN: 978-1-945863-81-3
Ebook ISBN: 978-1-62636-6671

Printed in the United States of America

*For Heather, the Kenemores, the Blissters, the Cougars,
and Mr. T. Banks*

One forgets that one is a dead man conversing with dead men.

—J. L. Borges, *"There are More Things"*

Hello.

I want to eat your brain.
Well, not *your* brain, necessarily. It could be anybody's brain.
I mean, let's be clear . . . Nothing about this is *personal*.
But . . . brains. Yes. I do want to eat brains.
Brains . . .
Braaaaaaaaains . . .

Sorry. You'll have to excuse me. I . . . drift a little bit sometimes.
These days, it just sort of happens, and I can't control it.

Don't let it worry you if I . . . list . . . on occasion. You're still
doing fine, and I'm not losing interest. I'm certainly not feeling
sick. Okay, to be completely honest with you, I do feel a little sick.
But I always feel a little sick. I'll be fine. It's not like I'm going to
die or anything.

I don't think I can.

So—what did you want to know about?
Really?
You're serious? You want to know about *that?*
All right, I'll tell you . . . sure.

Just give me a moment to . . . collect myself.

Revelation

I remember waking up ... or something ... by the side of the road, near a town I would later learn was Gant, Ohio. It was midwinter. My eyes were closed as I came to, but I could tell it was winter. I could smell it.

And I ... I opened my eyes and I saw the sky—a bleak gray and white Midwestern sky—and it was snowing just a little. Light, tentative flakes that drifted down absently.

I was on my back. My legs were crossed awkwardly, one atop the other, and my arms were spread out wide.

I untangled my legs slowly and sat up, pushing myself upward on numb, empty-feeling arms. I looked around and saw the trees and the road—empty winter woods, and a lonely country highway without streetlights. On the other side of the road was a wrecked car, impaled squarely against an old, gnarled buckeye tree that split into a "V" halfway up. One of the front tires on the car was still spinning. The headlights were on, and there was a massive, violent hole in the front windshield, like someone had been thrown through it.

I looked at it, and I looked at me. And I thought that maybe *I* was that someone.

I stood up slowly, feeling like a person who has been asleep for days. Like a patient coming out of anesthesia. Dizzy and light-headed, but also *empty*. A lingering emptiness that felt like it would soon give way—like I was waiting to come back and feel like myself again after a sickness ... get an appetite, and so forth. (Probably, I thought, this was shock, and what awaited me when it wore off was *horrible pain*.)

I took a step. It was okay. Not normal, but I could work with it. I took another. Walking felt like floating. It was awkward, but I could do it. I took another step, and then another.

I looked down at the road. Gray asphalt covered with snow so thin it blew in the wind. The sky above the bare, reddish-brown trees was getting dark. It was a late afternoon in winter.

It was also eerily quiet. No traffic and no people sounds. It felt like Christmas Eve, or some other holiday where everybody is at home. Slowly and carefully, I crossed the road and made my way over to the car. Not because I knew whose car it was—mine or someone else's—or because I wanted anything from it. Rather, I walked toward it because it was *what there was*. The headlights were like a beacon beside the lonely country road in the creeping dusk.

I walked gingerly, like a man with a hangover—trying not to provoke a throb or an ache. I looked myself over as I did. There was a little blood on my hands—a few cuts, but they weren't bad. The rest of my body seemed okay. I wore a jacket, a red-and-black-plaid shirt, and some jeans. The jeans were wet and clingy from snow.

I crept closer to the car.

It was a tiny import—a convertible with its flimsy canvas top raised heroically against the Ohio winter chill (and now ripped apart in several places from the accident). This was the kind of car that wouldn't have an airbag, I thought. The kind of car that invincible-feeling men tend to drive too fast down winter roads. The kind of car that, if you crashed it you were pretty much just going to be fucked (and maybe that was a perverse part of the appeal).

I moved closer, easing my way down the embankment to where the automobile rested. I could hear the radio or a CD playing through the shattered windshield. It was a classic rock song. I'd heard it many times before ("Oh yeah, *that* old number . . ."), and yet I couldn't place the artist or title.

Something about this inability to remember the name of the song really unnerved me. You know, like when you can picture someone's face, but just can't think of his name? What the fuck, right? It's crazy. And it was like that with this classic rock song. It seemed crazy that I couldn't think of it. Insane.

But I *know* this song, I thought to myself. Of course I did . . . Yet hard as I tried, I couldn't name it.

I just couldn't.

Keep in mind that I knew as much then as you do right now about where I was and what was happening to me. (You know more, actually. I didn't even know I was in Ohio, near a small college town called Gant.) Anyhow, that was when it hit me.

Amnesia. This must be amnesia.

I must be the man who went through that windshield, and *this must be amnesia.*

The driver's license was buried deep in the folds of the thick brown wallet I found in the back pocket of my jeans.

The name on the license was Peter Mellor. Though it listed a birth date, I couldn't pin down an age because I couldn't seem to remember what year it was. In the photo, he looked early fortyish, probably of Irish descent, with moppish brown hair and a drinker's redness to his cheeks. There were the beginnings of lines on his brow and circles under his eyes, but the face still had the confident jaw and steely eyes of a healthy man. In the right light, I suppose he might have looked handsome. In the right light . . .

The weight was listed as 175. Looking down at the bulge above my belt, I guessed this was being a bit generous. But was this, was *he* . . . really *me*?

I crept over to one of the car's side-view mirrors and woozily knelt down in front of it. In the dying light, I stared hard at the face it showed me. The visage I beheld looked fatter and more haggard than the one in the picture. The cheeks and nose even redder. The lines crossing the face even deeper.

But, yes. It was the same face. I was . . . apparently . . . Peter Mellor.

And Peter Mellor (said the State of Ohio Department of Motor Vehicles) lived at 313 Wiggum Street, in a place called Gant, Ohio. Zip code 43022. Well, fuck, I thought. Okay. So we've got *that much*. Not a lot, but something to start with.

And then another thought: Wiggum—like the incompetent, round cop on *The Simpsons*. *The Simpsons*—that TV show I like to watch! Yes, it was coming back. But when did I watch it? And where? I couldn't remember, but it seemed I was unable to think of this street name without thinking of the porcine, Edward G. Robinson–sounding policeman each time that I did. They were connected in my mind, now as then. I *was* remembering *some* things, I realized.

I patted myself down and found a cell phone in my right front pocket. I opened it. It felt familiar, like Wiggum Street, but the names saved in the phone's memory did not.

Jeeps.

Sam.

Mo.

Harvey.

I had no clue who these people were or who the phone would call if I clicked on one of their names. For a moment, I thought about dialing 911. (That was the emergency number; I hadn't forgotten that.) But what would I say? Where would I say that I was? I turned the phone off and put it back in my pocket.

Keys, I thought. That's what's missing. The third thing. I should have a wallet, cell phone, and keys. After some looking, I found them in the ignition of the car. I pulled the keys out (which also, finally, killed the radio) and shoved them into my right front pocket, where they felt familiar. At home.

Then, as I stepped back to close the car door, I saw the gun. It was on the floorboard, next to the gas and the brake. Maybe it had been secured when I'd been driving, and had only rattled loose after I'd gone into the tree. Maybe it had been in my pocket and had fallen out in the crash. Or maybe I *always* kept a gun next to the gas and brake pedals.

I stared at it for a long time, like I was trying to figure out what it was. Which was silly, of course, because I knew *exactly* what it was—a loaded revolver with a walnut handle. Cold blue metal. Heavy and new-looking. I had to admit, even then, in my dazed and unsure state, that the thing looked pretty cool.

For a second I wondered, "Am I the kind of guy who always keeps a loaded gun tucked in his car somewhere? One of *those* guys? A dude who has to pack heat when he's just going to the grocery store or picking up the dry cleaning?"

It didn't feel like I was. No, I felt more like the kind of guy who would only carry a gun if he had a reason for it. A *really good* reason. I decided that if I had a good reason to have a gun when I crashed my car into a tree, I probably still had a good reason now. I tucked the gun into my waistband and pulled my shirt down over it.

As I was doing so, I finally heard a sound that was not the snow falling on the winter road or the wind in the trees. It was an approaching engine.

Approaching *fast*.

By the time I looked up from tucking in the gun, it was already whizzing by. An ancient Ford pickup—the driver, an older man in overalls, wild and mean-looking—rocketed down the rural highway past me. A shotgun was propped next to him, and he gripped it with his free hand as he drove. He was speeding—going *very* fast considering the snow, I thought. As he passed (without slowing even slightly), he looked first at the wrecked imported car, and then at me—our eyes meeting for just an instant. His stare was cold and intense. Anxious, too—like he was running from something. Or *to* it.

I turned dumbly and watched the truck as it sped away, the taillights shrinking to ocher balls. I listened as the timeworn engine slowly faded into the distance. Then nothing. Just the snow and the wind in the trees.

That was when I decided I should start walking. Start walking and see what I found—like a hospital, or a clinic—hell, at that point I'd have taken a large-animal vet. Just someone in a white coat to tell me what was wrong with me. Tell me what was happening and who and where I was. I reasoned that if I walked, I might encounter familiar sights that would jog my memory.

Sure, I *could* sit by the car and wait for a passerby who might be inclined to stop, but the shadows were growing long and the temperature had to be dropping. I was still in shock from the wreck—that was why I didn't feel cold, of course—but it had to be 30 degrees out here. I knew I should seek shelter soon. Preferably someplace warm, with people.

Just as I was having that thought, I spied a simple black knit cap stuck to the side of the bifurcated tree, right where the car had hit. Was it mine, I wondered; did it come off my head when I went through the windshield? I walked over and plucked it from the frozen bark. Sure enough, the texture felt familiar. Warm. Comforting.

Pulling the black cap down over my ears (which, I noticed, *were* a little numb), I made my way back to the shoulder of the road, and faced west—presumably the direction from which I had been driving.

Then I did something that zombies have always done, since the beginning of time—something deep and innate which the undead have always been driven to do.

I started walking . . . in search of people.

Kenton College.

A quick search of the Internet will tell you all about it. (They groom a nice Wikipedia page.) It's a small, selective liberal arts school, set atop a hill in rural Ohio. Sizable endowment. Politically liberal, but with token conservatives sprinkled throughout. Trends upper-middle class. (Tuition is obscene. More than most people make in a year.) Its well-manicured campus has beautiful neo-Gothic humanities buildings, ultramodern science and athletic facilities, and dingy but venerable fraternity lodges that lurk in dark places. Kenton also has three or four very famous faculty members. (Or maybe used-to-be-very-famous faculty members.)

When you work there, most days it feels like you're playing for a really good AAA baseball team. Not the big leagues, sure, but you could do a lot worse. Then, other days, when a project goes well or somebody gets a little recognition in the *New York Times,* you feel better about it—like yeah, maybe you *are* in the majors, and even a pennant chase seems possible.

And unless you're a student, the community at Kenton feels almost incestuously insular. Everybody gets to know everybody's business. (It *is,* technically speaking, just a small town in a rural part of the state.) The grounds are a quiet, tranquil place, especially when the students aren't around. For many, it's far *too* quiet.

And that's just how it was as I approached Kenton on that dark and snowy evening. I had been walking west along the shoulder of the two-lane highway for perhaps five minutes, and the sun had nearly set. It was as silent and still as an empty movie set. No traffic passed me, and I saw no one. Then, suddenly, I found myself standing in front of the long drive heading up the hill from the highway to the college. The large Kenton College seal, affixed (somewhat gaudily, I thought) to a boulder at the base of the hill, loomed above me. I walked right up to it.

This seal is normally illuminated, I thought to myself. Lit up by decadently expensive spotlights from below. Even in the middle of the night. Even during holidays and vacations. They *always* keep it lit. (I didn't know how I knew this, but I did.) But it wasn't lit now. Something was wrong. The seal was dark. Almost *everything* was dark. Up the hill, I could see only one or two lights. I knew there should be many more.

Maybe, I thought, up this hill is the way to Wiggum Street and the address where I live. Maybe seeing it will help me remember. I straightened my black knit hat and started slowly up the steep incline toward the college. After a minute of walking, I thought I saw movement in the darkness above me. As I drew closer, I made out the silhouette of a man holding a rifle. He had stopped and was looking at me. Waiting for me.

I kept walking toward him. (What else could I do?)

As I neared the top of the hill, I began to discern the small college town unfolding behind this man. ("Village" might be a better word, actually. Again, see their Wikipedia page. Gant, Ohio: population two thousand—if you count the one thousand five hundred students.) From my position at the edge of the hilltop I could see small, dark houses, humorless administrative-looking buildings, and one or two cars. The entire campus was silent as the grave. Empty, as far as I could tell ... except for this man and his rifle. I drew close enough to make out his face in the growing darkness. He was black, middle-aged, and wore a thick mustache. On the breast of his puffy, blue jacket was emblazoned KENTON COLLEGE SECURITY. There was still a little sun left around the edges of the sky, but he drew a flashlight and shined it right in my face when I got close. Then he lowered it and smiled.

"All right then, Professor Mellor," he said genially. "You keeping it safe out here?"

"Uh, yeah," I said.

I had not spoken since awakening after the accident, and it suddenly seemed my throat was very dry. I could not remember what my voice usually sounded like, but my response to the guard felt guttural and hoarse.

"Good to hear," he said, as if he did not quite believe me. "Professor Puckett, Dr. Bowles, and I—we're keeping the watch on the graveyard tonight. You let us know if you need anything."

For a moment I hesitated.

This man, whoever he was, clearly knew who *I* was. It was enough to make me jealous. Part of me wanted to scream: "Yeah, I need something. I need somebody to tell me who I fucking *am!*" I wanted to shake him by the shoulders until he told me.

But something else told me that this was not the right thing to do. Not now. Not yet. Not until I knew more . . . It was clear— whoever I was and wherever I was—that *something was going on.* Something bad. There was this pervasive . . . *vibe* I was getting from everything around me. And it wasn't a good vibe. It was a profoundly, profoundly nasty one. I had stumbled into the middle of wrongness. Something had *disturbed* this place. This world. I could see it in the guard's eyes. Behind the courtesy and the forced smile, there were other things. Wariness. Weariness. Fear.

And now every part of my psyche told me that I needed to find out what this wrongness was without betraying that I hadn't a clue what was happening.

"Okay, thanks," I told him. "I'll see you later on."

Over the guard's shoulder, I spied a green street sign, just visible in the dying light. It said WIGGUM STREET. What were the chances?

The guard shouldered his weapon and moved on, giving me one final, skeptical glance. I waved at him and made my way over to Wiggum Street.

Professor Mellor.

That was what the guard had called me.

Well then, I thought . . . so I'm a college professor. And being a college professor is good, right? Probably beats being the college janitor. You get jackets with elbow patches and tasteful suspenders and so forth.

What did I teach? I wondered. Did I have tenure? Were my classes popular with the students, or merely something they endured? I thought again about the face I'd seen on Peter Mellor's driver's license, and tried to picture it at a lectern. It wasn't easy to do.

I entered Wiggum Street slowly and cautiously, gingerly creeping deeper and deeper into what I can only call a ghost town. Houses with dark windows. Shuttered, padlocked dormitories. Empty parking lots and empty driveways. My only companions were a pair of stray dogs that trotted about gleefully, like thieves given the run of the town. I suddenly wished I had a flashlight. It was very hard to make out anything, much less the house numbers.

At the very end of the block was a shabby, two-level home with a gambrel roof like a barn. It was one of the only places with any lights on at all. I felt like they had probably been left on absently, and that this might be a typical oversight. A generator hummed fitfully from somewhere inside. As I neared it, I felt increasingly like it was going to be number 313. My house.

I was right.

The crudely scrawled label on the mailbox left no doubt: 313, and underneath that, MELLOR.

I shuffled up to the creaky wooden porch and pulled open the screen door. The smell hit me right away. Home. This little house smelled like home. Whatever it was, the smell said this was where I lived.

I pulled out my wad of keys. I was ready to try them one by one, but the door wasn't locked. The knob turned easily and the door swung open in front of me. I went inside and walked around in the home-smell until I found a light switch. Flicking it on, I realized exactly what the familiar odor was. It was books. Hundreds and hundreds (or possibly thousands and thousands) of books. They were everywhere. Book on tables. Books on chairs. Books stacked into architecturally unsound pillars leaning precariously against walls. Books everywhere. I had been overrun. (Perhaps, I thought, the house had been abandoned to them. The arrangement had the feeling of a surrender. The books had won.)

I walked around turning on lights, now and then tripping over the smaller book stacks. Eventually, I found my way into a kitchen, and located a light switch next to the microwave.

Here, while books still held the upper hand, scotch was making undeniable inroads. Hard- and soft-bound volumes shared space on the kitchen table with empty bottles like opposing chess pieces on a board. Their combat had also spilled over onto the floor, I noted. Bottles with a variety of colorful labels cluttered an enormous recycling bin next to the fridge. (Apparently I wasn't loyal to any single brand.)

Finally, in an upstairs bedroom, I found what I was really looking for. A television.

Maybe some of you, if you're old enough, remember the news coverage following JFK's assassination. Or Martin Luther King's. Maybe some of you remember watching 9/11 unfold on TV over the course of a long, horrible morning, or what the CNN coverage was like during the opening salvos of the Iraq wars.

What I saw—after I made my way (through, yes, a sea of books) to the TV and turned it on—*destroyed that.*

First of all, half of the stations seemed to be down. The rest were channeling a news feed instead of their regular programming. I was planning to look for CNN, but that was hard because everything looked like CNN. Newsreaders, shaky amateur footage, crawls and tickers across the bottom of each screen. Homeland Security terror threat alert levels.

I flipped from station to station. It was a lot to take in.

One channel had a graphic that announced MOVING CADAVERS— WORLDWIDE CRISIS. Beneath the graphic, I seemed to see people in different countries running around in terror. And soldiers. Lots of soldiers with machine guns.

Another channel—just a news crawl. In part, it read: ". . . cadavers are dangerous and may attack. Do not attempt to confront a moving cadaver. Call the FEMA number at the bottom of the screen to make a report if you believe you see a cadaver that is moving. Do not attempt to contain a moving cadaver. Do not attempt to subdue a moving cadaver yourself."

Click.

Another network. This time, a flustered-looking doctor or scientist in a lab coat, seated opposite a newsreader. "Not at all," the scientist was saying. "There is no evidence that the cause of this outbreak, whatever the cause of this outbreak is . . . has had . . . has had any effect on the living. The CDC is loath to call this a disease, you understand, because the living are not affected."

"What about the living who have been attacked by the moving cadavers?" the earnest young newsreader asked. "Aren't they affected?"

The question appeared to flummox the scientist.

"Well, they . . . they . . . ," the scientist stammered. "Of course, they are . . . are going to be affected."

Click.

This time, maybe actually CNN. A sad-looking man with his name and a NASA insignia superimposed under his face sat talking to a familiar-looking host with a salt-and-pepper beard.

"What's this that we've been hearing—first on the Internet, and more and more in recent days in the mainstream media—about Comet 37-15, the so-called 'Arkham Comet,' identified by astronomers in Arkham, Massachusetts? Do you now acknowledge the existence of this comet that may have had a near miss with Earth, our planet passing, it appears, through its tail? Several independent sources outside of NASA have now confirmed this comet's existence."

The camera cut to grainy, black-and-white footage, as if from a website, showing a bright white ball streaming through black space, past stars and dust. Then it cut back to the rumpled NASA spokesman.

"We can, at this point, acknowledge that there was a . . . was a *point* at which this comet did . . . umm . . . did exchange an orbital path with—"

"So the comet *does* exist?" asked the host, forcefully.

The NASA expert looked distant and dead-eyed. He simply nodded—rocking back and forth in his chair.

Click.

". . . some of the most striking footage we've seen—and again, I must caution our younger or more-sensitive viewers that this is graphic—of one of the moving cadavers actually attacking a person. This is . . . this is from a parking-lot security camera at a retailer just outside of Indianapolis."

On the screen, an older woman with a four-pronged cane—apparently lost or disoriented, possibly senile—was absently strolling the length of an empty parking lot. From beneath the camera, a figure emerged and followed after her. It approached the ancient woman slowly, moving only slightly faster than she. The figure had long, white hair and horrible skin. It was also very, very thin. I thought of those "after" pictures of meth addicts. The figure walked funny—as though it were afraid, if it moved too quickly, that it might get distracted or lose focus. The old woman only noticed the figure at the very last moment, when it gripped her throat and easily bit her nose off. The station cut back to the troubled-looking newsreader. I changed the channel again.

Click.

"The federal government has now set up protection zones in virtually all major American cities," said a reporter. "The government invites all citizens who do not feel safe in their homes—especially those in rural areas—to proceed to the nearest protection zone. Citizens requiring transport can call FEMA at the number on your screen. If you would like to volunteer to assist those who need transportation, please call the same number, or go to the FEMA website and click on 'Volunteer.' "

Click.

I switched the TV off and sat down on the bed. For a long time, I just sat there in that dark room, smelling the books and thinking. In a horrible way, it made sense. This was why everything was wrong. Why everyone had a gun. Why no one was in their homes. Probably, it explained why I had been racing my car too fast on a snowy evening—no doubt on my way to one of the aforementioned "containment zones." Perhaps it also explained the unwillingness of my mind to cooperate.

The revelation that dead bodies were, apparently, moving around and attacking people was unthinkable. Enough to break your brain. Enough to make ignorance blissful—even a complete and total ignorance ... like of who and where you were.

Jesus, I thought.

I sat there, on my bed, looking at the black TV screen, until I heard a voice downstairs.

"Pete!?"

" ..."

"Pete, are you still here? Pete!"

I stood up from the bed and made my way to the top of the staircase.

"Yes," I called, in my scratchy, dry-mouthed voice. I clomped down the staircase and was suddenly face-to-face with a man holding a shotgun. The shotgun was enormous and the man was rather small, making their appearance together almost comical. The man looked about my age, though he was balding and a good deal pudgier than me.

"Pete?!" he said, lowering the shotgun.

"Yeah," I said, smiling at this man who was suddenly very familiar-seeming.

"I was over talking to the guys at the graveyard, and Starks told me he saw you come up the hill," he said. "I figured you'd be gone by now."

"I ... forgot something," I answered.

"Is everything okay?" the stranger asked. "Is that *blood* on your hand?"

"Umm, can we sit down somewhere?" I asked. "We should talk."

"*Amnesia?*" the pudgy man said. "You have *fucking amnesia?* Christ, Pete, that's just ... great."

We sat at my kitchen table, amid the battle of books and liquor bottles.

"Just tell me your name," I said. "Please. You feel really, *really* familiar. It's on the tip of my tongue."

"You're serious?" my somewhat diminutive guest answered. He had shouldered his shotgun and was lighting a cigarette.

I nodded solemnly.

"Fine," he said, taking a long, angry drag on his Winston. When he continued, it was in a sarcastic—and also, I noted, affected—tone. "My name is Gottfried Jurgen Horst, PhD. I'm forty-one years old. I'm a physics professor at Kenton College in Gant, Ohio.

I'm also *your* best friend—maybe the only friend of yours left in this town, if you want the truth."

"Sam!" I said, something in my brain firing. "I call you 'Sam'! You work in the big ugly building at the far end of campus, and you have a poster of Wernher von Braun behind your desk!"

"Bingo," he said.

"And this college ... I work here too?"

Sam took a skeptical drag off his cigarette and blew the smoke expertly out of the corner of his mouth. He stared into my eyes, waiting for me to flinch, waiting for anything that would betray this as some sort of sick joke. When nothing appeared, Sam leaned back in his chair and shook his head.

"You son of a bitch," he said slowly. "I ... I don't fucking believe it, Pete. Taking the easy way out like this ... How fucking convenient."

"Look, I'm not lying to you," I insisted.

"I know you're not lying," Sam said flatly. "That's what pisses me off. You lucky *son of a bitch.* You create this world of shit around yourself—thinking only of you, you, you—and then when things get to be too much, you just ... you just have this way of shutting down. Turning off. And now you've turned off your memory. This is typical *you.* Typical Peter Mellor. Tell me, do you really want to know who you are—who Peter Mellor *really* is? Because I can tell you, Pete. Oh yes, I can ..."

"I do," I replied, feeling, now, less than completely sure.

Sam placed his waning cigarette into an empty bottle of scotch, produced another from the pack, and lit it. His free hand went to his chin, and his eyes lingered thoughtfully in the top-right corners of their sockets. There was a pregnant silence as Sam tried (earnestly, it appeared) to figure out exactly where to start.

I, Peter Mellor, was a disappointment.

If anything was clear, it was that.

Once upon a time, I had had promise. Once upon a time, I had appeared to be the very horse upon which to bet. Once upon a time, I had been a bright young academic from whom great, great things were expected. I had earned a PhD in philosophy from Columbia University, specializing in the work of a Frenchman named Maurice Merleau-Ponty. After successful visiting appointments at Williams and Swarthmore, I had accepted a tenure-track position at Kenton. I was smart, capable, and handsome. Some said, very handsome.

In fact, when I'd first arrived, the female faculty members had been quite aflutter over me. In my first few months, I had broken hearts in more than one department. But everyone liked me—professors, students, townies. I got tenure quickly, and the college seemed pleased with me, despite my notorious romantic dalliances.

Then I had slept with a colleague's wife... and it was suddenly not funny anymore.

The couple divorced soon after our brief affair, and before that year was up, the husband—a serious old curmudgeon in the classics department—had hanged himself out of grief. Word spread quickly, and the part I had played became known to everyone. You didn't have to have a PhD to figure it out. By the time the body was interred, all of the faculty, most of the townies, and more than a few students knew that Professor Mellor and his wandering cock had driven an over-serious man to take his own life.

That was when, apparently, I had turned to the bottle. Hard.

"At first, I wondered if you were intentionally punishing yourself with the drinking," Sam said. "Like you were trying to pollute that good-looking physique that had gotten you into so much trouble. Then I thought, no, it's nothing that contrived ... You're just trying not to feel so bad anymore. That's all it is. You hate being here and you hate what people know about you. You hate what you did—and most of all, you hate yourself.

"I thought for a long time you'd leave—which I didn't really want; you're about the only friend I have at this place—but then things started with Vanessa."

"Who is Vanessa ... and why do *you* have no friends?" I asked. "You seem like a nice guy."

"I'll start with me," Sam said, pulling on his smoke. "Do you have any idea what it's like to be single and gay in a place like this? There are exactly *four* gay faculty members at Kenton College, Pete. *Four.* There's me, there's the morbidly obese lesbian who teaches math, and then there's Franklin and Jeremy, the 'perfect couple' in the English department. How I *loathe* Franklin and Jeremy, with their commitment ceremonies and their holiday parties and their coordinated ski outfits. Both tall and blond and wouldn't gain a pound if they ate mashed potatoes every meal for a month!

"So, ahem ... for me, that leaves ... gay students—whom I'm not allowed to date—and miles and miles of redneck farmers until you get to Columbus or Cleveland. It's pretty fucking grim, Pete."

"Ouch," I said. "I see your point."

"But *you* were always kind to me, Peter," he said. "You were there for me. I mean ... you didn't fuck me or anything, but you leant a sympathetic ear. You actually understood what it was like to be an outsider in this place—to feel you didn't fit in. And once—I might as well tell you—we were walking down by the trestle bridge and you were really drunk, and I'd been talking about how being here made me feel like such a shit ... Anyhow, you let me kiss you. It was just out of friendship. I know you don't feel ... *that way* ... about me, but I always appreciated the gesture."

"And so who's Vanessa?" I asked, as my companion lit smoke number three.

Sam smiled wryly, like I'd just asked what "unlimited ice cream" or "a winning lottery ticket" was. His eyes sparkled as he spoke.

"Vanessa is the best thing that's happened to you in a long time," Sam replied. "She's your girlfriend. She teaches at Dennisburg College, a little school down the road a lot like Kenton. You met at the library there, when you went to check out a book. She's divorced and has a couple of daughters. They have a house near the school. I think you were headed there when you crashed your car."

"Ahh," I said.

"Is it totaled, by the way?" Sam asked. "Your car?"

"Umm, I think so," I said. "The windshield's busted out. I didn't try to start it."

"She'll be expecting you—Vanessa will," Sam said. "We should get you there soon, or she'll worry. Maybe seeing her'll help your memory. You'll *want* to remember her."

"Okay," I said.

"I'll drive," Sam assured me. "I know the way."

"Thanks," I said absently. "Just ... one more question, if you don't mind. I was watching TV upstairs, and—"

"Three weeks," Sam said. "It's been going on for about three weeks. I just thank God the students were gone for winter break."

He stood up.

"Let's walk and talk," Sam continued. "I'll tell you all about it— and we'll drive you to Vanessa's—but first ... let's go see the doctor."

We trudged down the freezing, dark road, back toward the central campus buildings. Sam carried his shotgun across his shoulder like a soldier on parade. I still felt the heavy metal of the revolver tucked into my pants.

"At first, nobody knew what was happening," Sam said quietly. "The first pictures were just grainy footage on the Internet. Bodies moving around. Corpses in a morgue with twitching feet. We thought it was a prank or something, but big and coordinated. Some international group like 4chan or Scientology or, you know, shit like that. But it wasn't a prank. And it didn't go away. Just a couple of days after the first Internet videos appeared, it was the lead story on the nightly news. And then everything just started shutting down.

"The government has tried to keep things going for as long as they can. Keep people going to their jobs, kids going to school, businesses delivering goods and services and so forth. The people in the corridors of power talk about how we 'should not let a medical phenomenon create a global economic collapse.' The plan now seems to be to keep the cities protected and running, so things don't shut down completely—they could give fuck-all about what's happening out here in the sticks, mind you—but I don't know how long they can keep it up. Everything feels ... strained. The news is all bad. The Third World countries—the places we Americans buy everything from—are the least equipped to deal with this shit. Every day there are fewer and fewer boats coming in, and fewer docks functional enough to unload anything. Inflation's through the roof, and while they're not calling it this, *habeas corpus* is damn straight suspended."

"Jesus," I said. (I remembered what *habeas corpus* was. Sam was talking about martial law. You could be arrested for no reason.)

"We don't really know why it's happening," Sam continued. "Nobody does. Theories range from radiation to pollution to dust from outer space. But religious officials have responded predictably, as you might imagine. Apparently, every faith tradition has a line or two in their holy book somewhere about the dead rising, if you look hard enough. Now they all want to claim that this proves their particular prophecies true."

"Sounds like a good time to be a Bible salesman," I joked.

Sam only nodded grimly.

"Why is it so desolate here?" I asked.

"Most anybody from Kenton who had a place to go went there," Sam continued. "Those of us who didn't have anybody, or anywhere to go ... Well, we just stayed here on the hill together."

"How many are left here?" I asked.

"Maybe twenty-five," Sam said. "Food's been the biggest problem. There's what's stored in the cafeteria freezers, but they had to replenish that pretty constantly. We're not counting on it to last long. Mostly, we've been subsisting through our relationships with some local farmers and Amish. But the college hill is, you know, a hill—so it's quite defensible. That's the good news. Our only problem has been the graveyard behind the music building. We keep a steady watch, though."

"A *watch?*" I asked in a gravelly voice. "What do you do when you ... I mean, *have you* ... seen anything?"

Sam nodded, and began to light another cigarette.

As we walked across the darkened campus, I felt twinges of familiarity come and go with every other building. There were small cottages, stern academic buildings, a neo-Gothic dining hall that looked like a castle. At times, I would sense a strong association with a particular building or house, but I was never able to say exactly what it was.

"You can kill them," Sam said. "All you have to do is destroy the head—blow it apart or cut it off. And for some reason, the government isn't telling people this. I think they want to keep the army in charge, but you can't keep a secret with the Internet. So, yeah, you *can* kill them, and everybody pretty much knows it. We've had to kill three so far—two from the graveyard, and one that just walked into town from who-knows-where."

"I saw, on the TV, that they're calling them 'moving cadavers,' " I noted.

"Yeah, well ... ," Sam said, taking a long drag, "remember, that's coming from the same people who want you to call global warming 'climate change' or a barracks full of sleeping soldiers a 'target-rich environment.' Call 'em whatever you want. They are what they are."

"Can I say it?" I asked.

"Sure you can," Sam replied.

"Zombies," I said. "We're under attack by *fucking zombies*. The dead are rising from the grave and eating people! ... they *are* eating people, right?"

"Oh yeah," Sam said.

"*Zombies are fucking eating people!*" I shouted to the quiet Ohio town. My voice echoed across the empty campus.

"Feel better?" Sam asked.

"Not at all," I told him.

"Neither did any of us," responded Sam. "It's like ... It's like war or something—not that I've ever been to war. But all your life you wonder what it'd be like—standing there in the trenches, shooting and getting shot at—and it's kind of interesting and almost romantic in a sick, weird way. Then you get there and you find out: 'Oh, so *this* is what it's like ... It *fucking sucks.*' "

"You've thought about zombies happening before?" I asked him.

"Yeah," he said. "Didn't you ever?"

"I dunno," I told him. "I can't remember."

We turned down a connecting street and passed rows of tiny homes. Their uniform appearance extended beyond their clapboard construction and uninspired architecture. Everything looked shuttered, dark, dead.

"Do you remember any of this?" Sam asked.

I shrugged and shook my head.

"How about my house—the one on the left there?" Sam tried. "The one with the red roof?"

"No," I said. "Hell, I had to use my driver's license just to find *my* house. This is all foreign to me."

We crossed into an area of campus that appeared to be entirely composed of academic buildings. One of them, a large L-shaped structure with prominent columns, was being lit from behind by lights on a stand. I thought it looked like a roadwork site at night, without the pavement or steamrollers. As we neared, I realized that what was being illuminated was a small-town graveyard.

Perhaps a hundred headstones, most of them very old, jutted out of the ground like crooked teeth. Many of the monuments, too, stood at odd angles. Two or three modern mausoleums huddled like bunkers in the graveyard's center. At least one grave looked disturbed, as though something had pushed up and out of it. At the very back, against the far tree line, a row of cameras on tripods pointed back in toward the graves, their power lights shining like rows of red eyes.

In front of the graveyard, three men in heavy coats and winter hats sat together on cheap lawn chairs. Large guns rested at their feet. They chatted quietly and idly, like fishermen on a riverbank. One of them was the guard with whom I had spoken previously. One, a thin and intense-looking man, held a laptop that was plugged into a generator. There was an open case of beer on the ground next to them.

"Do you remember these guys?" Sam asked me softly. "Just be honest."

"No," I said. "I saw the guard before."

"Starks; his name is Starks," Sam whispered. "The one with the laptop is Professor Puckett from the music department. The other man is Dr. Bowles, from campus health services."

"Thanks," I said. "They feel familiar, but I appreciate the refresher."

We drew closer, crunching leaves and frost underfoot.

"How's the hunting, fellas?" Sam called.

The men turned and two of them smiled. Puckett did not look up from his laptop.

"No action just yet," said Starks, the security guard, indicating the motionless graveyard with a sweep of his hand.

"Can we trouble you for a moment, Doc?" Sam said.

Dr. Bowles—an athletic-looking man with a round face and small glasses—nodded and set down his Coors.

"Pete's run his car off the road," Sam said. "He looks fine, but he's having a bit of memory loss. I thought you should take a look. Could be amnesia."

Bowles smiled and wrinkled his nose, as if amused by this amateur diagnosis.

"Memory loss, huh?" Bowles said, rising a little unevenly. (I saw that there were more than a few empty Coors under the chair.)

"Yes," I said seriously. "I hit a tree on my way out of town. I feel basically okay—just got a few cuts on my hands and stuff—but my memory is . . . dodgy. I can't seem to place things."

"Well, you made it back *here*," Bowles said dismissively.

I nodded.

"A little memory loss can happen when you go smacking your head into things," the doctor said. "Here, follow my finger with your eyes."

I watched the tip of his gloved finger as it moved up and down, then left and right.

"Good," he said. "Now do it again without moving your head."

"Oh," I said. "Sorry."

I followed his finger again as he repeated the motions.

"Looks good," he said. "You're probably a little concussed." He gripped my arm, fiddling with my coat around the wrist to take my pulse. Then Professor Puckett dropped his laptop and started shouting at the top of his lungs.

"One in the back!" he called. "One in the back! Behind the Andrews crypt! Quickly—get the light!"

Everyone sprang into action. Puckett picked up a shotgun with one hand and a rusty sledgehammer with the other. He bounded lithely into the field of graves. Lights on stands were hastily moved in the direction of a crypt in the center of the graveyard. Next to me, Sam cocked his shotgun. I drew the blue metal revolver from my trousers. Together, we cautiously followed the other men.

Once the lights were placed near, it was easy to see what the camera had shown Professor Puckett. Behind a large marble crypt reading Andrews, the earth was moving. It was a plain-looking headstone, relatively new. The lettering announced that the inhumed man was named John Gypsum Beard, and that he had died at the age of fifty-six. All five of us crowded around, watching the patch of earth slowly move up and down.

"Beard!" said the doctor, with a laugh. "That old devil! He was the groundskeeper when I started here—used to drink himself insensible every night. I told him it was no way to live, but there was just no getting through to him. You remember Beard, right Starks?"

"Oh yeah," agreed the guard. "He's the one who ran the new mower into the side of the cafeteria. I was surprised they didn't let him go just for that."

"Shhh," said the intense music professor. He turned and made a hand-lowering motion, as if quieting a choir at rehearsal.

Starks rolled his eyes, but fell silent. All we could hear was the shifting of earth and a horrible scratching.

Then—penetrating obscenity!—a ghostly white finger poked its way up through the soil like an evil worm. I started, pointing my gun wildly in the direction of the single wiggling digit.

"Whoa there," said Dr. Bowles. "Not yet, Pete. You've got to wait for the head."

I lowered my weapon and tried to relax. We stood around the grave in a semicircle, stroking our chins thoughtfully like zookeepers watching an animal give birth. We didn't have to wait long. Soon an entire hand was out, grasping gently at the cool winter air. Then a wrist. Then half of a meaty white forearm.

It was hard to believe I was seeing it, but there it was.

"Wow . . . they usually take much longer," the doctor said. "This one is coming along nicely. No complications."

"The trick is to get them when they've just come up," said Puckett, still holding both the sledgehammer and the firearm. "At first, they're clumsy. They'll stumble and fall down a lot, like a newborn horse. But if you let 'em work things out for a little bit—get their sea legs, or whatever—then they get focused. And mean. *That's* when they decide to come after you."

I looked again at the pudgy white limb as it groped the empty air. The wrist bobbed and the fingers pinched, like the hand of a puppeteer who had lost his Punch or Judy. It was almost more comical than ominous. Almost.

Bowles walked away and returned with his half-full Coors.

"I'm impressed with the strength of this one," he said, taking a sip.

"Impressed?" I asked.

"Sure," said the doctor. "He had to go all the way through the coffin, then negotiate six feet of dirt. He's recently deceased, more or less, and modern coffins are heavy and strong."

"The Beard funeral was a charity case, I heard," Puckett responded, swinging his giant hammer like a batter in an on-deck circle. "The college paid for that nice headstone because he was an employee. When it came to the casket, though—something nobody'd see—I heard they gave him the same cardboard box they give *all* the vagrants who die in Knox County."

"Cardboard . . . ," the doctor said, stroking his chin. "Yeah, I could see him getting through that a little easier."

I looked back down. Now the hand was slowly attempting excavation—intentionally moving earth, widening the hole.

"Won't be long now," Starks said. "Let's all move back a little."

We stepped back as a second hand emerged from the grave. It, like the first, began clearing dirt away. The process was interminably slow. (At times, I had the impulse to go over and help the ghostly hands with their work, just to get it over with . . .) Eventually, however, the thing did it on its own, and we began to see the top of a bald pate emerging from the hole.

"Okay," said Puckett, excitedly raising his rifle.

"Wait for it," said the doctor.

We all readied our guns. Sam turned to me. He opened his mouth and winced, as though about to bring up something awkward.

"Peter, why don't you sit this one out," Sam eventually said. "You've never shot at one before, and you've just had a big blow to the head."

The other men looked over at me doubtfully as I stood there with my enormous revolver.

"Oh, okay," I said, lowering the gun. "Sure thing. You guys go on ahead."

"No worries, Pete," said Puckett, who clearly relished what was about to occur. "We got this. We got it *just fine* . . ."

In that instant, a horrible low moan came from the opening grave. It was subterranean and more animal than man, but it was still the moan of something *aware.*

I saw movement. The head struggled to free itself.

"I'm calling it," said Puckett, sighting the emerging pate. "This one is officially fair game."

They all took aim, but did not fire. Two arms awkwardly flailed above the top of a head. (It reminded me of a man trying to put on a turtleneck.) Then, suddenly, the body shifted and the head stuck out all the way up to the mouth. A heavy, flabby face turned toward us. The eyes opened and *saw.* The thing was looking at us. I had just a moment to meet those eyes before they were blown apart by Puckett's gun.

At the moment of impact, the face exploded completely and the head jerked backward violently. Then the other men began to let fly, and the rest of the head began to deteriorate. The noise of the firearms was deafening (although it did not, in any sense of the word, "hurt" my ears). The zombie's arms fell awkwardly, and the body stopped moving. All that was left protruding up from the grave was a jawbone and some spinal cord. The hands flopped once, then ceased all movement.

The men lowered their guns. Puckett picked up the sledgehammer and stalked over to the now-headless cadaver. He regarded the bloody stump thoughtfully, like a painter trying to decide if a canvas required one final brushstroke. Then he hefted the hammer high and struck like a man swinging to ring the bell at a carnival. Blood and brain matter splattered out and up. Part of the frothy spray hit me right in the face.

"Bastards," pronounced Puckett, spitting out the word.

"*Pffft*," I said, wiping blood from my mouth and nose.

"Dammit, Puckett," Sam said. "You got Pete right in the face."

"It's okay," I told him, more startled than disgusted.

"Damn, you got coated," said Starks, looking me over.

"Yeah, you should probably go wash that off," said Bowles, ejecting a shell from his weapon. "Nobody's turned into a zombie from eating zombie blood, but you probably don't want that stuff around your eyes and mouth."

"What the fuck, Puckett?" Sam said, still angry at the music professor.

"Sorry," Puckett said. "I'm just, you know, *making sure.*"

"I'm fine, really," I insisted. "Don't make so much of it."

The doctor handed me a heavy flashlight with plastic sides that glowed.

"The music building's unlocked," he said. "Go into the men's room and have a rinse-off."

"Yeah, then we'll get you over to Vanessa's," Sam said.

"That sounds like a good plan," I told him, and took the flashlight.

So anyhow.

I don't have to tell you that there are moments that change you forever—that blast apart your old world, and leave you trembling and alone in a new one. There are metaphorical doors through which you walk (hardly noticing at the time that they are doors at all) that nonetheless quickly close behind you, forever preventing a return.

There are accidents. There are tragedies. There are ill-considered tattoos and piercings. There are things we replay in our minds thousands of times, thinking of all the ways they could have been avoided or delayed.

But there are also first loves. Moments of self-discovery and moments of bliss. There are religious revelations. There are Eureka! moments in research. There are inspired performances that make you suddenly *know* you want to be a dancer, or a singer, or a didgeridoo player. These also have a way of shattering you and what you used to be, and replacing you with a new version. A "You 2.0."

In my case, one of those important doors—the *most* important door, in fact—turned out to be the one that led to the filthy student men's room in the darkened bowels of the Kenton College music building.

As I shuffled inside that cavernous, 1960s-style washroom and set the heavy plastic flashlight on a metal lip above the sink, my only thought was cleaning zombie goo off my face. The flashlight beam shone straight up, but the glowing plastic sides were bright and gave me a pretty good view of myself in the mirror.

Head to toe, I looked terrible. On a scale of one to ten, I was a .5 and sinking. The skin on my face hung flabbily. It was pale. Sallow. The circles under my eyes looked especially pronounced in the reflected glow of the flashlight. On the upside, there were only a few flecks of gore from the "moving cadaver" on my lips and chin. I turned on the faucet and leaned over to splash water on my face. That was when my hat fell off and I noticed that the top of my head was missing.

There is, frankly, no other way to describe what I saw.

Most of my head, clearly, was still there. My head and forehead were the same as they had always been. But the top was another matter. It had been removed by an almost surgical slice—a clean cut off of the topmost part. It was like a case of male-pattern baldness, except that my "bald spot" was now a "skull and top-of-brain spot."

When I had kneeled down to gaze into the side-view mirror of my wrecked car, I had been very, very close and had only seen my facial features. But now, in this large bathroom mirror, I could see my entire head. And my entire head was not entirely there.

I looked into that bathroom mirror for a long time, studying the ridges in my brain, and thought: "Is *that* the top of my *brain?* That's not the top of *my brain* . . . is it? It can't be. There's no way. But wait—is *that* the top of *my brain?*"

It was. It did not seem possible, but *it was*. Then I wondered: "How? How can I be seeing my own brain? How is that possible?"

It took only a few moments to hit me.

"Maybe I can see my own brain *because I'm dead*."

My hand shot to my throat. It tightened, and then tightened some more. Nothing. No pulse at all. I squeezed as hard as I could. I couldn't even choke myself. That reflex was also gone. No gagging, no matter how hard I gripped.

I tried my wrist next, where the doctor had been about to take my pulse. Once more, nothing. I reached my hand underneath my coat and shirt, feeling desperately for any movement in my chest. I placed my hand over my heart and waited. The answer was the same: Zero beats per minute, with a blood pressure of zero over zero.

What about breathing? It seemed to me that I drew breath—when I spoke, and so forth—but did I *need* to?

There was an easy way to find out. I took a deep breath and held it. Then I clicked the button on the side of the Timex Indiglo on my wrist and the hands became incandescent. I watched the second hand as it made a full circle of the dial, and then another.

When five minutes had passed and I felt nothing, I decided I must be cheating—unconsciously breathing through my nose somehow, or taking little sips of air with my lips. I pinched my nose and mouth closed like a cannonballer jumping into a pool. Still, the hands on the watch moved, and still I felt no impulse to aspirate. How long were you supposed to be able to not breathe, I wondered? How long had that flamboyant magician held his breath in the disappointing television special? I couldn't seem to remember. (But I did remember the disappointing television special, which was kind of cheering in a way ...)

As I neared the fifteen-minute mark, I decided that this was some kind of world record. I was the new champion breath-holder guy. Or else ...

Or else I did not need to breathe.

With a desperate hope that the matter was still somehow unresolved, I took away my hand and drew air into my lungs again. It did not make me feel any better or worse to do so.

No pulse. No sensation. No breathing.

I was dead.

Except, of course, I *wasn't*. I was walking and talking and thinking (to some extent, anyway). I just wasn't remembering things so well. But I *was*. I *existed*. Didn't I?

A line from my training in philosophy came to me: "I think, therefore I am." A Frenchman—not *my* Frenchman, but another one—had said that. I was definitely thinking. So I definitely *was*.

But *what* was I?

Then another line, this time from Arthur Conan Doyle, running something like: "When you have eliminated the impossible, whatever remains, no matter how improbable, must be the truth." (It's funny, you know, what you remember and what you don't. I can remember Conan Doyle, but not the last five presidents. You could bring in a photo of my grandparents right now, and I think the odds would only be about fifty-fifty that I'd recognize them. Other things—poetry, legal boilerplate, advertising jingles—I can sometimes recall with crystal clarity.)

I stood facing that mirror, my mind racing to find other explanations—to find *any* explanation—in which these facts could combine such that I was not a "moving cadaver." Yet there seemed only one solution to the puzzle. When I eliminated all the other possibilities, only one conclusion made any sense. (If being a zombie can be said to "make sense" at all.)

I began to feel like a lawyer with a bum case. The "My client's not a zombie" scenario felt less and less plausible. The evidence against him was mounting with each passing moment. It was my job to defend him, but Christ, he looked culpable.

Since I had awakened from the accident, I had not felt any pain. I had not felt hunger or thirst. I had not felt tired. And (as the line of empty urinals to my left reminded me) I had certainly not had to go to the bathroom. Add that to not having a pulse and the top of my head being shorn off, and, well, it was hard to find another explanation. Very hard.

After a while, it was impossible.

This conclusion, however, was less devastating than confusing. It was like waking up one day and finding evidence that (despite whatever you did for pay the day before) you're actually a fireman. Terrifyingly, you realize you know almost nothing about fighting fires. You've seen fire trucks before (you always pull over for them), but you have no clue how it works when they actually *get* to the fire. You have a vague inkling that ladders and Dalmatians are involved, but you've only got a stepladder for changing lightbulbs, and your dog's a Corgi who wets himself when it thunders.

But there's the protective yellow suit and fireman's hat staring back at you from the closet, and your name is printed on both.

Zombies killed people and ate them, for heaven's sake! Did I want to eat people? To *kill people?!* I didn't feel as though I did. Eating somebody's brain was not an idea that had ever occurred to me.

But as it happened, I was not to have long to consider my new vocation.

"Pete!"

Outside in the hallway, someone was calling my name.

"Pete, are you there ... ?"

It was Sam. I could hear his heavy footsteps getting closer. I hurriedly replaced my black knit cap and washed the blood from my face.

"Pete," Sam called, very close. He opened the bathroom door right behind me.

"Yo," I said, wiping my cheeks with a paper towel.

"You okay?" he asked. "You were taking a while."

"I'm fine," I said. "Had to make sure I cleaned off real good. That zombie out there was ... gross."

Sam cocked his head a little, as if he found something suspicious. He looked me over closely. For a second, I was sure that he knew. That in the light from the flashlight behind me, he could see through the hat—see the unnatural outline of my sheared scalp. I felt certain I had betrayed my condition.

But then all he said was: "You *really* look like hell, Pete. When we get to Vanessa's, maybe you should take a nap or something."

"Yeah," I said. "Sounds good to me."

I pulled down my hat and followed him out of the bathroom.

Sam and I crossed back over the dark campus, heading for his house. I was in a kind of stunned silence, and struggled to maintain the same chatty curiosity I'd managed just minutes before. I listened to the gravel crunch under my feet as I searched for something to say. I was glad for the darkness, and hoped it concealed any hint Sam might have had as to my status as a member of the walking dead. I nervously adjusted my hat two or three times—then made a point to stop touching it entirely for fear of drawing Sam's attention to my head.

As we neared the red-roofed home that Sam had indicated was his, a pair of expensive-looking blue headlights suddenly appeared in the darkness at the end of the street. A shiny luxury car, jet-black yet positively gleaming in the moonlight, eased gently toward us. Its tinted windows were utterly impenetrable in the darkness. Although the general look of the automobile was sinister, Sam's lips curled into a bemused smile as it approached, and he raised an arm to hail it.

"Who is this?" I asked him.

"Our boss, John Bleckner," Sam said. "We should say hello."

We stepped to the side of the road as the mass of polished steel and chrome pulled to a stop beside us. The passenger-side window slowly lowered, but revealed only the shadowy silhouette of a fat man in a dress shirt, the outline of his neck bulging like a giant dollop of sour cream.

"Gentlemen," said the figure. He addressed us in deep, sonorous tones.

"John, good to see you," Sam said. "You heading out?"

"Indeed I am," said Bleckner. The shadowy man acknowledged my presence with a nod, but did not address me directly.

"Headed north, was it?" Sam asked.

"Yes," Bleckner said. "To my brother-in-law's. The two of you are going to stay here ... in this place?"

"*I* am," Sam answered. "Pete's going to take his chances over at Dennisburg, actually."

"They may have the better football team, but they don't have our hill," Bleckner said. "You sure you don't want to just hop in and come with me?"

For a moment I flinched, afraid that I had been prompted to speak to this man whom I remembered not at all. (Was I jocular with him, as Sam was? Deferent, as to a supervisor? Self-effacing, perhaps?) Before I could reply, Bleckner put the car into drive and began rolling forward. I understood with great relief that he had been joking.

"Take care, you two," Bleckner said, and pulled the luxury car away. The car reached the end of the street and turned right, heading down the college hill.

"Bosses," said Sam. "Even in a zombie apocalypse, they're still dicks."

I sat in the passenger seat of Sam's new Scion xB and looked out the window. He drove down the hill past the still-dark Kenton College welcome sign and out into the freezing Ohio countryside. The snow fell absently, still struggling to accumulate. Sam's heater worked well, but I felt no change in temperature inside the car. Mirroring him, I removed my jacket. The black knit hat stayed on.

Now I had a secret to keep from my friend (who was strangely my new friend and my old friend at the same time). Also, we were going to my girlfriend's house at a neighboring college, about an hour's drive away, and I had no idea how I ought to be acting. Should I seem anxious? Excited? Pleased? It was harder and harder to think about how I ought to behave. I looked out the window at the dark, cold countryside and felt nothing.

Maybe Sam was right. Maybe a nap was in order. I had no idea if I could sleep (I can't), but had the notion that if I let myself shut down for a few minutes, perhaps things would somehow be all right. Before I could find the lever to recline my seat, we passed the wreckage of my car.

"Christ, Pete," Sam said as he slowed. "That looks pretty horrible."

"Uh, yeah," I told him.

"Did you go *through* the windshield?"

"I don't remember," I told him honestly. "But I think yes."

"Clearly totaled," Sam said, speeding up again. "If the cops come up to the college asking, I'll say they can just haul it off. Although something tells me they're not going to get to it for a while."

"Likely not," I agreed.

We drove on.

The countryside surrounding Gant is hoary and wild. There are sections of old-growth forest where it can feel like midnight at noon. There are forgotten train trestles that cross empty riverbeds where water has not flowed for a generation. There are abandoned farms, crumbling silos, and unkempt enclaves of Amish that the rest of the world is never meant to see.

In the right light, these things can look eldritch and terrible. This was the right light.

As we crept along the rural two-lane highways and connecting roads, I said to Sam: "You haven't once suggested I call her— Vanessa. That just occurred to me."

"You can try if you want to," he replied. "Most cell services have been down for a while, and the landlines are going too."

I shrugged and took out the unfamiliar phone.

"I don't see her name," I said, scrolling through the choices.

"Your nickname for her is Jeeps," Sam told me.

"Oh," I said. It was the first choice. But when I pressed call, the phone didn't even ring. Eventually, it flashed a NO SERVICE message.

"Told ya," said Sam.

"Are all the utilities like this?" I asked.

"They come and go," he said. "Water and sewer have been fine. I wouldn't count on trash collection anytime soon, though."

We drove on, and I kept thinking about how *dark* it was. Even along country roads—roads where there are no streetlights or traffic lights to speak of—you could usually count on seeing lights in houses or security lights near farm sheds. On this night, however, there was just *nothing*. It was like everybody had decided to use darkness as a camouflage, or like the countryside itself was hiding. It was so very dark. Only the trees along the sides of the road reached up out of the blackness to greet us.

"I never noticed how much light there was before," I told Sam.

He nodded, but made no answer. It wasn't nice to think about so much dark.

Then, after about twenty minutes, I did see electric lights in the distance as we drew near the intersection of two country highways. A pair of still-functioning streetlights that marked the crossing cast a bright and welcoming illumination. Then, when we got closer, I saw that there was more.

At one corner of this intersection, a long-shuttered gas station sat quietly. Diagonally across from it was a small, bunker-like country bar. The Labatt Blue and Budweiser neon signs were switched off, but a dim light from deeper inside showed that—although the dingy paper sign said CLOSED—there still might be inhabitants

within. Although there was no other traffic to be seen, Sam carefully
slowed the Scion as he prepared to carry us across the intersection.
Then he slowed more, and came to a stop. He put the car into
reverse and we began creeping backward.

"What're you—"

"I think there's something going on behind that bar," Sam said
to me, quiet and intense, like a concerned father. I craned my neck
and tried to see.

"There," Sam said. Then, after a moment, added: "Oh, fuck . . ."

I looked into the darkness. Sam had been right; there was
definitely something going on. I followed his gaze. In the shadows
behind the tiny country tavern, two skeletal figures crouched over
another, lying facedown on the pavement. The crouching figures
were eating the body on the ground, carefully and methodically
pulling flesh from its back.

"Christ," I said. "Should we do something?"

"That guy is already dead—got to be," Sam said.

We sat and watched, unsure of what to do.

I rolled down my window. This seemed to concern Sam. He
looked hard at me, but I just kept pressing the button until it was
entirely down. I could hear the sound of them eating, and it trans-
fixed me. It put a deep, profound longing in my soul. Or perhaps
the longing had always been there, and I had only just noticed it.

What can I compare it to? A symphony? No. It was nothing so
ordered. A couple making love? It *was* exciting, but not in *that* way.
If anything, it made me recall childhood memories of walking to
play tackle football with my friends in the park. Hearing them there
ahead of me, already playing as I approached, and knowing that
soon I would be joining in the game. I could hear the flesh being
pulled from the body. I could hear smacking and chewing and
methodical swallowing down a throat that did not need to breathe.

"Can you turn the car, so we can see them with the headlights?"
I asked intensely.

"What?" Sam said. "You want them to come after us or
something?"

"They won't come after us," I said. "We're safe in here." I had,
of course, no authority to know that this was the case.

"The headlights won't scare them off," Sam said, turning the car.

"I don't want to scare them off," I said. "I want to see them
better."

Sam reluctantly backed up and turned the Scion until the beams
hit the zombies square in their faces. (They looked up, but only for
a second. We were a momentary distraction, like flies at a picnic.
The creatures returned almost instantly to their food.)

I will remember those zombies forever. What a sight! One was an older man, dressed like a trucker in jeans and suspenders. His face was gaunt from rot, but he'd clearly been husky before passing away. While he ate, gore dribbled down his white beard like sloppy Joe. The other zombie was a younger, hale-looking man. In life he might have been a high school quarterback. He wore a dark suit and black shoes—certainly the clothes he had been buried in. The victim beneath the zombies was nearly torn apart, making it almost impossible for me to guess what he (or, I suppose, she) had once been.

I continued to struggle with the sensation awakening as I watched them. What more can I compare it to?

Do you remember your first sexual experience? You do? Then go earlier. Try to think of your first sexual inkling *at all*. The first time it occurred to you that maybe what was between your legs was, kinda, sorta, what it was all about. The first time you understood *why* the adults around you got so quiet and uptight when it came to fucking. Try to remember the moment when you understood why women were coy and men were brutes. Think about how your world changed.

Have you ever been addicted to a drug? Good. Then skip ahead to that part where you were *really* in the throes of it. When you stopped caring whether or not it was fucking up your family or your friends or your body. Go to that point where it was so incredibly good that your mind would find any way to rationalize it. Not that you ever thought doing smack or snorting blow was good for you ... just that it was *acceptable*. And even as your friends left you and your health deteriorated before your eyes, remember how you still found a way to decide that it was *acceptable?* Then think about eating dead people's brains, and think about how good it would have to feel for you to start rationalizing *that*.

Have you ever "found yourself"? Like, have you moved to a new place (maybe Manhattan, New York; maybe Manhattan, Kansas), and thought to yourself: "So *this* is who I am. Shit! So *this* is how I always should have been living."

Have you?

Because it was something like that.

Watching those zombies eat that raw red flesh, I understood that I'd encountered a thing that was going to be important to me for the rest of my days. I understood that I was feeling something that was going to change what and who I was forever.

It *was* me.

All the anger and fear that had filled me as I had looked into my own head in the music building bathroom began, somehow, to dissipate. I felt no fear or shame at all. Any trepidation was replaced by the excitement of being a part of something illicit and exciting, like a conspiracy. There were tinges of glee and delight. I was looking at something that was delightful. I felt delighted. These new feelings helped the hole in my head to "make sense" in some strange, unfathomable way.

At the same time, I had the sense of being overwhelmed. I was not completely ready for these feelings. Not yet. Not all at once. (*But soon,* I felt sure . . . *soon.* Yes. It would come sooner rather than later, I would be able to be a part of it. *This* world would also be *my* world.)

I began to feel a little sick to my stomach—a little pained all over. The sickness of the inchoate. The adolescent stickiness of strange new feelings. The sickness of one who is using new muscles for the first time. (I call it a sickness, but I trust I've made clear that I can in no way become sick.)

By the time Sam pulled the car away, I was shaking with excitement.

"Sorry, Pete," he said, mistaking my vibrations for tremors of terror. "I forgot you hadn't seen them eating before. We've all been inundated with it on TV for going on three weeks now. We're kind of immune."

He pulled the Scion across the empty intersecting highways and we left the zombies alone in the quietly drifting snow.

The village surrounding Dennisburg College looked remarkably like the village surrounding Kenton. Pleasant lawns and well-kept churches and academic buildings. Modest homes for professors. (And what was clearly an art professor's house—structurally like all the others, but painted ten colors and with a bunch of statues and shit out in the yard.) Dogs and cats were the only moving things. Sam had to slow the car as they darted across the road like squirrels. But they weren't squirrels. Many still wore collars and tags. It was clear that quite a few house pets had simply been released by their owners when the zombies had set in.

Sam said: "Not long now. Vanessa lives on the far side of town. Is this familiar to you, Pete? Any of this?"

I looked around at the night-washed buildings. They were utterly alien.

"Ehh, maybe a little," I told him.

"It'll come back," he said reassuringly. "Seeing Vanessa will help you remember. I'm sure of that."

"So here's a question . . . ," I said, clearing my throat. "These zombies . . . Has anybody, like, gotten better from it?"

"Gotten better?" Sam said, looking at me askance.

"Yeah," I said. "Maybe, like, they became a zombie and then they ... got better again? Somehow?"

Sam shook his head.

"Not that *I've* heard," he told me. "I don't think zombies 'get' better. I think they get you—or you get them."

"That's it?" I asked.

"That's it," Sam said.

"What about the government?" I asked. "Aren't they, you know, working on something? A cure. Something to get rid of all the zombies."

"I'm sure that's *all* they're doing these days," Sam said, "but c'mon—nobody expected this. They might know more than we do, but that doesn't mean they know much."

I turned away and put my head back, as though going to sleep, and looked out the window.

"Chin up, Pete," Sam said. "I didn't mean to sound hopeless. We've got the smartest people all around the world dropping whatever they were doing and working on this now. It'll be like Kennedy wanting to go to the moon. It seems far off, but in a few years, they're bound to have something."

I nodded noncommittally, and watched the snow outside.

My girlfriend lived in the woods on the far side of Dennisburg, in a house with a high-peaked roof at the end of a long gravel drive. The drive was decorated with flowerpots and planters on wooden stands. In front of the house, a large bower encrusted with grapevines and dead, frozen spiders shielded the front door from the road. The windows of the home were dark and shuttered, but a light at the doorstep had been left on.

"Does it look like she's home?" Sam asked. I smiled. He was *saying* that the house looked uninhabited, and not really asking me anything.

"Maybe she likes it dark," I told him. "I don't remember."

Sam pulled up close to the house and killed the engine. We looked around carefully before opening the doors. And we brought our guns. I remember thinking: This doesn't feel like a guy going to his girlfriend's house. This feels like we're marines on a drop, or maybe cops responding to a distress call.

"Watch over there," Sam said, gesturing to the woods. "We can't see much over there."

I kept my eyes on the impenetrable, dark row of trees that Sam had indicated, and took a superfluous breath to taste the cold, frosty air. We crept past the creaking grape bower and up the steps to the house. I went to knock, but Sam stopped my arm and pointed to a legal pad under a rock that had been left beside the welcome mat.

"Gotta be for you," he said.

I stooped and picked up the pad. The message—in a woman's handwriting that was usually flowery, but had had its fancy curtailed by haste—read:

Pete,
What the fuck? We waited and waited.
Going up to Kate's place.
V

I handed it to Sam and watched him study it.

"You have any idea where she means?" I asked.

To my great relief, something like recognition crossed Sam's face.

"Yeah, actually," he said, "I think I do. Vanessa has a sister named Kate. Lives on an eco-friendly farm or something, a few miles north of here. You took me there once for a cookout on Labor Day when I didn't have anything else to do. I think I could find it again if I had to."

"Good," I said. "Because you have to. I've got no memory of it at all."

"Yeah," Sam continued. "I mean, it was a few years ago, and it wasn't dark and snowing, but I think I remember the way."

We walked back toward the car.

"Good thing I was so nice to you all these years, eh?" I said. "Sure paying off for me now, isn't—"

I stopped. Dead.

A shadowy figure was lurking underneath the grape bower. It walked like a man with his legs in locks, and slumped forward as if nearly bereft of energy. But it *did* walk—and moan. Neither Sam nor I moved. We let it get a little closer and saw an ugly, flabby face, black with rot. Its eyes rolled, then focused, aware of us. The thing stank, even from a distance. (I didn't have to breathe to get a hint of the stench.) It moaned again and took another step forward. Its arms slowly stretched in our direction. I instinctively took the blue revolver from my pants and raised it at the lumbering hulk.

"Wait," said Sam.

"But it's a zombie," I told him.

"Look how slowly it moves, though," he whispered. "I don't think we need to shoot this one. Plus, we might hit the car."

He was right. It was a clear shot through the zombie into the hood of the shiny, new Scion.

"What, then?" I said. (I was also whispering, although I wondered why. Clearly, the thing was already moving toward us. Or, now that I looked more closely, was it only moving toward Sam?)

"Let's just go around it," Sam said. "We'll run in a wide arc out past the bower and around to the car. No way it'll catch us."

The figure took another step. It was still hard to see, but parts of it looked heavy and fat. I started to think they were breasts, and that this had been a woman. Massive rolls of flesh swayed as it walked. I began to reckon that I liked our chances, zombie or not. This person had been no great sprinter in life, and zombification would not have improved that trait.

"Okay," I said. "You go first."

My pudgy companion hitched up his pants a little, and began creeping forward like an animal stalking prey. When we drew closer to the bower, he quickly accelerated into a run, arcing wide around it. I stayed on his tail.

As soon as we started running, I saw that Sam had been right. This single, slow zombie would be easy to circumvent. No problem at all. If anything, we had over-thought it. It turned as we ran past, but did little else. I found running more difficult than I could remember. Some new primal sense told me that acceleration was dangerous—that moving quickly would put my body into some sort of "red zone" where I threatened to shake apart.

I slowed down and hazarded a glance back at the zombie. It was still lumbering forward slowly, a sad, awkward corpse of what had probably been a very obese woman. Then a mad curiosity overtook me, and I stopped, letting it close the gap between us a bit. Then a bit more. Then further still. I heard Sam starting the car, but paid it no mind. I turned and walked back toward the bower. Soon, the zombie was close enough to reach out and touch me. But it did no such thing.

The zombie regarded me for a moment with unblinking, idiot eyes. It *saw* me, but did not see food. I was just an obstacle, blocking its path. A moving piece of turf. The zombie looked past me, and lumbered on toward Sam.

More than my lack of breath or heartbeat or hunger, *this* seemed to confirm that I was, without a doubt, a member of the walking dead.

"Pete, you okay?" Sam called from the car. "Where'd you go?"

"I'm coming," I said, and loped through the bower after him.

Back in the car, speeding toward the house of my girlfriend's sister, I began to feel a new hesitation and anxiety.

When we met these people (whom, presumably, I would "know"), I'd have to continue the charade that I was alive in the same way that they were. I would have to pretend to eat and breathe and shit just like they did. And I would have to explain away my raspy voice and my cold, pale skin. As the black Ohio farms and hillsides rolled past, I wondered how long I would be able to keep the truth quite literally under my hat.

"I know that lake there," Sam said, gesturing to a round body of water at the base of a steep hill. Next to it was a crude roadside billboard that seemed to advertise homemade jams. "We're on the right track."

I looked where Sam had pointed, and suddenly a memory came to me. A woman. Mid-thirties. Half-Chinese, half-European. Short black hair and glasses. A substantial bust and nice hips, topped off by a devilish smile. (I would have said this memory-woman was attractive if I'd had any sexual feeling at all.)

Sam slowed and turned the boxy car down a drive that wound past the circular lake and into some very dark hills.

"Hey, does Vanessa wear glasses by any chance?" I asked. "Short hair? Maybe part-Asian?"

"Bingo!" Sam said, genuinely enthused. "Welcome back, buddy."

"Yeah, I ... wouldn't get too excited yet," I told him. "This isn't a full recovery. Something in that lake just made me picture her. I can't remember the situation, but we're outside and I'm standing very close to her and the sun is bright behind her. Almost blinding. I think it's reflected light coming off of that water."

"Could be," Sam said.

"And you're there, too," I said. "And there are other people with us."

"Sounds like you remember Labor Day," Sam said. "See, this is good. Memories build on memories. We'll have your brain up and running in no time."

"Uh, yeah," I said, a little uneasily.

The country road—poorly paved to begin with—soon exhausted itself, and gave way to side roads of gravel and dust. There was little light, but even less to see (apart from the odd silo or telephone pole). Dark, tree-shrouded drives led off to what I presumed were people's homes. There were no signs of life. No people. No loose pets. Certainly, no movement.

Then, when I thought the old gravel road could not possibly go on any longer, I spied the light of a single kerosene lantern hanging from an ancient oak that framed the entrance to a darkened drive.

"That's gotta be for us," Sam said. "It's been a while since I've been here—and it's hard as hell to see in this dark—but that lantern's got to be a signal for us. I mean, for you."

Sam turned down the narrow drive into an even darker forest, the gravel crunching noisily under the Scion's tires. As he did, he laid on the horn twice in quick succession.

I looked at him. "What'd you do that for?"

"So they know it's us," he responded. "*People* coming, and not . . . anything else."

"Do *they* drive cars?" I asked.

"Hey, anything's possible," Sam answered.

We crept slowly and crunchily along the drive. The trees folded in close to the car, creating a tunnel of dark wood, with the odd birdhouse or no hunting sign thrown in for variety.

After a couple of minutes, I began to make out electric lights ahead of us, and the tree tunnel opened to reveal a clearing. In it stood an empty garden, an ancient barn, and a modern-looking home with daring architecture and what appeared to be solar panels dripping off of every surface, like reflective moss.

"They have power—at least a generator," I pointed out.

"They've got more than that," Sam said. He gestured to the edge of the yard where three wind turbines captured the winter gusts and routed the resulting energy to the house.

"Well, damn," I said. "So they do."

"Do you remember Kate, Vanessa's sister?" Sam asked, pulling up to the house.

"Not a thing," I said. "Can't even picture her."

"She's like a smaller Vanessa; not as pretty, frankly," Sam said. "She married an older man who owned a factory that made matches. Seriously. Matches made him rich. Anyway, the guy died about a year ago, but she had a couple of kids with him."

"Oh," I said. "That's sad. I guess."

There was movement on the porch. Before Sam could kill the engine, a heavy, matronly woman stepped out of the house and was illuminated starkly and unflatteringly by automatic porch lights. She must have been three hundred pounds without her heavy winter coat. She held a shotgun, and looked not completely unlike the stout zombie we had circumvented at Vanessa's house.

Sam and I looked at one another.

"You sure this is the place, man?" I asked.

Sam shrugged.

We exited the car slowly, leaving our guns behind.

"Hello there," Sam called, waving both of his hands to show he was not armed. "Are Kate and Vanessa home? We're friends."

The woman frowned disapprovingly, as if we were children requiring to be scolded. Then she stuck her head back inside the house.

"Vanessa!" the woman called from the side of her mouth. "You said it was only going to be the one!"

Looking just as I had remembered her, Vanessa emerged from the house like a figure stepping out of a dream. She wore a tight-fitting black sweater and jeans, but no coat. She crossed her arms against the cold and looked at Sam's car, appearing momentarily confused.

"Oh ... hi, Sam," she said, addressing my friend first. Then she looked to me and flashed a cautious smile. I flashed one back.

"You said *one person*," the grumpy woman reiterated. "We had an agreement. If you all start changing things, I'll take my food out of your freezer and go back to *my* house. I mean that. Don't think I won't!"

I quickly guessed what the problem might be.

"Sam just drove me here," I called in my raspy voice. "He's not staying."

The matronly lady cocked an eyebrow (but not, at least, her shotgun). We gingerly approached the deck where the two women stood.

"Sam's not staying," I said to the woman. "He's just my chauffeur."

"Peter was in a car accident and got a little bump on the head," Sam said. "I didn't think he should drive. Besides, his car is totaled."

"Seriously?" Vanessa asked, suddenly alarmed and concerned. "Are you all right?"

"I've been better," I said with a smile. "But basically, yeah, I'm okay. Still walking and talking. You know."

"We had the college doctor look him over," Sam added. "He seemed to think Peter was okay—just a little concussed. From what we gather, Pete was on his way to see you, and he ran his car into a tree."

"You 'gather'?" Vanessa asked.

"I'm having some trouble remembering things," I confessed.

"Yeah, he's got a little memory loss," Sam said. "Doc made it sound like it wasn't a big deal. We expect it's temporary."

"Do you remember *me?*" Vanessa asked, half seriously.

"Yeah," I said, truthfully. "Of course I do."

"Well, that's a relief," she said, her mood genuinely brightening. "Then let's just be thankful you made it here safe and sound."

Her tone was gentle enough on the outside, but it was wrapped around something deeper and guarded. Something tender, that hurt. It said this was not the first time I'd fucked things up, and that surprises and shortcomings on my part were not entirely unexpected. (Maybe it was a lot to infer from someone's tone of voice, but somehow I knew it instantly.)

We joined the women up on the deck, and Vanessa hugged me.

"You look *really* terrible," she said matter-of-factly. "And you're cold."

"Thanks," I told her. "Sam says I need a nap."

"Pete, this is our neighbor, Matilda Kay," Vanessa said, indicating the stalwart and bewarted woman brandishing the shotgun. "Matilda is joining us for the ... duration of things."

"Our food supply is finite—limited, you know?" Matilda said, managing a tone that was apologetic and stern at the same time. "I didn't mean any offense to your friend. It's just that we've got to think ahead."

"Matilda's a hunter," Vanessa said, her arm draping itself naturally around my shoulder. "She brought over a freezer's worth of venison."

"You don't need to be concerned," Sam said. "I'm not staying here. A group of us are holding out just fine on the hill at Kenton."

"What about the graveyard?" Vanessa asked.

"That's the most exciting part," Sam said. "Seriously, though, we keep a watch on it. Things crop up, and we put them back down."

"But there are gangs and criminals loose now," Vanessa said. "They announced on the news that the prison in Mansfield had a huge escape—over half the inmates."

Sam shrugged.

"We're up on a hill," Sam said. "We see things coming. We've got guns."

Vanessa nodded, but still looked concerned for him.

"That's what we're hoping for here," she said, indicating the long wooded road leading up to the house. I couldn't help thinking that this only meant you could see cars coming. Anyone, or anything, that really wanted to could pick its way through the forest and up to the house from any direction.

"I'd have been fine to stay at my own place," Matilda offered, almost defensively. "Excepting it's right by the side of the road. It's too ... visible ... for what's likely to come."

"On TV, the president is saying it's going to get worse before it gets better," Vanessa said.

"Well that's his motto, isn't it?" I responded hoarsely. Vanessa smiled.

"Sam, do you want to come in and have a cup of tea or something before you head back?" Vanessa asked.

Matilda wrinkled her nose.

"We're not rationing *tea*, Matilda," Vanessa said sternly. "Besides, none of it is yours."

Matilda rolled her eyes.

"No, but thanks anyway," Sam said. "I should really head back before it gets any later. Starks and the others will be expecting me."

"How was the drive over?" Vanessa asked.

"Not bad," Sam said. "Snow was light. No accumulation. Not much ice on the roads."

Remarkably, Vanessa shot him an expression which handily telegraphed the entirety of *That's not what I fucking meant, and you know it.*

"Oh, right," Sam said, looking over to me. "I wouldn't say we saw . . . *too* much activity. What would you say, Pete?"

"Just a couple—behind that old bar by the highway intersection," I said, deciding to leave out the fact that we had also met a zombie on the very doorstep of her house. "And they could've just been drunks, for all I know. Drunks behind the bar. It was hard to tell."

"Yeah, good point," Sam said unconvincingly. "I bet they *were* just drunks, stumbling around. You know how it is."

Sam and I nodded in unison, as if to say that the matter was settled. Vanessa (and Matilda) appeared less than sold.

"*Whatever* they were, you be safe getting back, Sam," Vanessa replied. "Say, we've got some gas stored out in the garage. You want to top off, just to be safe?"

Yet another look of alarmed disapproval sprang from Matilda. Vanessa threw her back a cast-iron glare of her own. Matilda grunted and went back inside the house.

"I've still got half a tank," Sam said. "Take care, you two. You know where I'll be if you need anything. I'll try to call if the phones go back up."

"So will we," said Vanessa.

"Thanks again for the ride," I called as Sam turned to go. We waved as he walked back to the car.

Vanessa and I stood on the porch and watched Sam's taillights disappear down the thickly wooded country road. Vanessa held me around my waist. Hard. It was a tight feeling. Good. Secure. She could squeeze as hard as she wanted now. I wouldn't feel any discomfort.

Gentle snow fell just inches from our faces. I took a deep, superfluous breath. Vanessa smelled good—like perfume and warm laundry and food fresh from a kitchen. Even after Sam's car was well out of earshot, we stayed there, holding on.

The sensations were enough to make me forget my predicament (or perhaps it was *our* predicament) for the moment. I let my head swim, the snowflakes swirling like points of light in a disco.

But then she had to go and break the spell.

"Do you *believe* this shit?" she said, rocking a little as she held me. "I keep feeling like it's a dream. You know what I mean? Just a few days ago, I was worrying about finals and incompletes and who's going to be the new editor of *The Journal of Indo-Asian Studies*. Now I'm holed up at my sister's house with our kids and her terrifying neighbor, stockpiling food and guns."

"And me," I said, hoping it was a good thing. "You're stock-piling me. I'm here, too."

"And you," she said, pulling me down toward her face and giving me a kiss on the lips.

After a second, she flinched and pulled away.

"Pete, you're like ice," she said.

"Sorry," I responded.

"Let's get you inside," she said. "How are you not freezing? I'm completely freezing."

"Just warmhearted, I guess."

As I stepped inside the house, I was greeted by the inefficient glow of energy-efficient lighting. A geothermal-pull heating system provided something akin to an afterthought of warmth. I was not, of course, cold, but it was still enough to surprise me. Vanessa noticed my expression.

"Most eco-friendly house in the state," said Vanessa. "Or did you forget?"

"I *am* having some memory problems," I told her. "Sam wasn't lying about that. I mean, this house is familiar, but ..."

"Well then, let me give you the tour again," Vanessa said brightly.

Ahead of us, down a bamboo-floored corridor, four girls between six and ten years of age—Catie, Sarah, Elise, and Chaz—played together in a well-appointed family room. Kate, Vanessa's shorter and dowdier sister, sat playing Stratego with one of the older ones, and gave us both a wave.

"To start with, you've got your voltaic solar panels on the roof," Vanessa said, shifting in tone from harried college professor to genial contractor. "In the summer, they generate more electricity than they can use. The difference gets fed back into the grid, and Kate gets a little check from the power company. In the winter it's not nearly as good. You have to go up on the roof and knock the snow off.

"Moving to the interior, here you've got your bamboo flooring, your automatic blinds, and your low-VOC paint on the walls.

Recycled plastic for all the kitchen countertops, and recycled porce-
lain tile in all the bathrooms. Low-flow toilets too, which is gross,
so let's not get into that.

"Every room is connected to the Internet. So, theoretically, Kate
can go to work—not that she works—and she can use the Internet
connection at her office—not that she has an office—to turn off
lights or turn down the heat. And look, out the window there, you
can see all those trees they planted close to the house. In the summer
they're natural shade. In the winter they provide a windbreak."

"And that really makes a difference?" I asked. "A few trees like
that?"

"You'd be surprised," Vanessa said. "Little things add up. This
place has been profiled in magazines and newspapers. It was in
Architectural Digest when they first built it. One of the professors at
Dennisburg teaches a class on this stuff, and brings his students out
here once each semester."

In addition to its environmental benefits, the house was as
impressively modern-looking inside as out. (I couldn't remember
having read architecture magazines, but it certainly *seemed* like
something I'd see in one. Outcroppings were daring and angular.
Interior balconies seemed to overhang rooms at striking, M. C.
Escher angles.) As we ended the tour and returned to the family
room, Vanessa gestured to an empty metal square about the size of
a television or fish tank.

"This is a portable room heater that runs on clean-burning oil,"
she explained. "The floors are heated too. Geothermal. There's a
rain garden outside, and an organic greenhouse out back where she
grows vegetables. Oh, and the water in the taps goes through cycles.
Like, water from washing your hands goes to the toilet tank. Stuff
like that."

"Eww," I said.

I looked over to confirm that Kate was out of earshot.

"Whose idea was . . . all this?" I asked raspily. "Your sister, or—?"

"It was Kate's," Vanessa said. "He built the house for her. I
mean, we were all a little cynical when they started the project, but
now we're the only house left in the area with power that's not
from a generator."

"Little did you know you were preparing for a zombie outbreak,"
I said.

"Yeah," Vanessa replied. "Us and the Amish . . . We're the ones
who were living off the land, or at least trying to. Growing our
own food and not depending on the grid. Matilda, that neighbor,
used to come and gape at this house like it was the damnedest thing
she'd ever seen. She's not gaping now."

I smiled.

Then, disaster.

"I know it's not that warm in here, but *do* take your coat and hat off," Vanessa said casually. Then whispered: "You're liable to hurt Kate's feelings."

"Sure," I said, without moving to do either. Or moving at all.

"Oh," Vanessa said, as if she had forgotten something. "We're putting coats in the laundry room over there. There should be some empty hooks on the wall. I'm going to go make you some hot tea. You look like you could use it."

Vanessa departed for the kitchen, with its low-energy appliances, solar grill, and countertop composter. I slunk off in the direction she had indicated. In a nook by a side door, I found a washer and dryer almost completely covered in clothes. I put my hand to my coat, and stopped. I was all despair.

What had I been thinking, exactly? That somehow I would be able to hide the top of my head from these people indefinitely? (Of course I couldn't do that. It made no sense.) Maybe I needed to leave. Maybe I should just leave now.

I sighed. It was a depressing thought.

Vanessa was nice—*very* nice, actually. And I seemed to have something much more than a general memory of her . . . But could I expect her to, in any sense, "be understanding" when I told her I was one of these *things?* That I was a "moving cadaver"?

I looked, in my despair, through the small circular window in the nearby door. (Like many conventional homes, this eco-house had a side door in the laundry room that opened directly to the outside.) The snow fell quietly among the trees, unaware and uncaring. I seriously contemplated an escape on foot.

Then I saw it. Something small and round and blue and red. Twenty-five feet from the house, looking forgotten and lost at the base of a tree.

It was a baseball cap, and it was calling to me.

Even as a member of the walking dead, I was not yet forsaken.

I quietly unlocked the side door and stalked outside to retrieve the hat. It was faded and sweat-stained. CEDAR RAPIDS KERNELS was stitched across the bill in silver thread. The front of the hat bore an emblem of a baseball emerging from a cornstalk. It was perfect.

I picked the dirty, cold hat off the ground and quietly shuffled back inside. I paused and listened for a moment, but it seemed no one had heard me. The shrill voices of the children echoed in another part of the house. I took off my coat with some trepidation (forsaking the hook and throwing it on the pile with the others), then in a single, swift, Indiana-Jonesian motion, I removed my black knit cap and replaced it with the baseball hat.

There was no mirror handy, but I consulted my reflection in the window's glass, and thought perhaps I'd pulled it off. Moments later, Vanessa surprised me with a cup of tea.

Three of us, Kate, Vanessa, and me, sat in the kitchen, sipping our drinks. My ruse appeared to have worked, but I was not entirely off the hook. (Perhaps, I feared, I had merely delayed the inevitable.)

"The *groundskeeper's* hat?" Vanessa asked cautiously.

"He's not like a regular groundskeeper," Kate asserted firmly, between bites of whole-grain carob brownie. "Not like most people have. He makes his own loam and brings fertilizer and other things we need from the local farms. He has a degree in organic landscaping from the University of Minnesota."

"It's not like he's using it," I pointed out. "The hat, I mean—not the degree."

"Yes, but he said he lost it," Kate insisted. "He's been looking for it."

"Then I'm just hanging onto it for him, aren't I?" I countered. "Look, the doctor said I should keep my head warm. That's something you should do after you hit your head, apparently. Keep it warm. Doctors all agree on that. He . . . recommended hats."

"It looks *filthy*, Peter," Vanessa said. "At least let me get you one of the clean caps from the closet." She leaned in to touch it, but I flinched away.

"Look, I like it," I said, trying to sound playful (as opposed to terrified-that-she-would-see-that-my-brain-was-showing). "Seriously, I'm gonna leave it on. This is doctor's orders. You want me to get better, right?"

"Then you're washing your hair before you come to bed," Vanessa said. "And that's *not* up for debate."

"But Vanessa, all the water—just for that?" Kate objected.

"Where's Matilda, by the way?" I asked, to change the subject.

"Up in her room, I have a feeling," Kate said. "The guest room at the very top."

"Quite a personality on that one," I offered.

No takers.

Both women looked again at my filthy hat, I think only half-believing I was *actually* wearing the thing.

"How was it, on the hill at Kenton?" Vanessa asked. Finally, something I could answer. I told her about the empty campus with the group keeping watch over the graveyard. I described the dark, empty houses. The roving dogs. And I told them about killing the zombie.

"Dreadful," Vanessa pronounced, shaking her head.

Another awkward pause.

"It was nice seeing Sam again," Vanessa said. "He used to come around a lot more often."

"Did he?" I said, forgetting myself. "He made it sound like he'd only been here once."

Vanessa looked at me curiously.

"I mean, he sure did," I quickly amended.

"You *really* hit your head, didn't you?" Kate offered.

"No use pretending I didn't," I said with a nervous laugh.

Kate finished her brownie and let out an immodest belch. Vanessa wrinkled her nose reflexively.

"What?" Kate said defensively. "It's *natural.*"

"She's got us there," I said with a grin.

Vanessa smiled back at me, and something triggered in my memory. That smile! I had once loved it like nothing else. I had felt about that smile the way a zombie feels about brains. I wanted it like cats want mice, or like drunks want a drink. Yes . . . *that* had been *my* all-consuming goal. Once, I had been willing do whatever it took to see that smile.

I had craved it for the same reason addicts crave a fix—because it *made everything okay.* (But unlike drugs, there was no downside to it. No hangover. No sense that I really shouldn't be doing this. No danger of dying. It was all good. A non-zero-sum game, where I could just feel better and better and better.)

I liked seeing Vanessa's smile because it signaled that I had made her happy, and that was the goal.

Even as a zombie, apparently, I could still do it.

At least a little.

So we were talking—just like that . . . about burps and hats and how Sam was going to fare on the hill back at Kenton—when the din of little-girl ruckus from the living room increased considerably. Jarring screams echoed off the bamboo and recycled fiberglass. It sounded like a serious fight.

"Girls!" Kate called down the hallway. Her tone said that they had already been warned against becoming over-boisterous. The shrieks did not cease. Vanessa cocked an eyebrow.

Then we heard a door slam.

"Catie? Sarah? What's going on?" Vanessa called.

We heard a six-year-old's barefoot plod approaching. A

towheaded girl in a purple sweater presented herself. She was wearing a frown.

"Elsie left," the girl announced flatly. "She ran outside."

"What?" Kate said, springing up. "Outside? What did we tell you girls about going outside?" Kate took the girl by the hand and I followed the alarmed mothers into the living room. There, two other girls (Catie and Sarah, Vanessa's children) quickly indicated the door.

"Where's Elsie?" Kate asked Vanessa's daughters.

"She went to get Missy Madlangbayan," said the older girl, referring—I later learned—to an American Girl doll of Pan-Asian ancestry. "We told her no. We said not to go outside. She did it anyway."

The women cast their alarmed looks against the door, its foggy energy-efficient window, and the creeping emptiness beyond. Vanessa hurried across the room and threw the door wide open. Beyond it, we saw only the quiet snowfall, an organic garden shuttered for the winter, and the quiet forest. There was no little girl to be seen.

Vanessa stepped through the doorway, attempting to survey the scene beyond. She looked left and right desperately, but it was clear she saw nothing. "Elsie!" Vanessa shouted.

No response.

"Elsie," she tried again. "Come here right now! This isn't funny."

"Are there footprints in the snow?" I asked.

"I don't see anything," Vanessa replied. "It's all just mud."

"You girls stay here, understand?" said Kate, who had already retrieved a green Eveready flashlight from the kitchen. "*Stay here!*"

The mothers bolted out the door, one turning left toward the greenhouse, the other turning right and heading into the fallow winter garden. I shuffled after the lither, quicker woman, and was almost out the door when I felt an insistent tug on my pant leg. It was Sarah, Vanessa's youngest daughter. She looked up at me with deadly serious eyes.

"Elsie went up to the road," Sarah said matter-of-factly. "She threw Missy out the window when we were in the car before. She was afraid to tell Mom."

"Up the driveway toward the road?" I asked. "Where cars go?"

"Yes, stupid," the little girl said. "Where cars go."

I looked out across the yard into the darkened mouth of the wooded driveway. I saw nothing beyond—no movement except skeletal trees creaking and cracking in the winter wind.

I shuffled outside, feeling stiffness in my joints.

"Kate ... Vanessa!" I called, seeing no sign of either woman. "I think Elsie went up the driveway! Guys? I'm going up to the road!" Then I saw the flicker of Kate's frantic flashlight beam in the depths of the greenhouse. Perhaps she could not hear me. Perhaps neither woman could.

"Fuck," I croaked to myself, and hurried toward the drive. The wind picked up, and the woods chattered excitedly as I approached. The tunnel of trees loomed before me like an enchanted funhouse ride, anxious for me to wander inside once more, eager to come alive and scare me. The solid darkness of it grew closer and closer. I wished for a flashlight of my own.

I entered the dark tunnel. The driveway began crunching softly under my feet—an easy-listening version of the sound it had made under the Scion's tires. I slowed down to a kind of sprained-ankle shuffle. It was black and very hard to see. I started running into things. Branches whipped against my face in the wind. I had to pull my hat down hard to keep it on my head.

C'mon, I thought to myself, don't zombies have special night vision or something? Apparently, we did not. Before I had ventured twenty paces down the dark driveway, I slipped in the snow and (painlessly) fell on my face. I spat out snow and re-secured my Kernels hat. Then, as I righted myself via an awkward push-up, I saw it.

Faint in the muddy snow, and just inches from my face ... a child's footprint. I inspected it closely. Even in the near-total blackness, I was soon sure. This was no animal mark or random indentation. This was a child's footprint—and, from the way it had ground the new snow into the mud, it was a recent one.

I crept forward a few inches and found another.

I wondered what to do. Going back to tell the women would take time, but they also moved quickly and had flashlights. Then again, the little girl might be mere paces ahead of me. In that case, it would make no sense to go back and risk her wandering farther away. Surely, I thought, even a zombie can move quickly enough to gain on a little girl in the woods.

I began advancing forward once more, extending my arms to feel for errant branches and shuffling carefully on the icy gravel. I listened closely for any sound of the little girl. Every minute or so, I called her name ("Elsie ... !") into the nothingness. Shouting made my voice sound especially hoarse and—if I had to be honest—a little frightening, even for me to hear. I looked hard at every variation in the darkness, but never did I see a little girl.

Then, just as I was beginning to regret my decision not to go back to get Vanessa and Kate, I saw a light in the distance ahead. And movement.

"Elsie," I called, unaware of what I was seeing. (It was not quite headlights . . .) "Elsie, it's . . . it's Uncle Peter."

Then I heard a scream. High-pitched. A child's.

I began scrambling toward it.

The sound was soon followed by a forceful, "Eeeeek! No!" by the same voice. Then a sound of distant movement—clothing rustling, gravel splashing underfoot.

Then another scream.

Then: "Mommy! Mom—" The second *Mommy* was hideously cut off by the sound of a blow. Slipping and sliding, I broke into a lumbering run, making straight for the light and voices. My breath did not quicken with my pace, so my hearing remained sharp. As I drew closer, I could more distinctly detect violent, urgent noises. Pulling. Pushing. A struggle.

The light ahead of me came from the lamp left hanging at the mouth of the drive, but also from something else. There were two lights, and one of them was pointed like a searchlight *into* the forest. The scene soon came into view.

A young girl in a winter coat was being pinned against an ATV (with a single, blinding headlight) by a large man with an unkempt beard and a giant gut. He gripped a hunting knife and held the struggling girl against him. When she flinched away, he hit her hard with the fist that clenched the knife. There was a horrible noise. The girl fell back against the ATV, stunned and sick-looking.

"Hey!" I managed, still several yards away. "Hey you!!"

My voice startled the man. He released his grip on the child, and she began to squirm free. He looked around for me, but was blinded by the lights so near him. Then, he drew a handgun from his coat.

I felt an almost unbelievable lack of fear. This man was much larger than me, and armed with a knife *and* a gun—that I knew about. But I continued to charge him. After a moment, he detected the direction of my approaching footfalls and turned to face me, still squinting to see beyond the glare of the lantern hanging above him.

He was wild-eyed. He regarded me only for an instant as I came into view, and then looked not *at* me but *past* me. He wanted to see if I was alone or part of a group. The girl squirmed completely free and started sprinting toward me.

"Run to the house," I screamed at her. "Don't run to me! Run to the house!" She obeyed, and we passed one another on the fly.

The man looked over at his ATV, and then at me. This was the fight-or-flight instinct they talked about. I was watching it unfold in front of me. (Most would have hoped to induce the latter, but, as I say, uncannily, I felt no fear.) I closed within a few paces of the scruffy-looking man, and he could now make me out with perfect clarity. A contemptuous smile curled on his beard-covered lips. I could see him sizing me up. Middle-aged. Out of shape. Dressed like a city boy. Yeah . . . I should be *no* problem.

He looked past me again, but not to see if others followed me. Rather, it was a longing look at the backside of the little girl. It was a look that said not to wander too far. A look that said he'd be with her again in a moment . . .

I opened my mouth to say something to the crazed, hairy man, but in that instant he leveled his gun at my chest and fired. The weapon leapt wildly in his grip, and the bullet knocked me down.

(Look, as I hope is clear at this point in my tale, I'm not a "gun guy." Remember how in *Days of Thunder*, Tom Cruise's character didn't "know cars"? Remember that? Yeah. Well, I don't "know guns." I don't know anything about them beyond what I learned from going through this experience. I was a college philosophy professor, not a hunter. Was the gun that this woolly man used to shoot me "high-caliber" or something? I have no idea. Was it a .22 or a .38 or a Colt .45? Again, your guess is going to be as good as mine. Let's just say it was a giant, scary-ass handgun, held by a terrifying-looking man, and it sent me flying backwards.)

After a moment's disorientation, I opened my eyes and understood exactly what had happened. I had been knocked on my back. The bullet had hit high, stage left. Near my heart, actually. (But the joke was going to be on him, wasn't it?)

An evil smile spread across my face. There was no pain at all. Not even a tickle. The man above me was looking up the path again, toward the girl. He had already stuck the gun down the back of his pants. In a trice, he was advancing into the darkened wood after her.

All at once, I began to feel the strange sensations that had overtaken me as I'd watched the zombies feasting on that body behind the dilapidated bar. It was an awakening that seemed to come from the back of my eyeballs and flow through my entire body. I shivered with pleasure and anticipation. This time, it was my turn.

I stood up quietly and began to follow my would-be killer. He moved slowly, corralling (as opposed to chasing) the child. I crept ever nearer. He never once looked back. I sidled up near him, matching my footfalls in time to his own. The snow's soft powder concealed almost every noise.

When I drew within arm's reach, he sensed something and paused, lifting his head like a deer sniffing the air. I leaned in, and in one deft movement, pulled the heavy weapon from his pants. He spun on his heels and lunged violently, but stopped when he saw the gun in my hand. I pointed it at him.

He was clearly confused. He had just shot me. Had seen me go down. This did not make sense. I took a few steps back, turned to the side, and hucked the gun as far as I could into the woods. Wasting no time, my assailant drew his knife.

I threw off my hat and pointed to my lack-of-head. His eyes widened to pie plates.

"That's right, motherfucker," I shouted. "Come get some!"

They say you never forget your first time.

Know what? They're fucking right.

There *may* be subsequent occurrences that bring greater excitement or deeper pleasure. Yet, alas! It is these most pleasurable encounters which often prove the most difficult to recall, instant for instant, later on. The greatest ecstasy can be the most ephemeral. (The brain is a confounding and delicious thing.) But the first time . . . You remember *everything* about that.

But let's be honest, too: The first time is seldom the most pleasurable (if it is pleasurable at all). You don't know what you're doing. The other person doesn't know what they're doing. You're both scared. You just writhe around together on the ground for a few minutes, and then suddenly, it's done. It's over, and you think to yourself: "Gee, that was it? *That's* what all the fuss is about?" But then, after a little reflection (and recovery time), you start to think maybe it was pretty good, after all—maybe you *would* like to try it again. And again. Then you start to practice. You get better at it. Before long, you know what you're doing. And *that's* when it starts to get really good.

But I'm getting ahead of myself. (And one must not, in these matters, arrive prematurely.) *My* first time—there in those woods, with this nightmare wild-man struggling and fighting the whole time—is etched into my memory as if by lightning, every moment of it. I can recall each moment and stage as vividly as if they were pictures in a book. I can hit repeat and play the track again and again and again.

I can watch myself lunge forward, feel his knife lodging painlessly in my chest, and taste the spray as I bite into his throat. I can feel him flailing wildly, landing blows on my face and hands. I can feel the blows register, painlessly, all over my body. I feel him try to buck me, like an animal I'm riding. He whips his neck back and forth like a wet dog drying itself, but still I remain. I am attached to him—by a connection so firm I would not have thought it possible. I can taste the terror and confusion in his eyes as I taste his neck-blood with my tongue. Soon, he is paralyzed by his own pain and surprise, which allows me to bite deeper. I know that I've "struck home" when the blood begins to geyser out in time to his heartbeat from the mass of gore that used to be his throat. It's clear (to my remaining human sentience) that nobody comes back from this kind of injury. I've hit the right veins and arteries.

Before long, I am covered in his blood. I have a beard of blood spilling down my chin. I still wear his knife in my chest. He falls to his knees.

I am clearly the victor, yet there is so much life in him still—life that will not or cannot surrender. He fights and fights. Against it— the inevitable. It is a full five minutes before he decides to stop resisting and flopping like a fish. He understands that I have won.

His breathing begins to make noise. His lungs are full of blood and straining. It is the death rattle of old.

Then, even when he is still and cold and lifeless before me, I cannot stop biting. I know it is not the end. One task still remains.

Now ... Here's something important—something the movies (most of them, anyway) get dead wrong. Human heads are hard. *Very hard.* The skull is incredibly tough. You can't just bite through it like the crusty top of a *crème brûlée*. It takes *work* to get down in there. I mean, doctors—when they do brain surgery or whatever— have to use saws and fucking power drills to get through a skull. They use shit you have to plug in. It takes quite a bit of force and power. You can't just crunch through with your incisors.

It's a harsh truth, and one that I was about to find out.

When the hairy ATV-man was dead—really dead and unmoving—I wanted nothing more than to eat his brain. *Nothing* more. It was a romantic and poetic longing. I wanted to get inside of his head. To be inside him with my tongue and mouth, and then have him be inside of me. (In my stomach.) A wonderful sharing of inside and outside. Ahh, yes ... A divine communion of brain and tongue.

The problem was *how.*

I looked down at the motionless corpse and considered where I might start. His head was a complete mystery to me—a labyrinth with delicious brains hidden in the middle. How would I find my way in?

I'll tell you the way I did it, but please, don't judge me. I wasn't as suave and sophisticated as the zombies you see in the movies, chomping through papier-mâché heads. I'm a pragmatist at heart, I guess. I did it in the most practical way possible. Just try not to laugh. (First times are embarrassing for everybody.)

I stooped down next to him, took a grip on the ears, and brought his head up to my mouth. My first few tentative bites into his scalp proved fruitless. I knew there *had* to be a way to get in there. After all, eating brains was what zombies did. But *how* did they do it? Was there some trick they knew? Was my humanlike sentience preventing me from enjoying the full brain-eating advantages enjoyed by the rest of the walking dead?

Then my arm absently brushed against the knife still buried in my chest. Was there—I wondered—any rule that said a zombie couldn't use tools? I didn't think there was. Besides, nobody was looking.

Removing the serrated hunting knife (which, I had to grant, had been expertly and forcefully driven between my ribs by my foe), I took a knee next to the corpse and began to saw at the top of the head.

Nothing doing. I succeeded in little more than mutilating him.

Leaving my victim awkwardly half-scalped, I turned my attention instead to his neck, where I had bitten him to death. There, his skin gave way more easily. Soon, I felt the knife punch through into the windpipe, like I was punching it into the soft center of a pumpkin. I was elated. This felt like progress.

Before long, I had opened up the neck, and only the spinal cord connected the dead head to the body. I applied the knife's serrated side to the cord, carefully and forcefully, and made short work of it. Holding the severed head up to my face, I gnawed into the bloody hole. The taste was exhilarating, but the brains eluded me. They were there—so close, only inches away—yet still out of reach of my anxious lips.

I dropped the head and howled like an animal. This wanting was intolerable. I could not remember desiring a thing so intensely. I drummed my chest in anger, casting my gaze wildly into the snowy night. I looked for anything that might solve my horrible problem.

Just off the path, set back into the woods, was an ancient stone fence. It looked as though it separated long-forgotten property lines. Now it stood moss-covered and crumbling. Despite the ravages of time, the waist-high wall looked like it was still tough. Strong. Hard. *Harder than a skull.* For the second time that evening, an irrepressible smile curled my lips. Yes … *This* was something I could work with.

My first few ill-considered blows involved driving the head itself into the stone wall, which did not have the desired effect. (I only further mutilated the face.) Then, at my feet, I found a heavy stone that had long ago fallen away. I set the head on the top of the little wall, then hefted the loose stone and brought it down with all the force I could muster. Something gave. I did it again. And again. *And again.*

Before long, I had cracked the nut.

What I ended up consuming, as I ate the contents of his head, looked more akin to "brain paste" than the ridged, shapely brain that one is accustomed to seeing in medical journals. Still, the pleasure was not lost on me. I scooped him into my mouth hungrily. I chewed him like bubble gum. It was beyond delicious. I ran my finger around the inside of his head and licked my fingers, like he was a peanut butter jar.

It wasn't always pretty, but it got the job done.

Like I said, it was my first time.

When it was over, I sat on the ground, my back against the hard stone wall. I was covered in blood and bone fragments. The man's headless body rested only feet away on the driveway.

So *that* was eating someone's brain, I thought to myself. Not bad. Not bad at all.

Some part of my newfound zombie sensibilities told me that there also might be some enjoyment to consuming the rest of the man. His skin. His muscles. His guts. Yet it was almost too overwhelming to contemplate—eating an entire man. I had tasted brains for the first time tonight. That would be enough for one evening. (But tomorrow, perhaps, or the next day, I would be ready to investigate more.)

I knew not how much time had passed when I first heard the sound of approaching footsteps. They advanced down the drive in my direction. They were slow. Measured. Heavy. I looked up from my bloodbath, staring hard into the forest until I finally detected movement. It was a monstrous shape. Something massive. A miniature mountain that walked or stumbled.

I stood. The shambling shape sensed this and paused, and in its own movement betrayed itself for what it was—the neighbor woman, Matilda. She was wearing a strange hodgepodge of sports-equipment and body armor—a policeman's riot helmet, a vest, and what appeared to be skateboard kneepads. Her shotgun was at the ready. Though the sight was risible—and my first inclination was laughter—I became all at once hesitant. There was suddenly a lot to think about.

Part of me, still hungry for brains, wanted to eat this woman too. (She *had*, after all, been something of a bitch to Vanessa. And there was so *much* of her . . . It would be a grand buffet!) Another part of me—the rational mind still left—also understood that this woman could destroy me with that weapon she was carrying. She could destroy *my* brain, and then *I* would cease to exist. Another part of me still understood that there were people back down that road, inside a daringly designed energy-efficient house, whom I bore no ill will—one of whom, I even loved—and whom I wanted *never* to be eaten, by me or by any other zombie.

The mountain woman drew closer. I had to make a decision.

Already, I knew the answer. I would not eat this horrible woman. That was not something I could do. At least not tonight. But with the dead man's gore still warm on my face, neither could I go back to that house.

Matilda stalked closer, heading in the direction of the old wall. I could see her clearly. The mask of her riot helmet had fogged over with her breathing. She nearly tripped over the headless corpse, and when she *did* see it, the thing seemed to register as nothing more than an earthy inconvenience, like a pile of dog shit or moldy, rotting garbage. Matilda continued stalking forward into the gloom. This was a hard woman.

I cleared my throat. A little blood came up with the gurgles.

"Matilda!" I called. "Matilda, over here."

She started, and fell to one knee, pointing the firearm wildly. She looked in my general direction but seemed not to see me. (I think she only saw the stone wall, and assumed I was on the other side of it.)

"Who's that there?" she spat in a guttural whisper.

"It's Peter," I replied. "Look, don't turn on your flashlight. There . . . there still might be others around."

"What's going on?" Matilda whispered. "Elsie said she saw someone shoot you. And this guy's got no head."

"Uh, yeah," I said, choosing not to reveal exactly what had happened.

Matilda cocked her shotgun.

"Look," I said, "I can't go back to the house right now. Something happened. I have to leave. Please tell Vanessa I'm sorry."

"What?" Matilda said.

"Look, I killed one of them," I said. "I scared the others off, but they're going to come back for me. I think . . . I think I should take that guy's ATV and lead them away from the house."

Matilda seemed to think for a moment. "Okay," she said.

"We want to make them lose interest in this house," I said. "We've got to keep them away from the little girls. All these drive-ways look the same. You take that lantern down, and they're not going to remember this place."

"Aye, I'll do that," she said (suddenly Scottish). She began to edge closer to me.

"No," I said. "Don't come any closer. Seriously. I'm gross. Just go back down the path until I get out of here. Please."

"Uh-huh," she said, seeming to grow somewhat skeptical.

I stood cautiously, and began to pick my way along the stone wall toward the road. I had taken no more than four or five steps when Matilda's flashlight hit me in the back.

To this day, I can't tell you how much she saw. I have no idea. My face was a carnival of gore. But my backside? That's harder to know. I had not, of course, replaced my hat, so it was possible that she saw the missing top of my head. Yet I walked through the underbrush with a bit of a stoop, and this may have concealed my mutilation from her. Again, I cannot say for sure.

"Turn that off!" I shouted as the beam fell around me. "They are here and they will see you."

For a moment, the beam inspected my back, its invasive circle of light as obscene and violating as any lecher's grope. Then the hefty woman switched it off, and I heard her retreating back down the path.

"Just making sure," she whispered. "Just making sure . . ."

I returned to the drive's entrance and switched off the lantern. Then I saw about the ATV. A Kawasaki, keys in the ignition. A full tank of gas. It was the best option. The only option. It was my new ride, whether I liked it or not. (I wondered if I ridden an ATV before. I didn't think I had.)

Before I pulled away, I found the timeworn Kernels baseball hat on the ground, and put it back on my head.

It fit perfectly.

I drove and drove, to the top of the highest hill I could find. Ohio—even central Ohio—has its areas of hills and valleys, and I was definitely among them. I rode through the night for what felt like hours, along back country roads, until I found the tallest hill. I went up, up, up the lonely road toward the top. I found an empty place with a few farms on the hillside. Maybe a little Amish below.

The hill was bald at the top. Just a few shrubs and bushes, and an old forgotten spool that had once contained wire. I got off the ATV and sat down on the spool. Then I stood up again, and started pacing.

An interesting side note: So, okay . . . Have I made it clear by this point that I can't really feel pain? Because I can't. I have "sensation," but I don't really feel it in the same way I used to. It's like, say you walk up to me and tap me on the shoulder. I'll have the information, *You are being tapped on the shoulder*, but I won't really "feel" the tap. Not like I used to feel things. Same thing with being stabbed or shot. I'm aware when the knife or bullet goes in. On some level, I get the information, *There is now a great opening in your chest that wasn't there a second ago,* but the info comes without any sensation—positive *or* negative—attached to it.

Anyhow, the same thing sort of goes with exertion or getting tired or whatever. I don't get "tired" in any conventional sense of the word. I can sit down in a chair if I want to, but I never *need* to. I can walk (or jog awkwardly) for days without ever needing to "rest" in the way you do. Sitting is as good as standing. Walking is the same as sitting still.

Yet, lest you think that this feels like having a superpower—like I'm "Rechargeable Battery Man," a superhero whose energy can never be drained—allow me to also note the terrible "awareness" that goes along with being a zombie.

You see, even though I can't feel tired or hungry or like I have to take an enormous shit, I can feel my body breaking down. It's that same kind of "informational" feeling. It's like being handed a telegram saying: "Your toes are starting to rot away," or "The tip of your penis is turning black and hard." And I think it would be easier to take if I were less aware. Less sentient. (More on this later. Let me not get ... ahead ... of myself.) But, as it stands, I notice when the vitreous humors in my eyes start to molder, or my fingernails fall off, or my ears dry and shrivel like apricots. I am *aware* of all this, and yet, I can do nothing about it.

The more rotted and decomposed a zombie is, the more slowly it moves. This is because—on that animal level of "awareness"—a zombie understands how precarious its body is. Joints are ceasing to work properly. Synovial fluids have evaporated. A thousand functions and processes that have always kept things moving smoothly have forever disappeared. A zombie in advanced decomposition must feel like a snail with no slime left. (Whereas once, it never thought about having slime—it just moved without thinking about it—the snail now drags itself along horribly, feeling each grain of sand grate into its underside. I think that even the stupidest, least-aware zombie has some animal understanding that it can destroy itself if it's not careful.).

And so ... Zombies creep. Zombies shuffle. Zombies lurk. But zombies make a point not to overtax the precious sinews and muscles still holding them together.

Even I must face that this fate awaits me. I am not immune. One day my movement will become even more difficult than it already is, and then, impossible. My abilities to move and function will break down one by one until I am left a blind, shuddering, damned thing, perhaps inching my way forward like a worm along the ground.

My ability to anticipate this fate will not save me from it.

But...

At the point where our tale stands, I was in a body that was still working remarkably well. My lack of fatigue let me be as close as ever I would to feeling like I had a superpower. Also, it was cold. Freezing. And weather is important for zombies. I shudder to think of my poor colleagues born into tropical climes, for they have only a few weeks before serious and irrevocable deterioration sets in. The cold, you see, slows the process. It is natural refrigeration. And though it keeps one a bit stiff, the cold delays (or prevents completely) the many malfunctions of the body that come along with being a rotting corpse.

As I paced back and forth along that freezing hilltop in Ohio, the winter chill did me more good than I then knew.

I was angry and confused. I felt lost. None of this made sense. It was hard to deal with the feelings because my spotty memory gave me no frame of reference. Usually, when you're going through hard times, it helps to think of tight spots in your past that you've managed to survive. They give you confidence. You think to yourself: "Hell, if I got through *that*, I should certainly be able to survive *this* challenge." Or when you do something that makes you feel like a real bastard—stealing, lying, fucking around—maybe you think back and remember some of the *good* things you've done, and then you decide you might not be such a complete shit after all.

But I had no frame of reference. I could remember nothing more difficult than the situation in which I found myself, because I could more or less remember nothing. Period. Simply put, I did not know what kind of a man I was.

According to my colleague, Sam, I was a disappointment and a philanderer. According to the massive collection of scotch bottles in my kitchen, I was a high-functioning alcoholic. According to the suspicions lurking in my girlfriend's eyes, I was the kind of man who could or would wrong a woman.

Those were the negatives, but there were some positive traits too.

I was a professor at a good college with a fancy degree from an Ivy League. I was an only friend to a lonely man who felt like an outcast. And, despite my faults, there was a woman out there who loved me.

I had just eaten a man's brain, true—but even there I saw signs pointing toward a redemption of some sort. I had protected a small girl (and perhaps an entire houseful of women) from a rapist or murderer. And I had spared a woman I hardly knew (but whom I knew loved me) the angst of knowing that her beloved had become a member of the walking dead.

"The walking dead, indeed," I thought to myself. For indeed, I walked. I paced that hilltop feverishly, looking at the ground and, occasionally, at the empty wire spool, out of place and large as a coffee table. I walked in meandering lines, and I walked in tight circles. Sometimes I walked a crazy, crooked wobble. Sometimes I pivoted suddenly, as though trying to escape from an invisible tail.

Something in me—either human or zombie—told me to keep moving (even if it was only back and forth across the same hilltop). To pause and take stock of things in the middle of a crisis would benefit me in no way. "When you're going through hell, keep going." That was a famous quote. I had read it somewhere.

I had to keep going. But where?

I paced that hilltop long into what had already been a very long night. My only guest was a single wild turkey, ugly and wattled, with a face like a melted candle. Black as the night itself, it emerged from the frozen forest and lingered near the spool. At first, I paid it little notice, and for a while it only watched me. Then, as I made turn after turn around the top of the hill, it began following me. It trailed after me at a distance, like a balloon on a string trailing after a child.

At first, it was amusing. Then it became confusing. Was a turkey *following* me? Intentionally? I doubted it was happening. Did it think that I had food—or that I *was* food? Perhaps my dead zombie-flesh released an appetizing smell? But, no. Wild turkeys were not known as carrion birds. (I pictured them eating bugs and worms and things that scuttled on the ground.)

Only one thing was certain: This was a persistent turkey, and seemed as tireless as I. (There were no actual zombie-animals. I recalled Sam saying, during our walk from my house to the grave-yard, that animal corpses had been mysteriously unaffected. For whatever reason, it was only humans that rose from their deathly slumbers.)

Thus, the turkey was not explained. All night, it kept me company as I paced the hilltop. Now and then I would lose track of the bird, yet it always reappeared within a few minutes.

I sat down on the spool as dawn neared, if only to have a stationary view of the sunrise. The bird approached, and lingered perhaps five paces away. Forgetting my guest entirely, I let the only words I would speak aloud on that hilltop escape my icy lips.

"What . . . the . . . *fuck?*"

At whom this question was directed, I could not have then said. (Nor can I now.) I suppose a cleverer man—or zombie—would have asked the universe something useful, like: "What the fuck am I supposed to do with myself now?" Or: "What the fuck becomes of a zombie?" Or simply: "What next?"

The sun rose. There was no answer.

Then the turkey clucked. An ugly noise—almost as ugly as the bird itself. I smiled at the turkey, as if to say, No, that's not really the answer I was looking for, but thanks for trying. Then the bird walked down the side of the hill. I sighed superfluously and stood up from the spool. The bird toddled along ahead of me. Our roles reversed, I lumbered after it.

The grass was slick with snow, and the turkey passed out of sight for a moment ahead of me. When I caught up to it, I discovered the bird standing—deliberately, it seemed—on the seat of the waiting ATV.

It was right, of course. I could not stay here. Movement. Travel. Exploration. These were the only things that could sate the questions in my soul. These were the things a zombie knew. I was hungry for answers (and perhaps also brains). I wanted to know what the fuck had happened—what *exactly* the fuck had happened— and what it meant for me.

As I neared the four-wheeler, the bird hopped off, as if to make room for me. (It was all so uncanny.) Then I had another thought. Was I, Peter Mellor, a mystical type? (I remembered so little about my prior self.) Perhaps I had communed with animals like a Catholic saint or a *National Geographic* reporter. Perhaps I saw portents in the weather, in tarot cards, or in . . . the behavior of animals?

This bird was no doubt behaving strangely. I felt that if I were a living, heart-pumping, lungs-breathing man, I'd be inclined to interpret the actions of my odd avian visitor as a "sign" of something. It would be interpreted as a nod—a discreet *pssst*—from the universe or from God. (Whatever you like.) But did the universe have anything left to say to a zombie? Did a brain-eating, skin-rotting zombie get to have mystical encounters with the unknown?

I didn't feel like it did. Instead, I felt that my status as a member of the walking dead meant that my story was somehow *over*. Zombies were lost, lonely wanderers, weren't they? Our time in the world was *finished* in some crucial way (though we were still, quite clearly, standing right there). We were the *dead*. The used-up. The rotting.

Did the great, magical universe—the same universe that sent omens to kings in the clouds, or to witches in the form of tea leaves—have anything left to say to zombies?

I started the ATV and began my slow descent from the hill. When I remembered to crane my neck to look back and see what had become of the turkey, it had disappeared.

I piloted the Kawasaki down quiet back roads until I came to a two-lane highway. The sun rose, and it stopped snowing. The temperature also rose. My sense of smell was more or less still intact, and morning in the countryside smelled good. With no clear destination in mind, I headed west along the shoulder of the highway. I wondered if I knew these roads, or if this was the same highway Sam had taken as we'd driven to Kate's house. I could not be certain.

I let my first impulse guide me. I drove on autopilot, like this was a commute home from a job I'd had forever. This was the way I always went, I told myself.

And so I went.

For perhaps an hour, I saw no one.

The day was calm. The sky was gray, the road eerily quiet. Then, far off to my right in a field, I noticed an Amish man walking next to a horse. He was a hundred yards away, but I made out his dark form instantly against the field, as white as a page. The horse was dark too. They were impossible to miss. I had a feeling of déjà vu, and a thought.

"They always wave," my spotty memory said to me.

Huh? I thought. Wave? Are you serious?

"If you wave at an Amish person, they always wave back," my memory insisted. "They *have* to—it's like a rule or something. Even if they're busy. Even if they're plowing a field or working a butter churn. Even if they dislike you personally. If you pass an Amish person—on foot or in a car—and you wave to them, they *have* to wave back."

Okay then, memory, I thought. Here goes.

I slowed the ATV to a crawl and did a big back-and-forth "Hello" wave with my right hand. The Amish man turned his head and regarded me for a moment, and then kept walking. No wave. No nothing.

Nice job, memory, I thought to myself.

But although those were the words I consciously formed in my mind, another part of me knew that my memory was probably correct. Amish people *did* have to wave, and under normal circumstances, that *was* what you could expect from them. But these were hardly normal circumstances.

I looked at the Amish man again and discerned a shotgun tied to the side of his horse, along with a sack of cornmeal.

Could Amish people carry guns? Was that within "the rules"? My memory had nothing to say on this question. Clearly, however, at least one Amish guy *was* packing, and he was just a Hail Mary away from me.

I took the ATV back up to speed, and the Amish man soon vanished into the whiteness behind me.

I continued down the two-lane highway. To my right and left were muddied creeks and frozen, snowy woods. I kept my eyes peeled for man or beast (or zombie), but saw nothing.

(Speaking of eyes, it was at this point I noticed that my eyes no longer lubricated themselves. There was, for me, no pain associated with this, but it seemed my eyes rolled more slowly in their sockets than they had before. I no longer produced tears. At one point, I pulled over to the side of the road and put some snow into my eyes. This helped immeasurably, but the effects were frustratingly short-lived. Thus, I began to understand the physiology behind the "zombie stare." [You know the one. Eyes open wide, fixed straight ahead.] I began to envision a future for myself where looking to the side would only be possible by craning my neck. But then how long, I wondered, until my neck starts to go?)

After another hour, I passed through a small "town" called Galen, with an ancient welcome sign but no stoplight. It had perhaps fifteen homes and two or three businesses. No post office. One gas station. (This got me to thinking about fuel, but the gauge on my Kawasaki said I still had about half a tank left.) It appeared the posted prices had gotten up to $35 a gallon before the hastily scrawled NO GAS sign had been stuck to the door and the windows shuttered.

But at least one home in Galen showed signs of life: a three-story Federal-style monstrosity, replete with American-flag bunting. The lights were out, but healthy plumes of blue smoke roared forth from two red chimneys. I thought, as I passed it, that I caught a whiff of coffee above the stench of my own engine. An embroidered sign hanging on the side door of the house read JESUS IS WATCHING OVER THIS PLACE. Someone had propped a shotgun next to the sign as well—just to show that JESUS had some backup.

The sun drew higher in the sky. It was warming and pleasant, and a smile came to my frozen lips. I realized, with a little alarm,

that I was feeling good. I had relaxed. I was enjoying the ride—
letting my intuition guide me along the empty road. Seriously,
"enjoyment" is the word.

In some weird way, it felt good—not just having the highway to
myself, but being a zombie riding a four-wheeler. "Maybe I'm a
reanimated corpse with no memory," I thought to myself, "but
right now I am master of this universe. I don't *need* anything. I
don't want for anything. And I am damn-near invincible."

I stared at the shuttered farmhouses here and there, and thought
about how all the humans around me were terrified. They were
afraid of zombies, afraid of other humans, and afraid of starving to
death. I was above such concerns. I smiled down from my Kawasaki
with the swagger of the immune. I smiled like a New Yorker on
vacation—the rest of the world's "efforts" and "concerns" quaint
and provincial by my standards. In this grotesque carnival at the end
of the world, I took a definite pleasure from my seated position.
(Plus, ATVs are fun. Seriously. Have you ever ridden one? If not,
you're really missing out.)

Anyhow, about an hour past Galen, the highway crested a hill
and I saw a vehicle stopped on the shoulder. Truth be told, I was
distracted and almost crashed into it. It was a black Harley-Davidson
Road King with a sidecar. A man in a new-looking leather jacket
was slumped forward over the handlebars. He wore a motorcycle
helmet and a thin coating of snow. In the sidecar was a young boy
of perhaps five or six, bundled many times over against the winter
chill. In his right hand he held a bag of potato chips. He had heard
my engine approaching and was standing up in the sidecar, facing
me as I came into view.

I could tell the man was dead before I stopped the ATV.

I silenced my engine, dismounted, and approached the child
warily. The dead man wore a holster with a gun in it on his side. It
was unlikely a small child would have a weapon, too, but these
were clearly different times. Anything was possible.

I looked them both over carefully.

"My dad died," the boy said flatly. (I say "boy," but the child's
gender was unguessable at this point, he was concealed beneath so
many layers of coats and scarves.)

I nodded at the boy, and gently approached the body of his
father. The boy only watched.

I pulled the head up and gave the corpse a cursory inspection.
The dead man (perhaps fifty years old, bristly mustache, nicotine-
stained teeth, maybe Hispanic) wore no expression. His clothes
were thick against the chill like his son's, but I could detect no sign
of injury upon him. He did not look sickly or unwell.

"What happened?" I asked in my raspy voice.

"He pulled over," the boy said. "He said his chest was hurting, and he was holding his chest. Then he died." From the snowfall on the body, I guessed the boy (and the decedent) had been out here for at least four or five hours.

"Where were you going, you and your father?" I asked him.

"My aunt who lives in Columbus's house," the boy managed. "My dad says ... My dad said there aren't zombies in Columbus. They have the army and police."

"Are you cold?" I asked the boy.

He seemed to consider the question seriously, then shrugged.

"We should ... get you inside," I said huskily. And I was pleased at how easily this conclusion came to me—that saving this child's life was the first impulse I had.

First impulse ... Did I also have an urge to ... *do* things to that child, the way I had "done things" to the woolly man whose ATV I now rode? I have to be honest. That was there. Eating his brain would have felt good. I understood that I would have liked it, and I understood that it was obtainable. It would have been an easy thing to chow down on a cold, defenseless child, paralyzed by fear and the loss of his father. (And—let me stress this again—it also would have felt *really good*.)

But there was also a part of me that understood this was a child. You know? A fucking *child*. I stood back a moment and looked at the empty fields around us.

I had to get the kid inside. The only question was where.

I scanned the horizon in my direction of travel, finding only forest and more farms ahead. How many miles until the next town? I had no idea. (I hadn't really been paying attention to road signs as I passed them, and this part of Ohio all looked the same. Mansfield. Coshocton. Mount Vernon. Who knew what might lie up the road.)

Then, something out of the corner of my eye. Maybe nothing. But ... *Maybe* ... The fingers on the corpse of the father, twitching. I walked over and leaned in close. I squinted hard. The middle finger seemed to move a little. Then it *definitely* moved a little. Then it positively jumped. Did zombie corpses twitch before they awoke? I had no memory of twitching—only of suddenly waking up—but that didn't mean I *hadn't* twitched first. Maybe finger twitches meant the corpse still had hours to go before reanimation. Or maybe only seconds.

"Time to go," I croaked to the kid. "Come on. Help me."

"What's your name?" the boy asked as I began to move his father's body off the Harley.

"They call me Peter," I told him, casting his father's body to the side of the highway. "What's yours?"

"Billy Hernandez," he said. "They call me Billy."

I gripped the father's body around the shoulders and pulled it off to the side of the road. (I wondered—if, in fact, he *was* coming back—if the right thing to do might have been to find a way to put the body down. Mash in the head. Hell, run it over a few times with the bike. But I couldn't do it with the little boy right there. No matter how well he seemed to be taking the situation. Some things you did, and some things you didn't do. Even if you were a zombie. I decided that defiling a father's corpse in front of his little son wasn't one of them.)

I got on the motorcycle with no idea if I'd ever driven one before. I looked at the kid. "Billy, did your father ever tell you anything about how to start this thing?"

"You turn the keys," he said. "On the side of the motorcycle."

There they were, right in front of me.

"Ahh," I said. "That makes sense. Do you need to buckle up or anything?" I asked him.

"No," the kid said. "I just sit down."

"Oh," I replied.

"Mister," the kid asked, "where are we going?"

"Someplace warm," I said. I pulled my baseball cap down hard over my forehead and started the motorcycle.

Once I'd gotten the Harley going, I turned around and headed back in the direction from whence I'd come. The motorcycle was much faster than the four-wheeler, and it didn't take long to get to the outskirts of Galen.

I had no memory of having driven a motorcycle before, and I certainly wasn't good at it, but with the road deserted and empty, it was hard to feel like we were in any danger. The snow was light. The temperature might have risen above freezing—I couldn't really tell—and there didn't seem to be any ice. Even so, I kept it below fifty the whole way.

As we drove, I stole a couple of glances over to the sidecar to see how the kid was doing. He looked back at me each time I turned my head, seeming to study my features. I wondered if he could tell. Was I only a stranger, or was the zombie aspect of my appearance becoming apparent to the child?

The destination I had in mind for Billy Hernandez was Galen's Federal-style home—the forbidding, Christian one that had shown signs of life. I would not normally—as a human or a zombie—have even been inclined to approach it. Flags and Jesus and a shotgun. (It definitely seemed the kind of place where liberal arts professors didn't hang out.) And yet, in a zombie apocalypse, perhaps those were some of the things that would protect a child.

In a best-case scenario, I anticipated a gruff conversation at gunpoint with someone like the Matilda-woman. Worst case, they shot first and asked questions later.

We entered Galen, and I pulled the Harley into the abandoned gas station.

"Stay here," I told the kid.

I got off the bike, walked up to the glass door of the station, and cupped my hands to the window. Inside, on the counter by the cash register and the gum and the lottery tickets, I saw what I was looking for.

I regarded the door for a moment. There's a way to do this. There's a way to do this, and I know it, I thought to myself. Trusting my instinct or memory, I stood facing the door with my hands at my sides, pulled back one leg, and kicked hard next to the handle.

The glass began to give.

Several kicks later, and the door had fractured enough for me to reach through and undo the lock. I stepped inside the abandoned station and took the pen I found lying next to the cash register. Then I took a missing-cat flyer from the station window, turned it over, and began to write.

Moments later, I was back outside with the kid.

"Billy," I said to him. "Do you see that big square house at the end of the street? The one with the American flags that hang down in half-circles?"

Billy nodded.

"I want you to go to that house and knock on the door," I croaked. "Take this piece of paper and give it to whoever opens the door, okay? Here. And give them the side with the writing on it, not the cat picture. Can you do that?"

"Yes," he said, taking the flyer from me. "Not the cat picture. Are *you* coming?"

"No," I told him.

"Why not?" he asked. "Is it because you're a zombie?"

I hesitated, wondering if all kids were as perceptive as this one. "Yeah," I said. "Something like that."

Billy walked away from me, down the empty street. It took a good two minutes for him to reach the house. He carefully climbed the steps up to the imposing door and knocked hard with his twice-gloved hands. Nothing happened. He looked back at me. I motioned for him to press the doorbell. He gave me a reluctant glance, then turned and depressed the button. Moments later, there was movement from inside. Two windows on the upper level of the home opened slightly, and shotgun barrels emerged. I saw drapes pulled aside at other windows. And it may have been my imagination, but I thought I heard a woman's voice on the wind say: "It's a child."

The front door opened. An older man with close-cropped white hair emerged, rifle at the ready. At first, he looked not at the kid but past him. He looked all around, for any sign that this was a trick or trap or ambush.

I was way down the street, on the other edge of the little town, but he saw me right away. I gave a little wave, then gestured to the boy who was holding up the flyer.

The older man took it—cat side first, of course. Confused, he looked back down the street in my direction. I made a "flip it over" motion. The man turned the flyer over, where he would have read all or part of the following:

Sir or Madam,
I found this boy alone on the road. His father has just died. He has been outside in the cold most of the night. His name is William Hernandez. He has an aunt in Columbus. Please care for him until they can be reunited.
Yours in Christ.

Perhaps the final flourish was a *tad* patronizing, but it seemed to do the job. The silver-haired man lowered his gun and crouched down next to the little boy. They spoke. The two were out of earshot, but the boy nodded at what was being said. Then the man moved aside and the boy walked inside the house. The man stood and gave me an awkward half-wave before closing the door behind him.

I started up the motorcycle (noting that the shotguns—obviously aware of my presence—had *not* moved from the upper windows). I drove away slowly, as if trailed by a police officer. As I passed the Federal-style house, I gave a little wave to the shotguns.

Jesus and shotguns, I thought as I pulled away. They weren't good or bad, they just *were*.

Back along the highway, I approached the place where my ATV should have been, and found that it had been taken. I had been gone for no more than thirty minutes, and yet my vehicle had already disappeared. I slowed the motorcycle to a crawl and saw the body of Mr. Hernandez Sr. in a ditch. It had been moved.

I cautiously pulled the Harley over to take a closer look and saw that Mr. Hernandez's head had been cut from his body—I guessed with a chain saw, judging from the jagged flaps of skin. It sent a shudder through me that had nothing to do with the gore.

I was not as alone as I seemed. These fields and forests had eyes. (And, apparently, chain saws.) I wondered if Mr. Hernandez had come into his full presence as a zombie, or if the decapitation had merely been a precaution. I would never know.

Next to the body was a pool of water created by melting snow. I stooped over to put some of it into my eyes, and caught my reflection on the surface. The water was getting muddy, and the reflection it showed was a bit uneven, but one thing was clear: I looked really terrible. And not just a "You've been out all night drinking vodka and Red Bulls" kind of terrible. It was more of a "You're not going to be able to pass as *human* too much longer" kind of terrible.

My skin was a deathly shade of white. My eyes had a manic stare. My hair looked unhealthy—like it was an old, dried-out wig ready to slip off a bald head. Even with my Kernels hat pulled down low, the days of my being able to seem human were numbered. I looked, if not dead, then deathly ill.

And it had been such a short time! Only sixteen hours (give or take) since my accident, and already I was looking this bad. My eyes made no tears. My nose made no snot, so the dirt that went into my nose stayed dirt and didn't become boogers. My skin was bereft of all natural moisture and oil. They sounded like small things, but their combined absence for less than a day made me look like a sickly monster.

My one hopeful thought was that I'd still be able to pass—for a few more days—as someone with pneumonia or a terrible flu. Yet even playing sick would likely arouse suspicion. (There was not a flu epidemic raging across the land, but there *was* a zombie epidemic.) I would have spat down at my reflection if I'd had any spit left in me.

From here on out, it would be a game of proximity. I'd be able to pass as human at a distance—as long as I kept moving (and driving, it occurred to me, because most zombies didn't drive)—but up close, I'd be fucked. Within ten or fifteen feet, people were going to be able to see that something was *very* wrong with me. So I would have to be careful. I'd have to make sure I didn't let people near. I didn't know what this meant for my lifestyle in the long term, but in the short term, I decided it shouldn't be *too* difficult. I looked again at the decapitated corpse next to me, and considered the alternative.

Then I got back on the Harley and pulled away.

I rode the bike up and down rural highways for most of the day, exploring Knox County. (The thing sipped gasoline compared to a car, and apparently it had a full tank.) I saw very little in the way of signs of life—or "life"—until near dusk, when I crested a hill and saw a group of zombies wading through a snowy field of winter wheat.

As I say, the light was dying, but I could easily make out fifteen or twenty in their group. Maybe there were more. The zombies were all in the later stages of decomposition, and I could smell it from the road. Black flesh or mud clung to their bones. They moved slowly and stiffly. They made almost no sound at all.

How, I wondered, did a *group* like this happen? It was a mystery. Was there a single source for all of these zombies—like a country graveyard—or had they gradually found one another and banded together?

Then, another question: Even if they *had* been reanimated at the same time, what kept them together? I tried to imagine how it was that certain zombies did not veer off from the herd.

I pulled the bike over and watched them until the light died. They moved through the wheat like a flock of birds in slow motion. There was a formation to it. One in front seemed to lead the way, and the others followed like links on a chain. But even within that, there were small variations. Now and then, two zombies might seem to notice one another. They would adjust their courses for a moment, investigate each other, and just as quickly correct themselves to rejoin the group. They were not moving in my direction, but across the field toward a distant farmhouse. From where I stood, the home looked shuttered and lifeless. Perhaps, however, the zombies "knew" on some level that it would be worth their while to go and have a look-see.

Unlike my compatriots shambling in formation, I felt no supernatural ability to divine for humans. I could only look for movement or listen for human sounds. Unless these zombies had something I didn't, they were likely heading for the farmhouse because it was the nearest thing. Maybe the lead zombie could remember that humans usually lived in houses. Whatever the impetus behind their march, the zombies sauntered on, determined.

When it was completely dark, I started up the bike again and continued down the empty highway. Along one familiar-feeling stretch, a road sign announced GANT 15. Kenton College was only fifteen miles ahead. The sky was dark, but my incandescent watch told me it was only seven-thirty in the evening.

I decided to pay my friend Sam a visit.

I drove the bike for what felt close to fifteen miles, then turned off the headlight and pulled to the side of the road, edging the bike forward slowly through the darkness. To my dismay, it was still *very* loud. (I wasn't sure who I thought I was sneaking up on, but a clandestine approach just felt like the right thing to do.) After a few minutes, I encountered the welcome sign for Gant. This was a different two-lane highway than the one where I'd wrecked my car. I had little memory of it, but apparently more than one road ran through the little college town.

I piloted the bike to a clump of trees near the welcome sign and killed the engine. I covered the motorcycle's reflective chrome parts with brush and branches, and took the keys out of the ignition. Stand a few paces away, and you'd never know it was a motorcycle.

This way into Gant / Kenton College was utterly alien to me, but I knew that the town and the college buildings must lie up ahead. I also knew that a team of people was defending the college against zombies and strangers. After seeing my reflection in the dirty puddle by the side of the road, I no longer liked my chances at passing as "living human college professor Peter Mellor." Not even with people who had once known me. In fact, it might be worse with them. (To a stranger, I might claim to have always looked this haggard and ill. To an old friend, it would be apparent right away that something was very wrong with me.)

Based on these concerns, I decided to discreetly pick my way into town through the underbrush and find Sam's house with the red roof using backyards. I crept along the edge of the road leading into town, and then did my best to melt into the first clump of trees I found. Briars and branches grabbed at me, but I felt no pain as their hooks and needles found their way into my skin. The leaves beneath my feet were wet and snowy, and I was relieved to find this helped me move noiselessly. (There was no crunch—just a soft *gloop* sound to my steps.) I carefully maneuvered through the brush and eventually found a long, contiguous row of trees that seemed to run right into the center of town. I followed it like a trail. I moved slowly. Took a few steps, then remained still, sometimes for a full minute. I listened and looked for any sign of life. Then I repeated the process.

I passed an empty football field, covered with snow and strewn with trash. Then an abandoned student parking lot, and a massive athletic building. Except for a dead raccoon moldering at the foot of a tree, I saw nothing living or dead. Certainly, no movement.

But then, as I neared the top of the hill that was Gant, Ohio, I caught a flash of nickel and steel in the moonlight. I huddled against a tree and froze. Bowles and Starks, the college doctor and the security guard, were walking the perimeter of the town, weapons in hand. They chatted with one another but frowned seriously as they surveyed the woods with grim eyes. I ducked down and waited, certain they had seen me. Moments later, I saw that I had been wrong. They had noticed nothing. The two men resumed chatting, and moved away.

Still clinging to the trees as best I could, I moved on, entering a residential area. Here, I crossed from yard to yard until—finally!—I found the house with the red roof. I crept near the modest dwelling and saw the flicker of a single candle in the upstairs window.

Hoping I would not be simply shot on sight, I emerged from the trees and threw a stone against the window like a teenage suitor. I saw movement inside instantly. Moments later, the top of Sam's head peered out from the window.

"Saaam," I rasped, waving my arms.

He regarded me suspiciously.

"Sam, it's me . . . Peter," I said.

Sam left the window. Moments later, I watched as the candle moved through the house, through the upstairs, descending a staircase, and finally edged over to the sliding-glass door that opened into his backyard. He cracked the doors slowly, and cautiously looked to his right and left before addressing me.

"Pete, is that you?" he called.

"Yeah," I said.

"Well . . . what are you doing back here?" he asked.

"It's complicated," I told him.

"Is Vanessa with you?"

"No," I said. "It's just me."

"Do you want to come in?" he asked.

I thought about it. "No," I finally answered. "Can we talk outside?"

"Let me get my coat, then," Sam said.

He reemerged in a puffy jacket, carrying a pistol. "Do you want your gun back?" he asked. "You left it in my car."

"No," I said. "That's fine."

He followed me into the trees. When we both felt sufficiently insulated by the forest, we faced one another and crouched down confidentially.

"I'm a zombie," I told him.

"What?" he said. "No, you're not."

"Dude, look at this," I said, and removed my hat.

Sam's eyes went big. I watched as he absently mouthed "What the fuck?"

"Seriously, I'm a zombie," I told him.

"But ... but you *can't* be a zombie," he stammered.

"Dude," I said, and bowed as if to a dignitary. Sam shrank back from the top of my head. "*Yaaaah*," he ejaculated. "Okay. I see your point. Just ... put your hat back on."

I obeyed.

"I think when I crashed my car yesterday, I didn't just get amnesia," I rasped to him. "I also died and came back as a zombie. I'm not really alive anymore."

"But you're walking and talking," Sam pointed out.

"I know," I said. "But I'm also a zombie. My head's half gone. I don't breathe. My heart doesn't beat. And ..."

I hesitated like a nervous man on a date, afraid to go in for that first kiss.

"And what?" Sam said.

"I ate a guy," I told him. "This stuff around my mouth? It's blood."

"Jesus," Sam managed. He put his hand on his chest and began to look a little faint. "Are you going to eat me?"

"No," I told him.

"That's good, at least," Sam managed.

"He was a bad guy—the one I ate," I said to Sam. "He was going to rape Kate's little girl, I think. And he tried to *kill* me. So it was probably good that I ate him."

"Still, though," Sam said. "That's pretty fucked."

"Yeah, I know," I said. "I'm not exactly happy about it."

"So what ... What're you going to do?" he asked me.

I shook my head.

"I don't know," I told him. "I kinda hoped *you* would have some ideas in that department. That's why I stopped by."

"*M-m-me?*" he stammered.

"Yeah," I said. "Have you ever heard of anything like this? You're a science guy, right?"

Sam ran his hands through his hair and sat down against the foot of a tree.

"Jesus, Pete," he said after a sigh. "You should've found yourself a biology professor. I'm a physicist."

"Do your best," I said.

"Well, okay," Sam said, thinking for a second. "Maybe it's like AIDS. Do you remember what AIDS is? HIV?"

"Yeah," I said, recalling several harrowing impressions of a deadly STD.

Sam said, "There's a small group of people who get HIV—the blood virus—but they never get sick and they never develop AIDS. It's a small fraction of a percent. Like one in every one hundred thousand. But these people never get sick. They *have* HIV—they can pass it along to others—but it never makes them ill. Nobody understands exactly why it happens, but it does. Shit. I wish we still had a biologist on campus. They might be able to tell you more."

"So maybe one out of every hundred thousand zombies gets to keep talking and thinking?" I asked.

"It's a theory," Sam said. "But here's another thing: Right now, when people die, they come back as zombies. They're usually dead for a while, though. A few hours or a few days. But you came back right away. Like, almost instantly, from your description of things."

"The tires on my car were still spinning," I told him.

"Exactly," said Sam. "So maybe zombies lose their memory and speech and whatever because they're out for so long before reanimating. It's like brain death. Or maybe brain rot. But you weren't out for very long—maybe just for a second or two—so you're relatively untouched."

"So I just randomly got lucky, then?" I asked. "Assuming that 'lucky' is the right word for this."

"Freaks happen in anything, or in any group of things," he said. "It's like with batteries and lightbulbs. I know more about *them* than I do about biology."

"Batteries and lightbulbs?" I asked.

"Yeah," Sam said. "You know how whenever you see an ad for batteries on TV, it always says 'Duracell batteries last up to six times longer than the average Energizer battery,' or vice versa? That language is an advertising trick. They're comparing the top of a range to the middle of another."

"Explain that," I said. "And keep it simple. I'm a zombie."

"I'll try," said Sam. "So when they make a battery, it usually lasts for fifty hours, let's say. But there's always some variation. Some batteries last for fifty-one hours, or forty-nine hours. But sometimes, every few years or so, a *freak* battery comes along—one that's going to last three hundred hours. In those ads, they compare *that* battery to their competitor's *average* battery. See, even if their average battery lasts forty-nine hours and their competitor's average battery lasts fifty, they can still say that their batteries can last 'up to' six times longer. And it's because they're going by that once-in-a-decade freak battery, you see? It's the same thing with lightbulbs, too, but I won't go into that."

"What, then?" I asked. "I'm a lightbulb that burns for a really long time? A battery that can keep the stupid bunny going forever?"

"Yeah, sorta," Sam said. "Maybe most people, when they die and become zombies, have virtually no self-control or memory. They can hardly think or talk at all. But *you* ... Compared with a *human*, yeah, you've got a terrible memory. But compared to a zombie, you're an elephant. You're Funes the Memorious. You're ... you know ... somebody who remembers things really good."

"I see," I said slowly. "I'm some kind of statistical freak, is what you're saying? A freak that comes along once in many years?"

"In my opinion, it's a tenable hypothesis," Sam replied, the professor in him emerging. "It's ... remarkable, really."

"Hmmm," I said, unconvinced. "If you say so."

"You really don't remember me, do you?" Sam said. He seemed—somewhat abruptly—to want to make things personal.

"You seem *familiar*," I told him. "Lots of things seem familiar. But I can't remember us doing much together. Now and then I get a few mental pictures of you, but it's hard to know what they mean. I don't know the events surrounding them."

"No memory of, like, conversations we had?" Sam questioned. His eyes were searching, sad.

Suddenly, I felt for the awkward little guy. It would have been easy to tell a white lie. No doubt, he had invested much of himself in our friendship over the past few years. Hundreds or thousands of hours of his life. And though I was walking and talking right in front of him, it was also like the Peter Mellor he had spent all that time with was dead. That person he had been friends with no longer existed. All of the time and effort he had devoted to that friendship was wasted.

But I couldn't lie. Now was not the time for lying. Not to the one person I still hoped might help me.

"No," I answered. "Like I said, I just sort of have ... impressions of you. They're *good* impressions, though. They're really good."

Sam sighed and picked himself up off the ground.

"So what're you going to do with yourself?" he asked, changing the subject once again.

"I don't know," I said. "It's dangerous out here."

"Dangerous?" Sam said, incredulous. "Dangerous?! Are you serious? You're already a zombie, Peter. What're *you* afraid of? You ate a guy."

"Everybody I see has a gun, even the Amish," I told him. "Everybody is hunting zombies. If they realize what I am, they'll kill me. I'm all alone."

"Hmmm ... Maybe you should hang out with other zombies," Sam said.

"I'll assume that was a bad joke," I told him.

"Then how about keeping your hat on?" he said. "You're walking and talking and . . . obviously you can drive if you got here this fast."

"Dude, it was a Harley," I said with a smile.

"See, there you go," Sam said. "When you need to be a human, be a human."

"But I can only be a human in the shadows, or from very far away!" I protested.

" 'Not in perspective, and not in the light,' eh?" Sam said.

"Have you really looked at me, Sam? I saw my reflection in some murky water today, and it was terrifying. My skin is fucked up and too white. There's no moisture left in my body. Listen to how hoarse my voice is—and it's getting worse by the minute."

"I'm not saying there's an easy answer," Sam said. "But you can't just focus on the negative. In a way, I'm envious of you."

"Envious?" I said. "You, of me? You're kidding."

"Christ," Sam shouted, suddenly hostile. "The news is . . . it's bad, okay? *Bad.* Everything we hear—from the TV, from the Amish, from people passing through—it's all terrible. Violence everywhere. People acting like animals—fighting over food, hoarding, killing each other. Criminal gangs forming across the countryside. Bikers taking over towns like Brando in *The Wild One.* Jesus, Pete, there are twenty-five of us left here who can fight. Twenty-five. If a hundred Hells Angels ride into town and decide to go on a looting, raping, and killing spree, we're pretty much fucked. Even if the phones were up, and we could call the National Guard, how long would it take for them to send troops up from Columbus? And something tells me they might have their hands full down there."

I nodded, solemnly.

"And that's not even talking about the zombies!" he railed. "What's left of the news is showing some pretty horrible shit. The zombies . . . Hordes meet with hordes, and they decide to cooperate and grow stronger. They become armies. Out west, where people haven't been around to put down all the country graveyards, they're forming massive divisions out on the plains. When they decide to turn on a town, there's no way to stop them. The pictures I've seen—they can't be real—but it looks like zombies as far as the eye can see. They're going to have to be nuked or something. Apparently, the other day, one of those massive waves ate Iowa City. Like, ate the whole city. The people just aren't there anymore."

"Wow," I said, genuinely impressed. (And also horrified.)

"Don't you see, Pete?" Sam continued. "You're on the winning team."

"You can't believe that," I said to him. "The cities are doing okay. There are still Green Zones and such. I saw it on the news. They've got food, and law and order."

Sam sighed.

"I don't know," he finally said. "I just don't know. How long will the food last if people don't go back to farming? If we can't import anything? I hate to imagine being in a city when the food runs out. Nah ... I think I'll make my stand here on the hill with people I know."

Far away, a car horn sounded several times. It was an awkward cadence, like a code. Something told me it was being sounded in frantic alarm. It was very, very distant, but still definite. We both searched the sky, as if trying to judge from which direction it came—though neither of us, I think, knew what we would do with that information. After a full minute, it stopped with a sickly, final squeak, like the life leaving a trapped animal.

We both looked at one another as if to say *What the fuck was that?*

"Anyhow, I can't stay here," I continued. "I won't pass as human for long, and I can't trust that the others here would understand. You know? I'm a zombie, I already ate a guy, and I have no memory of them ... but I want them to take my word that I'm not a threat? That's a hell of a hard sell."

"I think you might be right," Sam said, taking a cigarette out of his coat. "Best-case scenario, they might chain you in a basement somewhere. 'Monitor' you."

"Yeah," I said. "I'm feeling—and don't ask me how I know this—but I'm feeling like a lost teenager. A runaway. Something tells me this is not the place for me. I've got to go somewhere, and I don't know where. But I'm just going to go."

"Follow your heart, huh?" Sam said, taking a drag on his smoke.

"Not that it beats anymore," I said, tapping my chest.

"It goes without saying, but you can come back and visit whenever you want," Sam said.

"Okay ... Thanks, Dad," I said, a hollow joke.

"Final question, then," Sam said. "Can I give you a ride anywhere? Do you *need* anything?"

"No," I said. "Got the Harley, remember? And I can't think of anything I need."

The truth of that statement really started to hit me. It was true. I *didn't* need anything. I was a zombie. The open road was my world.

"Look," I said, "I appreciate all your advice, but I should go now. I'm just going to head back through the trees here."

"See you around, then," Sam said, finishing his cigarette.

I shook his hand.

"See you," I said, and picked my way back into the thicket.

Halfway back to the Harley, they were upon me. Seemingly from out of nowhere, I heard the sound of automobiles and shouting men, and saw flickers of flashlights or headlights through the trees. They did not appear to know where I was, but something had put the residents of Gant on alert.

I picked up the pace of my picking. Had someone spotted my motorcycle? Perhaps they had seen me leaving Sam's place and raised an alarm. I hadn't concealed my exit through the yards with the same gusto I'd used on my approach.

There was no time to consider it. I saw headlights approaching from the far side of the hill. The voices increased in volume and number. My motorcycle was close now. Did I hide or run for it? I needed to make a decision, and I could hear the townspeople nearing. It was only a question of whether or not they would head in my direction. Their flashlights seemed to shine all over—past me and above me—but never lit upon me. They knew I was here, but the specifics of my position remained undiscovered.

I made a break for it. The operative word being "break." My legs stayed intact, but the extent to which my body had stiffened became ever more apparent as I tried to move with speed. It was like running on stilts—horrible, arthritic stilts. I slipped and nearly fell.

Fuck, I thought to myself. What did I expect? Everybody knows *zombies aren't supposed to go fast.* I hustled down the rest of the embankment on iron legs and found the motorcycle by the coppice where I'd left it. It appeared to have remained undiscovered. I moved the branches away and got on. I started the engine. It was loud. There was an instant fluttering of the flashlights up the hill, and then they all began to shine in my direction. The Kentonites would not catch me, however. The bike was too fast, and I left Gant, Ohio, in a growl of snow and dust.

It was a quiet, cold night. The snow continued to fall in thin waves, never accumulating much, but always present. Aside from my single headlight, there was total darkness all around.

I rode the bike deep into the Ohio woods. First, I took the two-lane highways, then I turned down even darker country roads—the darkest I could find, the darker the better. When I came across an abandoned railroad track, I turned onto it and followed it for as long as I could. The bike ran out of gas atop a crumbling trestle bridge. I left it there, and walked deeper into the forest.

By the time dawn broke, I was in the middle of nowhere. It was just where I wanted to be. I strolled idly, enjoying the quiet forest and the snow on the trees. I had no idea if I was still in Knox County. The people from Gant had not pursued me, and I hadn't needed to stay on the highway for very long. I still had no clue how they'd known I was there, but I was impressed at how quickly they had been able to organize and come after me. Cell phones were down, but perhaps they'd had walkie-talkies. Perhaps they'd simply shouted to one another.

The sun rose higher in the sky. I reflected that not needing to sleep was going to give me extra time. Most people needed eight hours a night. I could keep going, twenty-four/seven. (Sure, it was extra time. No question about that. The question was, extra time for what?)

I walked and walked through the empty forest. Despite the silence and stillness, I encountered reminders that this was a settled country. Wherever I walked, I was on someone's property or on state land. Here was the broken head of a pickax. There, an empty bag of potato chips built into the nest of a bird. There was no "getting away" from humans, even in the most rural of areas. I followed a frozen creek until it terminated in a little pond full of Canada geese. On the other side of the lake, the woods thinned out and a farmer's field became visible. As I approached it, I saw an old hay cart with wooden wheels, forgotten and overturned.

Then: Astounding! Not zombies. Not people with guns. Something more unbelievable.

As I approached the overturned cart, a wild turkey emerged from underneath. It was jet-black, and disgusting to look at. And it appeared very much like the one who had kept me company the night before. His tread was slow—almost absent—much like mine. He had nowhere to go, and nowhere to be. My jaw dropped a little. I approached the bird, but it did not shrink away.

"What's up?" I said.

The bird, as if only hearing my second word, climbed the overturned cart and hopped to the top until it was face-to-face with me. It was creepy. (And here *I* was the zombie.) For a moment, I thought the bird might actually speak to me. It might talk, like something out of a fantasy movie. But it only stayed still and watched from atop the cart. It was just a bird.

"What?" I said to it.

No response.

I let out a superfluous sigh. "I went back and talked to Sam— who I guess is my friend—but he didn't know what I should do. It almost got me caught, though. People from the college came after me with guns. And I didn't get a better idea of what I should be doing—other than to keep moving."

The turkey nodded, or seemed to. Again, creepy.

"I don't think I can go back there anymore. I've got to, like, accept being a zombie or something. Maybe accept eating people." My stomach growled upon uttering these words. It took me aback. My stomach was supposed to be dead, like the rest of me. It wasn't making gastric juices anymore, or turning food into shit. I didn't even feel hungry anymore.

Or did I?

Thinking about eating brains again had definitely triggered something . . . down there. In my mind, I ran through the details of eating the ATV man's brains like paste. Nice.

"Wait . . . okay, just wait," I said, to my own stomach as much as to the turkey. The turkey cocked its head as if to say *What?*

"Eating brains feels nice. Really, really nice. But I can't just . . . kill people. People who don't deserve it. There are people that I like! I don't remember them much, but I still *like* them. Sam and Vanessa were—or are—good people who I cared about. I wouldn't want to eat them."

The turkey bobbed again. This guy approved of everything.

I made my monologue internal.

Maybe there was some way I could "help." I liked eating brains. I liked thinking about it. But I would be different. I would have rules. I would only eat the brains of bad people—would-be child rapists and such—as I'd already done. I had little memory of my past, true. But from what I could tell, I had loved others and others had loved me. These remnants of feelings told me that my girlfriend Vanessa was associated with love. If I could help her . . . be useful to her . . . save her—then perhaps my "life" would be worth something.

And then I could eat the brains of her enemies, which would be totally awesome.

Yeah, I thought. I could be a *moral* zombie, never eating the brain of a good person. (I had already shown that I was above eating the brain of a child.) I would use my murderous appetites to make the world a better place. Somehow.

"Yeah," I said aloud. "Maybe that's it."

I gave the wild turkey a little salute and walked out into the farmer's field, determined, in some vague and general way, to use my powers for good.

The bird watched me go.

I'll try to give you some sense of the way it felt to be there, in those lonely days that followed, stalking around the empty countryside, trying to be a zombie. I think I said somewhere before that it was like walking around on a holiday. There was the emptiness and quiet of Christmas Eve. Except it was Christmas Eve with guns.

Now and then, I saw farmers or Amish, always armed. My interactions with them were always the same. I was sure to wave, but was just as careful to keep my distance. I had to establish that I was human, but I did not want to look inviting. I didn't want to look friendly or approachable. Just *human*—nothing more. Never did I let anybody get close.

I stayed on the roads. They were deserted. Nobody was using cars—there was so little gas to spare that car travel was for emergencies only. In a week of wandering, I saw four (moving) vehicles total. One sedan. Two motorcycles. One pickup truck. In every case, I disappeared into the winter wheat or forest at the first sound of the approaching engine. (There were concealment-related advantages to being a zombie. I could jump into a pond and stay below the water indefinitely. I could conceal myself in places that were full of freezing ice or itchy brambles, with no concern for personal comfort. If necessary, I could, with considerable skill, pretend to be dead.)

A couple of times, I passed gangs of humans. These terrified me, and I just stayed away. They'd be mostly men, and always armed to the teeth. I hesitate to call them "hunting parties," like they were a group out hunting for food, or hunting zombies for sport. They were gangs. Something in their membership looked mean and criminally inclined. Whenever I crossed a hedge or valley and encountered one of these slow-moving, weapon-toting groups, I just turned around and headed the other way. If I had any notion that they might've seen me, I found a pond and sank below the waterline for a couple of hours, just to be safe.

The real trick was the small towns. (I had some memory of having once called them "blink towns," because they were so small you could miss them if you blinked when you were driving through. Sometimes they were just four or five houses. Maybe a store and a post office.) Some of them were completely dead and empty, but some—like Galen, the town where I'd left the kid—had at least one house where folks were holding out.

At first, I approached these places with curiosity and longing. Was there some clue here? Some sign among these clapboard homes and quaint country stores as to what my next step should be? Would some way to be a "helpful zombie" present itself? I longed for a friend. I longed to find someone like me (or who liked me). Ideally, another zombie who could talk. A kindred spirit. Yet, time and again, these tiny clumps of homes did nothing but let me down. Sometimes residents emerged to confront me, armed and threatening like a posse. Once, as I meandered innocently down a main drag (such as it was), a sniper from a roof put two bullets in my legs, and it was all I could do to hightail it into the woods. Other towns I avoided altogether upon seeing gun barrels emerge from upstairs windows.

After a while, I just started to go around them, circumventing them completely if I could. Nothing good was waiting for me in those places.

After a very lonely week, I found myself on the outskirts of Mount Vernon, the largest city in Knox County. Mount Vernon's population was close to twenty thousand. It had a Bible college, and was the birthplace of Dan Emmett, the guy who wrote the song "Dixie" as a joke to make fun of Southerners (and then they took it seriously and made it their national anthem [or else maybe he ripped it off from some black guys who lived in the area, which is also kind of ironic in its own fashion—but either way, anthropology PhDs have gotten involved in the debate now, so it's boring and not fun anymore]). There's a statue of Emmett on a pillar downtown in a traffic circle. In the summer, teenagers cruise around it in cars with Confederate flags, trying to pick each other up. Churches outnumber ... everything else. It's the kind of place where people still talk about the time Rob Lowe came to stump for Walter Mondale. (I don't think he changed any minds.)

It's also the kind of place where people get left behind. Where you can't understand why people would ever decide to stick around once they've turned eighteen. But enough of them do that they form a tight-lipped clique of sticking-arounders. And that clique will look at you cross-eyed if you begin to suggest that anything's wrong with sticking around a place like Mount Vernon. It's like a big horrible cycle. Pretty soon, everybody's uncomfortable. It's the kind of place that gave up on trying to be "charming" or "quaint" a long time ago.

It is what it is. And also, go fuck yourself.

As I approached Mount Vernon, these impressions—I won't say "memories"—came flooding back. I'd been here before, many times, yet I hadn't looked forward to any of the trips. This was where I'd come when I needed to go to a real supermarket, or hit the state store for some scotch, or send something by UPS. It was a "have-to," not a "want-to" kind of place.

But I was lost. I was lonely. I was sick of the "blink towns" where people took potshots at me. It had been a disheartening week. Mount Vernon presented a change. Something new. The only game in town, but a game no less. In a perverse way, I found it attractive. (It had only taken an apocalyptic zombie outbreak for Mount Vernon to finally become a "want-to.")

I crept to its edge along some railroad tracks. Then I climbed a tall hill and stared down into the town enviously, like Grendel looking into Heorot. There were puffs of smoke coming from several of the chimneys, and I often saw flittering flashlight beams pierce the night. Once or twice, I heard far-off shouts. Most of Mount Vernon's twenty thousand residents had apparently not fled to the Columbus Green Zone. (Like I said, these were not the kind of people who left. Not to get a real degree. Not to get a better job. Damn straight not for zombies.)

These people were taking the President of the United States up on his challenge to keep going to work. And they were probably doing a lot more than that. (I pictured them holding church services and AA meetings and city council hearings as zombies sauntered past. I wouldn't have been surprised to see mothers down below me on their way to a bake sale.)

I saw fast-food restaurants. A movie theater. A hotel. I stared into these places hard, sensing the familiarity, yet I was hesitant to venture in completely. I didn't want to risk just strutting down Main Street. I needed to take my time, I decided. I needed to enter slowly and carefully.

For the better part of a day, I crept around the edges of the city in a circle, like the hands on a clock. A few people saw me, but I kept my hat pulled low and always gave a wave. Once, I passed a city graveyard where a larger-scale version of the Kenton College watch was going on. Twenty or thirty men milled about the headstones with flashlights and rifles. At least one of them was reading aloud from a Bible.

Then, on the south edge of town, I stumbled upon an auto impound lot set back into a valley. It held maybe fifty cars surrounding a single, ancient trailer home with a generator. An older man in a Russian-style hat with earflaps stalked through the lot, drinking from a steaming cup of coffee. He carried a hunting rifle and made periodic stops back inside the trailer. I stayed and watched the scene carefully, because one of the impounded cars that he guarded was mine.

A tag had been placed on one of the side-view mirrors, and a sheet of copy paper in a plastic sleeve had been taped to what was left of the windshield. But there it was. My car. Still totaled, but no less mine.

I was intrigued.

I concealed myself in the trees for hours, watching the guard's patterns. In the late afternoon, a red tow truck appeared. It had the words Final Notice crudely stenciled onto the passenger-side door. It hauled a decrepit Dodge Neon into the lot, and the driver got out and greeted the man in the Russian hat. The car was deposited unceremoniously, inspected and tagged, and then moved to the back of the lot next to mine. The driver got back into the truck and drove away.

Toward sunset, another man pulled up in an aging Firebird and honked the horn. The man in the Russian hat emerged from the trailer, locked the fence around the impound lot, and got into the Firebird. The tires squealed as the car tore away into the darkness.

I now had the lot to myself, but could hardly see anything. The winter night had fallen quickly, and most of Mount Vernon was without power. There were no streetlights or lamps. Nothing. I fumbled toward the lot in the darkness, my hands outstretched to feel my way. I reached the fence, and began to consider a way to scale it. The top was lined with evil-looking barbed wire.

I was a zombie, so just saying "fuck it" and climbing over anyway was a real option. The barbs wouldn't cause me pain, but they *would* probably rip me all to hell—probably worse than a living person because I would feel no pain when the barbs entered my skin. Also, something about carrying Peter Mellor's 175-plus pounds over a wire fence with just my hands felt like a bad idea. I pictured pulling the skin off my fingers—or losing entire limbs—without even noticing. That would fucking suck.

In the end, I decided to tunnel under the fence like a dog. I picked what I hoped was an inconspicuous place in the back of the lot and started digging. The ground was hard. I used sticks to help me dig, my movements slow and methodical.

It took all night. Just before dawn broke, I finally shimmied my way underneath the impound lot fence. I had no clue when the guard started his shift, but something told me I didn't have much time. (The Mount Vernonites seemed like the kind of people who rose at dark-thirty.) Already, I seemed to hear the distant din of an approaching engine.

After taking a moment to brush the dirt off my clothes, I made my way over to what was left of my car. The thing was ruined, of course. Destroyed. Totaled. (I was impressed, in fact, that they'd been able to haul it to this lot in one piece.) The tag on the side-view mirror appeared to be a storage number, written with a black permanent marker. The photocopied page, however, was a more interesting matter.

It was an accident report, filled out in an almost illegible hand with a ballpoint pen. A series of notes at the top outlined the basics: The make and model of the car. The license plate number. (Then they *would* know whose car it was, if there was still any way to run a license plate ...) The location where the car had been found. The date upon which it had been taken to the impound lot. Then, at the bottom of the form, under Other, had been hastily scrawled: "Brake lines cut!" It was underlined three times.

I read it again. Then again.

Brake lines cut!

My breath had already been taken away, but this idea affected me deeply. I began to feel light-headed. Brake lines cut? Like, on purpose? All this time, I'd assumed I'd crashed my car because I was driving too fast on a snowy road. But there, in my cold, dead hands, was striking evidence to the contrary. I'd crashed (and had *died*) because my brake lines had been cut.

That meant ...

That meant ...

Murder.

Had to be. There were a million more sensible ways to commit suicide. Nobody—not even alcoholic, oversexed college professors—cut his own brake lines. College professors probably didn't know *how* to cut brake lines. (I searched my patchy zombie memory for anything on car maintenance, and found little beyond the replacement of gasoline and washer fluid.)

But then there was no time to consider it further. More suddenly than seemed possible, a Firebird with two armed men inside was pulling up in front of the impound lot. Though still distant, the car's headlights fell upon me. Both men jumped out.

"Hey you!" a voice called angrily from the Firebird.

I grabbed the photocopied form and took off running. I heard anxious footfalls, and someone hastily fiddling with a ring of keys.

"How'd he get over the fence?" one man said to the other.

I ran through the rows of cars and headed for my hole at the back of the lot. The two men struggled to get the gate open. I could hear their frustration. I looked back over my shoulder as I ran, and saw that one of them had readied his rifle.

"Stop or I'll shoot!" he shouted.

I did no such thing.

Three seconds later, I was rewarded with a rifle bullet through the shoulder. The Vernonites could shoot—I had to give them that. (Some part of me had *known* they would be able to.) The slug didn't slow me. I kept on going. A second shot rang out, but this one zinged past me and ricocheted off an ancient Oldsmobile Cutlass Ciera.

"It's okay," I heard one of them say. "He's trapped back there. He's not getting out."

"I think you hit him," the other said. "Let's let him bleed for a while."

An instant later, I was on my belly and shimmying underneath the fence. I heard the men finally get the gate open as I scuttled away into the woods.

There was no doubt about it. My ability to move quickly was getting worse and worse. My legs and joints seemed to be growing unnaturally stiff, and not just when I tried to run. Half the time, they operated as though they had minds of their own. Going along at any clip faster than a stride was dangerous. It felt like dancing in leg braces. (You could do it, but Jesus, why would you?)

I fled the city and trekked into the forest. I walked until I could hear no horns, smell no smoke.

It began to sleet. I stopped in the shelter of a wildly twisting tree in a clearing. Without any breath to catch, I needed no recovery time to turn my attention once again to the piece of paper I still clutched in my hand. *Brake lines cut!* The words hadn't been scrawled in the clearest of hands, but I'd be kidding myself to think they said anything other than that. It was right there. Underlined three times.

Even so, I stared at it like a magic-eye picture, hoping that if I relaxed my eyes, another picture—another message—might become clear. As much as I wanted to see something else, it was the same every time. *Brake lines cut!*

Whoever Peter Mellor was—whoever *I* was—somebody had wanted to kill him.

I stayed under that tree until the sleet let up, thinking about being murdered and absently fingering my new bullet hole. It was a lot to take in. Here, I'd been having fantasies of being some kind of "good zombie," waxing fanciful about finding a way to use my powers to help people. I now found myself feeling less beneficent. Being murdered will do that to you.

I hadn't thought that I—or the original Peter Mellor—had been a *good* man, exactly, but neither did I think I'd been some sort of Hitler. I was an oversexed disappointment who'd started drinking too much, true. But I had called only for the annexation of liquor bottles and vaginas, not Poland. There were far worse things one could do . . .

But this piece of paper in my hand said another thing entirely. It said that I was the kind of guy whom somebody wanted dead. That

I had done something to make somebody want to *kill me*. And not just want to—to actually go through with it. I regarded the piece of photocopied paper through a zombie's cold, nonlubricating eyes. I *was* dead. The car accident *had* killed me. I *was* a murdered man. Yet, like in that old song by The Highwaymen, I was still around. (I seemed to hear Willie Nelson singing "I was a zombie ..." somewhere in a memory.)

Who had wanted me dead?

My list of suspects—like my mind—was hazy and full of holes.

Sam had said something about a classics professor at the college killing *himself* after I'd slept with his wife. That felt like the most obvious lead. Maybe the wife had decided to take me out. Maybe one of her friends, or one of their kids. Maybe just someone in the community who thought I was a fuck for sleeping around. (This part of the country was rife with scary churches. A zealous congregant could have heard of my case and decided I should pay the ultimate price for coveting my neighbor's wife.)

And all of this assumed that there was not *something else* I'd done. Something worse than transgressive sex. Something, perhaps, that I'd kept secret even from Sam.

I tried to think of things that got people killed. Gambling debts. Blackmail. Vendettas. Consorting with criminals. All of these were possibilities. I looked down at my pale hands and wondered what they had done in a previous life. Had they strangled someone? Stolen money from a gangster? Bet the company payroll on black?

People wanted to kill me because I was a zombie, but apparently they'd wanted to kill me as a human too.

I was a wanted man, both ways.

I stayed there, letting it sink in. It took most of the day.

Around dusk, a zombie approached me. He was a loud, blustering fellow (as zombies go). I heard his moans and heavy footsteps as he stalked through the woods. I let him approach, hoping the company might do me good.

He emerged from the trees and stepped confidently into the clearing, walking right up to me. He had been a tall, barrel-chested man. He wore a blaze-orange vest and hat, and a rattling canteen was still strapped to his waist. Half his face had rotted away, and the rest of it had turned blue. His hair was full of wet weeds and worms. It looked like he'd been underwater, and for some time. As he drew closer, I spotted two old wounds where rifle bullets had gone into his back. A hunting accident. (Or—considering the placement of the wounds—more likely a "hunting accident.")

The zombie regarded me cautiously, emitting a low moan.

"Yeah," I said. "You and me both."

The idea made me smile. We had both been killed. Murder will out—and here it was, "outing" right in front of us.

The visiting zombie sniffed the air for a moment, then began to walk slowly in the direction of the impound lot. Likely he had scented the humans. I let him get ten feet before stopping him.

"Hey, buddy, you don't want to go there," I said, taking him gently by the shoulder. He regarded me with genial confusion, like a doddering grandfather pleased to be set right by a nurse or caretaker.

"Here," I said, tugging him east. "C'mon. Let's go this way instead."

And we did.

It didn't take long for me to name him Hunter. It was a bit easy, true, but nobody was around to criticize obvious puns. They were only around to shoot at us.

We made our way east, away from Mount Vernon, through woods and across farms and fields. But that's not to say we were safe from humans. We stuck to the trees as much as we could. For most of the walk I heard no one other than ourselves, but these were dangerous times. Sometimes humans just suddenly appeared, and even the Amish were packin'.

I moved slowly, but Hunter moved slower. One of his shoes was gone, and the exposed foot had rotted away into a kind of crumpled meat-claw. He was quiet compared to a human, but loud for a zombie. His moans ranged from gentle and tentative—like a confused engineer, puzzling over a blueprint—to anguished and urgent—like a woman in labor.

"Hunter, Jesus—You're creepin' me out," I'd say when he lingered too long in this latter category. Sometimes that worked and he shut up. Other times, it didn't, and he just wailed on.

In case I need to remind you, neither of us slept. In our first twenty-four hours of walking, we covered several miles. We just went and went. We were walking machines.

As dawn broke in the woods near some farms, we encountered a "dead" zombie, shot through the forehead and lying in a snowy puddle by the edge of the tree line. It had been a young man wearing only a hospital gown. I prodded it a bit with my foot. Hunter failed to notice our fallen compatriot at all.

Less than an hour later, we saw the humans that had likely put down the zombie: a teenage girl with a ponytail and an older man whose gait was sickly and slow. They both wore plaid shirts and carried rifles. Neither looked to be in a very good mood. They were walking away from us, heading south, and I intended to let them go. With considerable difficulty, I made Hunter sit down on a snowy log as we waited for them to move off.

Eventually, I got my courage up and peeked out at the nearby farmland. There was no sign of them—or of anybody—but that didn't mean we were alone. We sat there for eight hours, continuing only when the moon had risen.

A few days later, Hunter and I met up with another pair of wandering zombies. They were knee-deep in unharvested corn, in a field out past Coshocton. Both had been male. One was tall, wore a leather jacket, and had long black hair and neck tattoos like a heavy-metal singer. The other was short and pudgy with a mustache—Italian-looking—and wore expensive grave clothes.

Hunter and I approached them cautiously. I waved my hands above my head to get their attention, and they began moving in our direction. Like cats, they seemed to notice movement before anything else. When they got close and I stopped waving, I could tell it was sort of a letdown for them. They had been hoping for something to eat.

I tried making conversation. "What's up, friends?" I asked. "I'm Peter . . . or I used to be. This guy, I'm calling Hunter. Would you like to join us?" I knew that they couldn't understand me (and wouldn't respond), but introductions still felt like the right thing to do. The Italian remained motionless. The taller one in leather drooled some goo from the corner of his mouth. Hunter moaned, as if in assent.

"Looks like you're in," I said. "I'm calling you Rock Star," I said to the tall, tattooed one. "And you can be Mario," I said to the other. "Hang around long enough, and maybe we'll find you a Luigi." (Nintendo games! It was astounding. I could remember fucking Nintendo games, but not my girlfriend's last name! Ahh, the ticks and tricks of a zombie's memory . . .)

We continued through the corn as a group of four. Hunter stuck close to me and moaned. At first, Rock Star and Mario trailed at a distance, but trailed nonetheless. After a couple of hours they seemed to get the idea, and joined us in a tight formation.

The land became hilly and steep. The only humans we saw that day were in an SUV that sped past in the distance along a dirt road. I didn't think there was any way they could have seen us, but I still halted our little party for the good part of an hour before continuing.

The fields and forests began to feel familiar. At first, I couldn't put my finger on it. Lots of forest looked like lots of other forest. That was how forest looked. You couldn't see it for the trees. (Or rather, you *could* see it, but it all looked identical.) *This* forest, however, was uncannily close to a memory. Of that, I felt sure. Perhaps this was an area I'd visited in life. I'd picnicked here with Sam, or perhaps with Vanessa.

Vanessa ... and her sister Kate. Yes! That was it! My zombie band had wandered back near Vanessa's sister's environmentally friendly house. *That* was where I had seen these woods before. We stopped walking. My compatriots gathered near me, looking around absently. I realized I had some considering to do. Should I take them back there, my little zombie band? Could I even *talk* to Vanessa about what I was? Did she already suspect—or know—that I was a zombie? I nervously pulled down my Cedar Rapids Kernels hat and tried to guess what Vanessa might have concluded from the circumstances surrounding my Judge Crater–like departure.

And then I had these zombies who were following me—I certainly couldn't trust *them* to behave. I closed my eyes and tried to think.

Maybe it was the smell of the woods. Maybe it was the feel of the ground underfoot. Maybe it was the memory of Vanessa's voice that came tumbling back into my brain. But, for whatever reason, the answer hit me like a ton of bricks.

Of course, it said.

Of course you go. This is a woman who loves you. Every positive memory or association you still have up there involves her in some way.

Maybe it'll work out, and maybe it won't, but you won't know that until you try. You've thought about trying to be someone's helpful zombie, right? Well, this sure looks like your chance.

So you go.

You damn-straight go.

It was a pretty persuasive voice.

No sooner was I thus resolved than I chanced to remember Matilda—first as the rude neighbor on the porch, and then as the defender wearing the improvised body armor and stalking me with a gun. Had *she* seen that I was a zombie? I couldn't be sure. And who knew what she might have told Vanessa.

Despite all of this, going back to the house was a chance I wanted to take.

I led my party of zombies through the snowy woods toward my girlfriend's sister's home. I kept us close to the roads, so as not to lose my bearings, but always stayed a few feet into the underbrush.

It was a tricky act, sighting the road out of the corner of my eye and trying to keep level with it. We took a couple of wrong turns, but before long I had us back to the gravel driveway entrance where I'd fought the man on the ATV. It was mid-morning, and the tunnel of trees was more welcoming than forbidding this time.

I pulled my hat low over my forehead and started cautiously down the drive. My band followed after me. I knew there was no way I was going to get them to stay and wait. Instead, I hoped to alert anyone at the house that we were friendly and not dangerous. (Well, at least *I* was. Perhaps the other zombies could be left clawing at the front door whilst I slipped in through the side laundry-room entrance.)

"Hello! We're friendly!" I called out, quickly realizing my voice sounded terrifyingly hoarse and sickly when I tried to shout. I kneeled down by a puddle of melting snow and drank. The other zombies looked at me oddly.

"Hello!" I tried again. It was a bit better with the moisture. A little more human-sounding.

We made our way down the long drive with me halloo-ing all the way. Around every bend, I waited to see Matilda, poised with a shotgun at the ready. But we saw and heard no one. Just the quiet trees. Soon, the house came into view.

I could see that something was wrong, even from a distance. The windows of the energy-efficient home were broken, and the front door was off its hinges. It also looked as though someone or something had sprayed mud or sawdust across the house. I took a few steps closer, then stopped.

That wasn't sawdust and mud. Those were bullet holes. A great gun battle had happened here.

"Hello, Vanessa?" I called into the ruin. "Anybody?" There was no sound or movement. The place was dead. Confident that we were alone, I ceased my shouting and walked directly into the clearing and up to the house. It had been subjected to an incredible amount of firepower. That much was visible from the exterior. Even the environmentally friendly greenhouse in the back had had its glass smashed and plants uprooted.

On the ground by the side of the home, near where I'd found my hat, was a body. It was an older man with tattoos and a salt-and-pepper beard. He'd been shot clean through the forehead, probably as he'd crouched behind a tree. He wore an ancient leather jacket and had a pair of jeans awkwardly belted around a fifty-inch waist. I kicked him over until I could read the lettering on the back of his jacket. "The Frogs" was all it said.

It took me a while to get up my nerve to look inside the shot-up house. The other zombies showed no interest at all, leading me to conclude that no living person remained. (At one point Hunter shuffled inside through the wreckage of the front door, but shuffled back outside again a moment later with the same bored look on his face.)

I entered the house not through the front, but through a sliding-glass door in the back. I went through it literally—the panes had been knocked away, the glass shards mixed with the snow. The inside was a mess of bullet holes and a little blood. Surprisingly though, there was only one body. It was Matilda, and she still wore her riot helmet. She had been shot several times through the chest, and she lay slumped beneath a window. A pool of spent shells was at her feet.

"At least you got one of them," I said softly.

Then, an unexpected movement right next to me. I started, and turned to see a fat raccoon sitting on the kitchen countertop, reveling among the ruins of a loaf of bread. I raised my hand threateningly. The raccoon hissed and scampered out of the house, a slice of bread still in its mouth.

Aside from any pilfering that animals had done, the kitchen looked remarkably untouched. I cautiously made my way through the rest of the house. It was odd. Nothing had been touched. Aside from the damage caused by the bullets, the home and its contents were mostly unmolested. I opened every door and every closet. There was no sign of anybody else.

I walked out the front of the house and sat down on the steps. I put my head in my hands.

"Woooagh?" Hunter asked, coming up next to me.

"Be quiet," I told him. "I'm trying to think."

And that was when I really lost it.

I mean, I "lost it" by your standards—by your human standards. A zombie might say that it was the moment when I really came into being ... when I became my real and true zombie self. Vanessa and my half-memories of her were the strongest things left tying me to something like humanity. And now she was gone. Killed or taken. Probably by a biker gang called the Frogs. (Stupid fucking name. C'mon, rural Ohio rednecks. Was that really the best you could do? Awww, what? Was "The Barely Literate Bearded Fatasses" already taken? Fuckers ...) Her sister and all their kids had been killed or taken, too. Or worse. And even if they weren't dead, how would I ever hope to find them again?

So, yeah, I "lost it." And another thing I lost was my desire to connect with whatever my humanity had been. Seeing the ruined, bloody house, I had been instantaneously relieved of any further curiosity about Peter Mellor. I no longer cared about who he had been before I woke up in his body by the side of the road near Gant. What were his likes and dislikes? What were his loves? His hates? His strengths and weaknesses? *I no longer fucking cared at all.*

Those things were theory and speculation. They were all in the past. But I'd been shown a new world of delight that I could have *right now.* So what if it involved eating someone's brain? Eating brains felt *wonderful.* It felt better than anything I could recall. Better than sex. Better than drugs. Damn straight better than rock and roll.

You know how sentimental people say that their job or whatever is "what they're supposed to be doing"? Well, it was dawning on me that maybe eating people's brains was what *I* was supposed to be doing. There was some pretty fucking strong evidence for that position—not the least being that brains tasted incredibly awesome to me.

When I stood up from my seat on the porch, I was a new man. A new undead man. I was a zombie—ready to *be* a zombie, and to do the things that zombies did.

"All right, guys!" I announced. Hunter looked up. Mario and Rock Star wandered over from beside the biker's body. I looked them over seriously, like a general reviewing his troops.

"Gentlemen," I said sternly, "let's go eat some brains."

II.

Rampage

It's an unfortunate truth that sometimes the more you want something, the harder you make it for yourself to get.

When you're unemployed and a month behind on your credit cards, you drip desperation and smarmy, false alacrity at the job interview. People can smell it on you, and it poisons your chances to get the gig. When you're already pulling down six figures and you just won a big industry award, you nail that shit—projecting confidence, competence, and general awesomeness.

And when you're a twenty-year-old virgin who obsesses day and night about getting laid, then that's going to come through when you try to play it cool at the beach bonfire or the frat party. But if you're some sort of Casanova who's got bitches throwing themselves at you all day, then yeah, you're gonna come across as a little more relaxed and natural when you're trying to talk to girls.

When I decided to give in to my zombish impulses—to allow myself to eat all the brains I wanted—I found myself no less subject to this law.

For days now, my entire object had been to avoid humans. I hid from them whenever possible. I skedaddled generally whenever they approached. I avoided towns and settlements. But now I'd made this little "mental changeover." I was, physically, still the same zombie. I had the same abilities and handicaps. But what had changed were my desires. And wouldn't you know it ... Now that *encountering* humans was number one on my to-do list, they were suddenly nowhere to be found.

My zombie band departed the gunshot-strewn energy-efficient home and headed directly for the first neighboring residence. We found a farmhouse covered in flaking blue paint, padlocked and empty. Hinges rusted. Windows broken.

We stalked on, and found another just like it. Then another. Then another still. All were empty. Some of the houses had obviously been pillaged, and others merely shuttered. Some appeared to have been destroyed by the residents themselves. But there was no sign of life in any of them.

It was enough to make me laugh. We had spent the last few days taking these great pains to avoid people. (The humans we *had* seen, even at a distance, had terrified me.) And now that I'd decided that *they* were the prey—and *I* was the predator—there was nobody around.

I began to realize that most of a zombie's day is spent in fruitless search; it was an endless hunting trip where you searched for animals that were hiding and smarter than you. Viewed one way, this was . . . well, boring. Horrible, boring tedium. It was lots and lots of walking—slow walking—between generously spaced houses, all of which proved bereft of life.

But I began to notice that there was a thoughtful—almost Zen— acceptance of these grim prospects in the silence of my traveling companions. House after house proved empty or abandoned. Distant movement that looked hopeful would turn out to be a curtain blowing in a broken window, or a barn door banging in the wind. It was like opening gaily wrapped packages and finding only empty boxes inside. Yet these failures never fazed my companions. There was apparently no zombie equivalent of "Awww, nuts."

I tried to learn from my companions. I felt sure that it was my own anxious nerves that were jinxing us. That I was moving us too quickly, and expecting too much to happen. That I was somehow still thinking "like a human," and not like a zombie.

Then, as dawn broke one morning, Rock Star and Mario became excited by a doubtful-looking dirt footpath on the outskirts of some farms. I tried to redirect them at first—there appeared to be nothing down there—but they were insistent. I gave in and decided to see how it played out. I could hear, see, and smell nothing. Possibly, it was a path used to move farm equipment. I collected Hunter, who had veered off in yet another direction, and we followed Rock Star and Mario.

The dirt path wound down the side of a gently sloping hill that seemed to separate two farms. The underbrush near the trail had been recently removed—hacked away with machetes, it looked like to me. The trees and bushes around it were thick, and this clearing-away had taken no small amount of deliberate work. The path beneath our feet also appeared recently traveled. There were foot-sized indentations in the muddy snow that belonged to neither Mario nor Rock Star.

Looking up ahead of them, I spied a small blue box—like a car battery—perched beside the path. It looked . . . out of place. Alarms went off in my head.

"Hang on guys," I shouted, pushing my way to the front. I put a hand on Rock Star's chest to stay him. Then, keeping my compatriots at bay with one hand, I swiveled my neck to examine the blue box.

It took no great powers of inspection to spot the trip wire that extended from the box and terminated around the base of a tree on the other side of the path. A trap. It was some kind of trap. Something that a human would see right away—it was bright fucking blue, after all—but something into which a zombie would obliviously stumble. Rock Star almost had. Was it a bomb? Was it an alarm? I had no way of knowing, and didn't want to hazard a guess.

There was a thin opening in the underbrush adjacent to the tree to which the trip wire was tied. This opening was just wide enough for a person to shimmy past. I carefully pushed my intractable companions through, one by one. Mario was a little thick around the middle, but I braced myself and kicked him in the back, and sure enough, he squeezed out the other side. He stumbled and moaned, but the blow kept him clear of the wire.

"You don't even know I just did you a favor," I said with a smile.

Ahead of me, the zombies continued to lope down the path. They were obviously aware of something up ahead of us. Something good.

I kept an eye out for additional traps, but found none. At the bottom of the hill, the path terminated and the forest opened into a clearing. On the far side was a barren farmer's field with recent-looking tire ruts leading away. In the center of the clearing was a huge American-made SUV. Next to this was a stone well with a metal bucket, and next to the well was what I can only describe as an improvised bunker—a pair of storm-cellar doors that opened into a concrete foundation in the ground. My compatriots were *very* interested in the bunker.

It was instantly clear to me: There must be people inside, holding out. Not an entirely bad place, I reflected. Water, transportation, and a way to batten down the hatches if unfriendly elements arrive. These humans were well hidden from the forest side, and could presumably make a getaway into the farmer's field if the need arose.

A pretty good setup, all in all. And we were going to fuck it up. (I tried to contain my nervous excitement at this idea, but it was hard.)

I watched as Rock Star and Mario staggered closer to the cellar doors. Rock Star regarded them cautiously, as if looking for an opening, or—more intriguingly—trying to remember what they were. Mario dropped awkwardly to his knees and began to paw at them, like a dog trying to open a door. He made no progress. These doors were bolted from the inside. But this fact—perhaps unknown, or, more likely, irrelevant to Mario—did not deter him in his pawing. Before long, I started to hear voices from inside the bunker. I crept closer and listened.

"Do you hear that?" It was a young woman, possibly just a girl. "Wait? Do you hear that? Do you hear that? Seriously . . ."

Then another voice—also a young woman: "Omigod, yes. Is it an animal, d'you think? It's digging like an animal."

First voice: "Do you think it's one of *them?*"

Other voice: "Omigod. Omigod. Omigod. Seriously . . ."

This conversation amused me deeply. Soon, I was smiling from ear to ear.

I moved closer, until I was almost next to Mario.

First voice: "Omigod, when the fuck is Chet going to get back?!"

Other voice: "We never should have come with him. We should have gone to Columbus. I can't take this much longer."

First voice: "Look, maybe it's just an animal—an animal that smells your Doritos or something."

The girls stopped talking. One of them seemed to be weeping. It was a plaintive sound, and made me think of an animal caught in a trap. (Indeed, that might have been close to the truth of the situation.) I walked over to the well and inspected it. There was water in the bucket. I picked it up and took a long drink, using my swallowing muscles for the first time in days. It felt good, like flexing a limb that's been in a cast for a while.

I returned to the bunker doors and gently moved Mario out of the way. He seemed more confused than annoyed, pawing the air awkwardly.

"Hello, there!" I shouted into the doors. "Is anybody there? Is there anybody inside?"

A stunned silence from the young women. The crying was hushed.

"Look," I said, going for an Academy Award–worthy performance, "my name is Peter Mellor. I'm lost and I need some help. I was going to my girlfriend's house, and I ran out of gas. I'm unarmed, and there are zombies out here. Please—can I come in? I'm just a nice, middle-aged man."

Again, no answer.

"Please," I tried again. "You're not going to let me *die* out here, are you?"

I heard indistinct mumbling from within. They were discussing it. Behind me, Mario, Rock Star, and Hunter cast impatient glances at the doors. I moved as if patting an invisible dog just behind me, encouraging them to be patient. Then I heard the sound of padlocks being unfastened.

"Oh, thank you," I said. "Oh God, thank you so much."

The unfastening continued, and the door opened a crack. Then a hunting rifle extended out of it to greet me. Its barrel was shaking.

"Hello?" one of the girls said tentatively.

"Yes ... hello," I said. I moved myself directly in front of the opening, hoping to block their view of the motley crew behind me.

"Back up some," the girl said nervously.

"Sure thing," I said. I pulled my hat down over my eyes and stood right in front of the gun. I raised both of my arms at the elbows, like a person in a holdup.

The storm-cellar door opened wider, and a second, identical gun barrel extended out and trained on me. Also shaking.

"I'm unarmed," I said (honestly, I noted). "I don't have any weapons."

"Okay," one of them said. "Is someone with you? I can see something behind you."

"There are zombies, and they're very close," I said (ever truthful). "Can you please let me in? I don't want to get eaten." There was a pause, then more whispering. Nothing happened for a full thirty seconds. They were trying to figure out what to do next. (I was glad I was not *actually* in danger of being eaten by zombies, because this indecisive pair would almost certainly have doomed me.) The zombies behind me had regained their foci, and were almost at my back. I had to act fast.

"Here," I said, advancing toward the gun barrels. "I'm going to head right toward your guns. They're pointed right at my heart, see? You're safe. If I do anything wrong, you can shoot me dead."

I reached for one of the trembling barrels, and gripped it with my fingertips. I pulled it to the center of my chest. Then, with my other hand, I gripped the second barrel and made the same adjustment.

"See, right at my heart," I said. "Now, can you just open up the doors a little? Obviously, I'm not going to try anything."

Another pause. Then one of the two storm-cellar doors opened completely, and I was confronted with two frightened-looking sorority girls (one of them actually wearing a pink sweatshirt inscribed with Greek letters). The closer of the girls (in the pink sweatshirt) took a step toward me. Then my compatriots spilled forward over my shoulders.

"Omigod, zombies!" Pink Sweatshirt said.

In that instant, I tightened my grip on the rifle barrels and held them fast to the center of my chest. Pink Sweatshirt screamed. The other girl—standing beside her, but lower in the bunker—pulled the trigger of her weapon. The slug jolted me, but I kept my grip tight on the guns.

Fortunately for us zombies, so did they.

The girls screamed and pulled back hard, but did not drop their weapons until it was too late. As desperately as they pulled, my grip was always stronger. In an instant, Mario, Rock Star, and Hunter were upon them.

Their shrieks were unbelievable.

In my period of aspiring to be a "good" zombie, I would have tried to excuse or reconcile our consumption of those two young women as a kind of self-defense. They had pointed guns at us. They (or, more likely, "Chet") had set up some kind of trip wire device to foil or kill us. And we? Well . . . We were just doing what came *naturally,* weren't we?

But I was past making such excuses. The moment those girls' brains touched my tongue, it felt right. It felt like I was doing what I was supposed to be doing. The universe *made sense.* (And if, by someone's estimation, what I was doing was "wrong," then— believe you me—I *did not want* to be right.)

Also, that morning I learned that zombies aren't very good at sharing. They're greedy and pushy and shovey. Luckily, I was faster and more nimble than the other three, and enjoyed the lion's share of the brains at our banquet—leaving the others to chew on skin and guts. (For this selfishness, I felt absolutely no guilt. After all, I'd been the architect of our little operation.)

When we were done, and there was nothing left to chew or swallow, I explored the inside of the little bunker. There were crates of food, generators, and bottles of water (to supplement the well, I supposed). There were also stacks and stacks of women's fitness magazines. A small TV/DVD player was connected to a generator, and stacks of DVDs were piled next to it. The entire interior smelled of a dusky perfume. It turned my stomach.

I took one of their rifles and a heavy Maglite finished in a dull red metal. I shouldered the weapon, and stuck the flashlight through my belt loop. That was all I took.

And we got out of there before Chet could come back.

That night a full, rich moon rose over the Ohio plains. I howled at it out of pure joy, in love with my existence. It felt good. It felt better than good. We wandered north, drunk on murder and brains, and hungry for more.

As we walked, I replayed our encounter with the sorority girls in my mind with an almost pornographic salaciousness. It had not, by any stretch, been a fair fight. We'd "won" because I had not played by the rules, and it occurred to me that my ability to do this was going to be a very powerful thing.

In the animal kingdom—and don't ask me how I remembered this—it takes only a tiny variation to make one animal vastly superior to the others around it. A giraffe with a neck just a few inches longer than its friends' can feast while those around it starve. A gazelle that's just slightly faster than the rest of the herd will never have to worry about being caught by lions. Whenever an animal can see better, move faster, or think more quickly than the others—even if it's just to a tiny degree—it will always have an enormous advantage.

As a zombie, this idea applied to me. But my powers were not just a slight advantage. I was off the damn chart. If I'd just been *a little* faster or *slightly* smarter than an average zombie, I'd have been at the top of the "food chain" for sure. If I'd been able to surprise humans just by being able to speak, or just by using tools, or not walking straight into the path of concussion grenades, then I'd be the most talented zombie out there—the Michael Jordan of zombies, or whatever. But it wasn't just that I was able to read signs or run a little bit. I could do *all of these things*. And most problematic of all—for the humans—was the fact that I was *aware*.

Any animal can think—at least a little bit—but humans excel because they understand that *other things are thinking too*. When an animal encounters a hungry tiger in the forest, it has two options: fight or flight. (And when you're faced with a tiger, both of these choices are pretty lousy and usually get you eaten.) A human, on the other hand, when surprised by a tiger, understands that the tiger is thinking too. That the tiger has needs and wants. The tiger needs food. It wants a nice dinner, and wants it with the least effort possible. Sure, a human's first instinct might—like an animal's—be fight or flight, but a human will also *understand* the tiger. This may, for example, lead a threatened human to reason: "Gee ... If I give this tiger the rabbit I just caught, and then back away slowly, maybe the tiger will eat the rabbit instead of me, and I'll live to fight another day." The ability to notice that *other things are thinking too* has allowed humans, despite a marked lack of claws and fangs, to dominate all other animals for thousands of years.

And humans also dominate because they categorize. They are list-makers. They are stereotype-bestowers. They are racists, and species-ists, and genus-ists. Able to recognize and "know" a thing because they have seen others like it, humans are masters of the split decision.

"Those things can fly."

"Those things are poisonous."

"These are good eatin'."

Humans react quickly because they assume that the things they encounter are probably similar to other things they've encountered before. Living by stereotype—especially in dangerous situations—is what comes naturally to a human.

As a zombie, I knew I would be subject to this "instant stereo-typing" by every human who met me. And all of the stereotypes about me would be negative (dull-witted, slow, unable to move evasively when subjected to artillery fire). More important, *all of them would be wrong.*

When I was on the attack, I was going to be a complete surprise to humans. I was going to break all of their rules. Everything they thought they knew about me would be incorrect. I would be like a lion that could fly, an eagle that could breathe fire, or a shark that could walk on land. I was going to have my teeth in their brains while they were still protesting "Wait a minute! Zombies can't do *tha—*"

But I could. And I would.

I would take their prejudice and use it against them.

The night drew on and a mist descended. We traversed a swampy, snow-covered fen and found a lonely state highway on the other side. It was barren and dark. We followed it. West, I think. After a few miles, a sign confirmed we were on State Highway 36.

We walked until just before dawn, when I saw a figure in the distance silhouetted against the moon. I stopped my little herd to observe it at a distance. Something about the figure's shape was ... *familiar.* It was ovoid. Vaguely female. And, most important, unarmed.

I conducted my little party toward the figure. When we drew within fifty yards, it, likewise, began to move in our direction. Its gait betrayed it as a zombie, even though it was no more than a silhouette. (This was more than the slow, falling-forward step and outstretched arms. Unlike humans, zombies move with supreme self-assurance. There is no caution. Nothing is tentative. Zombies don't doubt themselves, or second-guess what they're doing. Zombies are confident. It is, perhaps, an idiotic confidence, but a confidence nonetheless. [Many humans could stand to adopt the confidence of a zombie.]) Even before I hit it in the face with the Maglite, I could tell the zombie was—or had been—Matilda.

It stood to reason, I supposed. She had been killed in the shootout at the house, but only hit in the chest. Her brain was unharmed. No reason she shouldn't reanimate.

"What's up, Matilda?" I said jocularly, as we met. "Fancy meeting you again. Are you here to enlist?" She looked at me absently, her dead eyes squinting in the glare of the Maglite. (Somewhere along the way, she had lost her riot helmet.) The other zombies gathered around, waiting patiently.

I shone the flashlight over her, noting some blood around her mouth. Perhaps she had already fed. (Perhaps on the bearded man in the "Frogs" jacket, or on some other unlucky soul.) I also noted with a wince that her shirt had been ripped away, and two grossly distended breasts now swayed pendulously in front of her with each stumbling step forward.

"Yikes," I said, averting my eyes. "I don't dig *those* dugs."

I chuckled, and looked to the mustachioed zombie next to me.

"Get it, Mario? Dig dugs? 'Dig-Dug'? C'mon, dude . . . It's a video-game reference."

I nudged Mario's ribs, and he managed a little moan.

"Just bustin' your balls," I said to the Matilda-zombie. "I don't think we have much in the way of recruiting standards."

Rock Star gnashed his teeth, and Mario groaned again.

"Well, that's a quorum," I said. "Welcome aboard."

I took Matilda's hand and gently turned her. Together, the five of us headed west.

My band was steadily growing.

Two days of nothing. Silence. Frost.

Walking. So much walking. Yet never a muscle ache—never a shin splint. Not so much as a sore toe assailed us.

We walked and walked. We were like machines.

I became bored with the tedium of Highway 36 after the first day, and turned us once more into the pastures, empty farmland, and small tracts of forest that covered the countryside. It was wild and interesting, but—alas—abandoned. My adolescent desperation and hunger began to grow. I wanted so desperately to feed again soon, but we found no one—living, dead, or undead. It was a world of emptiness. Empty houses. Empty trails. Even an empty hunting lodge, picked clean and bolted shut.

Then, as dawn broke on the third day, a sound.

We were plodding through snowy muck, following the side of an old-growth forest that edged a cornfield, when I began to discern a mechanical din on the wind. It was distant, but nonetheless real. I stopped walking and listened closely to the sound. It went *whop-*

whop-whop. It was a chopping sound. And it was getting louder. At first, I pictured a car with a flat tire racing frantically along a barren highway. Then the source drew closer, and I recognized it for what it was. A helicopter. An *approaching* helicopter.

There was almost no time to act. I considered attempting to hide my band of zombies (or at least myself) in the forest of giant buckeyes and maples. But I knew it would be a challenge to get the other zombies to plunge in in pursuit of nothing. This difficulty aside, I also had to grant—if I was honest—that I was curious about the helicopter. We'd encountered nothing and no one for two whole days. I sort of wanted to see it.

Then it crested the horizon and shot out over the forest—and I saw that it was a military helicopter.

I was ready to flee anew.

The military was about attacking and killing hostile, murderous things ... like groups of zombies. Yet, observing the craft more closely, my alarm began to melt away. There were no missile launchers or mounted guns on this machine. Neither were there turrets or bomb-bay doors. It was an observation helicopter—small, army-green, and bearing a single white star.

As I stood and watched, the other zombies—perhaps interpreting my hesitation as a cue to change direction—spilled past me out into the field, where they made very conspicuous targets. After a moment, the helicopter appeared to notice the little zombie parade. It visibly changed course, and began a wide circle back toward our position.

"Well, fuck," I said hoarsely. "I guess we're making new friends." I decided that unless one of the pilots wanted to roll down a window and take a potshot at us, we were probably safe. I remembered my own rifle—taken off the sorority girls—as I studied the helicopter. Hell, I thought, *I've* got more firepower than it does.

I cautiously followed my compatriots out into the field and watched the helicopter hover above us. It drifted over slowly, and took up a steady position about fifty yards away from where we were standing. I could see two men—soldiers—in the cockpit. They were chatting. Smiling. One of them appeared to be making notes on a clipboard. From time to time, this note-taking soldier pulled a pair of binoculars to his face and observed us through them. Then he took more notes.

After few minutes of this, I began to feel uncomfortable—like I was an animal in a zoo, or a freak on display in an old-timey carnival. It was like these soldiers were on zombie safari, and I was supposed to be some sort of exotic beast for them to document. I hated this thought. I was nobody's zoo animal, I reminded myself. I was a proud, All-American zombie.

I suddenly wanted to eat the helicopter soldiers with a furious intensity. (I understood that this was not practically possible, but the desire was there.) That would show them! I wracked my brain for a way to get at them, but they were hovering just out of reach. What was I gonna do, shoot them down with my sorority girl's rifle? I was no marksman. It'd be dumb luck if I hit anything at all. I hated to admit it, but these smiling, floating men were safe.

And still looking at me.

Impetuously, I gave them the finger. Just one firm digit, raised firm and high. I let it linger there defiantly, and I glared over it at the helicopter. Sit and spin, boys. Sit and spin.

I might as well have fired off an RPG.

The helicopter swiveled crazily on its axis. The soldiers' heads turned back and forth, and they gestured frantically. Their lazy-safari smiles fell away, and were replaced by masks of incredulity. The one with the clipboard trained his binoculars on me—looking again and again, as if he could not believe what he was seeing.

"What," I said aloud, "you've never seen a zombie before? Fuckers!"

The one who was not at the controls next produced a camera and began to train it on me.

Enough's enough, I thought. I lowered my defiant digit. With both hands free, I shouldered my rifle and pointed it menacingly at the helicopter. I did not intend to fire, but my anger and annoyance were real. Reacting instantly, the whirlybird shot up and backward, clearly taking no chances with my desire to shoot.

"That's right," I shouted. "Get the hell out of here. Dicks . . ."

The helicopter departed by making wider and wider circles around us—cautious, but still clearly intrigued.

"Fuck this," I said. "Let's get back into the forest, guys. Nothing else to see here."

I took Rock Star, who was nearest, by the hand and pulled him after me into the trees. Before long, the other zombies followed. I could still hear the helicopter's cavitations in the distance as we disappeared into a canopy of snowy branches.

Hours later, we were out of the forest and walking through the open countryside again. I was still trying to decide what our encounter with the army helicopter had meant.

"What was *that* about?" I asked Mario raspily. I had taken to speaking with Mario because he tended to moan in response to things—as opposed to randomly—making it feel the most like having a conversation. Also, I liked his cool mustache.

"It's like, first they're taking pictures of us like we're lions at the zoo or some shit, and then they go crazy when I give 'em the old up-yours. What's up with that?"

Mario moaned in what I took for agreement.

We eventually moved out of the trees and into an empty soybean field just outside of West Lafayette. A giant, abandoned enamel factory loomed on the horizon south of us, though I had no inclination to explore it. As we marched, I played the encounter with the helicopter over and over again in my mind. I felt like a businessman who is worried he has just said the wrong thing at an important meeting and queered the deal. I considered what else I could have done—or should have done. What had the men been saying to one another so frantically? If only I could have heard.

"I would've liked to have eaten their brains," I said to Mario. "I just couldn't think of a way to do it. I kept hoping they would crash or something—that would have been awesome, right?—but they didn't."

Mario moaned again.

Then his forehead exploded.

I made a noise like *Whaaaggh?* and ducked instinctively. Then I heard the rifle report echoing across the grim, gray farmland.

Fuck, I thought. We're being shot at. But from where?

A quick scan of the horizon told me. Someone was shooting from the old enamel factory. There was thick forest in one direction and sloping hills where a marksman might have concealed himself in another, but I glimpsed a flicker of movement in one of the bashed-out factory windows. We were being hunted. Maybe one person. Maybe a couple. Definitely with scopes.

Suddenly, I wanted very much to save the rest of my little band. (Maybe they weren't much, but they were mine. And fuck me if I was going to stand by and let strangers gun them down for sport.)

Hunter was nearest. I grabbed him by the sleeve of his blaze-orange jacket and started running for the trees. A second shot crackled out over the empty soybean farm. This time, a miss. (I didn't see an impact, but nobody else went down.) Hunter was a poor choice for a running companion. His ancient, water-corrupted flesh and muscles were weak and rotted. For him, just a simple amble was a calculated dance to avoid coming apart. Pulling him after me was like pulling a sickly, arthritic mule.

Another shot rang out. It missed us, but this time I saw the impact in the dirt nearby.

"Fuck it," I said. "Hunter, it was nice knowing you."

Determined that at least one of my compatriots should be saved, I retraced my steps, and this time gripped Rock Star by the wrist and began to pull on him. He was more solid—stiff, but solid—and responded to my urgings that he should attempt a run. We made for the nearest swath of forest. There was still a lot of open field to go. As we passed Hunter, a bullet lit up his chest and knocked him over. Another hit the ground nearby at exactly the same instant. Multiple shooters, then. At least two.

I tugged Rock Star into a lumbering half-run. His leather jacket was slick against my grip. Hunter and Matilda were trying to follow us, but I didn't give them much of a chance. The rifle reports became more and more frequent. I took a look back, and saw dirt dancing at their feet.

Rock Star and I neared the woods—brown, barren trees, but densely packed and replete with undergrowth that looked well-nigh impenetrable. If only we could reach it, the foliage would provide more than adequate cover.

We neared the edge of the copse, and as unexpectedly as it had started, the rifle reports stopped. I entered the underbrush, tugging Rock Star after me, and then chanced another glance behind me. Miraculously, both Matilda and Hunter were upright and still moving. They had new holes in their chests and abdomens, but were basically intact. For whatever reason, the shooters had elected to grant them a reprieve.

I stepped out from the trees and risked a quick inspection of the enamel factory. No movement. Windows still and dark. All quiet on the Western Front. Matilda and Hunter loped their way over to the underbrush, only vaguely aware—I think—that anything out of the ordinary had just occurred.

Mario's body was left on the soybean field. He had fallen facedown. In his fine clothes, he reminded me of a drunk passed out at a wedding.

Not wishing to take any chances, I ushered our group deep within the trees. Then, after a few minutes, I began formulating our plan of attack.

Now, you see, it was personal.

The basis for most of my video-game-based puns had been taken from me. (I mean, I still had Rock Star, and there was actually an incredibly popular video game franchise called Rock Band, which was *very close* to Rock Star ... but I still missed Mario. His moans had felt like interplay. Rock Star was just silent and mean-looking, like Lemmy after a fifth of bourbon. [I remember Lemmy! Remarkable! And something called "Ace of Spades!"])

I waited in the trees until dusk. Then I went scouting.

On one side, the trees ran to within fifteen yards of the enamel factory's loading dock. Bluish-white metal doors with (climbable?) ridges looked out on snow-covered parking spaces where no trucks had backed in for many years. There were windows above, dark and empty.

When darkness fell completely, I risked leaving the wooded area and scouted along the side of the building until I found a padlocked emergency exit. I thought about the little bunker with the sorority girls again. The key to success was defying the expectations of the humans inside. According to them, zombies couldn't talk, reason, or take cover in the woods to scout for openings in an old enamel factory. They certainly couldn't use the butt of a rifle to smash an ancient, rusted Master Lock. But that's exactly what I did.

First, however, I waited.

Humans needed sleep. We did not. Best to catch our enemies when they were as groggy and disoriented as possible. As I waited to attack, I sought to ensure that no other zombie would be picked off as Mario had been. I led my band of undead brothers to the far side of the thick woods, a good distance from the enamel factory. We waited there until my Timex Indiglo said that it was three in the morning. Then we slunk back through the twists of tree and thorn and emerged in front of the factory's emergency exit.

At first I thought about just shooting the lock. People did that in the movies, and it wasn't likely the bullet would ricochet back and hit my brain. However, the lock looked *so* old—positively calcified—that I decided to give it a go with the butt instead. It took only four forceful whacks to send the thing into a pile of rusted pieces. Its rusted guts looked mealy and vaguely chemical, like the inside of an old battery.

I surveyed the dark windows above us. I saw nothing, but my blows had been loud. There was no way to tell yet if any residents had been roused. The humans might still be sleeping soundly in their cots, or already strapping on Kalashnikovs and grenades. There was no way of knowing. As I stood there, listening and considering, the Matilda-zombie brushed past me and walked toward the door. She smelled something. They *were* close.

I opened the clasp where the lock had been hanging. (I did this in complete silence. So far, so good.) Then I gripped the cold metal handle and began to pull. There was a sudden shriek. At first, I thought an alarm had gone off. But no. It was only the squeak of hinges that had not seen WD-40 since the late 1950s—the angry, metal scream of iron parts pleading to be left to entropy and oxidization.

I threw the door wide. It screamed epically, like a murder, then ceased just as suddenly. In the silence that followed, I heard reverberating sounds like footsteps on a metal staircase. Any fantasies I'd had of sneaking in like some kind of zombie-ninja were not coming true.

Through the doorway in front of me, I saw a short hallway leading into a large room that appeared to be full of moldering pallets. I hesitated. Defy expectations. Defy expectations. I repeated it like a mantra in my head. Win through treachery. Ask yourself: What would zombies *not* do? Then do *that*.

Soon, I heard whispering in the darkness far above us. I chanced a look. The roof of the factory appeared to be a nest of ladders, precarious walkways, and pulleys. If our guests were in position above, setting foot on the factory floor would only turn it into a killing floor. Going inside in a blind, murderous rush was not going to work.

I gripped the incredibly squeaky door—inciting further protestations—and pulled it closed again until only a two-inch crack remained. Keeping my curious compatriots at my back, I did my best to impersonate a zombie.

"Braaaaaains . . ." I moaned into the crack. "Br*aaaaaaa*ins . . . *Want . . . eat . . . braaaaaaaaains.*"

I nudged Hunter in the ribs, and got him moaning a little too. Matilda clawed at the door, which also helped.

Before long, I heard muffled voices approaching (once distinctly making out the word "zombies") and footsteps cautiously padding down the metal staircases. As the human sounds drew closer, I moved us so that we weren't visible through the crack. We huddled behind the iron door, moaning and clawing.

"Braaaaains!" I shouted again, then slammed the door with the butt of my gun a couple of times.

As the reverberations ceased, I caught the end of a whispered sentence from inside: ". . . the zombies from yesterday?" Then another voice said: "Flamethrower?"

And I thought: *Flamethrower!?!*

But then another voice whispered: "No sense wasting it on zombies."

Whew.

These humans were aiming to conserve their resources. There were things in this world worse than zombies. Like other humans. (Like, I also reflected, me.)

The footsteps approached. Soon, I was sure there were humans very close to the other side of the metal door. I heard somebody whisper, "Don't see anything." Soon, as I had hoped it would, the barrel of a rifle emerged through the crack in the door, just an inch or two. I heard the same voice whisper, "Still don't see."

Then—delight of delights!—one of the humans kicked the squeaky door open from the inside, and I saw that we still had numbers.

Ranged before us were three nervous-looking humans: A bearded farmer in a plaid shirt and overalls, a pretty thirty-something woman with long blonde hair, and an older Asian man with a buzz haircut and big muscles showing underneath his flannel pajamas. All were armed. The farmer and the woman carried rifles, and the Asian man held what appeared to be a long metal sword with a thin blade and no cross-guard. ("Asian guy with a samurai sword?" I almost said aloud. "Way to be a stereotype, dude.")

Anyhow, I was loaded and ready, and I shot all three of them in the face before they knew what had happened. The farmer went down instantly, stone dead. The blonde woman managed to get one shot off as she fell, but it only hit Matilda in the thigh. The Asian man—though I had shot off part of his jaw—remained standing, and managed to stumble backward and begin a retreat back into the factory. I lumbered through the doorway and shot him again in the back as he ran.

The zombies behind me were squirming and bucking to get at them. I felt like a man trying to keep a group of large, hungry dogs from assailing a Christmas ham. When the last human went down—with my bullet in his back and his sword clattering across the concrete floor—I quickly moved out of the way and let the horde descend.

"All yours, boys," I said with a smile.

The zombies charged past me and were upon the humans in moments. The blonde woman—as I could soon hear—was not quite dead. But after Rock Star's dedicated efforts, she soon claimed that honor alongside us.

I, like all zombies, was hungry. And I, like any zombie in that position, had an almost uncontrollable urge to stop and eat the brains of the newly dead humans on the floor. However, I was also the only one in my party with the sense to understand that there could be more humans ready and waiting to kill us if we weren't careful.

Thus, with what I do not hesitate to call a supreme effort of will, I forced myself to pass up the feast that presented itself. Instead of stopping for a meal, I cautiously crept past the dead swordsman's body and into the depths of the enamel factory, my rifle at the ready.

The factory floor was a mess of heaped, broken pallets and giant presses. I tried to imagine the factory floor as it had been long ago—loud and profitable and full of workers and enamel. Now it was only silent and dark. Suspended high above the factory floor was an office—about the size and shape of a trailer home—set against the roof and accessible only by a series of ladders and metal staircases. It was very, very dark inside the factory, but I was certain I made out a flicker of movement in one of the office windows.

I had to take it out. Whatever or whoever was still up there, I had to take it out. Proud of myself for having resisted the strong urge to stop and feed, I began contemplating my next assault. From those interior windows, anyone left inside would have a clear shot at us, especially when dawn came and light began streaming through the factory windows. Attacking it would be difficult, but not impossible.

I gripped my rifle hard, advancing carefully across the factory floor, using the giant machines and presses—some over twenty-five feet tall—as cover. I poked around and explored. Soon, I found a set of stairs that ran straight up to the elevated office, on a side where there was a door but no window. I decided to make my assault using that staircase. The iron steps were loud under my feet, and the entire network of ladders and suspensions around me seemed to vibrate as I ascended. The door, as I neared it, moved slightly, jostled by my own approaching footsteps.

I stood before it, feeling some trepidation. Then I remembered that a bullet to the heart would not fell me. (Hell, I thought, protect my own brain, and I've got nothing to fear. And from the way I'm walking and holding a gun, whoever's inside will think I'm alive, and probably aim for my chest.) Emboldened by this thought, I kicked the metal door open as hard as I could and bounded into the little trailer. Inside, I found an office that had been converted into something like a dorm room, with beds, clothes, and other necessities. Food and hot plates were stowed against the wall. There were also weapons—lots of weapons.

In the far corner was a boy, shivering and curled, as though he hoped the wall itself would absorb him. His brains would be delicious, and yet I knew—instantly—that I would not kill him. Kids were off the menu. Off mine, at least.

"Well, fuck," I said.

I approached the boy. He was unarmed. He curled tighter and tighter into the wall as I stepped over, as if willing away reality—willing himself into oblivion.

"Hey kid," I rasped. "I'm not going to hurt you. Hey! Listen to me kid, would ya?"

He seemed to consider it, and slowly uncurled from his ball. He looked up at me, his face a mask of fear. He was red-haired and freckled. His searching blue eyes scanned my alien face. I self-consciously pulled down my hat a little.

"What happened?" he asked.

"Uh, some zombies came," I said. "You should probably get out of here. Is there another emergency exit or something?"

The kid paused for a long time, then said: "There are some back stairs, but we boarded them up."

"Show me," I said.

The kid took a flashlight off of the wall and walked me down the noisy iron stairs. We reached the factory floor, and he conducted me through it to a row of planks in the back of the factory.

"What's that sound?" he asked.

Me missing delicious brains, I wanted to say.

"I don't know," was what I actually said.

We pulled away the hastily nailed planks to reveal a metal fire door that opened easily. Outside was only darkness.

"Okay," I said to the kid. "I want you to walk through that door and keep walking till you're far away." The kid obeyed. I closed and locked the door behind him.

Just a few yards behind me, my compatriots were still working their way through the corpses. I noted with relief that they had yet to open the heads in any substantial way. I decided, finally, to allow myself to join them.

"Here," I said, picking up the samurai sword. "Let's do this sashimi-style."

With just a few forceful chops, I opened the skulls of our three victims—keeping one for myself. It was delicious. This time I didn't stop at the brain; I ate most of the face and some of the neck. It wasn't the same as brains, but I still had that feeling of "Sure, I could eat."

And eat I did.

Afterward, leaving my companions to stumble aimlessly around the factory floor like slow, lost pinballs, I returned to the trailer room at the top of the staircase and began to search through the group's possessions. I took a new flashlight and a pair of binoculars, and I traded my rifle for a pair of heavy revolvers and a box of bullets. The revolvers came with holsters, so I strapped them on. I also kept the samurai sword; it would come in handy for opening up heads.

As I was tying the sword to my belt loop, I heard a knocking sound at the bottom of the stairs. The zombies below instantly started moaning. I unholstered one of the loaded revolvers and cautiously made my way down to the factory floor. The sound was coming from the fire door. I opened it and found myself pointing the heavy revolver right in the freckled kid's face.

"What?" I said, annoyed.

"Can I have a coat?" he said. "It's freezing out here."

I hadn't thought of that.

"You need a coat?" I said.

"Yeah," the kid said. "Mine's upstairs in the room where you found me. It's blue and puffy."

"Okay," I said. "Wait here, and *don't* open the door."

I returned to the trailer office and found the kid's coat. I hesitated, then filled the pockets with food—Pop-Tarts, granola bars, and pull-top cans of soup. I also grabbed a flashlight with a built-in compass. Then I took my old rifle, removed the bullets, and slung it over my shoulder.

"Here," I said, back downstairs. I handed the kid the coat full of food, the flashlight, and the gun.

"A gun?" he said.

"Don't get too excited, chief," I told him. "It's unloaded. It's not for zombies—zombies, you can outrun—it's for pointing at people who might not be friendly."

He took the gun and looked at me, hard.

"Those people in there are dead, aren't they?" he asked.

I nodded, and said: "I hope they weren't your parents or anything."

He shook his head.

"My parents sent me out here to live with my uncle," he said. "He was the man with the beard. Don't worry; I didn't like him much. My parents thought it would be safer out here in the country. It turned out the opposite was true."

"You got that right," I said grimly.

"Are you a zombie?" he asked.

"Why?" I said. "What makes you ask me that?"

"You have blood all down your mouth that wasn't there before," he stated flatly.

"Oh," I said. "Yeah, I guess I am. But I'm ... I'm not exactly like other zombies. It's complicated." I stumbled a bit on this last line, like a lover trying to describe an open relationship.

"You don't look like a zombie, except in the face," he said.

"Thanks ... I guess," I told him.

Behind me, Rock Star moaned, curious about my guest. I decided to redirect the conversation and get the kid on his way as soon as possible.

"Look," I said, "this flashlight has a compass on it. See? I want you to follow it south. Got that? South. Eventually you'll hit

Columbus, or at least the suburbs. If you see any soldiers or police, you drop the gun and go toward them. If they're in a car, then try to flag them down. If you see zombies, just run away. If you meet a person and they don't feel right, stay away from them. Just run."

"Okay," the kid said. "Thank you."

He turned, and I closed the door behind him.

So, let me just get this out of the way, here and now: I harbored no illusions about that kid—about his fate. About what probably awaited him. I'd chosen not to eat him, true, but it wasn't like I'd saved him. He was a *kid*. A fucking child. Maybe ten. At most, a young-looking twelve. And I'd sent him out into an empty, cold wasteland-world full of things that wanted to kill him. He had only enough food for two or three days, and no real way to defend himself.

This was not selfless or kind. This was the act of a coward—of someone too afraid and too weak and too drunk on his lust for human brains to do the things that would *actually* ensure a child's safety. I knew this kid would probably be killed out in the wilderness beyond . . . just not by me. If I didn't do it myself—if he didn't die by my hand, or gun, or tooth—then I could wrap myself in a warm lie. I could tell myself that it was not my fault. Not my responsibility. That I'd had nothing to do with it.

But between you and me—yeah, some part of me knew that it was bullshit. A cop-out.

I hadn't killed him myself, but that didn't mean I wasn't his killer.

For the next few days, we stayed in the enamel factory, exploring. (Not that there was anything very interesting. Empty closets, dusty typewriters, cans of oil . . . and hey, you see one enamel press, you've seen them all.) But for a while I had the idea that we might be able to make it our headquarters and lure people into the factory. After all, why muddy our feet and risk being shot when we could feed just as regularly by staying in one place?

I imagined erecting a banner reading WELCOME! FRIENDLY HUMANS AND FOOD THROUGH THESE DOORS! Then, when curious visitors wandered inside the factory, I'd pick them off from above and we'd feast on them below. If a group looked too unruly or hard to handle, we'd just batten down the hatches or escape out the back.

If only the factory hadn't been set so far away from everything else, it might have worked. But this factory was the kind of place that didn't see a lot of foot traffic. My band of zombies had been an aberration. It was where you went when you wanted to *avoid* people. And zombies.

How long would we have to wait here between seeing visitors, I wondered; a month? Two? Three? That would not be enough action to satisfy me, or my hungry companions. And I knew it. Ineluctably, I soon decided that the right move was to move on.

For a while, I feared the freckled kid might return—having run out of food and with nowhere else to go—but that never happened. He never showed up. After a few days in the factory, we lit out in the middle of the night, back on the hunt.

Short and bleak days followed—mysterious mornings of blue and pink that gave way to gray, profitless-feeling afternoons. Mold grew on us where the ice had melted, frozen, and melted again. Our skins grew slack and spongy like old, wet wood. We walked and walked.

We saw dead zombies—that is, zombies that had been shot through the forehead—more than we saw "living" zombies or humans. Some had been shot and then burned, leaving behind only piles of white bones with telltale holes in the skulls. Other times, we found dead zombies that had been tied up, or tied to fence posts or trees. Twice, we encountered orderly piles of dead zombies, stacked according to size. (I chalked these up to the Amish and their Germanic meticulousness.)

It was one big circular hunt, all of it. The humans hunting us. Us hunting the humans. Humans hunting each other.

I assumed that—as the days wore by—the humans would sort of "get better" at surviving in this new, zombie wasteland. That they would improve. Become accustomed to "survivalist mode" or whatever.

It was too early to tell if this was what was happening; it was certainly clear that a lot of them couldn't take it anymore. Many of the humans went stir-crazy. (I mean, rural Ohio, in the middle of the winter—that'll do it for some people right there; no zombies needed. But add a zombie outbreak to that, and you've got a situation ready to make inroads on the steadiest of nerves.)

Like one morning, a few clicks outside of Utica, we came across a man who'd killed his wife and daughters with an ax. Then he'd piled the bodies inside the family trailer and set it on fire. He was sitting on a stump, just watching it burn, as we approached him, the cruor-coated weapon resting at his feet. I wondered—after bringing him down with a bullet and eating his brain—if this murderer had always wanted to kill his family. Had it been a goal of his for a while? Something he'd always harbored, but never had the gumption to execute? (I imagined him as one of those henpecked husbands, imprisoned by a mortgage and stuck with a mean wife who found fault with his every foible. I imagined that his daughters had been shrill, self-centered, and irritating. Perhaps murder had been the liberation from this prison.)

Or, perhaps this man had truly loved his family and been happy here, despite the relative isolation and penury. Maybe he'd enjoyed his folksy, rural existence. It was possible, I had to grant, that it was only the outbreak of zombies that had driven him to this. (Not *just* to insanity, but also to murder.) Zombies had unhinged him. Zombies had warranted that he should kill the very family he had raised and loved.

Or—a third idea—maybe he was "saving" them from being eaten by zombies by killing them himself. Or saving them from rape and murder at the hand of gangs.

Alas, he was in our stomachs now, and not around to ask.

As we left the steaming, smoldering trailer, I saw the bodies of the two young daughters—charred and smoking, and with visible ax wounds in their chests—rise up and begin to walk. Their crisp, ashen bodies edged awkwardly through the rubble, leaving coal-black footprints in the snow.

Another time, we saw a fat man wearing only boxer shorts and an expensive fur coat running through a snowy field. I instinctively lifted my pistol to bring him down, but hesitated. This one was also a mystery. Was he running toward something, or away from it? Was he just running to run? We were on the edge of the woods, and there didn't appear to be anything around for miles. I could see the prints made by his snowy, bare feet extending back across the hills to the horizon. It was like encountering a big fish swimming in a tiny puddle. How had it gotten there? How could it live there? What was it trying to prove?

Nothing made sense until I saw the man's eyes.

He was insane. This man's brain was broken. A mania, ancient and terrifying, possessed him. He was not running to or from anything. He had ceased to need "reasons" for doing things. We surrounded and confused him, and I was able to bring him down using only the sword. He did not speak during the entire affair.

As we ate him, I noticed that his feet had turned blue from frostbite. His fingertips, nose, and penis also showed signs of having been frozen. Luckily, an insane brain tasted just as sweet as a normal one.

In yet another strange case, we encountered an overturned luxury car lying in the center of a field. (I could not have sworn to it, but it looked very much like the car that Bleckner—the Kenton College administrator—had driven.) There was no indication as to what force had flipped the automobile, but I reckoned it must have taken many men. The really remarkable thing was that the car's surface was almost completely covered in lines of poetry, etched hard into the paint.

At least, it appeared to be poetry. The sentiments were certainly poetical (though I could remember very few poems, and these were not among them). There seemed to be thousands of lines, and they had been painstakingly carved, as if with the tip of a sharp and exacting knife. The car was recently rainwashed, and the silver lines of verse stood out iridescently in the sunshine. It must have taken days for the author to have covered the surface of the car. I had to get in close to read them. Many of the verses were so small as to be nearly illegible. The ones I could make out tended to disturb me.

One line ran: "My head is heavy, my limbs are weary, and it is not life that makes me move." Another declaimed: "Horseman, your sword is in the groove!" Another still read ominously: "A ghost wants blood." I stopped reading before I'd finished a single door.

There were other instances of insanity. Weird things we found or saw: A missive to Satan ("our dark father below") written in blood on the side of a silo. A group—it appeared to be the remains of several families—who had shot up one another inside a recreation center just outside of Newcomerstown. A tiny house, deep in the woods, with recently skinned and mutilated animals hanging from all the trees around it . . . and inside, a man in a rocking chair who'd blown his own brains out.

These grisly pastiches were like clues in a mystery that made no sense.

Clearly, these people had started out okay. They'd been holding their own as the dead rose from their graves and society broke down around them. They'd managed to avoid being eaten by zombies. They were hanging on. And yet, undeniably, here they also were—or parts of them, anyway—undone, insane, and dead.

For a while, I felt like an investigator. I'd see something like the skinned animals hanging from the branches at that house and think: "Aha! Another clue for the file." But these were not clues, and there was no file. There was no *use* for this information. If these instances "pointed to" anything, it was that life sucked out here. Sucked big-time. Especially for humans.

I felt luckier and luckier to be me—whatever I was. I embraced my inner zombie more and more each day. I felt a real contempt toward these humans. Not only did they hunt me; not only were they delicious to eat; they were also broken internally and couldn't handle reality. They were, in a word, losers. At least, compared to zombies.

I mean, we all had to live in the same shitty world. We had to walk through the same mind-numbing countryside day after day. We had to find ways to endure in this ugly snow globe filled with blood and gray dishwater and a little WELCOME TO KNOX COUNTY! sign. And yet, zombies, despite it all, could suck it up and keep going.

Humans—as was being made increasingly clear to me—were broken and could not. They *lacked* something. They were incomplete and broken. They went insane and turned on themselves, or on one another. Zombies, in contrast, were focused.

Alone, zombies were competent and resourceful and never gave up. In a group, zombies were harmonious. There was no infighting or disagreement. We stayed sane—sane and hungry, but sane.

We might have rotted from the outside in, but humans rotted from the inside out.

A few days later, I was leading my band west through a string of farms outside Pipesville, located along the southern border of Knox County. It was a warm morning, and there were signs of an early spring. Birdsong, the scent of tree buds on the wind, warm wafts of air—the whole nine yards. It was nice, nice in a way above and beyond being able to sense hot or cold. My cell phone—which formerly displayed time and date—had long since died, but I estimated the date as late February or early March.

Wherever the sun could reach, the snow had melted. The ground was wet and muddy, and it clumped to our shoes (and, in many cases, bare feet). The snow lingered only in the shadows under the trees.

I led the way when we were in forest or underbrush, but hung in the middle of the group whenever we crossed open terrain. (I was ever alert for snipers. *Ever* alert.) I was learning that zombies were like windup toys. If you could get them walking in one direction, they would pretty much go until they ran into something.

My band had grown. Our group now boasted numbers safely into the double digits. I still had Hunter—my original traveling companion, still decked out in his bright blaze-orange—and all of my original members (except for Mario [RIP]), but we had picked up others along the way. A formerly beautiful young woman with wispy hair, bright blue sandals, and a gaping shotgun wound in her chest. A teenage boy in a tuxedo who, judging by the dried gore running down his face, had already made a few kills. An ice fisherman who appeared to have frozen to death.

There was never any ceremony or pomp to the enlistment proceedings. Zombies simply tended to follow other zombies. Was that such a strange thing? I saw it throughout the animal kingdom— from the flocks of Canada geese that soared above us and shat on the fields where we roamed, to the deer that loped after one another when we disturbed their solitude deep in the Ohio forests. Things followed other things that were like them.

We usually encountered lone zombies, not other groups. They would watch us approach without alarm, and we would pass them by like a slow and bedraggled parade. Then, after a few minutes, I'd look behind us and see that—sure enough—the stranger-zombie had become our rear guard. Some zombies moved faster than others, but no one was ever left behind entirely.

I had the sense that the growing numbers were making us stronger—more effective—and I wanted to keep it going. (Getting my share of the brains was never a concern. My companions were easy to outmaneuver when it came down to it.) With a group of fifteen or so, we could surround a house or building, block off passageways of escape, and confuse humans. Also, fifteen zombies meant fifteen noses (okay, really more like thirteen) and thirty eyes (actually, 27.5—and you *really* don't want to know about the .5). More noses to smell you with, and more eyes to see you with. Even though my compatriots were dense as hell, they often smelled or saw things that I missed. These other zombies seemed to have an ability to detect humans that I, for some reason, lacked. (I assumed this was connected to the other ways in which I was atypical for a zombie.)

So, anyway, the smells ... As I was saying, it was a springlike morning outside of Pipesville. Gradually, I began to sense something on the warm wind, something more than the melting snow and wet earth. It was the scent of people. A lot of people. Like a rock concert or a sporting event. But not *just* the scent of people ... There was also a low undercurrent of something else that was sickening. Rot. Decay. The stifling musk of death. In my former life, I might have mistaken it for a freshly manured field.

My companions seemed to notice nothing at all.

Cautiously curious, I began to guide my group toward the source of the strange smell. I could see and hear nothing, but the intensifying odor was unmistakable. Where I had first only caught the odd waft as the wind blew in our direction, I soon smelled it constantly. It was powerful and wild. Then, as my band crested a row of man-made hillocks dividing two farms, the source came into view.

It was a battalion—a *battalion*—of zombies. Easily four hundred of them spilled across the plain in front of us. It was a walking forest of zombies. They moved slowly and implacably, their gaits unhurried and confident. They moved like time. Like inevitability. Like a force of nature. It was breathtaking. I had never seen so many. I felt no trepidation, only curiosity. What happened when large groups of zombies met? Surely, one absorbed the other. And my group being smaller by far, we were doubtless the appointed absorbees.

My position as leader and commander had always come naturally in my group. (I mean, who else was going to pick locks, shoot a gun, and lead us away from ambushes?) Perhaps, I thought, I would be able to insinuate myself as the leader of this new, giant throng. In that instant, I began to imagine what we might be able to accomplish. Entire towns surrounded. Bunkers starved out. Snipers and well-armed survivalists overwhelmed by the sheer force of our numbers.

My zombie compatriots had also paused to regard the approaching throng. They looked surprised, if not necessarily uneasy. Hunter, especially, seemed confused by our visitors.

"Now, now," I said warmly. "Nothing to fear here. We're among friends. C'mon, Hunter. Wade in with me!"

At first, I had the impulse to strut through the rows of zombies like a newly minted CEO inspecting his workers. Who would have thought there could *be* so many? The zombies were diverse in both appearance and character. Some were old corpses—little more than walking skeletons, flesh and rags hanging down from their bones like wet mud—while others were recent additions, still strong and hale-looking. One delegation wore bright-orange prison jumpsuits with lettering that read MANSFIELD CORRECTIONAL. Another subset was comprised of police, fire, and prison guards. (I imagined a prison riot in which these two groups had fought one another bitterly and to the death. Now they stood side by side, united in purpose.) A smattering of children and teenagers—and at least one "little person"—were interspersed among the living dead.

Some of the zombies regarded me curiously as I passed. Others failed to notice me at all, their gazes fixed forward, locked on the horizon. Others still (perhaps the majority) seemed to notice me with only a corner of their attention, like a man or woman engaged in an all-consuming task who is momentarily pestered by a fly.

Almost all of them had blood around their mouths that was not their own. An army marched on its stomach, and this army of zombies was no exception. There could be no doubt; this was a group that fed.

I was wading against the current, and before long I was through it and standing at the tail end of the parade. Behind them, the zombies had left a swath of footprints in the snow fifty yards wide. In addition, they had left behind scraps of clothing, splotches of blood, and even the odd body part. This group was a force to be reckoned with. It was like a slow-moving snowball, growing larger as it rolled. Adding new members. Using up and spitting out everything that lay behind it.

These were my kind of people.

It was a few days before I found him. (I say "him," but it could just as easily have been a "her.") I had resolved to search the entire horde, if necessary. At times, I walked at the head of the pack. Other times, I lost myself in the center of the great bolus, or skirted around the edges of the grim formation. I was looking for any sign of dominance or influence. I was looking for any action or reaction that would denote intelligence. In short, I was looking for someone like me.

Did I expect a chatty, reasoning, gun-toting zombie? Of course not. But I *did* expect to find one who was smarter than the others. One who was more advanced. A leader. And this leader—as I eventually discerned—came in the form of a bald, overweight, Middle Eastern zombie in a golf shirt and khakis. He wore several gold chains around his neck, and had sandals on his feet. His eyebrows were heavy, and a placid smile lingered on his face. He appeared to have been embalmed, but bore no visible injury, and I could not discern his cause of death.

He was one of the zombies who looked back at me as I walked by. And as the days of searching the ranks went by, I noticed how his gaze lingered longer than most. His eyes stayed on me when I approached him, and sometimes his expression changed. Though silent, his mouth sometimes opened as though he had something to say.

There was another clue to his strength and superiority: He wore far more gore down the front of his face than any other zombie in the crowd. When it was feeding time, this one clearly knew what to do.

He walked at the head of the group, though not at the very front. That honor went to three giant zombies. As I watched the leader (for the good part of a day), I observed how he interacted with these huge zombies. Before long, I could have no doubts—he was using them. There was an *intentionality* to it. The leader allowed the three large zombies to clear the way, to move obstacles, or to feel out dangerous situations. He never spoke to them with words, but directed them with expressions, gestures, and the occasional nudge. He was conscious of the situation. He knew he was in a group—on a team—and that he was the captain. There was a responsibility to it, as if he understood that he *must* lead for the good of all. He had a lust for brains—the still-fresh gore upon his chin was ample evidence of that—but he also had an understanding that he was not alone in this lust.

He was not as cognizant as a human (as I, more or less, was). He was more like a dog—a smart, happy dog. He was pleased to be among friends, and pleased to reap the benefits that came with being leader of the pack. Accordingly, my first action was to stroke his head gently. He smiled back pleasantly, and we strolled together for a time. He seemed to appreciate my company.

"Who's a smart zombie?" I asked cooingly. "I think *you* are . . . Wes, I do. Wes, I do. I think *you're* a clever little zombie."

He smiled again and looked bashful, as if to say I must stop because I would make him blush.

"What's your name then, I wonder?" I said to him. "You're a mystery, you are. Looks like you aren't from around here. You look like you're from the Middle East. Maybe someplace like Iran or Iraq or Turkey?"

He smiled at this last word. It was more than the idiot-dog smile. There was definitely something to it.

"Turkey?" I said. He smiled again.

"Nice," I said. "So you're from Turkey, maybe. What if I call you 'the Turk'? How would that be?"

He appeared, more or less, to accept the idea. I continued to stroke him gently.

"So, Mr. Turk, I have to say: This is quite an impressive array of zombies you've got here. Believe it or not, it's about to get even more impressive. See, I'm a zombie like you are. That's why you don't smell me. That's why you don't want to eat *my* brain. But I can do things you can't even imagine. It's clear that you're very smart, but I can do things even you can't do, like shoot a gun and read road signs. And I think if we can combine forces—as it appears we already have—then wonderful accomplishments are going to be possible. Wes, they are. Wes, they are, indeed."

The Turk smiled and even nodded a little. I returned his goredripping grin.

Something told me it just might be the beginning of a delightful—if not exactly beautiful (at least not in the classical sense)—friendship.

The next day we attacked a grocery store in Pipesville. I had taken up a position alongside the Turk in our marching order, near the front of the pack. We were not exactly the lead dogs, but forward enough to steer the group when we needed to. The road into Pipesville ran through a hilly stretch of crevasses and crags, making it feel more like southeastern Ohio than smack-in-the-center Ohio.

We walked through the town slowly, an obscene parade of rotting flesh and naked bone. All the windows were dark, all the houses empty. I felt safe with the Turk and his three giant zombies leading the way.

A few cottages and modest farmhouses dotted the outskirts. Past these, the town revealed itself as one long street. A VFW hall. A hardware store. A couple of horrible-looking diners. One tiny church. About fifty houses in all. And, intriguingly, a grocery store around which a ten-foot-high fence (topped with barbed wire) had been recently erected.

The Turk and I steered the group slowly toward the grocery enclosure. There were no humans to be seen, but there *were* several automobiles inside the fenced perimeter. A gate at the front of the fence had been fastened shut with bike locks. (This frustrated me. Those were the kind you had to saw through.) To the side of the gate, but within the fenced perimeter, a makeshift watchtower had been erected in the crook of a giant maple. Like an armored tree house, it featured metal plates and a homemade turret that could rotate.

"Whaddaya think, Turk?" I said. "Looks like a tough nut to crack, but I'll bet it's worth it."

He looked at me and smiled. That was all I needed.

The fence would be the only real problem. I began thinking about a way to breach it. If I could find a car, I'd be able to run it down. But there did not appear to be any vehicles left outside the fence. Every car in town seemed to be inside the perimeter of the grocery store's parking lot. ("Frederick's Fresh Produce" it was called, or so said the sign affixed to the structure's tin roof. I wondered how fresh the produce could be—even pre-zombie-apocalypse—in the middle of winter in rural Ohio.) As an alternative, I wondered if there might be something—trash cans, boxes—that I could stack up beside the fence to make improvised stairs.

As if from out of the ether, I distinctly heard a voice from above cry, "Oh shit!"

The Turk heard it too. We began looking around. Some of the zombies in front of us began lumbering toward the fence, as though they had scented something.

I detected movement in the tree house above us. At first, just a shuffling. Then a man with a rifle slung over his shoulder popped out from a hatch in the bottom. As he scampered down the wooden slats nailed to the tree, he looked disbelievingly at our horde and began turning white. He dropped to the ground and took off toward the grocery store.

"Oh shit!" the man shouted again. "It's the big one. It's the fucking big one. They finally found us, dudes!"

The man wore an unbuttoned parka that flopped awkwardly behind him as he ran. He was thin and bearded and had enormous, expressive eyes that looked very, very afraid. His face also looked tired, and I decided that this sentry had likely been napping. As he neared the door to the grocery store, a surprised-looking man opened it and they collided, falling back inside the store together. This display of cowardice was not entirely unamusing. I elbowed the Turk in his fleshy ribs and laughed.

The bulk of our zombie battalion began to gather around the grocery-store perimeter. (A few drifted off to explore the houses and empty buildings, but there was nothing for them to find—no humans, dead or alive—and they soon joined us back at the fenced perimeter.) We nearly encircled it. The windows at the front of the grocery had been sandbagged with sacks of cat litter and rock salt, but I saw slices of faces peering out at us.

For a while, nothing happened, and this, I decided, was important. If the humans had had a flamethrower, or unlimited ammunition, they might well have begun the task of picking us off through the fence. We were easy—albeit numerous—targets. But they did no such thing. This bespoke limited resources. That was good for zombies.

I wondered, as the four hundred zombies crowded around, moaning and scratching, if *we* might not be the ones with the appearance of unlimited resources. Only the scared man in the parka had actually seen us from any perspective. Once we got to be a few rows deep in front of the fence, it might appear to the humans inside that we went on forever. We were a huge group, true, but through a fence we might look like we numbered into the thousands.

After a few minutes, a group of humans emerged from the grocery store: five of them—three men and two women. The shaky man in the parka was not among them. These humans had the grim, steely-eyed stares of soldiers on their third or fourth tour of duty. The types who would crack under the pressures of a zombie-world had long since fallen away here. These were the strong ones who had made it their business to survive.

Each member of the little band carried at least one gun. Two had machetes that looked somewhat similar to the samurai sword I carried. One of them appeared to be ex-military, and wore the fatigues to prove it. Unlike the screaming, wide-eyed man in the parka, this group appeared confident that we posed little threat. They made no aggressive moves toward us, instead seeming content merely to observe. I decided to do the same.

They began speaking to one another. I sidled up to the fence—through the rows of hungry, gibbering zombies—until I could hear what was being said.

"God, they're ugly," one man was saying. "I never get over it."

"You were right about the fence, Don," said one of the women. "It's holding up just like you said it would."

"How many do you think there are?" asked another. "A thousand? Two thousand?"

"Not hardly," the military-seeming man said flatly, and spat from the corner of his mouth. "Just a few hundred. I'd say less than five. They look like more than they are. Roger, do you still have those dowels from the hardware store?"

One of the steely-eyed men nodded.

"Righty then," the man in fatigues continued. "I reckon we can take 'em out through the fence."

I was intrigued. What *did* they think they were planning?

"But we can take them out through the fence right now, with bullets," one of the women said after a moment. "What do you want with dowels?"

Thank you, I almost said. That had been my question.

"Sure, we could," said Fatigues Man. "Shit, we prob'ly even have the bullets to do it, too. But what about when the next group like this one shows up, and it's bigger? And then the one after that? We'd be out of ammo before we knew it. Then we open ourselves up to the gangs."

I had to admit, he made a good point. (There was a definite pleasure to be taken in this kind of eavesdropping. It was like being invisible. I was so close to them—probably less than fifteen feet away—but I might as well have been a tree, or an animal, or a part of the fence itself. Little did they know... Little did they know... [I forced myself to suppress a smile.])

"The U.S. Army will have to come for us soon," one of the men said. "The helicopters could air-drop something, or pull us out and take us to one of the cities."

I detected a longing in some of the faces—especially the faces of the women—at this idea. The military-looking man, however, appeared half-ready to vomit.

"Is that what you really want?" Fatigues said. "To move to the city and pay that price? To suckle on the teat of the government—the fucking federal fucking government?!"

Aha! There was some tension here! This was getting good.

"Answer me this," Fatigues continued. "Why didn't you people move down to Columbus *before* this all happened?"

"Are you serious?" one of the men answered him.

"Sure I am," Fatigues said. "You ask yourself that, and you'll find the answer. You wanted to be free. You didn't want to get dependent and lazy and fat. You didn't want to be a ward of the damn-blasted *federal government*. You wanted to be a self-sufficient American."

"Jack, I live here because my family's farm is here," the man replied.

"You can go down to Columbus if you want to," Jack/Fatigues said, as if the other had said nothing. "Anybody can leave at any time. You know the rules. You're always free to go ... But all Columbus is, is a bigger grocery story running out of food, with a bigger fucking fence around it."

"And bigger assholes in army uniforms telling folks what to do?" the man quipped.

Jack stared at him hard. His hand that was not on a gun curled into a fist.

"We'll try the dowels," one of the women said, hoping (much to my disappointment) to diffuse the tension. "No sense in not giving an idea a try, right?"

"Need to do it soon," Jack said. "I want to make a dent in them before it gets dark. They dig under the fence in the middle of the night—I feel like *some* of us might not know what to do if that happened."

They went back inside the grocery store. They were planning something.

That was all right. I was planning something too.

For the next hour, I heard the intermittent sound of hammers and power saws coming from the back of the store. It was like a reality show or something—where each team has some lumber and odds and ends and a couple of hours to build things. The two teams are separated by a fence, but can kind of guess at what the other is doing.

I went exploring, though there wasn't much to explore in a place like Pipesville. Most of the homes had been pillaged for everything valuable or useful. Other houses had just been respectfully locked, but I found a toolshed behind a ranch-style home and cut through the moldering wooden door with my sword. Inside was an assortment of garden tools. I took a pair of pruning shears with a long wooden handle—the kind that could cut very thick branches.

I stuffed the shears down the leg of my pants and walked stiffly to the back of the fenced perimeter behind the grocery store. There were a couple of windows facing the back of the store, but they looked like they'd been boarded up with sacks of charcoal and pet food. Most of the other zombies were still in front of the store, but a handful were milling around in the back. I had to chance that we were unobserved.

As furtively as I could, I took the shears out of my pants and began to cut the fence. The "snaps" when I clipped the wire were louder than I would have liked, but it was quick work. In under a minute, I'd made a hole big enough for a zombie to wander through.

"Hey, buddy," I said, grabbing a nearby zombie by the scruff of the neck. "In you go."

I guided two or three other zombies through the hole in the wire, and watched them wander absently around the back of the building. Trusting that more would soon follow, I dropped the shears and returned—at what I hoped appeared to be an unhurried zombie's gait—to the large group at the front of the fence.

After a few minutes, the same group of humans reemerged from the store armed with an assortment of homemade spears—dowels with very long, very thin nails at one end. I had to grant, they looked perfect for driving through a zombie's skull.

The humans approached the fence. I noted—with some excitement—that they had not brought their firearms with them, only the spears. Jack, the one in the fatigues, took one of the spears and slid it through the fence. He didn't have to slide it far, the zombies were right there, inches away. In his other hand was a flathead hammer.

"Now watch this," he said. "It's two motions. You're going to stab into the forehead in the first, and hit the end of the dowel with your hammer in the second. That should be enough to pierce the skull. Then you just keep hitting until the zombie goes down. Most of these guys, the skulls are old and brittle. You'll get through on the first try. The newer-looking ones, like ... *that* one," he said, pointing directly at me, "those fresher ones may take a few more blows."

The other humans nodded grimly at the thought of the work ahead. Behind them, I saw the first zombie peek its head around the side of the grocery store, *inside* the fenced perimeter.

"So—watch me, here—I'll start with one of the easy ones," Jack said. "Watch how I do it, and then y'all give it a shot."

Jack took a new stab through the fence and found the forehead of a crusty, skeletal zombie standing just a few feet from me. As

Jack closed one eye and raised his hammer, I extended one finger and began to gesture.

Jack contemplated his hammer blow like a golfer preparing to make a difficult shot. As he raised back the hammer to strike, my gesturing became more insistent.

"Hey Jack," one of the humans shouted to him, "take a look at that."

"Yeah," said one of the human females. "That zombie looks like it's trying to tell us something."

"What?" Jack said skeptically, lowering his hammer. He watched my gestures and I pointed back toward the grocery store behind him. He was completely confused.

"Now it's smiling," the human female said. "Look! It's totally smiling."

"It looks like it's ... pointing at the store," one of the human men said.

"Now why in the God-lovin' world would a zombie point at the store?" Jack growled.

But then he looked behind the group, where three zombies now milled about, clearly on the wrong side of the perimeter.

"Oh, son of a *bitch!*" Jack exclaimed.

"Shit!" one of the others said, and began heading for the store. And as they turned, I drew both of my revolvers.

"Hey!" I shouted in an angry rasp.

Some of the humans regarded me.

I winked.

Then I started pulling triggers, shooting with both hands at once, like something out of a Western. The recoil of the guns jarred my numb hands, but I did not let go. I shot and shot until the guns were empty—six bullets from each weapon.

One of my shots hit Jack, and he spun around and fell. The rest of the humans had started running, but I still brought down three of them, leaving just one lithe female unharmed and sprinting back toward the grocery store. (Let me say that again: I hit four out of five, and I was shooting from the hip. Given my total lack of training with firearms, I think this was absolutely remarkable.)

"Omigod!" the running woman screamed to whoever was still inside the store. "Get your guns! Get your guns! There are people out here too!"

Only one of the humans I'd shot actually looked dead. The rest, including Jack, looked wounded—just temporarily down. I took my time reloading the revolvers.

"C'mon guys," I rasped to the zombies around me. "There's an entrance around back. Follow me." A few of them seemed to get the idea. We walked to the back of the perimeter behind the grocery store where more zombies had started making their way through the hole. I tried to encourage even more of them to follow me, and ducked through. I rounded the side of the store in time to see a new human—a skinny man armed with a rifle—emerge from the grocery entrance. He was running fast. He dodged zombies skillfully, weaving this way and that, making his way toward the group lying prone on the ground. The moment he reached his colleagues, I shot him in the back.

Most of the zombies were still at the front of the fence—the humans so tantalizingly close, yet so far away. A zombie sidled up next to me. It was the Turk.

"I knew I could trust *you* to figure it out," I said to him.

Screams began to erupt. A few zombies were already upon the humans. The others, across the fence, gnashed their teeth angrily. Jack, however, was fighting them off with his pointy dowel. I'd hit him in the thigh, but he was still able to hop around a bit. Now he was back on the offensive. He used the dowel like a spear—fighting with overhand thrusts. Mostly, he just kept the zombies at bay, but now and then he struck home on an older, more-brittle zombie, and sent it down with a hole in its forehead. Worst of all, I could see there was real joy in it for him.

Some part of my memory triggered. I knew this man, it told me. Knew his kind. A survivalist.

Not *all* survivalists were problematic, of course. I mean, soldiers needed survivalist skills in case they became stranded in the course of a mission. The same was true for explorers or people who traveled in isolated regions. But this man, Jack, belonged to that peculiarly cynical variety characterized by a pervading feeling that the world was on its way out. According to these men and women, things were crumbling and society was doomed—and the only solution was to hide on the side of a hill with a bunch of canned food and guns.

It was, in a word, solipsism. I remembered *that* word from my philosophy classes, and I remembered that it was what I hated about these guys. They had given up on everyone but themselves. You say your community's not what you'd like it to be? Your government seems wasteful and impersonal? Each day, the world feels a little less like a place you can relate to? The solution isn't to stockpile food and prepare to shoot your neighbor if he tries to climb inside your fallout shelter. No. That's beyond insane. The solution is to try to *improve* society, not run from it. You interact with that world. You try to make it a better place. You run for city council. You mentor. You don't just *give up*.

And that was what really upset me about the expression on his face. It was more than pleasure at having an opportunity to use his obviously well-honed spear-fighting skills. It was the pleasure of validation. The pleasure of having been right all along when those around you said you were crazy.

I wondered how many relationships this man had severed in his life—how many friends and family members who loved him he'd alienated—all for the sake of militant preparedness. And now, of course, he felt vindicated. It seemed he'd been right all along.

The thing was, he *wasn't* right—not at all. The federal government *was* the last, best hope for people, and from every report there *was* at least something *akin* to order down in Columbus. It was people like this guy who'd chosen to "go it alone" and let the rest of the country go to hell who'd been taken to hell themselves. The fate Jack had wished on others was the one he'd received himself. I sauntered over at an unhurried pace that contrasted sharply with his war cries and manic stabbing.

"Hey," I said to him, gently pushing the other zombies out of the way. His eyes were boiling with rage and terror, and he did not seem to hear me at first. "I'm talking to *you*," I said. "Hey, you! Spear guy. Jack."

Then he looked at me, javelin raised. Startled. Terrified. As I watched, the terror became confusion. Then anger. Then wonderment. He took a step back.

"You're with *them?*" he asked, unable to understand who or what I was.

"Just so you know," I said, taking careful aim at his forehead, "you're dead wrong. You would've been *much* safer down in Columbus."

Crack! I put a bullet between his eyes, and the back of his head exploded. He went down—big and mean and camouflaged and dead. The other zombies were upon his corpse almost before he hit the ground.

I stood there quietly, looking at Jack's corpse and debating my next move, when I heard a gunshot and my left shoulder jumped in a puff of grime and dust. I fell to one knee and swiveled around. Behind me, three more humans—including the lithe woman and the scraggly man in the parka—had emerged from the store. They were armed—two with rifles, and the lithe woman with an Uzi, which she nervously leveled in my direction. They were perhaps fifteen yards away.

There were more than twenty zombies in the yard with me now, but these humans had seen enough of my interaction with Jack to understand (correctly) that I posed the biggest threat to them. I dropped completely flat against the ground and steadied my guns against the cold concrete. We all fired our weapons at once. The woman's Uzi went *brrrrrap!* and made the concrete dance around me. It was terrifying, but only lasted four or five seconds. If she hit me, I didn't notice it. I emptied my guns again, and they jerked violently in my hands. I hit one of the men square in the chest, and he went down, dead. I hit Parka Man in the leg. He fell to one knee and started screaming. ("OhGodOhGodOhGod ...") His kneecap had exploded and yellow matter was leaking out.

Then, a new group of zombies emerged from the side of the store. One of the quicker ones shuffled toward Parka Man as hastily as it could. Parka Man was completely oblivious, and the zombie pounced before the human knew what had hit him. The other zombies followed, and made short work of him.

The lithe woman was unhurt so far—by bullets or by zombies— but looked terrified by this new group of undead that had rounded the side of the store. She cast one final, sad glance at her friends who were being eaten, and ran back inside. She slammed the glass door shut and began stacking sacks of water-softener salt against it, until I could no longer see inside.

I carefully rose from my prone position and reloaded my guns.

More zombies spilled inside the perimeter, and then more still. They made their way to the front of the grocery. When I felt concealed from view, I holstered my guns and took off my hat. I had no clue if it was possible for the humans to shoot from inside the store, but I didn't want to risk her taking potshots.

Finishing off this woman was going to be a challenge, but I was up to it. We all were. I ate Jack's brain and considered the best course of action.

Moments later, I was in back of the grocery store, and my ear was against the glass window. Inside, I could hear the lithe woman talking on a radio. It wasn't like a conversation with someone who was there, or someone you were talking to over the phone. It was like someone operating a ham radio, calling hopefully into the emptiness. She kept saying things like "Come in" and "Do you copy?"

Occasionally, she also described the attack that had just decimated her group and left her the only survivor. (That was good to know.) She described me in some detail. (I was properly flattered.) My race, sex, and physical characteristics. My clothes. My guns. She theorized that I was a human who had learned to live among the zombies, or who could possibly command zombies. She stressed that for some reason, zombies did not attack me. Perhaps I had mastered some sort of repellent. (Never did she theorize that I was just a zombie who could shoot and think and talk.)

My stomach was full of brains, but I suddenly wanted this one more than I could say. She knew me. She'd shot at me. She had even told her friends about me. This was practically a relationship. We were a star-crossed pair, destined to meet.

I idly wandered back around to the front of the building. After a little looking, I found a zombie who looked about my height and weight. I unloaded one of my revolvers and tied it to one of his hands with an old shirt. Then I managed to get my jacket on him. (Should have done that first. Hard to get it on over the gun.) I put my Kernels hat on his head as a finishing touch.

"You look good," I told him. "Now let's do this." I conducted my newly dressed zombie to the front door, and stood off to the side, in a position I hoped was out of sight.

"Hey, lady," I called, a little like a gravel-throated Jerry Lewis. "Hey, lady, it's me!"

There was no response. I knocked hard, then stepped away. "Hey, lady," I tried again. "It's ... the guy you were just shooting at. Remember me? I'll bet you do." Again, there was no response. The zombies milled about listlessly. (If she were near the door, they would likely smell her and become excited.) The Turk wandered over and looked at me curiously, cocking his neck like a confused dog.

"I heard you talking about me on the radio," I shouted. "I'm flattered. Completely flattered." Finally, a noise from inside. I looked up. So did the other zombies. They began to gather around the front of the store. I had her attention.

"Hey, can we talk?" I asked.

Silence followed. Then a voice, shaky and broken.

"What do you want?" she screamed.

It was a good question. (What to say? What to say? This woman desired life. I desired her death. And there, the impasse.)

I could not simply begin with the fact that I wanted to eat her brain. Instead, I knew I must begin by establishing the commonalities that create a rapport. After all, it was not as though we had *nothing* in common. We were both residents of Knox County, Ohio. We were both fumbling our way through a zombie apocalypse. And, most specifically, we were both hanging around the grocery store in Pipesville.

"A little like spring today, isn't it?" I said.

A. Very. Long. Pause.

Then: "*What?!*"

"The weather," I clarified. "I mean to say that it's a little like spring outside. A little warmer than it has been, no?"

"What?" she said again, as if she had misheard me.

"Not that it's going to last," I continued. "But that doesn't mean we can't go ahead and enjoy it, right?"

"Are ... Are you trying to talk to me about the weather?" the lithe woman asked, beginning to get the picture.

"I mean, unless you have something better in mind," I said. "We don't really know each other, but folks can always talk about the weather. Are you from Ohio? I am ... apparently."

"Why aren't the zombies attacking you?" she shouted. "Can you command them?"

Command was such a formal, official-sounding term. I kind of liked it. "Yes," I rasped after a moment. "I command them. They are my *army of the night*. Except ... umm ... They don't always do exactly what I want them to. I can get them interested in a direction usually, but they veer off whenever they smell something interesting. Sometimes they obey me and sometimes they don't—but hey, even a stopped clock, right?"

"How do you get them to do that?" she asked.

"Uh, it's complicated," I said hoarsely, wishing there were something around for my parched throat. No pool or puddle presented itself.

"Excuse me," I tried again, "but have you got some water in there? Like some bottled water? That you could throw me?"

"*What?*" she said, harshly.

Back to this again.

"Could you please throw me a bottled water—maybe crack a window and throw it out?" I asked. "It's hard for me to talk."

Another. Very. Long. Pause.

"Am I crazy, or did you just *shoot all of my friends?*" she said.

I smiled. She had me there.

"Umm, as I recall, you were getting ready to stab my zombies in the forehead with your little homemade spears," I countered.

"But they're *zombies*," she said.

"They're *my* zombies," I corrected her. "And you were just going to kill them."

"They're *zombies*," she said. "I can't ... I can't even believe we're talking about this. I can't believe I'm talking to you. *You killed all of my friends, you stupid fuck! Go fuck yourself!*"

Go fuck yourself.

That sentiment was cold—cold like my flaccid zombie penis. (I had not achieved tumescence once since being reanimated. She didn't know what she was saying, of course, but it still felt like a hit below the belt.) This was quickly devolving into a standoff. I decided to change my approach.

"Can I apologize?" I asked. "I feel bad about this now."

"*I'll fucking kill you*," she shrieked.

"You can kill me if you want to, but I still want to say I'm sorry," I told her. "I really do feel terrible about all of it. How about this: You just open the door a tiny crack so I can apologize in person. If you want to shoot me, you can."

"I can already shoot you," she said.

I decided she was bluffing. There were no openings that I could see anywhere in the sandbagged front of the store. If she were truly looking out, she'd see that the zombie wearing my clothes and "holding" my gun was facing the wrong way. His lips weren't even moving.

Suddenly, like automatons brought to life with a restored flow of electricity, the zombies nearest to the store took an interest in the front windows. Even the zombie I'd dressed as me turned and began pawing at the front door. They could smell her. She had moved very close.

"Come on," I said, calling as loudly as I could from the side of the store. "Just open up a tiny crack."

"I'll open it up and I'll *shoot you!*" she screamed.

I was close. So close.

"Go ahead, if that's what you really want," I told her. "Do what you gotta do."

I drew my gun and crept near. From out of nowhere, there was a shattering of glass and the sound of blistering gunfire. The zombie dressed as me began to shake as if a seizure had taken him. The lithe woman had spread apart the sandbags and was firing through the glass door with her Uzi.

As the fake-me disintegrated before my eyes, I watched the woman's weapon spit its fiery fury. Seconds later, the Uzi ceased, its clip emptied. The fake-me was bent double, virtually cut in half. "Die, you *stupid motherfuck!*" the woman screamed. "*Die!*" Her voice was telltale, betraying her exact position.

I leapt forward, stuck my revolver through the hole at an angle, and started pulling the trigger. There was no way for me to miss. At such close range, she more or less exploded in a shower of hair and blood. The other zombies looked on in genial assent, like pedestrians pausing to watch city workers using impressive-looking tools. I heard the lithe woman's body—what was left of it—slip down the line of sandbags and fall hard against the floor of the grocery store. I used my gun-butt to break the rest of the glass, and gently pushed my way inside.

After I had eaten the lithe woman's brain, I returned to the parking lot and retrieved my hat and other revolver from the destroyed zombie. Then I opened the door to the store and let the zombies wander inside to finish any leftovers. The sun was setting, and I let out a long belch.

It had been a full day's work.

The interior of the store had been rearranged, obviously, but the place still looked discernibly like a grocery. Something about its geography was familiar to me. Fruit and vegetables to your right as you walk inside. Meat and seafood in the back. I was unable to recall where I'd shopped for food as a resident of Gant, but I decided it must have been a place like this. Even without power, the smell of freezers and produce was strong and recognizable.

At the back of the store, I found the area where the humans had made camp. There were cots, clothing, flashlights, ropes, ladders, and the battery-powered radio that the lithe woman had been using. There was also a considerable cache of weapons, and I was able to rearm and upgrade once again. (I kept my revolvers—I liked them, and the holsters were nice—but added a semiautomatic M16, a sawed-off shotgun, and a green camouflage backpack full of ammunition.)

Most of the shopping carts had been piled in a corner. For a while, I considered filling one of them with ammunition and other supplies, but quickly gave up on this idea. It would be almost impossible to push such a cart if we went off of the main roads, which we almost certainly would. (Not to mention that I'd look like a zombified homeless guy.)

At one point, the Turk walked past and I got his attention.

"Hey, Turk, look at me," I said, pushing a cart down an aisle. "I'm a human in a supermarket, and I'm shopping for food. Look, I'm opening this glass freezer because there's human food in here that I want to purchase and consume. Look at me."

The Turk smiled and nodded.

"Oh, wait," I said. "I almost forgot something."

I palmed one of the lithe woman's eyes that I'd been keeping in my pocket as a snack, and then seemed to pluck it from a produce display.

"I hope these grapes are ripe," I said, inspecting the orb. "They do come all the way from Chile. I'm sure the manager won't mind if I eat just one."

The Turk grew excited, and actually began to applaud.

I popped the eye into my mouth and chewed. After a few bites, I felt it pop. Various humors dripped from my lips like grape juice.

"Oh yes," I said. "I absolutely *must* have these. They are *divine*. Now to push my grocery cart to the front and pay for things with money. Then I'll put my fat ass into a minivan and drive back to my house with all my whining kids."

The Turk moaned in approval and laughed. It was not like a human laugh—it was a horrible, undead groaning approximation—but I still appreciated it.

For all the killing and eating, perhaps I'd never felt more fully a zombie than at that moment. By "a zombie," I suppose I have to mean "not human." Yes, then. Perhaps that *is* what I mean. Humans were the other. The thing to be lampooned and eaten alive whenever possible. I didn't look at them and think: "There is some of me in that." Rather, I thought only: "How do I get some of that in me." My immersion into zombiedom was closest to total when I felt a real contempt for the living. I wasn't just *different,* I was *better. We* were better.

It felt wonderful to embrace this concept: Not just different. *Better.* Some things are *better* than other things. And *we are better.* Zombies *are better.* It felt so good to say. Yes. We were obviously better. *A priori* better. All of us. Better than anything else. Superior. Masters of this world. And where, I wondered, were the humans? Where were the people who might have called this position "unfair" or "species-ist" or "undead-ist?" Where were they?

In my stomach. In my fucking stomach.

Objection noted. Now I'm going to eat the brain you used to think of it.

Better than. There could be no question. We were *better than* humans. That was what we were. I wanted to shout it from the rooftops (and perhaps would've, had my voice been more than a husky growl).

"Fucking humans," I said, tipping over my shopping cart ferociously and making the Turk jump back a little. "We are better than them. We're far, far superior. They are *our food.* It's obvious to any smart person who takes a look. Zombies aren't just 'different,' zombies are *better!*"

So, anyway, you see some pretty cool things when you travel in a group of four hundred zombies.

Like one morning, right after we moved on from Pipesville, we edged along a barely paved, intensely potholed rural route, and saw an SUV cresting the horizon and heading toward us very fast. It suddenly slammed on the brakes. The tires shrieked. The frame shuddered. Dust kicked up in a fifteen-foot plume. It was like something out of a movie.

I could see the driver's jaw literally drop as he took in all four hundred of us. Then he pulled a U-turn and hauled out of there, kicking up another cloud of dust and frost in the air behind him. It wasn't as dramatic as a battle or anything, but it was sort of cute, I thought.

Another time, I saw our old friends in the military observation helicopter again. Our zombie horde was fording a shallow stream when we heard the helicopter coming. Some part of me hoped it might be the same helicopter from before, and I was delighted when they came into view. The contraption hovered close, but not *too* close. This time, they were strangely cautious for men safely suspended hundreds of feet in the air. They took notes and photographs as they had before. I let them linger for five full minutes before becoming annoyed enough to take a shot at them. This time, I used the sawed-off shotgun I'd taken from the grocery store. My aim had not improved—and damn if the gun didn't buck like a mule—but I heard the tinny pings of buckshot against the helicopter's metal belly.

It moved off with all speed.

Fucking humans, I thought. We're better than you. How many photographs do you have to take before you figure that out?

Dumbasses.

Other times, traveling in a large group of zombies could be frustrating. Zombies aren't good at communicating generally, and they're really lousy at raising an alarm or telling other zombies when they see something important. (If they do see something good, they just quietly change course and lumber toward it. That's all the notification you can expect.) If you walk in the back of the horde, you can sometimes watch this happening. One zombie in the middle of the pack will see or smell something (like a human) and veer off. Then a few others will follow. Then the horde sort of splits and reconstitutes, the side, say, becomes the front, and suddenly you're all headed in a different direction.

I can remember—back when I was alive—reading about dinosaurs that used to be a hundred feet from tip to tail. These dinosaurs were so big and so dumb that if you stepped on the tips of their tails, it would take a full minute for them to register it. It took that long for the signal to travel from their tail tips to their brains. Anyway, that's kind of what it feels like, leading a zombie horde.

I'd be walking with the Turk, near the front of the pack, and the zombies in the back might get shot at, or smell some food and go off after it in another direction. You'd be climbing a hill and stop to take a look at the group marching behind you—and there at the back would be four or five dead zombies, and off to the side you'd see a guy scampering down from a deer stand and running off into the forest. And there was nothing you could do. It was one of the hazards of being the brain of an enormous thing, lumbering across the plains like the dinosaurs had. Sometimes people stepped on your tail, and were gone before you knew what had happened.

Other times, the wind might change direction, and the back of the group would get a whiff of some humans in a hidden cabin or forest hideout. When that happened, I'd look back and see our horde separating like an amoeba. It was all I could do to turn my half around and follow after the ones who'd caught the scent. It was like herding cats. Undead, rotting cats.

One day (in what must have been late March), we were walking through a lonely forest stretch by the side of a giant quarry and this amoeba-separation happened. As was usually the case, the Turk and I were two hundred feet in front of the split before we realized what had occurred. I looked back and saw the rear guard of our battalion veering away from the blasted-out quarry and heading into the forest. I sighed and carefully turned the rest of the horde back around to join them. It took a while. I sometimes had to spread my arms and "shoo" the zombies, like a man trying to urge chickens into a coop.

I'd glanced into the forest as we'd passed it and hadn't seen or heard a thing. My first impulse was to bet it was a false-positive. Usually, when the zombies smelled something like this—and there were no other signs, like noises or movement—it would turn out to be a freshly dead human, or a cabin where humans had been the night before.

As if reading my skeptical thoughts, the forest resounded with the echo of a gunshot. It caught me quite by surprise. Then there were more gunshots. Then gunshots and screaming—seemingly from just inside the canopy of barren trees. I quickened my pace, cursing myself. They had been there—hiding from us—and I had missed them. Walked right past and missed them.

I lumbered toward the trees, seeing nothing but other members of the walking dead. The zombies around me steadily became more and more excited. The gunshots continued, intermittent but steady. Then, as I closed in on the trees at the edge of the forest, a resounding shotgun blast exploded, and a zombie's head—cleanly severed by buckshot—rolled out of the forest, coming right at me. I stopped it with my foot like a soccer ball.

"Fucking zombie assholes!" I heard someone scream.

I readied my semiautomatic M16 and crept inside the trees. I didn't have to creep far. The situation was right in front of me, crystal-clear. The zombies had surrounded a tiny hunting cabin on the edge of the woods. It looked very rustic; likely no water or electric. Two men were standing on the roof of the hunting cabin—one was balding and pudgy, one rough-looking and bearded. The pudgy one was nervously reloading a shotgun. The other was taking careful aim with a composite hunting bow, and shooting zombies through the head. Several dead zombies already lay scattered at the door to the cabin. Many others (who were still "living") had arrows sticking out of their chests and arms.

These men were lost—floating on a little raft in a sea of four hundred zombies. (Or, by the look of it, maybe more like three hundred and ninety now.) Zombies are not natural climbers, so the pair was safe up on the little roof, but there was also next to no way for them to escape.

The pudgy one finished reloading and fired the shotgun wildly into the circle of zombies six deep around him. One zombie's rib cage opened up as he was torn in half. Another's head exploded. Three eighty-eight.

"Fuck this," I said to myself, and began to draw a bead on this larger of the two targets with my M16. As I did, he dropped the shotgun and produced a walkie-talkie from his back pocket. He flicked it on and called into it: "Hello? Hello? This is Terry! Is anyone coming?! We're on the roof of Derrick's cabin now. Jesus, there are hundreds of them!!"

Who was he calling, I wondered? I did not wait to find out.

I pulled the trigger three times, hitting him in the chest at least twice. His body blasted backward and he fell off the roof and into the mob of zombies below. He dropped the shotgun and radio. They clattered against the logs of the roof.

When he saw what had happened to his friend, the bearded man dropped his bow and fell flat against the roof of the cabin. I took aim at him and fired, but a prone man proved much harder to hit. I decided to move closer, assuming I could do so safely now that he was pinned. While I strode nearer, the bearded man crawled to the radio and called into it.

"Hello?" he shouted wildly. "This is Derrick! Do you come in? Look, there's a man with them who can shoot. He shot Terry. Do you copy me? A man with the zombies. He shot Terry!"

A voice talked back at him through the static. A familiar voice. (Where had I heard it before?) I sauntered closer through the writhing ocean of zombies, trying to find an angle that would get me a clean shot at beardo.

"No," Derrick continued. "No, I can't. Look, can you try the Guard—see if they can send a helicopter? Tell them we're right by the Lockport Quarry. They can't miss it."

I raised my gun and took three more shots at him. Nothing. Wood danced and splintered around him, but the angle was still all wrong.

"Jesus, they're going to fucking kill me," Derrick shouted. "They're fucking shooting at me. I don't know how, but one of them has a fucking gun! Can you send somebody, please?"

I crept closer and found an old stump, covered by moss and with snow still decorating one side. It was thick enough for me to stand on, and when I did so, it gave me a clean line of sight on the bearded man talking into the radio.

I lifted the M16 carefully and drew my bead. My undead finger tickled the trigger.

Then, disaster.

Have you ever locked your keys in your car? (Sure you have.)

You know that moment where you watch yourself doing it, but you still can't stop? Where you're looking at your keys, still in the ignition, *as you shut the door?* And then afterward you think, "Why the fuck did I just do that?!"

You know *that* moment?

Well, this was a little like that—only much, much worse. As I began to squeeze the trigger, I heard the familiar voice coming back again on the bearded man's radio, and realized it was Vanessa's. Then I shot the man—six times through the chest. Another bullet hit his forehead, killing him instantly. And then another bullet hit the radio.

Hit the fucking radio that had just had Vanessa's voice on it.

In horror, I dropped the M16 and put my palms against my forehead. The gun hit the ground and went off, shooting the zombie nearest me in the foot.

I had just heard my girlfriend's voice again. What had she said? It had sounded like: "The other group." Something about "others" or "other group." But . . . Vanessa. There was no question. It had been *her* voice. She was still alive. She had not been killed by bikers (or eaten by zombies). And I had just severed any means of communicating with her in the foreseeable future.

I stepped off the stump and fell to my knees, crushed.

I had lost my appetite. (Temporarily.)

While the other zombies happily feasted on the bearded bow hunter, I meditated over the wreckage of the destroyed walkie-talkie. It was square and heavy, like a cell phone from the 1980s. My bullet had passed through the earpiece, leaving an opening through which I could see red wires and part of a battery. When I depressed the largest button on the side, it made a hissing noise, but nothing else.

"Hello!" I tried calling into it. "Hello? Vanessa?"

No one came back. After a few minutes, the battery seemed to drain and the small red light on the side of the walkie-talkie faded to the color of dull plastic.

To distract myself, I turned my attention to the inside of the small cabin. It provided little in the way of clues about Vanessa, but there *were* points of interest. One wall of the cabin had been covered in maps—maps of Knox County, and also maps of the entire state of Ohio. Color-coded pushpins had been placed strategically around the maps. Green pushpins seemed to be concentrated around Columbus and Cleveland, with a few also spaced along Highway 71 between the two cities. Other green pins dotted Highway 70 east toward Wheeling, and west in the direction of Indianapolis. Blue and red pins appeared less frequently, and seemed to dot the countryside more than the population centers. Then there were the yellow pins. These appeared in only three places, and—as I consulted one of the maps closely—appeared to include the cabin I now occupied. There was something to conclude from all of this. These were important clues, and I knew it. I took my time and tried to puzzle them out.

Green pins were the army. Had to be. They were in all the major cites, and they also had presences at the rest stops along the major highways. (Plus, they were green. I think, when you have a bunch of pushpins and one has to represent the army, you go with green.) The cities made sense—they were the Green Zones—but the highways?

And then I recalled what Sam had said about the government trying to keep the economy going and encouraging people to keep going to work. It also made sense, then, that the government would want to focus on keeping the main arteries flowing.

For not the first time, I began to consider how little I knew of the world outside of Knox County. I'd seen the images from across the country on my television—chaotic and militant and things overrun by zombies generally. The government hadn't been saying much, hadn't wanted people to know how they could kill zombies, and certainly hadn't seemed like it had a plan. And that had been months ago.

I'd imagined that in the subsequent weeks the cities had "gotten worse" (for the humans, that is). I'd pictured mobs of newly homeless humans fighting against mobs of zombies (or fighting one another for food). But now, for the first time, I wondered if my estimation might be wrong. Overly cynical.

These green pushpins, if they did in fact indicate the presence of the army—I had no proof that they did—showed that the humans had succeeded in creating militarized Green Zones where perhaps soldiers kept order, and maintained commerce between major cities. This made me curious. I had the sudden urge to move my band west until we hit Interstate 71, just to see what we'd find there.

There were still so many unknowns. Was this a recent map? Did the pushpins reflect verified locations of military personnel, or was it only an idealized rendering of how people on the radio had said it was supposed to be?

Perhaps the highways and cities *were* safe, and people were punching in and punching out every day despite the threat of zombies. Though my days were now spent cultivating murderous chaos, I wondered: Could humans be comporting themselves with relative civility and discretion just a few miles away?

Knox County—this land where I was free to conduct my zombie battalion from one encampment to another, razing and killing at will—was all that I knew. For an unsettling moment, I considered that it might be the exception and not the rule.

Then I thought of the humans that were being devoured just outside the cabin where I stood, and instantly felt better about things. Even if there *were* military presences in the cities, so what? We were still the dominant animals. We'd be like the Chinese communists—conquer the countryside first, then the cities! (I remember Chinese communists! Ha! Perhaps some remnant of a serious book on the subject remains ... but honestly, it feels more like something left over from watching the History Channel.)

I took a step back from the map. I thought: Contemptible thing! I should not allow it to unnerve me so, or to tempt me toward these dubious considerations. I should *certainly* not allow it to convince me that I was anything other than a dominant life form, playing on the winning team. It was just a map of Ohio with some pushpins in it. Nothing more. Some ink on paper and some painted metal pins. Was I going to let a little paper and ink and metal change my whole view of the world?

I decided—for better or worse—that no, I wasn't.

But even so ... it was *interesting*.

In addition to a few camping supplies and some food, I found a stack of legal pads and a box of pens in the drawer of a little wooden desk. I drew myself a quick-and-dirty version of the pushpin map and put it in my pocket, before continuing on.

We headed west, more or less, along Highway 229 toward Interstate 71. Just to see, I told myself. Just to take a peek at it and maybe get a general idea of what the humans were up to. It would take a few days of walking, but hey, I was a zombie. I had all the time in the world.

We kept well south of Mount Vernon as we made our trek westward. I had a feeling that that place hadn't changed, and I saw no advantage to leading my parade of three hundred and eighty-some zombies past their rifle scopes and Bibles. Mostly, we picked our way through farms. The map I'd scrawled let me know where we were in relation to towns and highways. The hills and fields around us stayed quiet, and the weather turned cold again.

Amid all the banality of the (mostly) gray days, there were still more weird things to see. More things that made no sense. More things I can't—to this day—explain.

When crossing a muddy patch by a farmhouse outside of a town called Bangs, we heard rock music playing on a loudspeaker in some nearby woods. It was "Don't Stop Believin'" by Journey. I stopped and listened for a bit, absently tapping my foot in time to the music. Was it a signal from humans to other humans? Was it a lure for zombies? Just a guy rockin' out in the middle of a zombie apocalypse? I decided not to investigate. Then, as suddenly as it had started, the music ceased. As we were walking away, I thought I heard it cue up again for a split second, but then it was gone.

On a different day, this time close to Sparta, we watched as a farmer—far in the distance—stood on the top of his silo and pulled live cats out of a burlap sack, dropping them to their deaths below. (I thought about stopping to eat his brain, but reckoned that a silo would be pretty defensible, especially if the farmer was armed with something other than cats. I drew a bead on him with my M16, just for fun, but decided in the end to walk away. The cats continued to rain down as we did so. More and more of them. Soon, it was almost beyond crediting. How many cats could you fit in a burlap sack? We didn't stick around to find out, but the answer, apparently, is: *A lot*.)

Other things were not insane or beyond explanation. Other things made perfect sense. Ghost towns. Abandoned homes and abandoned farms. Houses that were burned or looted or both. Piles of burned corpses that were, on closer inspection, actually dead zombies, each one shot carefully through the forehead.

In addition to the piled-up dead ones, we periodically saw signs of giant zombie conglomerates, like our own; trampled swaths in the fields where large groups of zombies had passed through, their slow, unanimous treads leaving deep indentations in the mud. Other, smaller swaths showed places where human gangs had passed, leaving food wrappers, apple cores, and shell casings. My hunch about this—this landscape, this world, this endless combat—had been right. Both sides were improving. Getting better.

What humans needed to do to survive a zombie apocalypse was move carefully and fight effectively (against zombies, but also against other humans). The humans who weren't "good" at this were mostly dead by now. They'd been claimed in the first few weeks of the outbreak. The humans that were still around were more dangerous. More crafty. The survivors. (But being a crafty, violent survivor didn't necessarily mean you were a well-adjusted person.)

On the zombie side, the "improved" survivors would include zombies like me—who might be able to think a little—and zombies who had, out of sheer luck, massed into large, unstoppable groups. Individual or "loner" zombies who made easy target practice had been brought down by humans early in the game. But huge groups of zombies—who might be able to overturn a car, break down a hastily improvised barricade, or exhaust somebody's supply of ammunition—were more difficult to fuck up. Most humans thought twice before risking an engagement with a large zombie group.

Things were definitely getting more lethal out here, not less. As the weeks crept on, this would only continue. Soon, only the largest zombie armies and the most well-armed, clever humans were going to be left.

There was no doubt about it. Things were gonna get even more interesting.

I was at the head of my battalion of zombies—now swelled to perhaps four hundred and fifty in number—and we were crawling along Township Road 213 near Marengo, closing in on Highway 71 (and its purported Green Zone), when I began to see thick plumes of greasy black smoke wafting up into the morning air in the distance. They appeared to be coming from the base of a far-off water tower, perhaps a mile ahead of us, inside Marengo proper. The burn was unhealthy. It was like the smoke from an industrial or tire fire—not like somebody burning leaves. Not organic. (Maybe, I conjectured, someone was trying to burn down the water tower in just another act of madness.)

We were close to the Green Zone now. So very close. According to the map I'd copied, Marengo was right next to the highway. We approached the village warily, eschewing the main roads and cutting through fields instead. Part of me wanted to ignore the smoke entirely. (What if it was a trap, or a signal between groups of humans?) My goal was to reach Highway 71 and learn the extent of the Green Zone, not to be discovered. Unless the smoke was from an unwise cookout being held by delicious humans, I was hardly inclined to investigate it.

But as we neared the edges of Marengo, I found I *could* discern the source of the smoke, even from a distance, and I had to admit, I was intrigued by what I saw: A military helicopter had crashed into the legs of the water tower. (It was, I later learned, an AH-64 Apache.) This was not the kind of innocent-looking, observational craft I'd flipped off and shot at before. This one had missiles mounted under the wings and large, circular cannons like giant Gatling guns. It was the kind of helicopter that, when operational, could fuck up a big group of zombies with ease.

Now, however, it seemed in less than a position to do that. While the craft appeared more or less intact, it rested at an odd angle within the legs of the tower, and plumes of smoke continued to spill out of its engine. (It looked very heavy, and I was impressed that the legs of the water tower had not simply given way beneath its weight.) The helicopter's blades were still and its motors silent, but I thought I glimpsed a quivering movement within the cockpit.

Curiosity got the best of me, and I directed my zombie battalion toward the smoking wreck. I soon got a completely clear view, and saw that the helicopter was hanging about five feet off of the ground. When the wind picked up, it rocked back and forth and the girders of the tower groaned. If the pilots *were* alive, it was a precarious situation for them (even without the four hundred and fifty zombies milling about below).

"It's like a piñata," I said to the Turk. "We just smack it around until some people fall out." I mimed hitting a piñata with a stick, using my M16. The Turk seemed to know what I meant. He walked over and began pawing at the base of the helicopter with his fingertips. A few other zombies joined him. The helicopter began to sway.

Then I heard a voice coming from inside the body of the craft. A pilot talking into a radio. I motioned to the Turk to stop his banging, and pushed the other zombies off. Then I cupped my ear to the hull and listened.

"This is Lafayette Zero Six; come in, please," the pilot said. "This is Lafayette Zero Six; do you copy? I'm half a click outside of the Green Zone in Marengo. I'm in the center of the town, underneath the water tower. Total instrument failure. Gunner is . . . I think he's dead. Looks like I've already got a pretty good crowd of moving cadavers. Request evac. Request evac. Do you copy?"

I'd heard enough.

Half a click from the "Green Zone." That could only mean Interstate 71. The map with the pushpins had been right. This was just as I had hoped. The helicopter pilot's words had piqued my curiosity. (Hearing anybody's words did. As a zombie, I was accustomed to traveling for days in dead silence, with only my own quips and bad puns to keep me company.)

Here was a human who was not only talking, but talking about the Green Zone. I decided I wanted to know more about what was going on, even if it meant letting the man live for a while. I stepped away from the belly of the suspended helicopter and began, carefully, to climb the network of girders that comprised the legs of the water tower. The helicopter continued to sway and wheeze in the wind.

Like all zombies, I was not adept at climbing. Only by careful contortions and gentle shifts of my weight was I able to make my way upward through the girders. Really, it was *very* slow going. It took five minutes for me to climb five feet. When I was more or less level with the craft, I approached the cockpit from behind so the pilot would not see me. The glass around it looked impenetrable, but I drew one of my heavy revolvers anyway. Moving as furtively as possible, I edged around the side of the helicopter and peered inside. There were two seats in the nose of the machine. The front seat contained a man who was unmoving and slumped forward against his controls. Unconscious or dead. Likely dead.

The rear seat—the one closer to me—contained a young man in a pilot's uniform who was still very much alive. He looked perhaps twenty, Caucasian, and had a gaunt face with a lower lip that frumped forward, making him look sad. He didn't appear to be armed. I decided to take my chances.

"Hey," I shouted, rapping on the window with the butt of my gun. "Hello there!"

The man spun around wildly—shocked to see someone up in the girders—and looked me up and down.

"I've got some questions about Highway 71," I said. "We can do this the easy way or the hard—" I stopped mid-sentence because the young man had turned white and pressed himself against the far side of the cockpit, as if attempting to flatten himself. He stared at me with terrified eyes, his mouth agape. You would have thought he'd never seen a zombie before.

I mean, I wasn't about to win any beauty pageants, but as zombies go, I wasn't all *that* bad. There were no holes in my face. All of my limbs were present. I still had my skin and hair and both eyes. Even my teeth were still intact. I doubted seriously that I could be the *first* zombie this pilot had seen. (Maybe he was only used to regarding them from the air at great distances, or perhaps it was the fact that I was talking and holding a gun.)

The pilot's face was the very picture of terror, and yet he refused to look away from me. He edged his hand over to a button on his control panel and depressed it, never once dropping his gaze, his hand visibly trembling.

"This is Lafayette Zero Six," the young man began. He spoke slowly and soberly, as if every syllable were absolutely vital.

"Repeat: This is Lafayette Zero Six. I'm half a click east of the Green Zone in Marengo. I'm staring at the Colonel. Repeat. I am *staring at the Colonel.* He is on the other side of the glass, talking to me. The Colonel is standing right here, talking to me. Request . . ."

He dropped the radio button for a moment, then brought his hand back to it.

"Request air strike."

I didn't completely understand what was going on, but felt proud that I was being called a colonel. (It was almost a general, wasn't it?)

I tapped on the window again.

"Seriously," I said raspily. "Let's have a little chat."

The pilot released his radio button, but he remained flattened with terror.

"C'mon," I said. "Talk to me, kid. It'll kill time while we wait for the air strike. I know you can hear me."

He looked at me, still very afraid. I had the feeling his radio was dead. Nobody was talking back to him, and there was surely no air strike coming. Yet that's not to say I felt it was a completely safe situation. Many things could happen, and scared humans usually got violent. Also, I didn't want to stand on the water-tower girders any longer than I had to. I put my gun back in the holster and steadied myself against the gently swaying helicopter.

"Look, I'm not gonna eat you . . . but you've got to talk to me," I told him. "I can't think of a better deal for you than that. I'll let you live if you talk to me." My logic appealed to the pilot. He was about to give. I could see it in his eyes.

"Or," I continued, "if you like, my guys and I can rock this bird back and forth until you fall to the ground, and then it's four hundred and fifty against one, give or take. Up here, you've got much better odds. Trust me. If I'm lyin', I'm dyin'. You know . . . again."

"What do you want to know?" he finally asked, the fright making his voice almost as hoarse as mine.

"Okay, so the Green Zone—that's the highway, right?" I asked. "That's 71?"

"Yes," he said. His reply was confused and slightly contemptuous, like I'd asked him to confirm that water was wet.

"And the Green Zone," I continued, "it runs from Columbus to Cleveland? And those cities—they're also part of the Green Zone?"

"Of course," he said. "Everybody knows that. What are you asking me *that* for?"

I decided to try a new line.

"Okay, next question," I said. "Who is 'the Colonel'? You were just talking about him on your radio. Is that me?"

"Look, why are you making me tell you things you already know?" he stammered, still clearly terrified. "What kind of game are you playing here? Is this like *Saw* or some shit?"

"Just tell me," I said sternly. "I'm letting you live, aren't I? Now tell me . . . who is 'the Colonel'?"

"You are, of course," he said.

This assertion confused me. But a moment later, as I absently reached to adjust the brim of my hat, I instantly understood what the soldier was telling me.

He had not said "the Colonel." He had said "the *Kernel*." He was referencing the Cedar Rapids Kernels hat that I'd worn since the first day of my reanimation.

"Okay," I said to the frightened soldier. "Like we agreed, I'm gonna let you live."

"Okay," the scared soldier answered.

"But first, you're going to do one thing more," I continued. "You're going to tell me *everything* you know about the Kernel."

Apparently, I was famous.

Not good famous, like George Washington famous or Bruce Springsteen famous (or even Britney Spears famous).

I was bad famous. Maybe a better word is "infamous." Like Keyser Soze, or Bigfoot, or Benedict Arnold. My fame (or infamy) had begun when observational helicopters had first recorded me.

Pilots had brought back wild tales and shaky photographs of a zombie they claimed had gestured and communicated like a human. At first, their peers and superiors had not believed the pilots, but corroborating reports began to trickle in from different sources. Civilians communicating over radio said things about a talking zombie in a Kernels hat. Eyewitnesses who had made it to the Green Zone recalled having seen a large group of zombies headed by a gun-toting zombie who was talking to himself. (Bad puns, as they recalled.) The one constant in all the reports—always—was a red-and-blue Cedar Rapids Kernels baseball cap.

"The Kernel" became the name jocularly assigned to me by the military pilots who patrolled the edges of the Green Zone near Knox County. Whether I existed for real, or was only a fairy tale, was the subject of some heated debates.

True, there were a handful of hastily snapped aerial photographs featuring a zombie in a Cedar Rapids Kernels hat who *appeared* to be holding a gun or giving the finger. These had been circulated widely and posted in many of the pilots' lounges. However, a zombie with a gun in his hand did not mean a zombie with full sentience, and the military higher-ups were loath to acknowledge the Kernel as a phenomenon worth pursuing. (At least, officially.) Yet interest could not be repressed among the army helicopter pilots and National Guard soldiers who ran missions in and around the area.

The facts, such as they were, became speculations that soon transformed themselves into something approaching mythology. Just as soldiers in the Iraq wars had turned camel spiders into two-foot monsters that could bite off half your face as you slept, the airmen in rural Ohio soon turned the Kernel into an undead criminal mastermind of epic proportions.

It was said that the Kernel liked to sneak into the Green Zone late at night, slip into a tent, and eat the brain of just one sleeping soldier, leaving the others to find their dead comrade the next morning. Some pilots claimed that on dark and stormy nights they had seen the Kernel piloting a phantom helicopter (or even an airplane), like some sort of zombie foo fighter. Others still said the Kernel commanded an army of zombies, and ruled over them like a god—or that he was not *like* a god, but *was* the God of Zombies. (He had risen from his grave after exactly three days, and would someday lead his zombie followers to a promised land.)

Many of the things said about the Kernel could not possibly be true—or at least, could not possibly be true concurrently—and in a way, these irreconcilable contradictions made him more of a bogeyman and less of a real, tactile threat to be feared. The Kernel could sometimes be invoked as a humorous specter. A googly-eyed bogeyman. A caricature.

"Don't let the Kernel get you," soldiers along the Columbus/ Cleveland Green Zone might say to one another before going out on patrol.

I was a myth. A monster of the Ohio backwoods. Like the New Jersey Devil, but for Knox County. And yet I was plainly not a legend at all, but a real flesh-and-blood zombie. I was standing right here, before this shaky young pilot. I was talking to him.

The pilot—his name was Carson, his flight suit said—took a full half-hour to finish telling me about myself. (I suspected he genuinely believed the air strike was on the way, and that he was succeeding in keeping me fixed until it struck.) His sentences were long and wandering, and delivered with the machine-gun cadence of a man on a speedy drug.

"One last thing," I said, when he had finished. "Your friend there . . . I need you to give him to me."

"*What?*" the pilot said.

"Look," I told him, "it's one thing for me to climb down and leave you in peace, but the other zombies can smell you. I'm going to need your friend's body to lure them away. Let's just hope he died recently enough that they're still interested in his brain."

"No way," the pilot said. "If I open the window you'll shoot me."

"You'll have to trust me," I told him.

"No," the pilot said again.

"I'm *not* going to eat you or shoot you," I insisted. "I just want to pull your buddy's body out through the hatch."

"No," he said a third time.

"You're armed, too, aren't you?" I asked him.

He nodded.

"Well, pull out your gun and point it at me," I said. "If I try anything, you can shoot me dead. You'll be the guy who killed the Kernel. But I need your help, and I think you need me too. Think about what'll happen to you if I don't lead these zombies away. Sooner or later, the wind is going to blow you down from these girders. You should survive the fall just fine, but when you *do* hit that ground . . . Well, do you want a crowd of zombies waiting for you, or do you want to hop out into an empty Marengo with no zombies and jog a half-mile back to the Green Zone?"

There was a pause as Carson considered it.

"I'll shoot you in the head if you try *anything*," he said, taking a handgun from his belt and leveling it at me through the glass.

"All I wanna do is pull your friend out of there," I reiterated. "It'll save your life. I'm the only hope you've got."

"I wouldn't go that far," he said, and cautiously depressed a lever in the back of the helicopter. A hatch near the front popped open with a pneumatic sound. The pilot motioned with his gun, and I lifted the window nearest me. With the pilot's gun trained hard on my forehead, I hefted his companion out of his seat and carefully hitched the body up over my shoulder.

"Okay then," I said to the pilot, once again closing the window hatch. "I'll see you later."

"We're gonna get you," Carson said as I turned to depart. "You know that, right? Now that we know what you are, we're totally gonna get you."

"I don't know," I told him. "I don't think you know *everything* about me. I mean ... *I* don't know everything about me, and I'm *me*."

This seemed to stymie the pilot (it was a bit cryptic, I suppose), and I took the opportunity, carefully and slowly, to lower myself back down to the ground.

In fits and starts, I conducted my zombie battalion out from underneath the helicopter. We headed away from the interstate, back toward the sheltering interior of Knox County. Now and then, the zombies would fail to keep pace or seem to tarry over the prospect of returning to shake the stranded helicopter some more. In these instances, I chopped off pieces of the man over my shoulder (who was indeed dead), and dropped them behind me like breadcrumbs. (The pieces were furiously fought over and devoured.) Thusly, we walked well into the night, until there was little of the soldier left. Just before dawn, we stopped briefly in a dense forest, and I ate his brain (still remarkably lukewarm), sharing a bit of it with the Turk.

As I ate, I considered my newfound celebrity status. There was nothing positive about being a famous zombie. (First of all, there aren't many famous zombies. How many can *you* name?) Zombies succeed by being one of many, by being part of a herd they can always blend into. Being famous meant I didn't blend in any longer. I was conspicuous. A target.

Despite this danger, I wasn't ready to throw away my Kernels hat just yet.

I recalled the terror my chapeau had inspired in the helicopter pilot's eyes, and dreamed of legions of humans brought to their knees through fear of "the Kernel." For a moment, I imagined a world where the remaining human encampments knew me and shuddered in my presence. Perhaps I would make them "pay tribute" to me in the form of brains, or else attack their settlements. Or I would inspire humans to wage war against one another, and then feast upon the resulting fresh carnage.

There were possibilities in this baseball cap. Oh yes, there *were* possibilities ...

As I finished eating the helicopter gunner's brains, I thought about how remarkable it was that the world could change simply through the transfer of new information. I had not changed since becoming the Kernel. I wore the same clothes, carried the same things, kept the same company; but this knowledge of *who I was* was—I certainly felt—changing things around me.

It was a pleasant idea.

As it turned out, I was more correct than I knew.

As it turned out, the world itself was changing.

When dawn broke, I again consulted the map I'd sketched on the page from the legal pad—wishing, now, that I'd taken the time to make it more detailed.

Humans ... Humans were contemptible, reprehensible, and dangerous things, but they also meant information and food. (And information was almost as addictive as brains. Learning about the Green Zone was fascinating. Learning of my own celebrity had been riveting. I had to admit, I wanted more.) One of the humans was my girlfriend, and maybe she was still alive.

If the yellow pushpins indicated other cabins full of other humans, I owed it to myself to pay them a visit. Food and information. Yes, that's what I wanted.

Although my map was terrible and homemade, the closest yellow pin seemed to be in a town called North Liberty, to the northeast. It would be like finding a needle in a haystack. There were houses there—even a suburb-like subdivision—and lakes. If one yellow pin could represent a tiny cabin hidden in the forest by a quarry, who knew what nook or cranny of North Liberty might hold the next human settlement?

Despite the long odds, I was determined to find out.

We started off again through the farmland, the Turk and I leading the way. The temperature hovered above freezing. The land was sparse and empty. We saw horrible things. The world was changing.

The world had changed.

I first noticed it outside of Fredericktown—perhaps halfway to North Liberty—when we came upon a dead girl in a field. She wore mittens and a hat and a white dress. Her body was next to an old stone well with a tiny thatched roof built over it. She had been shot several times in the stomach with a shotgun. It had almost ripped her in half.

The zombies were not interested in the girl, and neither was I. She had been dead for quite a few days, and her flesh was no longer an appetizing prospect. Her limbs were stiff and her brains were cold. They were also, however, intact. She had suffered no visible head wound. And yet she had not reanimated.

"Would you look at that," I said to the Turk. My companion moaned and stroked his chin thoughtfully.

"She's been out here more than a few days, but she's not one of us yet," I said. The Turk looked on as I picked up the girl. She really had been savaged by the shotgun. Her legs dangled from the half-waist left like hams on a cord. I opened her mouth and looked inside. It was solid. A normal mouth. No wound to the brain from in there.

"I'm genuinely puzzled," I said to the Turk. He shrugged. I leaned the body against the well, giving it a once-over, trying to solve this mystery. I considered every inch of her, searching every pore for some clue as to why she remained dead, and not undead. I ran my fingers through her hair, feeling for holes or indentations in her head, but there was nothing.

"She's dead, but she doesn't become a zombie," I said to the Turk. "What are things coming to?" It was a small thing—minute really—but nonetheless, it left me feeling that something was up. Not *all* dead bodies became zombies, right? Those with destroyed heads or brain-wounds didn't. So this girl might just be one of the ones that stayed down for whatever reason. Or maybe she was just taking her time. Maybe this girl would become a zombie after a couple of months of rotting, instead of a couple of hours or days. Nonetheless, it nagged at me.

I felt like—since the zombie outbreak—pretty much everybody who had died had become a zombie pretty quickly. Those felt like the rules. I couldn't remember seeing a human who had been killed with the brain intact and hadn't reanimated. If you went down these days, you were going to come back up. That was just how it worked.

Except this girl hadn't.

I looked across my zombie battalion as we left the well and the shot-up girl behind. They still looked as strong and hale as zombies could. Whatever force had possessed them to rise from their graves showed no signs of flagging. They lumbered along as they always had. And so did I.

But something about it still made me uneasy.

Then, another thing.

Closer to North Liberty, a smell on the wind. A noxious odor that hung in the air. Fire, but something more than that. An *unpleasant* fire smell. Different from the smoking helicopter we'd left in Marengo, too. I could smell flesh burning, and gasoline. It smelled bad. It also smelled recent. A new-fire smell. It reeked of the works of men—people in the vicinity who'd been up to something—not an accidental forest fire, and not a factory smell. I decided we should investigate, even if it meant a brief detour.

"Let's turn 'em," I said to the Turk, indicating the new direction with my outstretched finger, and we did our best to maneuver the group of zombies in the direction of the terrible odor. (I think the Turk understood what I was trying to do, but his heart was not in the task. His Spidey senses were tingling. Other things were too. The smell was sickening, even to a zombie. He knew something bad was ahead of us.)

We directed the battalion through an abandoned farm and toward a shallow hill that overlooked a field next to some woods. The smell intensified. The Turk continued to drag his feet. Then, over the crest of the hill, we saw it: a battlefield full of "dead" zombies. The most we'd ever seen. Hundreds of them. They had been torn to pieces, probably with powerful guns. Most of the bodies had been moved into orderly piles which had then been set aflame, but some—who were more "body parts" than complete zombies—were simply strewn across the field. A couple of the piles were still smoldering. Large-impact craters made by grenades or other explosives dotted the field. Here and there, the ground itself was still steaming. Every single zombie—even the "partial" ones—had received a bullet through the skull.

It was a harrowing and baffling sight. I was used to carnage, sure—both by and against zombies—but not on such a massive scale. This had been a zombie bloodbath. (None of the casualties looked like they had been living humans. The KIA were 100 percent undead.) I scanned the horizon, but could discern no other sign of the humans who had done this. I understood, however, that the mere fact of my not being able to see or hear any humans did *not* mean that we were safe, or even unobserved.

"Fuck," I said, looking around nervously.

I tried to understand what had happened in this place. Was it a repository, where a nearby encampment of humans had been dumping (and exploding?) the zombies they'd killed over time? Or—horror of horrors!—was it what remained of a single, massive massacre of hundreds of zombies, and had a group as large as ours been killed in one fell swoop? I suspected the latter, more-terrifying option. I reasoned that a strike this powerful would almost certainly have to have come from the military. This was beyond the means of local farmers with hunting rifles.

I waded into the steaming piles of zombies, genuinely impressed with whatever force had done it. Helicopters with missiles (like the one we'd just encountered)? A carefully aimed blast of long-range artillery from the Green Zone? But no. The zombies had clearly been arranged on the ground and moved into piles. Someone had been here *on the ground*, and recently.

"I'm beginning to think your Spidey senses were right," I said to the Turk. "Let's not spend any more time here." We maneuvered the battalion of zombies away, into the forest. It didn't need much urging.

We moved on, through forests and fields, looking for more people to eat. And suddenly, it was there, like a new neighbor you hadn't noticed, moving in.

Company. We had company.

Human company.

I suddenly understood the phrase. (I seemed to recall action movies in which people were always saying "Looks like we've got company." I also remembered that, mostly, they were not very good movies. But the sentiment was right. Company. Visitors. Unwelcome relatives. That was what it felt like. Humans were our cousins—our stupid, contemptible cousins whom we sometimes ate—but nobody wanted them to show up *like this*.)

Their company first came in the form of small movements on the very distant horizon, furtive rustlings in far-off trees, and the occasional hum of invisible engines. (It was the sound of humans being intentionally furtive, and succeeding at it.) This was not how we liked to encounter humans. We preferred disoriented, weak groups. Just enough of them to go around. Groups we could overpower through our sheer numbers. (The dumber and more frightened, the better.)

These humans were aware of us. They were watching us and, apparently, traveling *with* us. For hours and then days, they seemed to live alongside or ahead of our zombie horde. They were *there*. No question about it. I'd catch the glint of binoculars at the top of a hill, or see the smoke from a far-off campfire. At night, I sometimes made out the cherry of a cigarette in a distant row of dark trees. These humans were good at what they were doing, and this damn sure wasn't the first time they'd done it. They stayed far enough away that we never smelled them. They stayed downwind. They stayed quiet.

As the only zombie in our group able to think and reason, I struggled with what to do next. The responsibility was all mine. I could turn the group if I wanted, or—with some effort—even reverse our course entirely. However, that would mean diverting us from our destination: North Liberty. And, thus far at least, the humans had posed no threat. Though we were traditionally ranged as foes—or at least, as entities that wanted ... *different* things from one another—these humans had done nothing to provoke us. And we, certainly, were not about to provoke them.

Only late into the third day did I chance to wonder: "Could these be the same humans who had created the field of flaming, dead zombies?" I couldn't guess what manner of weapons they might possess. Were they military soldiers, with tanks and Hummers, who had made a land incursion into Knox County? If they were, it wasn't like we could run away. (There were disadvantages—as well as advantages—to being a giant, lumbering dinosaur of an army.) I could steer my zombies into the nearest nest of trees if the humans started shooting, but beyond that, my options were pretty limited. And every hour I didn't let the humans deter us was another hour's march toward North Liberty. Another hour closer to that yellow pushpin.

Closer, maybe, to Vanessa. To information. To answers.

A road.

Then a crossroads.

Then a sign that said NORTH LIBERTY 5.

I urged the zombies onward. An hour's shamble past the sign, dawn broke, and an eerie tension descended over us. (Over me, anyway.) We were nearing a population center. A place that might—like Mount Vernon—be peopled and defended. The zombies around me continued their march forward with the resigned steps of pack animals, oblivious to any danger. (They also gave no sign of having scented human prey.) We traversed an empty cornfield that ran alongside the highway leading into town. As we drew closer to the town proper, my hesitation overtook me, and I allowed myself to drift to the back of the group.

"You take it from here," I said to the Turk. "Copilot's big day." The Turk seemed to understand, and kept his place at the front of the pack.

We passed a lonely church with a single white steeple, and all at once the zombies seemed to quicken their pace toward North Liberty. It was harder to see things from the back of the group—a little like having shitty lawn seats at an outdoor rock show—but an object up ahead seemed to have captured their attention. It was a small wooden structure past the church—just four wooden walls and one large window. It looked like a tollbooth or a free-standing closet. (I later learned that they're for farm kids who have to wait for the school bus in the dead of winter.) The zombies at the front of the pack seemed unduly preoccupied with this little structure.

As we closed within fifty feet of it, I saw the barrel of a machine gun emerge from a crack in its window. Suddenly, there was movement from all sides. Armed humans in improvised camouflage were emerging from the fields on every side and closing in on us. They held guns and flamethrowers and who knew what else.

It was a nightmare happening for real.

I wheeled around, looking for a way out of the trap, but the emerging humans closed all escape routes. Even the little church now had two humans with rifles sitting on the roof.

"Fuck," I said aloud.

I fell flat on my face and covered my head (which, really, was my only vulnerable part). Sure enough, moments later they started shooting.

Machine-gun fire erupted all around us. Homemade grenades and incendiary devices were tossed, blowing the zombies ahead of me high into the air. Flame was then thrown, and zombies caught fire and stumbled around until their heads disintegrated. In a matter of only moments, I was covered in bodies that had fallen on top of me.

Then I heard humans barking orders at one another. The zombies groaned like confused animals, unsure of exactly what was happening, but dead sure that something was wrong. Some attacked, and others simply shuffled about. I peeked out from my prone position. Between dead zombies, I saw the heavily armed humans keeping their distance and firing. This was not to be close combat, at which zombies excel, but long-distance butchery.

Several zombies almost reached the wind shelter-cum-pillbox before the machine gunner inside tore them apart. An improvised grenade exploded near me, and I bucked in terror. The zombies nearest me moaned in confusion. Soon, there were more zombies on the ground than standing. Then there were very few standing at all. The humans grew confident, and began to close in for the final kills.

I could not believe it would end like this, and I hated them— these humans—for ending my dream so ingloriously. I hated their anonymous faces behind their camouflage masks. I hated the lack of sportsmanship to their violence. (This was not hunting—as we did—for food. This was butchery. It was artless, crude, and uncreative.)

More than anything, I hated them for their lack of curiosity. As I squirmed there, on that cold road outside of North Liberty, Ohio, covered in the stinking bodies of dead zombies who had, moments before, been my companions, I hated the humans for all the questions they were content to leave unanswered. I functioned in a world of intrigue and mystery, but these over-armed bumpkins were soulless trolls, without spark or imagination, content to merely kill from a distance. "See a zombie? Shoot it." There was nothing more to it for these types. They had no curiosity about the walking dead. The only question was how to kill them.

Speaking of killing, it also looked as though I had eaten my last brain. I would never again taste the fleshy miracle inside of people's heads. This, too, was a greatly distressing thought. I cried out at the injustice of it.

Ah, calamity! Ah, woe! Brains! *Braaaaaains!!*

Now the guns had stopped, and I huddled still against the cool ground in my pile of bullet-drenched, flame-scarred undead. Now the humans crept closer, and I could hear their footfalls in the spring grass. How I simultaneously loathed and wanted to eat them.

Blam!

Not far from me.

This was it then. They were finishing off anything that still twitched. And at close range.

Blam! And again, *blam!*

The blasts grew closer and closer. The footfalls too.

It was a desperate moment, and it called for a desperate act.

Of cowardice.

"Don't shoot!" I screamed. (It seemed hackneyed, true—like something I was half-remembering from a war movie, or, worse—and perhaps more likely—a television cop show, but it was all that sprang to mind.) "Don't shoot!" I repeated, raising my hands above my head. "I'm ... I'm ..." I paused.

What to say, what to say ... Somehow, "Don't shoot; I'm an unusually intelligent, self-aware zombie" just didn't feel like it was going to cut it.

Was I "human"? Did I dare make that claim? They would see right through it, just as they would see through my increasingly translucent zombie skin and the bullet holes that riddled my body. (The dried blood covering the front of my face probably wouldn't help matters, either.)

Something else, then.

Should I claim to be "one of them" on some level? (As in: "Don't shoot—I'm one of you.") It would be a lie, and an unconvincing one. I was *not* one of them. I was the one who had killed and eaten their fellow humans for the past few months.

In the end, I decided to tell the truth.

(Fuck it, right?)

"I'm Peter Mellor's zombie," I said, turning over and sitting up. "I used to be Peter Mellor. I was a philosophy professor at Kenton College."

Three camouflaged men carrying rifles—and one woman with an enormous Gurkha knife—regarded me cautiously. The men trained their guns on me but did not shoot. Past their masks, they looked as startled as I was scared.

"I was killed in a car accident," I said. "Someone killed me. Someone cut my brakes. I have no clue who it was."

"What the *fuck?*" one of the men said. "It fucking talks."

"My girlfriend is still alive, and I was kind of hoping to find her again," I said. "Her name's Vanessa. I think she's around here. Half-Chinese? Hot?"

"It knows Vanessa?!" another of the men said, incredulous.

"Just fucking shoot it," the woman said. "It's a zombie, like all the others."

"No, don't shoot me!" I said. "I'm *not* like all the others. I'm talking to you, aren't I?"

"Look at the design on its hat," one of the men said. "It's the Kernel. It's the motherfucking Kernel!"

"So?" the woman said. "It still eats people. It's a fuckin' zombie; just shoot it."

"Yeah, I'm gonna shoot it," another of the men said. He sounded unsure, but lifted his rifle and took aim at me. From this distance, he would not likely miss.

"Wait, don't!" I said, instinctively shielding my face.

"Yeah, don't," someone else said. It was a high-pitched voice. A woman's voice, but not Vanessa's. I heard quick footsteps. The three men (and the woman with the evilly curved knife) looked over. So did I.

It was not a woman, but a small boy. He wore a red bandanna over his mouth and nose, and was armed with a rifle.

A familiar-looking rifle.

"I know him," the kid said. He pulled down the bandanna, revealing his face.

It was the freckled, red-haired boy from the enamel factory. The one I'd . . . (What *had* I done? Helped to kill his relatives?)

"This is the one I told you about," said the kid. That was all he said.

We just stayed there like that for a while, frozen together. The humans looked at one another, their eyes scanning me nervously. I took my hands away from my face and waited for one of the guns to go off, but nobody shot anybody.

The kid eventually walked over and stood right in front of me.

"Yeah," he said. "This is *definitely* the one."

III.

Redemption

They took my guns and tied me to a tree—not taut against it, but like you'd tie up a dog. I had a little lead. They also tied my hands behind my back and put a collar around my neck. It was not my proudest moment, but at least I hadn't been shot.

The humans proceeded to have a meeting about fifty yards away. I was upwind and out of earshot. They stood in a circle—about thirty of them, all armed and exhausted—and they spoke in low, confidential tones. They rubbed their chins, considering me, and occasionally gesturing in my direction. They looked like construction foremen trying to decide how to tackle a difficult new project. We were still in sight of the "battlefield," if you even want to call it that. (It hadn't been all that much of a battle. My battalion had walked into a carefully planned ambush, and been destroyed. It was difficult for me to accept. My group of zombies—which had accomplished great deeds, ravaged the countryside, and had been growing at a healthy rate the entire time—had been destroyed in less than ten minutes.) What remained of my army had been piled into stacks and set afire.

There burned Rock Star. There, Matilda. And somewhere, in that steaming, smoking mass, burned the Turk—who had been as smart as a dog, or maybe even a monkey. Now they were stacked up and on fire. Slowly turning to ashes, an inglorious end. (But, then again, did zombies get to *have* glorious ends? It seemed like eating a bunch of brains before finally rotting into nothingness was the best they got.)

So the humans talked in their huddle. Now and then they debated or argued seriously. Other times, their palaver came across as relaxed and playful. Once, they even appeared to share a laugh. The humans also talked into radios like the one I'd seen (and shot) at the cabin by the quarry. Pickup trucks full of food and ammunition came and went. And still, clearly, nothing had been decided. Still, I was tied to a tree.

In all of my time as a zombie, I could not recall having been this defenseless. I'd been hunted, shot at, chased—sure. But never had I surrendered and allowed my fate to be deliberated by others. It was nerve-wracking. (I hadn't been shot on sight, but that didn't mean they weren't eventually going to take a vote and put a bullet through my brain.) Nothing good was going to come of this meeting, I quickly decided. It wasn't like they were going to vote to let me go. The longer they talked, the more concerned I became.

When the palaver adjourned, I was guardedly relieved to see the humans did not instantly gravitate toward me to carry out a death sentence. Instead, they dispersed in all directions—some tending to the burning bodies, some disappearing into the woods, and others leaving on the pickup trucks. They slapped one another on the back, spoke in casual tones, and shared food. None of them gestured at me and my tree any longer. It was as though I had been tabled.

A few of the humans did wander in my general direction, but they paid me no mind. A loose Peter Mellor memory left swimming in my brain told me: "A jury never looks at a man it has convicted."

Later in the day, a Chevy Silverado pulled up and a new group of humans got out. Among them was Vanessa. She wore an ugly yellow parka and carried a rifle like the rest of them. She looked apprehensive—her eyes were wild and searching, like a relative rushing to the scene of a loved one's accident. Then she saw me, a sad, wet zombie—muddied, bloody, and tied to a tree—and she just disintegrated.

She fell against the side of the truck as though her legs would no longer support her, and her hand went to her eyes—shielding them from the sight of me. Other humans had to rush over to keep her from falling. They comforted her as she cried.

"Let me get this *absolutely* clear," Vanessa said, restored by an hour's rest and now speaking like a trial lawyer aiming to establish a crucial fact. "When I saw you back at my sister's house, you were *already* a zombie?"

"Yes," I said. "I'd been a zombie for . . . I think for a few hours."

"Really?" she pressed.

I nodded back.

Night had nearly fallen, and the humans had built a small campfire. Vanessa kept her distance, like it was hard for her to look directly at me. Two other humans, weapons at the ready, stood to one side of her, listening intently to our conversation. I was starting to wonder if the humans had elected to have Vanessa determine my ultimate fate.

"Why didn't you *tell* me?" Vanessa asked.

"I don't really know," I said, being honest. "I guess I was scared, or maybe embarrassed. I woke up like this, and then everything started happening so fast."

"So, what you said about having amnesia ... ?"

"That was true," I declaimed. "My memory *is* really bad. I've forgotten most of the major parts of my life. I just remember random stuff. Sometimes, if I'm lucky, I get little hints about important things."

"Did Sam know you were ... a zombie?" she asked.

"Not when he dropped me off," I said. "He knows now, though. I went back to Kenton and told him. Look, what happened to you? I went back to your sister's house to find you, and it was destroyed. I thought you were dead. It made me crazy."

"A biker gang came," she said. "We had to fight them off."

"I saw that they killed Matilda," I stated. "We found her body." I decided not to mention that I'd also seen her become a zombie and that she'd followed me around Knox County for the better part of the spring. Instead, I wondered aloud if the kids and her sister Kate were okay.

"Yeah," Vanessa said. "We got out of there all right, but it was a miracle. All that time, I'd been thinking we'd be able to hole up forever in that house—that we'd be safe there—growing our own food, making our own power, and not needing to be on the grid. Kate really had me sold on the idea. I was such a fool. It was all an illusion. All it took was four or five guys with guns to send it all crashing down."

I felt for Vanessa, having lately seen my own illusions of security and strength dispelled with similar swiftness and cruelty.

"What exactly happened?" I asked, wishing for all the world that I could have been there to help—her (mostly) bulletproof hero.

"It was a gunfight," Vanessa said. "What's there to tell? They drove up and started shooting at us. We shot back with Matilda's guns. It went on for hours. In the middle of the night, they just left. I don't know if they were tired, or they went to get more guys, or what. It was our chance to escape, and we took it. We lit out into the woods, wandering and foraging like everyone else. Two women and four kids with no map or supplies or anything."

Then she stopped, and her face fell. Vanessa put her hand to her mouth, and it appeared she might cry again. (Obviously, there *had* been something ...)

But then she continued, and said: "The *worst* part, Peter, was that I thought you'd run off."

"*That's* what Matilda told you?" I replied. "I mean, that was *all* she said?"

"Yes, that was all," Vanessa answered. "She didn't say you were a zombie, if that's what you mean. I was gonna go looking for you the next day, but the biker gang attacked before I could."

She looked down and swallowed hard.

I felt like shit.

"Peter, I was so worried about you," she said, averting her eyes. "And I was furious with you, too. I couldn't understand why you'd leave us like that—why you would *do* this to me. To us. When I needed you the most."

Now it was my turn to wince at the memory of ancient injuries.

I might have been a zombie with near-total amnesia, but I could recall *some* things. And this tone of voice—like the whimpering of a wounded animal asking why you'd kicked it in the face—was one of them. I'd heard it from Vanessa, but from other women, too. It soaked back through my brain, making me feel sad and trapped and paralyzed by my inability to explain myself. Making me feel like a heel. I was being asked why I'd opted for an odyssey of cross-country mayhem and murder with a gang of zombies in the same tone of voice that had once asked why I'd been so late at the bar, why I hadn't noticed her new hairstyle, or why I wasn't spending more time at home.

"I ... ate a guy's brain," I stammered hoarsely. (Hoarse as a function of general physical deterioration, yes, but also as a function of emotion.)

"And you didn't think you could *talk to me* about it?" Vanessa returned sharply.

" ... "

"I'm waiting for an answer, Pete," she said.

"Well, no, frankly," I said. "I didn't."

"Do you remember *any* of those times we talked about complete honesty?" she asked sternly. "Any of those times we said we'd tell each other everything? Christ, Peter. Was there a thing I couldn't bring myself to accept about you? I knew about the women. I knew about the drinking. I knew that you'd once fooled around with Sam."

"Umm, okay," I said slowly. "But seriously ... I *ate* a guy's *brain*. And I liked it. I wanted to do it again."

"And?" Vanessa shot back.

It was dawning on me that my girlfriend was less concerned with my being a member of the walking dead than she was with how I had broken the news to her—or had failed to break the news.

"I didn't think *anybody* could accept that," I said. "I was confused. I was scared—"

"*You* were scared?" she retorted.

"I was," I insisted. "I'd never been a zombie before. I didn't know what was happening. I still don't. It's not like I've got this figured out, Vanessa. I'm making it up as I go along."

"Did you think about me *at all?*" she asked.

"Vanessa," I said in exasperation, "once I got over the initial shock, you were the *only* thing I thought about. You were the only thing that I figured could still make sense for me. When I got back to that shot-up house—and I thought you were dead, or worse—it fucking crushed me. *That's* when I started eating people for real. Like, *for real,* for real. The thought of you not being around—even if, yeah, my memories aren't so great—made me crazy. It made me wanna give up and say 'Fuck the world.' I didn't care anymore. I roamed around the county, and I ate people's brains. You want the whole truth? There it is. You got it."

Vanessa paused.

"Tell me the rest of *your* story," I said into the silence. "Who are these people? How did they find you? They look like they really know their stuff."

"*We* found *them,*" she said after a moment. "And it's a lucky thing that we did. I think we would have been dead after a couple more days, otherwise. Running into these folks was a godsend."

"Are they soldiers or something?" I asked.

"They're just a group of people trying to survive," she said, shaking her head. "They're folks from around the county who knew each other. Just people trying not to get killed, like us."

"You have a few groups, and you keep in touch by radio," I said. "One of your outposts was a cabin next to a quarry."

She craned her neck, as if straining to hear me completely. "How do you know about that?" she asked.

"I . . . that is, we . . . we ran into it the other day—the cabin," I said, opting for a half-truth.

Vanessa stared hard at me, tight-lipped.

"Was that you?" she asked. "Peter, did you eat those men?"

Again, the tone was familiar. It was the same voice that asked if I'd gotten drunk and slept through a daughter's piano recital, or forgotten a birthday, or eaten the entire pizza that had been meant for everybody. There was seldom a reward for answering this sort of question honestly. And yet . . .

"They attacked us first," I said. "They attacked my flank. That's how it all got going. We acted in defense, really. But yes, we killed them."

"Your *flank?*" Vanessa spat. "Like you're ... like you're a little army general, or something ... Peter, those people were my friends."

"I didn't know," I said. "At least not until after. See, I heard your voice on one of their radios, but then it got shot. I tried to get it to work again, but I couldn't."

"I don't know what to say to you, Peter," Vanessa said.

"Why are you guys out here?" I asked, attempting to change the direction of the conversation. "Do you know about the Green Zone they've got going out on the interstate? We almost walked there. I talked to a helicopter pilot about it. It's supposed to be safe and patrolled by the army."

"Oh, it's great—if you can get there," Vanessa said. "There are criminal gangs everywhere, killing and raping and pillaging like pirates. It gets worse every day. Now they camp out along the roads to the Green Zone, waiting to catch people who are making a break for it."

"I've seen *some* signs of gangs, maybe," I said, not actually recalling that many. "But *we* were able to walk straight to Highway 71 with no problem."

"They would have avoided you," Vanessa replied. "They don't care about zombies. They just want to prey on other humans. Zombies are a waste of ammo."

Vanessa gave me a withering look and walked away, joining a group of men holding radios.

Once again, I was alone with my thoughts.

Many minutes passed. I lost track of time. They'd taken my watch. (I know, right? What did that accomplish?) Vanessa lingered over by a campfire, talking to the radio men. While her back was turned, a man walked out of the darkness and stalked up to me. He was tall and gaunt and wore a short haircut. A white guy, about forty. Mean face.

"Vanessa said you killed them?" he said to me. "Our friends at the quarry—you killed them, yes?"

I nodded.

"I want you to know that the only reason we're keeping you alive is that the military seems to be interested in you," he said. "That's the *only* reason. If it were up to me, you would not exist. As far as I'm concerned the moment—the *moment*—that the army tells us you're anything less than our ticket out of here, I cut your head off myself. I don't know if I can make a zombie feel pain, but I'm damn straight going to try."

"I'm ... I'm sorry," I said quietly, as he turned to go.

"What did you say?!" he exploded, pivoting back around. "What the fuck did you just say, you stinking dirty zombie?"

He pushed me hard against the tree, then punched me in the chest. (I, of course, felt no pain, but I wouldn't say it was a comfortable situation. He was really, really mad.)

"I said I was sorry," I clarified. This only seemed to increase his anger. He reached behind me—where my hands were tied—and bent the little finger on my left hand until we both heard tendons creak and bones snap.

"George, what are you doing to it?" another of the humans shouted.

George released his grip on me.

"I'm serious," he said to me. "The moment you're not useful to us, you die. You're nothing. You're debris. You're flotsam floating in the river."

I leaned back against the tree and stared at him. He spat in my face, then turned and marched back into the darkness.

After a few minutes—when the rest of the humans seemed to have lost interest in me—I pulled my finger back into its socket.

It grew late. The fire was brought low, and many of the humans retired for the night—some sleeping in trucks, others in tents or on tarps on the ground. Others still remained awake, nervously watching the perimeter. A couple of them had clearly been assigned to watch me. They sat on a log—the pair of them—staring at me disappointedly like I was a television stuck on educational programming. At one point, they chewed Skoal from a tin. I tried waving hello, but the two just chewed like llamas, staring right through me.

Perhaps an hour later, Vanessa returned.

"I'm not mad anymore," she announced. "I won't say that I understand what you did completely, but I'm not mad. And I want you to know that. I really believe you were just acting according to your . . . nature."

So I had that much.

"Can I ask some more questions then?" I said.

"Of course you can," she said almost cheerily, as if my hesitation was risible.

"Even with the gangs, why don't you guys make a break for the Green Zone?"

"I think your idea of 'the Green Zone' is a little exaggerated," she said.

"Okay," I replied. "Then where are the soldiers coming from? Where's headquarters?"

"Columbus and Cleveland, as far as I know," she said. "But they've mostly got their hands full just keeping order and trying to feed the populace. Let me guess: You've seen a few helicopters fly over, and now you think there's an armada of planes and tanks out along 71. Tell me, Peter, have you actually *seen* 71?"

"Not actually," I told her.

"Well, it's pretty fucking sparse," Vanessa said. "Now and then you do see a military truck go by, but it's not like a communist military parade."

"Oh," I said.

"The army's top priority right now is *not* rescuing people who ignored the messages strongly suggesting they go to the nearest population center," Vanessa continued. "Frankly, I think they knew this would happen—that the countryside would become lawless and go to hell. I think they knew it was coming, and just wrote it off. They could save the cities, but fuck the people left out here. So we—those of us 'out here'—have to face the fact that we made the wrong decision, and deal with it."

"But what's happening now, with us . . . with *me*?" I asked.

She smiled, as though I had hit on something important. "We're in touch with the military a little bit," Vanessa said. "Sometimes we can raise them on the walkie-talkies. Turns out they're interested in the Kernel. You knew that, right? I think you did. Anyhow, the consensus is that we offer to hand you over in exchange for being airlifted to Columbus or Cleveland."

"That's fine," I said. "I know you're not asking for my permission, but that's fine. I'll go willingly. I don't know what the military will do with me—study me, probably—but it's not like they can hurt me, or make me feel pain, so whatever. What I'm trying to say is: If it helps you and these people get to somewhere safe, I'll turn myself in."

"We're still keeping you tied to the tree," Vanessa said matter-of-factly. "It's not my idea, but—"

"That's cool," I said, cutting her off. "I'm sort of bored with walking around, anyway."

"Thanks for understanding," she said, and actually touched my arm.

Feelings stirred.

"So the plan is, what?" I asked. "We call for the helicopters and wait here for them to pick us up?"

"It's not that simple," she said. "More than one gang is hunting us. The trick is finding a safe place where they can airlift everybody out. All of us. I mean, we made a good go of it, but if you're not constantly killing and looting, you run out of resources pretty fast out here. We want a helicopter big enough for everyone in this group."

"What about Kenton College?" I suggested.

"What about it?" Vanessa said.

"Well, it's up on a hill," I told her. "Seems like it would be easy to land a helicopter up there—even a great big one. Plus, it's easily defensible from all sides—which makes it safer than an open field or something. Because of the elevation, you can see people coming from a long way away. I haven't been there since I went back to see Sam, but I'd bet they're still holding out. A gang would really have to want it to try and take the college."

"Yeah?" Vanessa said, seeming, at least, to take me seriously.

"I'm totally serious," I said. "It's the best place around here. I may have amnesia, but I've seen a fuckload of this county, and Kenton is the best place in it for what you're talking about."

"Okay, hang on a second," Vanessa said, and drifted away to the other side of a dark minivan. Soon, I heard voices. My handlers, still chewing some Skoal, watched me absently from the log. One of them spat.

Vanessa returned, with George trailing after her. He looked even madder than before. I instinctively braced for further assaults.

"Oh, hell—" I began to say.

George pushed past Vanessa and shoved me against the tree.

"Are you lying, you sick, zombie bastard?" he shouted. "Are you lying, huh? Trying to get us all killed by your zombie friends at the college? Are you? *Are you?*"

He once again gripped my hand and popped out the broken finger I'd worked so hard to reposition.

"Why would I do that?" I shouted back, pulling away my hand.

"Because we destroyed your zombie army and all your little zombie friends," he said in a bilious bark. "That's why. Tell me you don't want revenge, you stinking thing!"

"I'd like to kill *you*, right now," I said honestly. "I'd like to eat *your* brain, but only because you're being a giant dick. As to the rest of your group—whatever, shit happens out here. It's not personal."

"What he said makes a lot of sense," Vanessa interjected. "I've been to Kenton College, and he's right. It's up on a hill. It's being defended by a friendly group, and they know Peter. It's a wooded hill, too, but clear on top. Nobody would know we were there. It's perfect."

"And I suppose that this 'friendly group' will also want an airlift out?" George said.

"So what if they do, George?" Vanessa countered. "What difference would it make if some other people got helped, too? There can't be that many."

This seemed to fluster him for a moment.

"I just don't like it," George said. "It's too easy. And I don't feel comfortable trusting—or even talking to—a fucking undead zombie."

He turned to face me.

"Tell me, fucking undead zombie, why are you giving us advice?" he said. "Why are you doing that, hmmm?"

"Because I care about Vanessa," I said. "Someone with as simple a brain as yours might not be able to understand that, but it's true. I have a few memories of her, and they're all good. I have *feelings* for this woman. I care about what happens to her."

"You're fucking lying," George asserted, pushing me against the tree again.

"No, I'm not," I said.

"I don't think he is," Vanessa said to George.

"Fine, so we're trusting zombies now," George said. "Is it that desperate? Has it all devolved *that* much? Fuck! I guess it has!" He punched the air and walked away.

"They've just talked to the military again," Vanessa said. "That's why he's so pissed off. This thing actually might happen. We've been moving from place to place for so long, hoping for something like this."

"Is that guy, like, the leader?" I asked.

"No," Vanessa said. "He's just a jerk who talks a lot."

Another hour passed. More cars and trucks came and went. Mostly, they went. Then official word arrived from the only remaining van—where, presumably, the radio was. The military had agreed. It was on. The next day at sunset, we would meet their helicopters at the hill at Kenton College. In exchange for the Kernel—the famous zombie that could think and talk—the military would airlift everybody present to Columbus. Word was passed through the quiet, sleeping camp.

Vanessa approached the tree where I was tied and sat down next to me. I remained standing. I wondered when Vanessa slept. I was a tireless zombie, but surely, Vanessa needed to rest.

As if reading my thoughts, she said: "I won't be able to sleep tonight. I'm so excited. This is finally all coming together. Hell, I might get to have an actual shower tomorrow."

"Heh," I said. "Shower. I can't remember my last one. And that's not a figure of speech. I honestly can't."

I tittered.

"Laugh it up, zombie boy," Vanessa said. "You have no idea what I'd do for a hot bath right now."

Because she seemed in a good humor, I decided to bring up something delicate that had been concerning me. "So, your sister and your daughters ... ," I began. "I haven't seen them around here. Are they okay?"

"Yeah, they're fine," Vanessa responded, much to my relief. "There are two camps in this group—there *were* three, before you killed our guys by the quarry. Kate and the girls are with the other camp. We're in touch by radio. They're going to meet us at the college tomorrow."

"How are your kids holding up?" I asked.

"It's all relative," Vanessa said. "I can't imagine going through this as a child, you know? It's crazy. But I think they're doing okay. They're good kids. I'm so relieved that I'll be able to get them out of here tomorrow. You have no idea."

"You didn't bring them along when you came here?" I said.

"They're safer where they are, with Kate and the others," Vanessa said. "This area has more gang activity."

"Yeah," I said. "Cool."

It was crazy. I felt like a guy on a first date, straining to make small talk with Vanessa. Though my memories were spotty, I could get glimpses of how I'd fallen in love with this woman. She was beautiful, yes. (Though, as a zombie, I tended to regard beauty in a somewhat more abstract way than I had in my previous life.) Yet while I was detached from several aspects of physicality, I should not give the impression that I was entirely unmoved by Vanessa's charms. Even if it had been a good three months since her last shower.

Looking into her face—strained and creased from the stress of the situation, but still undeniably comely and gentle—I found I still harbored the ability to feel romantic love. I had forgotten our first meeting and our first kiss, but these omissions did not detract from my impressions of the woman sitting in front of me. It was a face I could watch for hours.

As the night drew on, that was exactly what I did.

It was just before dawn when they attacked.

Most of the camp was asleep. The ones who couldn't sleep—or who had night watch—had settled into a trancelike predawn state. Vanessa had curled up near me like a little girl dozing next to the family dog in the yard. (Despite her protestations that she would not be able to sleep, she now snored soundly.) In the entire camp, I was the only one standing.

I was thinking about the roads leading up to Kenton College and the different approaches you could make. I wanted to make sure Vanessa's group appeared friendly, and that no one became alarmed.

(My cynical side envisioned nightmare scenarios where everyone got scared and fired on one another, and Vanessa and Sam were both accidentally killed.) As it turned out, I was getting way, way ahead of myself.

In the cold, blue-black moments before dawn, I heard something moving in the trees on the edge of the camp. A twig snapped. Then another. Then there was a shuffling of feet.

Then nothing, but a pregnant kind of nothing.

Not wanting to betray that I'd heard anything, I slowly turned in the direction of the trees and tried to look them over without appearing too interested. (I was, in fact, very interested. As my eyes began to focus, I also became terrified.)

Ranged along the nearby tree line were ten or fifteen shadowy figures. At least one of them wore the remnants of a bright-orange prison jumpsuit under an overcoat. They were not zombies. These figures were very much alive.

In alarm, I shifted my furtive gaze back to the sleeping camp. There were maybe fifteen or twenty of Vanessa's compatriots still here. Twenty-five, tops. (I couldn't see inside the van or anything.) Counting me, maybe two or three of us were awake. I had only moments in which to act.

"Vanessa?" I whispered from the corner of my mouth, and kicked her.

"Mmmm . . ."

"Listen to me," I began (my quiet, zombie-rasp finally proving to be an advantage). "Don't look right away, but there's a bunch of guys in those trees over there. Lean over really slowly and take a look. Are they yours? Do you know them?"

She groggily obeyed, then froze when she made them out.

"No," Vanessa responded. "Oh, Jesus."

"Okay," I told her. "The first thing I need you to do is untie me. This collar has a release. I can do it myself, if you just untie my hands. Crawl over now, slowly, and do it. Do it now!" Vanessa obeyed. I watched the tree line from the corner of my eyes as she fiddled with clasps and ties. If they sprang upon us now, it would almost certainly be a lost cause. The lurking men occasionally turned their heads—signaling or speaking with one another—but remained where they were.

"How many guns do you have on you?" I asked while she untied.

"Just my rifle," she said.

I had hoped it would be at least two.

"The only chance we have is to get them to take cover," I rasped. "If they start shooting first—or rush the rest of the camp while it's still asleep—you're all done for."

Vanessa freed my hands. I slowly moved my arms up and unlocked my collar.

"Here's what we're gonna do," I told her. "When I say so, I want you to start firing into the trees. I also want you to start shouting. It'll just take a second for people to realize what's going on and pick up their guns. In the meantime, I'm going to try to draw their fire."

"What?" Vanessa said, shocked.

"I mean I'm going to charge directly at them," I told her in a hoarse gurgle. "I'm bulletproof, unless they hit my brain."

"Peter, that's crazy," she said.

"Look, I had a good run—a couple, in fact," I told her. "Anyway, it's all that I can think of right now. So I want you to pick up your rifle very slowly, with your back to the trees." She obeyed, falling to one knee and snatching up the weapon. "Okay, here we go," I told her.

"Peter," she said, in a failing voice. "I don't know if you're still the same 'you' I used to know, but you're still a good person. And I still . . ."

Something stirred in the trees. The men were advancing, guns raised. We both turned and saw it. There was no time for words.

"Shoot!" I shouted at Vanessa. As she did, I raised my arms over my head like a playful parent impersonating a monster. Vanessa began emptying her gun and screaming that the camp should awaken. Her shots were loud, and the people around us started.

Meanwhile, I charged toward the aggressors emerging from the trees. They were a mean-looking crew, perhaps entirely comprised of escaped prisoners. (It was impossible to know for sure.) They were armed with a variety of implements. Handguns and rifles, sure, but I also made out a couple of glistening swords and at least one rusty ax.

"Look at me!" I shouted as I ran. "I'm a zombie! I'm coming to get you! *Yeahhrrgh!!*"

I was not about to win any auditions for a monster movie. (I could already imagine the director's notes: "Too cheesy, etc." "This is not a kids' film." "Zombies don't say 'I'm a zombie.'") However, my actions *did* have the desired effect. I was almost instantly rewarded with a variety of small-arms fire. Most of it missed, but a shotgun blast caught me in the chest and sent me sprawling on my ass. I was back on my feet again in an instant, as if spring-loaded.

"Is that all you got?" I cried. "You better shoot me again, fuckface!"

Behind me, Vanessa reloaded her rifle and continued firing. The gang of aggressors seemed to have retreated to the edge of the trees, but they had also started firing into the camp in steady bursts. Several of the camp members sprang up and started running. I saw at least two get shot down. My heart sank at this sight, and I redoubled my efforts.

"*Yeahhrrgh!!*" I screamed again, advancing once more. "You didn't kill me! Come and get me, you bastards!" A few more bursts erupted from the trees—clearly directed at me—but nothing else hit. More people from Vanessa's camp got up and were moving. Some got the right idea and shot back from their prone positions.

Then the gang charged out of the forest.

Suddenly, everyone was everywhere. Dark, confusing violence ensued. Almost every person—friend and foe—had guns, but it was nearly hand-to-hand combat. I thought of a Revolutionary War battle, where it's like, yeah, you've got muskets, but once the two armies meet, everyone's just screaming and stabbing and shooting up close.

All I could think about was Vanessa. The shots from her rifle were soon drowned out by bursts from other guns, and by screaming. I was drawing fire, but not enough. Everyone was running, and it was very, very dark. I heard horrible cries from people who were wounded or dying. I'm pretty sure there was also a lot of friendly-fire going on too, on both sides.

At one point, I spotted the attacker who still wore his orange Mansfield Correctional jumpsuit, and jumped on his back. He was carrying an ax, but he dropped it the moment I grabbed him. He thrashed in my grip, but I kicked hard at the backs of his legs until he went down. Then I got my hands around his neck and choked him until I thought my thumbs would fall off. He was a skinny, underfed-looking guy, and it didn't take long for him to go limp beneath me. When he stopped moving, I grabbed the ax and made short work of the back of his head.

I grabbed some of his brain and downed it before continuing. It galvanized me, like fucked-up Popeye spinach.

I spied a man hastily reloading a shotgun while taking cover behind the radio van. He did not see me, but I couldn't say if he was friend or foe. (I cursed myself for not having paid closer attention to the faces of those in Vanessa's group.) I hesitated until he raised the shotgun and fired. I followed the line of sight where he had aimed, and saw the red-haired boy from the enamel factory slumped over dead. That was all I needed to see.

I crept up behind the man—holding the aforementioned ax as I did so—and chopped hard into his face, right at the eyes. The blade went halfway through his head, and his body made terrific, spastic contortions, as if electrified. I chopped again and again, going deeper into him each time. Hunks of skin and fleshy matter fell away. He dropped to his knees, dead, but with his fingertips still spasming.

As I admired my work, someone shot me twice in the back. I felt the slugs pass through (not pleasant—not unpleasant), and I turned to see an older man with wild, white hair leveling an automatic pistol at me. He fired again, nicking my right shoulder. I raised the ax and chopped him hard. The ax head went halfway through his neck. He let out an astonished wheeze before falling face-first into the grass.

I looked around for more targets, but there was nobody standing upright. In the morning haze I could only make out dark bodies on the grass. Were they dead, pretending to be dead, or just taking cover?

A bullet *ping!*-ed on the van next to me. Then another. I scanned the tree line and saw a gunpowder flash as another shot ricocheted off the old Dodge.

"Fuck that," I said, and took off lumbering for the trees. I did not head directly for the shooter, but rather for the start of the tree line, perhaps fifty yards from him. He shot at me twice more, hitting both times. Once, opening a hole in the center of my chest (with a great *poof!*) and once nicking my ear. (A tiny piece of earlobe fell away.)

The positioning of this second shot—I considered as I jumped into the trees—might indicate that he had started aiming for my head. He might understand that I was undead. That was a serious concern.

I fell to the ground amidst the trees, holding my ax to my chest. I remained perfectly still, listening. A few shots popped in the distance, but the shooter up the tree line had fallen silent.

As quietly as I could, I began to crawl toward him. At one point, I put my hand on something fleshy and warm, and shrank back, thinking it was a living person. It *was* a person—a young man with corn rowed hair—but he was very dead. I crawled on, until I could look into the clearing and see the van I'd been standing near. I knew the shooter was close.

Then—disaster!—I saw Vanessa skulk around the edge of the van. No sooner did I make her out than a gun fired. Someone—less than five feet from me, but utterly hidden by the underbrush—shot at Vanessa. And connected. She spun and went down, right next to the van. I saw red. Literally.

My vision changed. My body became focused in a way I'd never experienced. It wasn't a good thing. It was terrifying.

I rose to my knees and raised the ax.

The gunman in the grass was quick. He saw me and got off three shots before I buried the ax in his chest. He got off another before I pulled it out and put it back in again. (All of his shots missed, but still, his resolve was impressive.)

I chopped him several times—his face, his chest, even his groin—until I was sure he was very, very dead. Then I picked up his revolver and marched out across the misty morning field toward my girlfriend's body.

Nothing moved. The guns had fallen silent. Dead people were all around on the ground like sacks.

I got close and said: "Vanessa? It's Peter."

She started upward—evidently still alive—and pointed her rifle at my face. She froze, breathing hard. Her face was pulled taut like a grotesque mask—all terror and teeth, bone-white in the cool light of dawn.

I looked her over. The bullet had torn through her coat and grazed her arm. It did not look serious. I took a knee next to her, shielding her against the van with my back. "Can I see?" I said.

She relaxed her gun and nodded.

I removed her coat.

"This doesn't look too bad," I said after an inspection. The bullet had skimmed down the side of her arm, plowing up a fold of flesh as it went. (Really, it was just one long scratch. Not that deep. Could've been much, much worse.)

"I think you'll live," I told her. "Here, wrap your coat around it."

She obeyed.

I surveyed the battlefield where nothing moved. It was silent.

I held her, seeking to give protection by wrapping my bullet-proof zombie body around hers.

We stayed like that for a long, long time.

Dawn finally broke, and it became apparent that everyone was dead. Everyone but us. (Okay, technically, just Vanessa.) Dead or gone. Disappeared into the countryside.

Vanessa winced a little when she moved her arm, but seemed to be adjusting. I thought it would probably be okay if it didn't get infected. The thing to do would be to get her to a doctor. Perhaps that Bowles fellow back at Kenton College would do.

"How's it feeling?" I asked her.

"Stings a little," she said.

"I'm full of so many bullets, I'm surprised I don't clink when I walk," I said, to cheer her.

"Yeah, well ... you're different," she replied quietly.

"I think everybody is dead, or playing dead," I told her.

"Yeah," she said.

The response was curt and solemn. It made me wonder if I didn't possess a zombie's supernatural coldness—if some of my more tender emotions had not been sapped along with my heartbeat and brain waves. Here I was, joking and starting to think about next steps. Here, too, was Vanessa, in shock and afraid, and utterly devastated by the grim scene of murder all around us.

The difference between us felt wider than ever. And still, something in my DNA, my dying cells, my silent heart, knew that this was someone I had once deeply loved, and still did, in my own way. Despite her emotionality (and complicity in my being tied to a fucking tree), she offered direction and meaning in a world of chaos and disappointment. I was ready to serve her, emotional or not. I had abandoned her before. I would not do it again.

Still hesitant to make myself a target, I surveyed all that I could from my side of the van. Still, nothing moved. Bodies decorated the grass like forgotten parcels.

"Do you think you could walk if you had to?" I whispered to Vanessa. "I mean, not right now, but maybe later?"

She looked displeased at the idea, but managed to nod.

"Okay," I said. "Look, I'm going to scout around for a second. We need to get out of here."

While Vanessa hid against the van, I began to pick my way around the battlefield. I don't mean to be dramatic, using that word—or, you know, to denigrate real battles—but that was the only word for it.

When the humans—these same humans who were now dead all around me—had shot and flambéed my zombie battalion, that had been a massacre, not a "battle." (I think for something to be a battle, both sides have to fight, at least a little bit.) But this *had* been a battle. Men, women, and even a few children were dead all around me. And they had fought and killed one another.

Some had fled, but more than half of Vanessa's group was clearly dead. I didn't know how many people had composed the attacking gang, but I counted a good ten of them dead too. (Some from this group had likely also slipped away when things had gotten too hairy.)

Once, I called "Hello?" as loud as I could, just to see if anything moved. But there was nothing. I returned to Vanessa. She looked up at me wonderingly, but I just shook my head and shrugged. She understood.

Later in the morning, we started talking about what to do. For a second time, I was stymied by a shot-up radio. It turned out that Vanessa's group had had just one radio to connect them to the army and the other group of friendly humans. We found it blown to pieces by a shotgun, a few feet from its owner, who had met a similar end. Next, we tried to start the van, and found that this, too, would be an impossibility. Several rounds had hit the aging Dodge, and colored fluids now pooled below it. I found the keys, but couldn't even get the engine to turn over.

"I don't know what's wrong with it," I told Vanessa.

"Looks like it could be about twenty things," she said.

Soon, we began noticing a strong gasoline smell, and decided it would be dangerous to try anything further. Wherever we were going next, we were walking.

"So the other group of humans—the one with your sister and kids—they're all headed for Kenton, too, to rendezvous with the military?" I asked Vanessa.

"As far as I know, they still are," she said. "Unless they come here looking for us. They might do that if they've suddenly lost radio contact. The other group knew where we were. God, this is so fucked up . . ."

"It feels to me like we've got two options," I said. "We can either wait here and see if your friends come after us, or we can head for Kenton College."

Vanessa grew skeptical.

"And what if we get to Kenton and they're not there?" she asked. "I'm not leaving Knox County without my girls, even if it is a fucked-up murder land."

"Wait," I said. "Let's think this through. *I'm* your ticket out, right? So if your sister and your kids get to Kenton but I'm *not* there, then the whole deal's queered. No sense trusting the military to let your people on their helicopters anyway."

"You're right," Vanessa said. (I was glad she saw my point.) "We have to go to the college. They might send somebody here to check up on us, but it wouldn't be the women and children. We'll have to leave a note or something. Say we went to Kenton."

"Good thinking," I said.

We scrounged around the back of the van and found a Bic. I ripped the cover off the van's owner's manual and used the flip side to write on. We left the note in a conspicuous place, but made the missive's content general enough that a hostile couldn't use it to follow us. (We were attacked, but survivors are headed to the aforementioned place, to do the aforementioned thing. The afore-mentioned zombie is still with us.)

Before we set off, I shouted as loud as I could one last time, and so did Vanessa. We shot our guns into the air as well. Gave any survivors (friend or foe) the opportunity to come out of hiding in the forest and join us on our pilgrimage. None did. There was no response.

Alone together, we moved off toward Kenton College and a meeting with the U.S. military.

It would not be a long walk to Gant, so far as I could tell. With luck, and if we kept a good pace, we might make it there by late afternoon. The maps put it more or less straight south, but it would mean a march across farmland and through forests.

I was inexhaustible and accustomed to this kind of travel. Vanessa, in contrast, was wounded and sleep-starved and scared. The trick would be helping her keep up with me.

We carried maps, a compass, and food and water for Vanessa. Also guns. I'd plucked as many as I could carry from corpses on the battlefield. Which was a lot.

"You look like a walking bomb," Vanessa said at one point. It was a lousy analogy. (Yeah, I thought, I'm carrying a lot of guns . . . Just like a bomb. [Still, I took the essence of her point. It *was* a lot of firepower.])

The morning was beautiful. No gray sky, only blue. The wind whipped up smells of trees with new buds and moisture and birds. Change. It smelled like change. The scent made me smile. (Not that the cold bothered me, or that the warmer wind would feel any better on my zombie skin, but it said that some things were older and stronger than even a zombie apocalypse. There were seasons. There was the Earth. There was the unstoppable cycle of snow and rain and water. Animals would still breed. Bears would still awaken from hibernation. Zombies were a force to be reckoned with, true, but we were nothing compared to spring.)

As we walked on through the sparkling morning, I stopped short of thinking to myself: "This too shall pass." The fact of its being spring did not change my status as a member of the walking dead. I was still technically dead, and with little idea as to what exactly the future held for me. I was a zombie, was a zombie, was a zombie. Full stop. I still had no heartbeat. I was decaying. And, boy oh boy, did I enjoy eating people's brains.

And yet there *were* changes—lesser changes, but ones that I could not deny. For one, there was the fact that whatever force had been reanimating the dead seemed to have stopped. When people died now, they just stayed dead. (None of Vanessa's friends—or their attackers—had risen from the battlefield.) There were still zombies, but there were no *new* zombies.

And if that could change, then what else might? I had noticed no lessening of my own zombie-prowess. I was still as brain-thirsty as I'd ever been. But if there was a sea change afoot, who was to say what the next manifestation was to be? Perhaps whatever force or spell had caused the dead to rise would likewise cease to function soon. Zombies everywhere might suddenly stop, falling down dead-again in our tracks. Yet that could just as easily be incorrect; we might also "live" for another ten thousand years.

This was new territory for everyone. Nobody knew what lay around the next bend, or what would ensue over the coming months and years.

As I strode through the forest next to Vanessa, I considered that it was only she who would have a chance at having a normal, human life after this. Humans had families, and societies, and they could reproduce and pass on who they were and what they stood for. They were something through which life-force and culture flowed—from their ancestors to them, and through them into their own children (and also into friends and other people they touched).

Zombies were different. We did not improve or nurture one another. We were . . . something else. I couldn't remember anything about Mama and Papa Mellor, or what they might have instilled in me, but it seemed like a zombie was largely his own man. Only recent events ruled my mind and my world.

And while I wasn't one of the humans, I was still something.

I was a thinking thing.

I was.

In conducting Vanessa safely to Gant, Ohio, I hoped that in some small way, I was making a contribution to a chain of humanity that would last.

It may well have been delusion or wishful thinking, and I understood that—then as I do now. I was a dead thing, and Vanessa was alive. However much I wished or hoped, whatever I did to help her along, nothing could change my status. In a way, I may have been angling only to betray my kind for better treatment. (Did I dream of becoming some sort of "house zombie," regarded as "one of the good ones?") I thought about it, and the answer was no. I had no wish to be elevated in the sight of humans, or to be adjudged separate from the rest of the zombie community. I was just a zombie who liked this woman, Vanessa. A zombie in love, but still a zombie.

The more I thought about it all, the less I cared, frankly. Whether I fell into one category or another. Whether I was accepted by humans or by zombies. Whatever.

I knew that I was a thinking thing, with feelings and hopes. (Often, I *felt* like eating brains, and I hoped humans would get confused and run into a corner so I could just take them out with a sword.) But right now, all my emotions wanted this woman who'd been my lover in another life to get to where she was going, and get there safe.

At mid-morning we stopped so Vanessa could rest and eat. I kept an eye out for anything that looked like movement. Besides just being generally wary, I feared reciprocity from survivors from the gang that had attacked us. (On the other hand, survivors from Vanessa's party might be able to help us if we ran into them—or at least increase our number.)

We kept walking—through fields and little strips of forest. The air stayed crisp. The sun stayed warm.

A little before noon, we encountered two lonely zombies near a toolshed on the edge of a farm. They had pale, sad moon-faces, and were picking idly at a clump of bones and rags that might have once been a human skeleton. I shot them both through the forehead with a revolver.

"You're an equal-opportunity killer," Vanessa observed as we walked past their motionless bodies.

"What does that mean?" I asked.

"You kill humans *and* zombies," she said.

"Yeah," I told her. "That's the gig."

"It's weird," she said.

"I dunno," I rasped. "People kill people all the time. Why can't a zombie kill a zombie now and then?"

"Fair enough, I guess," Vanessa answered.

She smiled at me.

And God, it was still a beautiful smile.

As midday neared, we slowed our pace to a crawl and Vanessa ate a candy bar. We edged onto a muddy dirt road surrounded by trees. I looked at the needle on my compass frequently, and checked what landmarks there were against a hyper-detailed map of Knox County that Vanessa had in her pocket. It was during one of these moments of map-checking distraction that Vanessa saw the van.

"Peter," she said, candy bar still in her cheeks, "wouldya look at that!"

Ahead of us, down a fork in the little dirt road, sat an old Dodge minivan. As I looked closer, I thought it might be the *first* Dodge minivan. A Caravan from around 1984. Light blue, with wood trim. It looked in surprisingly good shape for something so old. Somebody had kept it in a garage and hadn't driven it much.

Vanessa and I looked at each other.

"You suppose it still runs?" she asked. "I'm more than tired of walking."

I had to grant, it was a tempting idea. Steal a car and drive the rest of the way to Kenton. Get there early.

I looked closer and saw something.

"Are those . . . are those keys?" I asked.

"What?" Vanessa said. "Where?"

"On the side-view mirror," I said. "Dangling there in the sunlight—it looks like a ring of keys."

"That's *totally* a ring of keys," she said excitedly.

It was too good to be true. I didn't like it. Who would park a van in the middle of a dirt road like this, and with the keys on the fucking side-view mirror, of all places?

Vanessa began to walk toward it.

"Wait . . . just wait a second," I said. I readied my revolvers and advanced.

"Did you see something?" she asked.

"No," I said. "It just feels a little too easy. I'm getting bad vibes." I crept nearer to the minivan. My eyes were not on the van, but along the trees. I searched for any sign of an assailant or ambush, but saw nothing but bark and branches. Then an unexpected sound from behind made me jump.

It went *Gobblegobblegobble!*

I turned around, scanned until I found the source, and smiled a bewildered smile. Back at the fork in the road, coming up the path we had *not* taken, was a wild turkey—ugly and jet-black. And *very* familiar-looking. "Hey, stranger," I called. "What's up?"

The turkey approached us. I waited patiently as it toddled over. Vanessa's jaw dropped.

"Peter, what *is* that?" Vanessa asked.

"An old friend . . . I think," I told her.

The turkey approached to within ten feet. It looked at me—I mean, right at me. Right into my undead eyes.

"Creepy," Vanessa said.

"I know, right?" I told her. "I wonder what he wants this time."

"This time?" Vanessa asked.

Vanessa slowly walked around the turkey, examining it. It showed no fear—ruffling its tail feathers only once as she leaned in close. Vanessa made an entire circuit of the bird. "Creepy," she said again.

The turkey bobbed its head, as if to say "Thank you."

"Well, then, it was good to see you once more," I said to the turkey. I turned to the minivan and extended my arm toward the dangling ring of keys.

"Gobblegobblegobble," went the turkey.

"No?" I said.

I tried again, this time taking another step toward the Dodge.

"Gobble*gobble*gobble," went the turkey.

I stopped in my tracks and smiled.

"I don't think he likes the idea of our taking the van," I said.

"What, like it's *his?*" Vanessa said sarcastically. "He's a turkey. He can't drive a van. Or *have* a van."

"Tell me," I said to Vanessa, "are there lots of black turkeys like this in Knox County? I have no memory of how frequently you see these creatures."

"I dunno," she responded. "I think I've seen maybe one or two. Never black like this one, though."

"That's what I thought," I responded, rubbing my chin.

"*What's* what you thought?" Vanessa asked.

"I mean to say that we're not taking the van," I told her.

"You're trusting a turkey?" Vanessa asked.

"I guess," I said. "I mean, *you're* talking to a zombie. But yeah, I'm not taking that van."

"So, what then?" Vanessa asked, putting her hands on her hips to rest.

"So we take the other fork in the road," I told her.

I hefted my enormous arsenal of guns and set off after the turkey. Eventually, Vanessa followed.

The turkey (perhaps by this point in the tale he deserves a title, like "Mr. Turkey" [...perhaps not]) bobbed along the dirt road at a steady clip, now and then passing out of sight, but always reappearing. We'd round a bend in the road and lose it, then find it patiently waiting for us at the foot of a tree. It would look directly at us, like an anxious dog, then hop up and continue down the path.

"You were right," Vanessa said at one point. "I'm glad we didn't take the van. This is so much trippier."

"That's one word for it," I said. "I'm still trying to figure this guy out. All I know is things have sort of 'worked out' whenever I've trusted him."

"You've seen him before?" Vanessa asked.

"A couple times," I told her.

"Makes me think of Buddy Duke," Vanessa said. "You must have heard that old story."

"If I did, I don't remember it," I said.

"Funny," she said, "it seems like you were the one who told it to me. Back in the 1950s there was a serial killer in Mount Vernon who was poisoning people. Putting arsenic in milk that the milkmen delivered, putting cyanide on the food people bought at stores—things like that. This was before all the tamper-proof packaging you have today. Once every few months he'd strike. Someone would drink a glass of milk or eat a peppermint candy and fall down dead. Eight people died. Everyone in Knox County was paranoid and terrified. People were driving to Columbus just to buy a jar of pickles."

"And Buddy Duke was the name of the killer?" I asked.

Vanessa shook her head.

"Buddy Duke was a local kid—I say 'kid,' but he was nineteen when it happened—who had severe brain damage. In second grade, he'd fallen through a frozen lake and been trapped under the ice for several minutes. They eventually got him out and got his heart beating again, but his mind was never the same. It was beyond being mentally retarded or slow, apparently. It was like some part of him had been left down there underneath the ice.

"Anyhow, at the height of the poisonings, Buddy Duke killed an old widow named Charlene Crawford with a hammer. He said that a wild turkey had shown him proof that Charlene was the poisoner, and that the turkey was the spirit of a witch who lived in the woods and talked to the dead.

"Everybody in Mount Vernon was furious at Buddy, of course. Charlene was a pillar of the community. She ran a ladies' luncheon club, volunteered at the YWCA, and so on. And the furious towns-people knew that a judge would never convict Buddy of murder because of his soft brain. He'd almost certainly just be sent to a mental hospital for a few years.

"So, despite never having shown any suicidal signs, a few days after he'd turned himself in for the killing, Buddy Duke hanged himself with his shoelaces in his cell. The whole town knew that the sheriff and his deputies had done it, and the whole town approved.

"After that, it took people a few months to notice that there had been no new poisonings in a while. Then, a few years later, Charlene Crawford's daughter sold the widow's property and a new owner installing some landscaping in the back of the house found a secret cellar. In the cellar was a store of twenty different kinds of poison, a journal detailing each of the poisonings, and a lengthy screed against the people of Mount Vernon—written in Charlene Crawford's own hand."

"That's a good story," I said.

"It's not a story," Vanessa said. "I looked it up after you told me. All true."

I thought about this for a while.

"You know what's weird?" I said.

"Ummm, *everything*," Vanessa responded, indicating the whole of Knox County with a giant sweep of her hand.

"Well, yeah," I told her, "but also—and I'm not saying this is the same witch-turkey the guy saw in the 1950s—I felt like being a zombie meant that I was supposed to be like an empty shell. That the special part of me that might get to be in touch with mystical and supernatural things was gone. Probably, I thought, it was the first thing to go. But maybe that's not the case at all. What if the opposite is true?"

Vanessa shrugged.

"Lots of people see things when they're near death," she said. "You know, when they're fevered and injured and so forth. I reviewed a paper for a journal about how the Lakota Indians used to do this thing called a Sun Dance where you suspended yourself from a tree for four days without eating or drinking until you saw spirits."

"Stuff like that though—don't we *know* that it's just the brain reacting to stress or something?" I asked.

"Maybe," said Vanessa. She indicated our avian guide with her hand.

"And maybe not."

Wherever the bird was taking us, it was more than simply a quick detour.

I tried to check the turkey's progress against our maps when I could. It was not always possible. For several hours, the turkey led us down steep inclines that descended into creek beds and through irrigation ditches that fed farms and seemed to curve in large circles. I could use the compass to tell which way was north, but the turkey changed our path so frequently that it was hard to discern in which direction we'd been progressing (or if we'd made "progress" at all). Once, it took us into a cave.

"A cave?" Vanessa asked as we slinked inside.

"This is the real test," I told her. "Do we trust this turkey, or not?"

The cave proved to be little more than a mossy passageway that opened into a wooded valley, and we navigated it easily. Then, at the end of a forest path that terminated at the top of a hill, the turkey was suddenly gone. The field that sloped down in front of us was covered by a thin spring grass in which a mouse would have had trouble hiding—much less a turkey.

"Do you think it flew away?" Vanessa asked, reading my thoughts.

"I was just wondering that," I told her. "Maybe a cougar ate it or something."

We looked around for signs of the turkey (or signs of a cougar).

"Oh fuck, Peter," Vanessa gasped, putting her hand to her mouth. "Would you look at that!"

Vanessa gestured off the side of the hill. I followed her finger, half-expecting to see our feathered friend in the jaws of some predator. Instead, I saw an encampment of humans on a distant field. Small and hostile-looking. Motorcycles. Leather. Guns. (Lots of guns.) They had circled their wagons, and appeared to be seated together, eating and drinking.

"Some kind of biker gang," I said dismissively. "I don't think they're likely to see us up here, though."

"But Peter, that's the way we came," Vanessa said. "Look! We were just on the other side of that ditch, looping around the edge of that field."

I thought about it. I wasn't 100 percent sure where we were, but it felt like Vanessa was right. The turkey had taken us along a long, scythe-shaped curve around the edge of that field, keeping us under the cover of elm trees and hillocks. If the bird hadn't done this, we would have walked right into them. Or, had we taken the van, driven right up to them.

"Fuck," I said, genuinely astonished. "I think you're right."

We moved off the other side of the hill, away from the biker gang, and continued, generally, toward Gant.

Bereft of our black-feathered guide, I was once again forced to rely on my map and compass. It soon became clear that the turkey had indeed wended us close to our ultimate destination. Vanessa increasingly required breaks to eat and rest her legs, but even with these, I calculated that we would reach Gant well before sunset.

One of these breaks took place on an upturned wheelbarrow in the shadow of an abandoned barn. As Vanessa drank from a bottle of water, I drew two revolvers from my considerable selection of armaments and kept watch over the fields. The inside of the barn was empty, save for a few stray tools and what I guessed were tractor parts. A lone tire propped against the barn door got me thinking.

"Did I tell you I found out how I died?" I asked Vanessa.

"In a car accident, right?" she said, between gulps.

"Somebody cut my brakes," I said. "I was fucking murdered."

I told her the whole story—seeing my car in the impound lot in Mount Vernon, sneaking under the fence, finding the accident report.

"So I still don't know who it was," I told her. "From what Sam said, I made more than a few enemies in my first few years at Kenton. You know, right, about the guy who killed himself after I fucked his wife? I'm assuming we talked about that back when I was alive. I figure it was someone close to that family."

Vanessa stopped drinking her water and became very still. Her eyes were unfocused, and an uneasy expression came to her face. I turned and scanned the horizon—afraid she had seen something dangerous approaching—but the coast was clear.

"You okay?" I asked, assuming her nauseated expression derived from the subject at hand. "I mean, *I've* gotten to be okay with the fact that I was murdered. Hell, maybe I even deserved it. I don't remember."

"Are you sure your brakes were *cut?*" Vanessa said, in a voice that was surprisingly sober. "They didn't just fail or something?"

"Like I said, the report at the impound lot said they were cut," I told her. "It was underlined three times."

"Fuck," Vanessa said with a sigh. She put her hand to her forehead like an overwhelmed Southern belle.

"What?" I said, genuinely curious.

"Sam worked on your car for you," Vanessa replied. "It was like a favor thing. He did it for a lot of people around Gant. He'd worked as a mechanic to put himself through grad school. He couldn't do all the major surgeries, but he did oil changes and replaced spark plugs and things like that."

"You think *Sam* cut my brakes?" I asked.

"Sam was working on your car the day of your accident," Vanessa said with icy coolness. "He was supposed to be fixing it up for you to come over and see me."

"But Sam's my friend," I protested. "I have a few memories of him, and they're all good. Why would Sam want to kill me?"

"Umm, *me*," Vanessa stated flatly.

"But you seemed to get along when he dropped me at your sister's house," I said.

Vanessa shook her head, like I'd just betrayed massive idiocy. "You know he wanted to be more than friends with you, right?" she asked.

"Yeah," I said. "I got that idea. But I don't think I swung that way, and he knew it. Not that I can swing at all, anymore ... I was just friends with Sam."

"He's a lonely man, Peter," Vanessa said. "And you're his only friend. When I showed up, it threatened that—threatened the only thing he had. Think about it. You were giving me all the things that he couldn't have, right in front of his face. We were friends *and* lovers. We held hands. We went to dances. You and I had even talked about moving somewhere together, maybe when the girls got a little older. You wanted to make a fresh start at a new school. Get away from Kenton and all the judgmental eyes. Sam knew that was coming."

"But if he coveted me ... why would he *kill* me?" I asked. "I mean, why not kill *you?*"

"It makes sense to me," Vanessa said, taking a tug on her bottled water. "If he can't have you, then nobody can. Isn't that how a lot of crimes of passion go?"

I sat down next to her on the wheelbarrow. Vanessa looked lost in thought. I think we both were.

"So, what do we do?" I asked her. "Sam's going to be at Kenton when we get there."

"Fuck if I know," she said. "I don't know how you'd prove he killed you, and even if you did, what then? It's martial law in the cities, but here in the countryside, it's anarchy. I haven't heard about courts out here hearing cases, but there might still be something operating in Mount Vernon. Maybe, if we convinced the people still at Kenton College that he killed you, they'd string him up. Lynch him. Is that what you want?"

I took a deep, unnecessary breath. It didn't help.

"I don't know what I want," I said. "But not that."

I took another breath. My lungs croaked like a broken bellows.

"As all this goes on, I have fewer and fewer friends," I said. "My world gets smaller and smaller. I don't like it."

"I know what you mean," she said.

"Now that I'm with you again, I'm trying hard not to give up on this world, you know?" I sighed. "The last time I did that, I ate a bunch of people."

"I know you did," Vanessa said. "I know you did."

"As it stands now, you and a wild turkey are the only ones who've treated me right," I said. I took a few more broken-bellows breaths. Vanessa threw her water bottle on the ground, and a gust of wind blew it away across the fields.

We got up and moved on.

When you approach Kenton College from the northeastern fields at the bottom of the hill, the first college building you can see clearly is the tower. It looks dramatic, but it's really just the top of a cafeteria. Like a lot of college buildings, its architecture is vaguely neo-Gothic. One tall gray tower with a big Harry Potter-style dining hall underneath. Vanessa and I sighted the tower in the late afternoon. I couldn't believe our luck. We had found it. Had done it. We had navigated a world of hostile humans and zombies and mysterious turkeys, and had found our way to Kenton College. The only question was: *Had it held?* Was it still a place ruled by free men and (relatively speaking) good people? Or had it fallen? Was it now the province of gangsters and murderers? We would soon find out.

"How do we make this approach, d'you think?" Vanessa asked as we marched toward the tower. We were still several hundred yards away from the start of the campus proper. In between here and there were parking lots, paved streets, gravelly service roads, jogging trails, soccer fields and lacrosse fields, football practice fields, folds of wild forest, and intricate college landscaping . . . all of which made a clear view of our approach impossible.

Before I could articulate an answer, we heard three steady rifle shots—*Crack! Crack! Crack!*—from up near the hill. Vanessa ducked a little.

"Carefully," I said, cocking my eye at the tower atop Kenton College. "We approach it very carefully."

Using the cafeteria tower to keep our bearings, we crept through the underbrush, staying away from even the jogging trails, until we reached a large clearing that had once been the school's lacrosse field. Aluminum stands rested to one side of the field, along with a tiny clubhouse where vendors could sell refreshments at games. On the roof of the clubhouse, facing away from us, an elevated chair (like a tennis line judge might use) had been erected. In it, a rough-looking man holding a pair of binoculars and a rifle sat facing the hill.

"Let's get down," I said to Vanessa. We fell to our stomachs, and I began unpacking some of our ammunition.

As I'd thought might be the case, the man in the high chair was managing a kind of lazy search pattern with his binoculars, the last phase of which involved a quick sweep of the woods behind him, where Vanessa and I were hiding. The watchman's glance was less than cursory, however, and there was almost no chance he would ever detect our presence if we stayed prone.

"Do you recognize him?" Vanessa whispered.

"No, I don't," I said. "He doesn't look like anybody from the college."

"I'd hope not," Vanessa said. "He looks evil. His smile is mean."

She was right. His smile *was* mean.

We watched the guard for a while. Most of his attention seemed to be focused on an area many yards off where the road approaching Kenton College fell away into a little valley. Near the mouth of the valley were three or four colored clumps on the ground. I couldn't see well, but I guessed they were clothes—maybe clothes with bodies inside of them.

"Strange that he should be focused in that direction—*toward* the college," I said.

"What do you mean?" Vanessa asked.

"Well, he's a watchman, but he's watching *in,* not out," I said. "What sense does that make? People could sneak up behind him, just like we did."

"What's he doing, then?" Vanessa asked.

"Something's over there, by that valley," I said. "Can you see?"

Vanessa followed my decaying finger.

"Are those dead people, those things on the ground?" Vanessa whispered.

I told her I thought they were.

"You're right about where he's looking," she whispered. "If you watch him, he's mostly focusing on two places: the college—up the hill—and that valley off to the side where those bodies are."

"I bet there are more people down in the little valley," I said. "And when they try to come up, he shoots them."

"So this is like a siege?" Vanessa wondered.

"Something like that, yeah," I agreed.

We heard the sound of distant gunshots and shouting from up on the hill. The sentry in the tennis chair heard it too. He fixed his binoculars on the college, and the evil smile returned to his lips. After the shots—a quick cluster of maybe twenty or twenty-five—a noise of distant engines became audible.

Four ATVs carrying armed men emerged from out of the woods at the side of the hill. They waved to the sentry, hailing him as they approached. The sentry raised his gun and began shooting intermittently—not at the ATVs, but *past* them, in the direction of the valley.

"That's covering fire," Vanessa said. "You're right. There *are* people down in that valley."

We ducked low in the grass as the ATVs pulled up. I only caught glimpses, but they appeared to dump the limp body of one of their colleagues. The limp man was not dead, but twitched his fingers and moaned a little bit. He'd been shot somewhere. The man in the chair smiled. The men chatted in casual, jocular tones. Their voices were low-class, criminal, and crude.

"Fuck these guys," Vanessa whispered. "These are murderers."

"Seriously," I said quietly.

"I have a guess about what's happened here," Vanessa whispered. "But I really hope I'm wrong."

"Tell me," I said.

"The other group—the one with my sister and our kids in it— was traveling in a school bus we'd found out by Coshocton. When the bus approached the college, it would have come by that road there—driving toward the hill from the south. But let's say they pull up in their bus and find the college is under siege from these murderers. They aren't able to turn around, so they veer off into that valley."

"You think a *school bus* is down in that valley?" I whispered.

"Exactly," Vanessa responded.

I tried to judge the depth of the little valley. I guessed it might *just* be deep enough to conceal something like a bus from our perspective.

"So?" I said, trying to put it all together.

"So they're trapped," Vanessa said. "They can't get to the college, which is up at the top of the hill. And your friends at the college can't get down to them. Look at those bodies by the lip of the valley. Those have to be ones who made a break for it."

I remained thoughtfully silent. None of the clumps of clothes had looked particularly female, but there was no guarantee that Vanessa's sister and children were not among them.

The men in the ATVs shared a final evil laugh with the sentry in the tennis chair, revved their rides, and headed back toward the hill. The sentry made a quick sweep with his binoculars—including in our direction, though there was, again, little chance he'd notice us—then took up his gun and laid down covering fire in the direction of the valley.

"They must be fighting back," I said. "Your people in the bus— they must be shooting back from the lip of the valley if they have to do suppressing fire like that. That's where these guys are vulnerable—when they have to cross the field."

"Well, what do you think?" Vanessa asked. "Can we take them?"

It was the obvious question. I had been wondering the very same thing. The answer, however, did not feel obvious at all.

"I don't know," I said, thoughtfully stroking a shotgun wound in my belly. "I just don't know."

It would be nothing to creep up and shoot the tennis-chair sentry in the back, but what then? How many of these hooligans had taken up positions around the college? And what of the far side of the valley? Might they have stationed another sentry (or several others) on the opposite side? I could make out a few clumps of trees and a small maintenance shed beyond the valley. Though I saw nothing else, it stood to reason that they'd have to watch it from more than one place.

Straight out from us, the men on ATVs crossed the far edge of the field and made their way into the cover of the woods at the base of the hill. The sentry in the tennis chair put away his weapon and relaxed back into his seat.

"It'd be easy to take him out," Vanessa said. "*I* could hit him. From *here*."

"I know you could," I told her. "But I think we should stop and think."

"Don't take too long," Vanessa warned me. "I know it feels like spring, but sunset still comes earlier than you think."

I swallowed instinctively. She was right.

Vanessa and I stayed low, covered in the grass and dead leaves and muck. The sentry also stayed where he was, getting up only once, to piss. Far in the distance, the ATVs could be heard revving. Now and then, distant gunshots were also discernible. When this was the case, the sentry in the tennis chair would put his binoculars to his face and gaze intently up at the hill, but I don't think he could actually see anything. The trees were too dense up there.

Then, after perhaps half an hour, we heard a rustling noise in the woods nearby. It was to our immediate left as we faced the college.

My first impulse was to sit upright and grab my revolvers, but undue movement might be noticed by the sentry. Vanessa and I looked anxiously at one another.

I motioned that we should retreat backward into the woods, and as gingerly as we could. She nodded, and we crawled back, keeping our eyes on the sentry's back the entire time. He did not turn as we slunk away.

Back inside the folds of forest, I drew my revolvers. The rustling, though tentative, continued. It sounded as though the other person (or persons) was also trying to remain quiet. That made it worse.

Then we heard whispering. Indistinct at first. One man, then two.

We were matched, if not outnumbered. I quickly decided that our only hope would be to surprise whoever had crept into these woods with us.

"Stay here," I whispered to Vanessa, who was intently clutching her rifle. "If you hear shooting, turn and run. That sentry on the chair will be coming." Vanessa nodded, and I slunk away on my knees and elbows in the direction of the whispered voices. They were near. Very near.

I edged along the forest floor—stopping whenever I made a sound, then proceeding quietly as I could.

I pushed through a hollowed area between two tree trunks and encountered a man's legs (inside of camouflage pants) dangling over the side of a log. I drew a bead on them, and continued to edge forward. Before long, I made out three men. They were bearded and looked haggard and sad and worried. Two were wiry thin. The other, thicker one was my old friend Sam.

My bead changed from Camo Pants to the forehead of my "friend."

And I wondered, "Do I just take the shot? Do I just kill him now, and get it over with?"

I recalled that in movies—though my addled, zombie brain could recall no specific films—heroes (and villains) always erred by opening a dialogue with their enemies, instead of killing them right away. I also remembered old philosophical thought experiments about whether or not it would be moral to kill Hitler in different situations—like if you meet him back when he was just a failed art student who hadn't yet called for the final solution to anything. (And you always think: Of course you do. Of course you kill Hitler. It doesn't feel neat and tidy, or like it all wraps up in some kind of moral syllogism, but of course you do it. Of course you kill him.)

And here I was, with the man who had murdered me—or at least murdered the first me—in my sights (and he was *German* to boot).

Calling yourself Sam ... Whatever, Adolf ...

And I might have done it. I might have pulled that trigger, then and there, and ended his life. (Probably, I could also have shot the other two, and Vanessa almost certainly would have been able to beat a safe retreat.) But my head suddenly lolled as if I had become drowsy. I lost my bead on Sam.

At first, I didn't understand what was happening. My neck seemed to have grown a mind of its own. Then my eyes—though it hurt to turn them so extremely in their sockets—found the source of my confusion.

The long barrel of a rifle was pressing itself *hard* against the temple of my zombie-numb forehead. I didn't move. Not even to lower my guns.

"Don't fucking move," a voice said. It was gruff and belligerent. And I thought I recognized it.

"Music professor," I said, not even daring to turn my head and look at the man. "You're the music professor. We've met. Your name's ... your name's ... Puckett."

A beat. Then the gruff voice again. "Jesus ... *Pete*? Is that you? Oh my fucking God ... It is."

"I'm gonna lower my guns now," I whispered, and did.

With my weapons pointed at the ground, I turned and looked up into the face of the stunned music professor. His stubbly face looked tired and sallow. (Compared to me, of course, he looked like a fashion model who'd just had a ten-hour nap. But still . . .) It had been a difficult few months for the man, and I could see it all over him.

"What the fuck happened to you, Pete?" he asked.

"I'm a zombie," I said. An instant later, I wondered if it was the right thing to say. I remembered Puckett's evident pleasure at smashing in the zombie's head in the Kenton graveyard.

Much to my relief, he lowered his gun. Then he called to the other men, including Sam.

All of them looked exhausted, and all shared aspects of Puckett's grim countenance. Sam's face lit up when he saw me. (Though I would have guessed such a sad visage might never smile again, that was exactly what it did.)

"Peter, what the fuck are you doing here?" asked Sam, bewildered.

For every part of me that still wanted to say "Fuck it" and shoot Sam in the face, there was a part of me that knew it would bring us no closer to helping Vanessa's sister and children. "I got here like an hour ago," I said. "Vanessa's with me. Wait . . . Vanessa!" The men looked in the direction where I'd rasped. A moment later, we heard her kneefalls as she edged her way over to us. "Vanessa, it's safe," I rasped.

She came into view, clutching her rifle hard to her chest.

"Vanessa?" Sam said.

"Hi, Sam," she managed, pulling herself up and sitting on a stump. I noticed her wincing as she did this, and thought again about getting her wounded arm to the college doctor.

"What the hell is going on here?" one of the thin, bearded men asked. "What is this thing?"

"This 'thing' is Peter Mellor," Sam replied.

"Jesus," said the bearded man. "*That's* Pete from Philosophy?"

"Don't worry," I told him. "I'm not going to eat your brain. I'm still like a regular person—I just can't remember much."

"But you've got bloodstains all down your mouth," the bearded man said.

"I said I'm not going to eat *your* brain," I told him.

"Oh," he replied, suddenly thoughtful.

"How did you die?" asked Puckett.

"Somebody killed me," I said, matter-of-factly, hazarding a glance Sam's way. "But let's not get into that right now—"

"What are you doing back here?" Sam asked, cutting me off.

Vanessa and I explained how we were set to rendezvous with another group of humans, and how our own group had been attacked by hostiles. I told them that everyone had scattered or was dead. "And let me guess," Vanessa added. "There's an old yellow school bus stuck in that big ditch over there?"

"Exactly," said Sam. "The bus pulled up a few hours ago. But we were under siege from these goddamn bastards on ATVs."

"We've been fighting them for almost a week straight," said one of the bearded men.

"They come and go, and they've staked up a perimeter around the hill so we can't leave," said the other bearded man.

"That's right," Sam added. "When the bus pulled up, there was a little firefight. Nobody knew exactly what was happening, and we all shot at one another. Now we've realized that the people in the bus—or, I should say, in the valley—are friendlies. They've been trying to reach us up on the hill, but they're pinned down too tight."

"But that ends tonight!" said Puckett, just a little too loudly. "The four of us are going to fan out into the woods and outflank them. As soon as the sun sets, we're going to take out the sentries all at once."

"Fuck," I said.

"What?" Sam said. "What's the problem?"

I explained about the government airlift coming at sunset to take us to the Green Zone.

"Really, they just want me," I clarified. "I'm famous with these guys, or something. I expect they want to study me. Learn how it is that I'm a zombie but I can still talk and think. I'd like an explanation myself, come to think of it."

"We were going to take you all, too," Vanessa added. "The government said they'd bring enough transports to lift out both our groups, and anyone else on the hill."

"So *you're* the bargaining chip?" Sam said.

"Fuck you," I told him. It was the first time my rage at the man had boiled over. It came out easily. It felt good.

"Whoa," Puckett said.

"I'm nobody's *bargaining chip*," I said to them. "I'm doing this to help these people. Because some of them—*some* of them—were, and are, my friends."

"So this is good, then," Puckett said. "We take out these son-of-a-bitch bastard sentries, get the people out of the bus in the valley and up the hill, and bingo—we're outta here. Everybody wins."

"Except the helicopters are coming at sunset," Vanessa said.

"Won't they wait?" said Sam. "Won't they get out and help us fight?"

"I think the answer is no," Vanessa said. "They aren't like the army used to be. They had to be cajoled into coming here and doing a quick 'get in, get out.' If they show up and anything's amiss, they're liable to leave. I think they already half-suspect this is some kind of trap."

"Do you have a radio up on the hill?" I asked. "Anything we could use to contact them?"

"Fuck . . . No, we don't," Puckett said.

"We only have cell phones that don't work," said one bearded man.

"And are out of batteries besides," said the other.

"So what do we do?" Sam said, looking genuinely curious.

"I'm not leaving without my daughters, and my sister and her kids," Vanessa said. "And as far as I know—*if* they're still alive—they're with that group pinned in the valley. We have to get them out."

"We'll get them out," I reassured her, resting my hand on her shoulder. She smiled nervously and looked away.

Puckett blanched a bit at my display of physical affection, and the two bearded men exchanged a pregnant glance. I suspected they had thought of zombies as subhuman—as walking offal—for so long that it broke their minds a little bit to see one comforting a woman near tears. (Or were they going one step beyond, and imagining Vanessa making love to this rotting, cold-blooded version of me?)

"We've got to get them out from the school bus, and we've got to do it before sunset," I told them. "I'll do it myself, if I have to."

"Can you take a bullet?" Puckett said, looking me over. "I mean, I don't want to be rude, but it looks like you already have. Like, more than a few."

"Uh-huh," I told him. "Like I said, I'm a zombie."

"So a head shot can still take you out, then?" asked Sam. There was an awkward pause. I just stared at him. Puckett looked back and forth between us, confused.

"Yes," Vanessa said, breaking the silence. "He's like any other zombie, as far as we know. A shot to the head can kill him."

"We'll help you, obviously," Puckett said. "I want these guys dead, too. They're fucking murderers. I'm sick of being shot at."

"Okay," I said. "How many of you are there? How many that can fight?"

The four men looked at one another, and there was some shrugging. The consensus was around twenty-five, counting themselves.

About twenty up on the hill, and then their little expeditionary party.

"And how many of *them* are there?" I asked, motioning in the direction of the man in the tennis chair.

"I think there are slightly more of them," Puckett said to nods all around. "But just slightly. I'd put it at thirty. Four of them are staked around like snipers—like our guy over there in the chair—and the rest are on ATVs, trying to find a way up the hill."

"Why are they attacking Kenton in the first place?" Vanessa asked no one in particular. "It's so horrible."

"Why did that gang attack us the other night?" I asked rhetorically. "We have stuff—or *appear* to have stuff—and they want it. There aren't cops around to stop them. Even the army's shit-scared to go very deep inside Knox County."

"He's right," Puckett said. "You'd be surprised how a few local cops were the only thing keeping some people from killing and raping and stealing. Not to wax, you know, philosophical ... ," Puckett glanced at me before continuing, "but I think the dead rising has made some people think that maybe no god is watching either. Like you can do anything you want, and nothing matters."

"Say, did you *learn* anything from being dead?" one of the bearded men asked me. "Like ... what's it like?"

I thought for a moment, but only a moment.

"Hmmm," I said. "I didn't see God or anything, if that's what you mean. As for what it's like ... I think the technical term is 'sucks.' It really sucks. My body's numb and dying and feels weird, and things don't work like they should."

"Oh," said the bearded man. "Sorry."

"So we need to figure out a plan," I said, hoping for no further existential queries. "It has to be something that gets all the friendlies out of the valley and up to the top of the hill by sunset."

"When's sunset?" Puckett asked. "Because, you know, it changes. And then there's the start of the sunset, when it's just getting dark, and the very end of it, when the sky is almost dark but there's that blue sliver left where the sun is just shining a little."

"We don't know," Vanessa said. "Back when we were talking to the army, we agreed on 'sunset' so that nobody would be confused. A lot of people don't know if their watches are right anymore. You know how it is."

"I think we ought to be ready at the *start* of the sunset," I said. "That leaves us, what? Two or three hours, tops."

"Has anybody tried *talking* to these guys on the ATVs?" Vanessa asked. "All we need is a temporary truce."

Puckett rolled his eyes.

"I don't think they'd negotiate," Sam said. "Besides, what would we offer them? What would we say? 'Could you please let those people join us at the top of the hill so we can all be airlifted out together?' "

"Well, now . . . it *sort of* makes sense," I said. "They want to take the college, right? If they agree to that plan, then they *get* the college—plus anything left over after we're gone. The supplies. The food. Everybody wins."

"It's not much; the supplies, that is," Sam said. "And what makes you think they'd believe us?"

"Yeah, I don't want to *talk* to them," asserted Puckett. "I only want to *kill* them."

"I agree with you," I said, seeming to reverse my position. "I know I just got here, but I think you're right on the money with that one. We need to kill these guys. If we negotiate, there are too many chances for them to betray us."

"What about the plan you guys had before?" Vanessa asked. "Can't we just do it a little earlier in the day?"

"Yeah," I said. "Take out the sentries all at once, then rush the people from the valley up to the hill before the ATV guys know what happened."

"Not possible," Puckett said.

"Why?" I asked.

"First of all, we need it to be dark to get to the sentry on the farthest side," Puckett said. "There are four of them. Three—like this idiot in the chair—have their backs to the woods, so it'll be easily done. But the sentry on the far side is set up in a lawn chair by the maintenance road. There's no real way to sneak up on him. The only cover on the approach is a couple of shrubs. Even in the dark, taking that one out will be real dangerous. Sam had volunteered to do it."

I gave Sam a sideways look.

"We also need the cover of darkness to get the people in the valley safely back up the hill," Sam said, unfazed. "Once you hit the base of the hill, you're into the trees and you're covered, but it's a good hundred yards from the lip of the valley to those trees. I wouldn't like to have them try it while these gangsters can see them. It'd be a shooting gallery."

"Okay, fine," Vanessa said. "But where does that leave us?"

"We can still do it," I insisted. "That plan will *still* work. Just substitute me for Sam."

"Huh?" Puckett offered.

"I move slow, but I'm safe, barring a head shot," I said. "Let me handle the one out by the maintenance road. You guys take out the other sentries and concentrate on getting the people out of the valley and up the hill. I'll keep this guy so busy with me, he won't have time to think about shooting anybody else. Then we just hold out on the hill until the army comes."

"Might work," said Puckett, rubbing his chin.

There was general cautious agreement all around.

"Somebody should sneak back up the hill and tell people up there what we're gonna do," one of the bearded men said. I couldn't decide if he was volunteering to do it himself.

"Is that easy to do?" I asked them.

"We're getting better at it," said Puckett. "These fuckers can't secure the whole perimeter of the hill the whole time. You just figure out where they aren't, and make a break for it."

"But don't choose wrong," Sam said. "Somebody already died that way."

"I'll do it," said the first bearded man. (My guess had been right. He *was* volunteering.) "Unless the gang is trying some kind of offensive up the hill, I can direct everyone over to the side nearest the valley, to be ready to help. I'll leave right now. Just give me half an hour or so to find my way back up there before you start shooting."

"Sound good to everyone?" I asked.

I wanted to keep things moving along. Too much hesitation and planning, and everything could be lost. I wanted to strike first and strike hard. Who knew if the military would actually come? They had had no radio contact for almost two days with the parties who had promised to deliver me. The military might presume them dead at the hands of gangs, or other zombies, or even me. (I was, after all, the Kernel.) They might not even be coming.

But then again, what if they did come? This airlift was the only hope for these humans for a while. The more I thought about it, the more I wanted to be sure they got their chance.

There was more deliberation. Some still had doubts. But Puckett, who seemed almost unnaturally moved to favor scenarios involving violence, was quick to stick by the idea of attacking as soon as possible. Though there were pros and cons—and certainly, risks—nobody could propose anything concrete that would have the same effect.

"Let's do this," Puckett said. "C'mon. Let's go fucking kill them. Before the situation changes."

"I agree," I said, though in measured tones. Puckett warranted no encouragement. (Indeed, I guessed that any additional stimulation would be dangerous.)

"I'm off then," said the bearded man who was itching to head back to the hill. "Good luck, guys."

After he had crawled away into the woods, the others explained to me where the shooters were and what their assignments had been.

"So it all stays the same," I said. "Except Sam and Vanessa can stay here and take out high-chair-guy, and I'll charge the one sitting out in the field."

"Yeah, that works," said Puckett.

"And Vanessa, maybe you stay *behind* Sam," I added.

"He's the man, so he goes first?" Vanessa quipped.

"Something like that," I said, looking hard at the man who had cut my brakes.

After a brief review of our attack plan ("When you hear Peter shooting, then *you* start shooting"), we moved into the forest to creep to our respective positions. I would have the longest, loneliest walk to the outcropping of trees from which I had to emerge.

As we trudged away, Sam attempted to take me aside.

"Look, Peter," Sam whispered. "I don't know what's with these sidelong looks, who told you what—or what you *think* you know—but *I* didn't kill you."

"Sure, you didn't," I told him. "You just had the motivation and the opportunity and were the only person at Kenton who knew how to cut brakes."

"Look, I didn't do it," he countered. "And I can *prove* that to you."

"What're you talking about?" I asked. "A witness puts you somewhere else at the time of my accident—and oh, let me guess, that person just happened to get eaten by a zombie?"

"No," he said. "I can prove, 100 percent, that I'm not the one who killed you."

That phrasing unsettled me. I stopped walking and turned to face him.

"You say that like you *know* who it was," I told him.

"Well . . . ," Sam waffled. "I do."

I bit what was left of my lip in consternation.

"But look, that person *is* dead," Sam continued. "I would never kill you, Pete. You've got to believe that. You were my only friend out here."

"So wait," I said, needing some clarity. "You thought I was alive when you found me and drove me to Vanessa's sister's . . . But now, when I come back here as a zombie, you know that I was murdered?"

"It's complicated," Sam stammered.

"You're telling me it's complicated," I returned.

"When we get back to the hill, I can give you all the proof you'll ever require," Sam insisted. "Until then, you've just got to trust me."

I looked hard into his eyes. For a long time. Sam did not look away, nor did he blink. For the life (*life?*) of me, if I hadn't known better, I might have gotten the impression he was telling the truth.

"Whatever," I said, turning away. "We've got a lot to do before we get back to the hill."

I walked away, leaving him standing there, staring at my back. After a moment, I caught up to Vanessa.

"Is everything okay?" she asked.

I shrugged.

"He says he didn't do it, and that he has proof," I told her.

"But who else could it have been?" Vanessa asked. "Someone related to that professor who killed himself?"

"It's possible," I said. "The list of suspects is pretty damn short."

I cast another suspicious glance back at Sam. He was holding his rifle awkwardly and looking at an early-spring toadstool.

I wondered: Was this really the man who had volunteered to make the dangerous charge against the shooter in the lawn chair? In that moment, as Sam stooped a little to examine the mushroom's glistening bone-white top, he hardly looked capable of killing anyone. Me included.

"Just keep an eye on him," I said to Vanessa.

This next part is hard to tell. We came so, so close.

At first, things went perfectly. We fanned out through the woods just as agreed, positioning ourselves as close as possible to the shooters guarding the valley. Puckett and the remaining bearded man each took a shooter for themselves, Vanessa and Sam shared the one in the high tennis chair, and I crept around to take out the one on the far side of the valley.

I'd been told my job would be difficult, but was not prepared for what I saw when I stood at the edge of the woods. The task before me would be very dangerous, even for a zombie. There was a tremendous amount of distance between the trees and the guard in the lawn chair, and virtually no cover in between. For a normal human, it would be suicide to attempt a charge in daylight. Yeah, maybe you'd have a *chance* at night, but even then, unless the guard was sleepy or distracted or something, it'd be a very risky thing. Again, I found it hard to believe Sam had volunteered. Maybe he'd wanted to die.

For all the advantage his position afforded, the man in the lawn chair was not an imposing figure. He was around fifty, oafish, and decidedly porcine. He wore a leather jacket against the chill, and held a rifle in his lap. Beside him on the ground was a cooler and several empty beer cans. He alternated between eyeing the valley and rotating his girth toward the hill to see if there were any new skirmishes to watch.

Before I charged (I was to "set things off," with the others commencing their attacks when they saw or heard evidence of mine), I studied the man's search pattern, aiming to charge at the opportunity calculated to afford me the most time.

At first, I had considered that some kind of ruse might be appropriate. I could conceal a single weapon in my belt and walk up to the man as though I were a lost traveler. I'd get as close as I could, and then whip out my piece and hit him at close range. So what if he beat me to the draw? As long as he hit my chest and not my brain, I'd be fine. (And I would definitely kill him.)

The problem with that plan was that I anticipated a hell of a firefight before the last friendly was rescued from the valley, and I wanted *all* my guns for it. (I'd carried them all this way, hadn't I? Why not use them.) Sure, I could sneak up on one person with just a pistol down my pants, but what about after I'd emptied it? What then? Even if I took the guy down with the first bullet, that left only five more shots—a situation which simply would not do. I wanted all of my weapons with me, even if it meant charging this guy head-on.

However, as it turned out, I *did* end up using a bit of subterfuge.

When I felt it was time (I was loaded down with all my weapons, and the sun had grown heavy and low in the clear spring sky), I emerged from my spot in the woods and began crossing the until-recently manicured college landscaping. The paunchy man in the chair had turned to check out a flourish of loud skirmishing up on the hill. I walked as quickly as I could, but my zombie bones had grown old over the winter and my muscles were stiff and stringy. It was hardly a run. Even to call it a jog goes too far. At best, I managed a kind of lumbering dance, like a slow-motion vaudeville performer imitating a running man.

Eventually, he saw me. His first reaction was clearly confusion. I could read the thoughts on his face. Who was I? Why was I coming in his direction? (Most people ran from gangsters, after all.) And why was I walk-running in such a strange, awkward way?

Then he noticed my guns. My many, many guns. (I could still read his face.) He raised his rifle nervously.

"Stop right there!" he said. "You! Stop!"

I did no such thing.

The man hesitated—looking around, as if for someone to tell him what to do. Soon, I was within fifty yards.

"Stop there!" he shouted, taking aim at me. "I don't know you. Don't come any closer."

I kept coming. I'd decided to go with a shotgun first, and I brought it up and leveled it at the man.

"Shit!" he shouted, and beat me to the draw. He might have said more, but I couldn't hear it over the crackle of his gun.

His first two shots missed, but the last one hit me in the chest. High in the chest. Almost my neck, really. Much too close to my brain for comfort.

I staggered under the impact of the bullet, but did not fall. My attacker had seen his weapon connect with me, and hesitated for a moment. Then he fired again. This blast also connected, striking my lower torso.

He hesitated again, waiting to see if I would go down.

Suddenly, shots rang out in what seemed all directions. The paunched man lowered his rifle and cocked his head, as if smelling the air. He wanted to look away, but dared not while I still stood. I saw my chance.

As dramatically as possible (even managing a theatrical [if raspy] *Arrruugh!*), I stumbled as though one of his bullets had struck home, and fell forward into the grass, unmoving. (I made sure my head was cocked forward and to the side, giving me a more than adequate view of my target from the ground.)

More gunshots rang out around me.

"What the fuck is going on?!" the gangster yelled, clearly growing alarmed. Seconds after I'd fallen, he felt comfortable enough to survey the horizon. (The different sentry posts were not close to one another.) As quickly as it had started up, the sound of shots died away completely. I hoped it signaled that my companions had been successful.

"What the fuck?!" the man said again, looking back and forth like an anxious animal. I considered trying to move my weapon up slowly and taking a shot at him. However (to my delight), he began approaching *me*—all the time turning around and around, scanning the horizon for the source of the gunfire.

He drew closer. Twenty yards. Fifteen.

I looked directly at him all the while, but mimicked the straight-ahead stare of the dead. (It came quite naturally.)

Finally, when he was within a first-down, I sprang up and leveled my shotgun at him.

"Shit!" he screamed, fumbling for his rifle on its strap.

I empted both barrels. *Blam! Blam!* The first blast tore through his gut, removing his defining feature. The second tore his face apart, splitting his skull and opening the side of his face into one giant eye. He fell to his knees, and then to his side. I smiled and reloaded my shotgun. Then I took off toward the valley.

So, okay, we'd all been calling it a "valley," but don't picture this giant incline or anything. It was a gradual, sloping hill. Maybe ten feet. Just barely deep enough to conceal something like a school bus.

As I approached it, I saw others running too. They were all friendly. The remaining bearded man was emerging from a line of trees. Puckett and Vanessa and Sam were making their way toward the valley too, but I was closest.

Hurdling the dead body of an old woman who had been shot through the neck, I reached the lip of the valley and looked down into it. And indeed, I did see a bright yellow school bus and an assemblage of weary-looking people. I also saw a police-style Glock pointed right at me.

"Wait!" I rasped, throwing up my hands.

I was too late, and the terrified man holding the weapon began firing.

I fell backward, taking one to the arm and another to the shoulder. I decided to stay on the ground.

"Pete!" cried Vanessa.

"Stop shooting!" I heard Puckett shouting. "Stop shooting! Goddamn it ... We're from the college! We killed the sentries! We're friendly!"

I decided to get up, just to show Vanessa I was all right.

"Don't shoot!" I called raspily, echoing Puckett. "We're here to get you out."

A few tentative heads poked up furtively from the lip of the valley, like wary groundhogs.

"Omigod!" one of the heads cried. "Vanessa!"

Weapons lowered on both sides. A woman emerged fully from the valley. It was Kate, Vanessa's sister. They reached one another and embraced.

"We thought you were dead," Kate cried.

"Everyone else *is* dead," Vanessa told her sister. "Peter and I were the only ones who made it out."

"Peter?" Kate said.

Vanessa pointed at me.

Kate looked me over, and slowly put her hand to her mouth.

"Is he ... ?" Kate began.

"Yes," Vanessa responded. "But he's friendly. It's complicated."

I gave a tentative wave, and a bullet fell out of my elbow.

"Are the girls okay?" asked Vanessa.

Kate nodded.

"They're on the bus," Kate said. "They're fine." The women embraced again.

"No time for love, Dr. Jones," quipped Puckett. "We've got to get going, people."

"Yeah," I said. "Everybody needs to get up the hill. Now. Just run. Forget about your stuff. The other gangsters could come back any minute now."

The call was repeated throughout the valley camp of about twenty people, and they too began to move. The exhaustion and terror on their faces was sad to see. These folks looked like they'd been up for days, and terrified for every instant of it. I smiled when Vanessa and Kate's girls emerged from the bus. They had lost, tear-filled eyes, but they looked pleased to finally be freed. Vanessa's daughters ran to embrace her.

"No time—no time!" reiterated Puckett. "Head for the hill!"

On exhausted legs and empty stomachs, the group of twenty or so began running for the base of the hill that was Kenton College. I waited until the last one had left the little valley, then took up a position as the rear guard. As I lumbered forward, I searched the hill ahead of me for any sign of life or movement (or gunfire), but saw nothing. I also heard nothing. All the guns and ATV engines had fallen silent. I hoped, desperately, that this boded well and not ill.

I could think only of the task at hand. Get these people into the cover of the trees, then get them up the hill and into the college proper. Then defend the hill for a couple of hours, and bingo— we're outta here. With the ranks of the good guys swelled to double their number, I reasoned that this should be an eminently accomplishable task. For all of their exhaustion, most of the bus group looked like they knew how to use a weapon.

The front of the group reached the tree line and began working its way in. I breathed an unnecessary sigh of relief. The gang would have no way of knowing that the army was on its way. Perhaps they would retreat for a time, and there would be no additional fighting.

No sooner did I have this thought—this inkling that a peaceful denouement might be close—than a new crackle of gunfire erupted from the hill.

I turned toward it, and heard a scream, and people began spilling back *out* of the tree line. I was confused, but not for long.

A great group—a posse of angry-looking men—emerged from the trees. It appeared to be the entirety of the criminal gang, and with them marched the disarmed Kenton defenders. I recognized Bowles, the doctor, and Starks, the guard, among them. They had been taken prisoner.

"Drop your weapons," commanded a sonorous voice from among the gangsters. It was a voice I'd heard somewhere before . . .

"Drop your weapons, or we start shooting!" the voice called again. "This is over. You can accept that fact, or you can die. Right now. It's your choice."

"Holy shit!" I heard Puckett cry. "Bleckner? Is that *you*? *You're* with *them*?"

I tried to follow Puckett's gaze from my position at the rear. The music professor appeared to be addressing a heavy man with severe eyebrows and white hair. He was older, perhaps sixty-five, and looked out of place among the others. Was this the same man I had met on the day Sam had driven me to Vanessa's house? The outline looked right, yet here he was, almost impossibly out of place. The rest of the gang members looked like—well, gang members. They had a criminal leer in their eyes, unkempt hair, and beards. A couple had face tattoos. At least one swastika was on display.

Bleckner looked more like a pregnant woman *pretending* to be a gang member, with his great belly and soft, womanly hands. His skin was pasty, well preserved from a lifetime of careful sunscreening. His nails, even from this distance, looked manicured (or at least, not bitten). And yet, like some of those around him, he wore a crudely fashioned headband and greasepaint under his eyes like a football player. A black leather vest had been placed over his white collared shirt, now grievously pit-stained. He might have been an improvised pirate at the office Halloween party, except the shotgun in his hand was very real, as was the maniacal glare in his eye as he leveled the weapon at Vanessa's terrified children.

The girls froze where they were, and the fat pirate approached.

"All of you: Set down your guns or you die," Bleckner cried. His double chin wobbled as he gripped Vanessa's daughter Sarah by the shoulder and put his shotgun barrel into her ear. That was all I needed. I dropped several pounds of metal to the ground as quickly as I could. My compatriots did as well. We raised our hands like a row of tellers in a bank stickup. In moments, we had gone from being steps away from freedom to cowering in front of an armed gang. (Now I felt bad for having even provided a brief glimmer of hope for these people, who had been better off in their valley. But this feeling only lasted for a moment. The new terror of what was happening was overwhelming, and there was no time to reflect.)

Only one of us did not seem terrified. Although he had tossed his weapons down like the rest of us, Puckett, the music professor, still appeared more angry than frightened.

"I don't fucking believe this, Bleckner," Puckett roared, addressing the man with no fear. "You said you went to Toledo!"

Bleckner smiled back evilly, with obvious relish. The gangsters began to collect our guns.

With my hands still raised high, I walked over to Puckett.

"Who is this guy?" I asked. "I met him, but I didn't really *meet* him. Sam said he was my boss."

"He's the Kenton College provost," replied Puckett. "I always thought he was a real dickhead, but Christ, I never thought he was capable of something like *this*."

Bleckner appeared to be taking stock of our defenseless group with evident glee.

"This place was going to be yours, one way or another, eh?!" Puckett said to him, baiting the man. (This Puckett was brave—or suicidal.) Bleckner strode over to Puckett. Then the fat provost saw me, and his jaw dropped.

"Lord!" Bleckner cried, genuinely stunned. "Pete Mellor? Is that *you*?"

I stepped forward and allowed him to examine me. The startled provost looked me up and down like I was a magic trick and he was trying to guess how I was done.

"You look like you have become a zombie, Peter," he said matter-of-factly.

I nodded.

"And yet you can understand me?"

I nodded again.

He met my eyes, and the smile returned to his face. He began laughing through his teeth. It was alarming—a deep, evil, and profoundly insane laugh. A laugh that told you to look out, because this person was capable of doing anything to anyone if it so pleased him—PhD or no.

"Well, hell yeah!" Bleckner cried, moving his hand away from Vanessa's daughter to slap me on the shoulder like an old friend. Puckett backed away from us, disgusted.

"Just when I thought this day couldn't get any better!" Bleckner said. "A tame zombie! Hot damn! Now tell me, can you talk, Peter?"

"Of course I can talk," I told him. "Just not loud."

Though I would have declared it a physical impossibility, his smile widened even further. "Wonderful!" the gleeful provost cried. "Pete, you were always one of my favorites! You know that, right?

But what happened to you? You weren't like this the last time I saw you."

"Actually, I was," I told him. "I died in a car accident. I just . . . hadn't realized it yet."

"Astounding!" quipped the provost. "Wonderful! I love it!"

"Uh, yeah," I said. "Say, how about you point that gun at me, and not at that little girl? Point it right at my head, if you want. That's a kill shot for a zombie."

"Oh, Pete," Bleckner said, declining to reposition the gun in any way. "You were always so *serious*. Don't you see that it's not *that* kind of a world anymore?"

I shook my head no. It was true. I didn't see that at all.

"This wonderful *thing* has come along," Bleckner said. He leaned in to me. For a moment, I thought he might actually kiss me—right on my moldering zombie lips.

"*You* have come along," said Bleckner, with what seemed to be heartfelt appreciation. "You wonderful, magical, undead creatures came along, and you wiped it all away. All the pretense. All the bullshit. All of the egos. All of it's gone! Because of you! You purified this place—*this world!* You created a world that made sense again."

"What 'makes sense' about putting a gun in a little girl's ear?" I asked him rhetorically.

"Yeah," Puckett agreed from next to me.

Bleckner's smile adjusted itself. (The expression was tireless, as if induced by a drug.) His face now seemed to say "Aha! But I have found the solution!," like a detective hitting upon an important clue.

"I take it that your memory isn't what it once was," said Bleckner. "Is that right? Have I guessed it? You cannot remember everything from life?"

"I remember enough to know you don't shoot children," I told him. "But sure, I've forgotten some stuff."

"I *knew* it," Bleckner cried. "For if you *had* your memory, you would recall the many evenings we spent together, you and me. The faculty parties where the mulled wine had loosened your tongue—along with the flask of scotch you always carried in your jacket pocket. 'Flasking it,' you used to say. Ha! You offered it to me on more than one occasion when we were out of sight of the college president and his buffoons . . . Like Puckett here.

"I take it, Peter, that your zombified brain has let these memories fade?"

"I guess so," I said, feeling no sympathy for this man, even if we had once shared liquor. He looked like a joke—an evil joke—and he was holding a gun to a child.

"I'm sure we had a few drinks together," I told him. "But from what I've heard, I probably had a few drinks with a lot of people."

"It was more than that," he said. "We saw eye to eye on a lot of things. On the *important* things."

"Why don't you let the little girl go?" I asked him again.

Bleckner shook his head to indicate my error, but with an avuncular smile. His expression said that I was a generally bright child who had, nevertheless, just suggested that two plus two was five.

"No, I've got a better idea," he said. "Why don't the three of us take a walk together, eh? You, me, and the girl."

He turned to the rest of his gang. Some of them were standing stationary, pointing their guns at their new prisoners. Others were milling about, or were still picking up the weapons and equipment that had been dropped.

"All right," Bleckner said to his new colleagues. "Get these people up the hill. Put them in Gunther Hall, in the old dance building. I'll be with you shortly. And listen! No fun begins until I get there—got it?"

I cringed as I imagined what "fun" might encompass in this situation.

The gangsters turned their guns toward the prisoners and they all began a slow, deliberate march up the hill.

"Sarah—" began Vanessa.

"She'll be fine," I said in a hoarse shout. "Don't worry."

A wiry, mustachioed gang member pushed Vanessa in the back with a rifle butt and got her moving. As she began her reluctant uphill trudge, she repeatedly turned toward the three of us: Sarah, Bleckner, and myself.

I had once saved a young member of Vanessa's family from a rapist on an ATV. I was determined, now, to prove myself a protector a second time.

"I'll watch out for her," I shouted up to Vanessa as she climbed the hill with the others. "I'll keep her safe!"

"Good," Bleckner said from next to me in a quiet voice. "I'm counting on that."

People like nice landscaping. Colleges know that, and behave accordingly. It helps with the final sale when visiting high school seniors can imagine themselves striding to class across newly mown lawns, attending outdoor study sessions in hillside gardens, and generally frolicking among topiary.

It was clear that Kenton College had taken great pains (and expense) to cultivate and maintain the grassy areas on the side of the hill where

Bleckner marched us. There were fancy shrubs and hedges and even a couple of statues. The leaves from all the nearby trees had been collected and removed at the end of the fall. The lawns, where they abutted a roadway or a path, had been nicely edged. The paths themselves had been replenished yearly with fresh gravel, and even a boulder that was spray-painted with the insignia of a fraternity had been encircled respectfully with cedar chips.

But even a few weeks of unsupervised growth could leave things looking amiss, and it had been *months* since the college gardeners had reported for work. The lawns beneath our feet were long overdue for their first spring cutting. The topiary bushes were shaggy and in need of a trim. Twigs and trash had blown across the fields and lingered there. This subtle degree of disrepair added to the feeling of wrongness or brokenness at the college. Bleckner looked it over and seemed to derive deep consolation from the disorder.

Mostly, I just looked at Sarah and tried to think of a way to get her away from the man with the gun. Vanessa's daughter seemed to be holding up, but anybody would be terrified in that situation. (Maybe, I reasoned, she's just too hungry and tired to care.)

"What do you think, Mellor?" Bleckner said as he strode, the little girl still held firmly at the end of his arm. "It's all ours, eh?"

"Okay, stop," I told him, rather like an adolescent. "Just stop. What makes you think you and I are on the same team? I still remember a few things about my life at this college. You're familiar, but I damn sure don't remember being friends with you."

"We weren't fast friends, maybe, but we agreed on so much!" Bleckner insisted. "The oppressiveness of the college culture. The censorship of our lectures. The increasingly thick veil of political correctness."

"Political correctness?" I returned. "*That's* what this is about? They want you to say 'Native American' instead of 'Indian,' so it follows that you should kill little girls?"

"Don't you see . . . it's just one more *denial of reality!*" Bleckner boomed, and then his face fell. "It makes me so sad, what happened to this place. Colleges and universities used to be about the search for truth. I'm old enough that I can remember those good old days, back when *I* was an undergraduate. Search for truth. That was the gig, since they founded Oxford in the 1100s, and probably earlier than that. Search for truth. But then these damn hippies came along—they don't wear flowers and beads and those little dresses that look like welder's smocks anymore, but they're certainly hippies—and they decided that the project of a college is not the search for truth. It's the search for *nice.*"

I regarded him absently, thinking it would be "nice" if he pointed the gun away from Sarah.

"The hippies went *poof!* And suddenly, it wasn't about the real world anymore. And you, as a professor of philosophy—where things are either true or not true—were quick to agree with me on this point, whether you remember now or not. Instead of searching for what was true in the world, our job became painting a picture of a world that was 'nice' for all of these nice tuition-paying students. Our task was to create a phony world for them, where facts that aren't 'nice' were swept under the rug, whether or not they were facts!"

"Sounds terrible," I said, trying to comport sarcasm through a zombie's breathy rasp.

"You jest, but in a few short years this college became Bizarro World," said Bleckner. "Giving dumb students Fs wasn't 'nice,' so you had grade inflation, and suddenly everybody who came to class had to get at least a C. Whites and Asians were 90 percent of the Kenton College student population, but only 75 percent of the national population—so of course we relaxed our standards for certain minority applicants and created Affirmative Action policies, because the idea that some groups got better SAT scores than others wasn't 'nice.' We decided we had to 'correct reality' to fix this lack of niceness.

"When I got the chance to become provost, I thought getting out of the classroom and into administration would save what sanity I had left. But it only got worse! The absurdities compounded! The college added a women's studies department, as though it were math or music. The fact that women weren't studied as much as men—because they *hadn't done as much as men*—wasn't 'nice,' so I had to approve this new department to correct the truth. And shamefully, I did! And with their appetites thus whetted, it couldn't stop there, could it? Men talked more than women—or apparently they did; it was news to me—so I allowed a female professor to forbid men from talking in her classes. Even the hard sciences were smothered by 'nice.' Forget studying human biology. So what if it could lead to cures for sickle cell or Tay-Sachs? Studying ways that human races were biologically different from one another wasn't 'nice,' so it was *de facto* forbidden!"

"Killing people isn't nice either," I told him.

"Which is why I'm doing it," Bleckner returned. "Don't you see? It's funny . . . You and I always used to say how we wished we could get rid of these people. Wash them and all their hippie bullshit away. And now it's happened! Now the 'nice' police are gone! And I'd love to take all the credit, but in truth, it's *yours*. You walking dead have made it happen. In a world of zombies, there is no time for 'nice' and no room for postmodern tyrants. The forbidden ideas are now ... bidden! I can do what I want, and say what I want, even if it isn't 'nice'."

"So that's why you fell in with a gang of killers?" I asked aggressively.

"'Fell in with' is hardly sufficient, Peter," Bleckner returned stuffily. "Clearly, I am their leader."

"Fine," I said. "You became their leader, then. Why? Because these bikers and ex-cons are somehow. . . *authentic*?"

"Exactly!" Bleckner boomed.

"Look, maybe I once agreed with you on *some* things," I told him. "Maybe I wanted to give stupid kids Fs and just say black instead of African-American, but I'm pretty sure I didn't want to kill people."

"The dried blood down your gullet says otherwise," chided Bleckner. For the first time, Sarah looked up at me with the detached expression of terror she had previously reserved only for Bleckner.

I hated him even more.

"Look, I'm not perfect," I said, as much to Sarah as to her captor. "Yeah, I ate some people. But most of them were bad and deserved it. One of them was trying to rape this little girl's cousin. Some weren't bad, though, and fine, I admit that. I shouldn't have eaten good people who were just trying to survive, like everyone else. I'm sorry I did it."

"Ahh!" seized Bleckner, "that's where you're wrong. Don't you see? It's in your nature to eat people—just as it's in the nature of my gang to take what we want, to kill our enemies, and to fuck good-looking women—whether or not they're receptive to the idea. These are things I've always wanted to do, but I've never before been allowed to acknowledge I even had these inclinations, much less carry them out. Now, not only can I say it, I can do it!"

I frowned.

"I see you're not convinced," said Bleckner, changing his tone slightly. "I'll make my intentions plain. I like the idea of a walking, talking—well, I suppose all zombies walk—then, a talking, thinking, *aware* zombie in my gang. And if it used to see eye to eye with me in life, then so much the better! Now, I understand that your girlfriend and your friend Sam are dear to you. We can arrange it so they are not hurt."

"Fuck Sam," I said (without thinking). "I think he's the one who killed me."

Bleckner's characteristic smile returned. I instantly regretted my candor, though I didn't know how he would use the information.

"Vanessa, then," he said. "I think I met her at a couple of faculty functions, actually. Just before all this started happening. Charming woman."

"Her sister and their daughters, too," I said. "Any deal has to involve them as well."

"Of course, my friend," Bleckner said, without taking his hand off of the little girl. "Whether or not you believe me, this is the best way things could have turned out for them. It was a hopeless fight against us. Maybe you're wondering what allowed us to finally overpower your friends at the top of the hill? Here, take a look."

He opened his ill-fitting vest. Inside were secreted a number of powerful-looking hand grenades.

I had the urge to reach over and pull the pin from one. To kill him, even if it meant exploding myself in the process. That would show him.

But then, Sarah was here.

I suddenly realized that this was why he had brought her along on our walk. A zombie's attachment to physical existence might be questionable; dying might be nothing to something that was already dead. But a zombie who had taken great pains to rescue little girls was another matter entirely.

I looked at the grenades and nodded.

"Just delivered from the National Guard armory in Danville," he said. "If you hadn't shown up and killed my sentries, we would have eventually pitched these little guys down on that school bus and made short work of everybody. They'd have been exploded before they knew what was happening. These little things are quite remarkable."

Bleckner prattled on, chummily. I began wondering what was going to happen when the military helicopters showed up—*if* they showed up—and if we still had some sort of a chance. I reasoned that the gang would be alarmed when the U.S. Army unexpectedly descended from the sky at the top of the hill. (The foliage on the Kenton College hill was rather like a monk's tonsure, with the top bare to the sun.) An alarmed gang could do many things. It could run away, true. But it could also start the indiscriminate killing of hostages.

It was a difficult situation. The fact that the gang *did not know* that the military was coming—unless someone in the captured group had already blabbed—was the one thing in our favor. The one ace still up our sleeve. (Though the more I thought about it, the less sure I was that it was an ace. Maybe it wasn't even a face card.)

"They're remarkable," Bleckner said, concluding a lecture on the benefits of fragmentation grenades. "All it took was a couple of gentle lobs up the hill ahead of us, and all your Kenton College friends came out to surrender."

I knew I had to act fast.

"To return to the matter at hand: It seems like *you* want something, and *I* want something," I said.

"Yes, that sounds right," said Bleckner, obviously pleased that I was willing to get down to brass tacks.

"You want me to join up with you, correct?" I said. "You want a zombie in your gang."

"Yes," said Bleckner. "But it's more than that, Peter. I believe that you'll eventually come to see eye to eye with me again. Maybe your memory will come back one day, and you'll recall the way we used to agree on what kind of place the world of Kenton College had become, and what we'd like to do about it. I think you'll be pleased when you realize that now we actually can *do* those things."

"Okay," I said. "I want something, too, though."

Bleckner sighed. "I know what you're going to say," he told me. "You're going to ask me to release Vanessa and her girls here."

When he said "girls here," he patted Sarah's head gently. It turned my stomach, and a dull anger inside of me, which had been growing since I'd met Bleckner, now threatened to boil over.

I did my best to keep cool.

"No," I told him. "That's not what I want at all."

"Oh?" he said.

"I want to kill Sam," I told him. "I want *revenge*."

It was clear this pleased Bleckner greatly.

"That sounds like something I can arrange," he said brightly. "Yes, indeed, it does."

He extended his hand.

"Have we a bargain then?" he asked.

Nobody had offered to shake my hand since I had become a zombie. I had to admit that there was a seduction to it. Though I was operating, now, under false pretenses, it felt right and real to shake on an agreement with somebody. It was like being invited back to the world of men.

Since giving in to my brain-eating desires, I had started thinking of humans as less than zombies. As food. After being captured by Vanessa's group, I'd started feeling less than human. They had treated me like an animal and tied me to a tree. Now, Bleckner's chubby, womanly hand beckoned to pull me out of the lower echelons of existence and back into the world of men—the world of contracts, and brotherhood, and equality.

It was seductive, but I was not seduced.

I made my conditions clear to Bleckner. Both of them.

I wanted it public, and I wanted it now.

As the aggrieved party, I desired something more than physical revenge. More than "a life for a life." I wanted to humiliate Sam, I told Bleckner. I wanted to establish myself as dominant in front of the others. I wanted to show everybody what happened when you messed with Peter Mellor—that even when you killed me, I would come back for you.

"Now you've come around," Bleckner said when he heard this, slapping me jovially on the back. "You see the importance of establishing yourself as a powerful force before the rest of the pack. That's the spirit! You know, it's funny—the zombies seem to have died down recently, but gosh, I hope that when I die, I'll come back as a zombie just like you, Pete!"

Bleckner lost some of his good humor, however, when I continued to insist that my justice must be delivered instantly. Within the hour.

"Of course you desire swift reciprocity, but we still need to secure the rest of the college," Bleckner returned. "There could still be a few holdouts in some of the buildings. We can't be too careful. And what if another group should arrive and attempt to take the college before we've had the chance to fortify our position? No, let's wait until nightfall. Hell, we can even build a pit, get some torches—it'll be appropriately dramatic to your purposes, I think."

"No deal," I said. "It's got to be now. Right now."

Bleckner cocked his head, as if suspecting something. I decided my task was to convince him of my bloodlust.

"Listen," I said, "I want to kill that motherfucker right now. I want to eat his brains in front of everybody."

"I know you do," began Bleckner. "You said that."

"Then prove it," I said. "You want me on your team? Fine. But you're going to have to show me that you're not bullshitting."

"I'm offering you a life of killing and eating brains and doing whatever you want, for as long as we can hold out here," Bleckner said.

"Yeah," I told him, "with strings attached. I already had that life when I was on my own."

Bleckner sighed.

"It really can't wait?" he asked in distress.

I knew that I had won, and indicated that no, it could not.

"Very well," said Bleckner. "We'll get her going, then. There's a little rock garden outside of Gunther Hall, in case you don't remember. It should be perfect for the primal, *authentic* sort of justice you're seeking."

"Then let's stop wasting time, and fucking get there," I told him. Bleckner smiled, and we were away.

We walked, silently, up the side of the Kenton College hill to Gunther Hall—a small, squarish building, hewn long ago from rough-looking stone, where the school's modest dance department met to pirouette and waltz (and possibly Electric Slide; I didn't remember). The fifty or so hostages had been rounded up into the building and the doors locked with chains. As we approached, I saw a couple of nervous faces peering out from one of the tiny glass windows. One was Vanessa's, and it became visibly relieved when Sarah came into view. (Vanessa's eyes also lit upon me, but only for an instant.)

Several of the thugs milled about. Like those they had captured, they looked exhausted and spent. I might have looked piteously on them, had I not known better.

Vanessa's take from the building window must have been confusing at best, as Bleckner began to bark orders, and the thugs hopped up and began tipping stone statues and moving benches to create a kind of fighting pit.

"I want everybody to see this," I told Bleckner.

"I'm not letting the people we captured out of Gunther Hall, if that's what you're getting at," he responded. "They killed many of us. I expect my men will want to exact their own revenge when yours is complete."

"The hostages can watch through the tiny windows there," I said, as if I didn't care. "But this is about establishing me as a member of your gang. I want all the members present. Do you have a name, incidentally? A name for the gang?"

"No, we ..." Bleckner began. "That is to say, I hadn't thought of it."

"You should really consider it," I told him. "Breeds terror among the populace. Gets your name out there with other gangs. Might help with recruiting."

"I'll think upon it," Bleckner said seriously.

"But this fight," I continued, "is about establishing me as a member of your gang. I want your men to see what I'm capable of. No, that's a lie. Really, I want them to see what I do to somebody who fucks with me."

"Ahh," said Bleckner. "It's to be an initiation and a warning, all in one. Delightful! Yes, of course! I see your aim."

"Good," I said.

"Though it would be a good deal more dramatic at night," Bleckner tried, clearly still wishing to postpone the proceedings. "I imagine torches and so forth would really create a spectacle—create something that will stick in the men's memories for a long time."

"What I want sticking in their memories is that justice from me comes swift and deadly," I said with all the bile I could muster. "I want them to know that if anybody fucks with me, then *they get eaten alive.*"

"I suppose that's something that might also stick," granted the provost.

The fighting pit was soon completed, and the gang gathered around. Some of them had evidently found a vending machine and smashed it open. The gangsters were circulating sodas and chips among themselves, and soon exhibited the restored spirits of a junk-food high.

The hostages inside the dance building began crowding around the two small windows that faced the improvised pit. Their nervous expressions betrayed a true terror of whatever was being prepared. They also looked askance at me, for it was clear from our body language that something had transpired between myself and the leader of the gang. We were definitely looking chummy. Though Bleckner still held one of Vanessa's daughters at gunpoint, his weapon never once pointed in my direction.

With the men relaxing and eating on the ground around us, Bleckner raised his hand and the group fell silent.

Bleckner addressed the men sternly, his tone harsh and commanding, his voice deep and powerful. I realized in a trice that *this* was what had allowed a chubby, weak college administrator not only to make himself accepted by a collection of felons and killers, but also, to establish himself as their leader. These men had been used to verbal commands since their earliest days, from school principals, policemen, and prison guards. They knew a voice of authority when they heard one. And yet, *this* voice was not berating them, pointing out their faults and transgressions, or laying out the conditions of their parole. This voice of authority accepted them for who and what they were, and for the things they liked to do. (It even gave them advice on how to do it collectively, to create better outcomes.)

"Gentlemen," Bleckner said, leaning against a gnarled ironwood tree. "This man next to me is Peter Mellor. I knew him in life, and now he is a zombie. Yes, question?"

One of the gang members had extended a Cheeto-stained hand.

"If he's a zombie, how come he can talk and stuff?" the man asked.

"You want to field that, Peter?" Bleckner said, stepping side.

"I just can," I told them.

"He just can," said Bleckner. "There you have it! Yes ... a follow-up question?"

"He's not going to try to eat *us*, is he?" the gang member asked.

I shook my head.

"There, that's a clear no," said Bleckner. "You're safe, Fred. Now, to continue, Peter was killed by a man inside that building. Though he's been on the wrong side lately, I've asked Peter to join us, and he has accepted. His condition is simple: He has asked to kill the man who killed him. What say you all?"

Bleckner held out for a rousing cheer, as from a crew in a pirate movie. There was only a confused silence. (I guessed this was not the first time that Bleckner's wax toward the dramatic and formal had made his meaning quite lost on these men.)

"Should we let Peter kill the guy who killed him?" Bleckner tried again.

"A'ight den," offered one gang member.

"Yeah," said the man with the Cheeto-stained hands. (There were several men with Cheeto-stained hands, but this was the one who had spoken before.)

"Yeah, totally," said another.

"And shall this be his initiation into our band?" Bleckner said, resuming his theatricality. (I have no idea why he tried this again. Did he need, in his mind, to be some kind of pirate king?)

There were only quiet nods of agreement.

"Very good, then," said Bleckner. "We'll bring forth the condemned and ... and ... How did you want to do this exactly, Peter? Just shoot him, I suppose?"

"Not at all," I said. "He turned me into a zombie, so I want to kill him like a zombie. More poetic that way."

"You propose hand-to-hand combat?" Bleckner asked.

"I was thinking more tooth-to-brain, but yeah," I said. "I don't need a weapon."

"Fair enough," said Bleckner, with an evil smile. "We shall now bring out the condemned. Or, I guess ... I guess I shall, because nobody else is going to recognize him."

Bleckner stepped toward Gunther Hall, and I followed after him.

"Wait one second," I said, putting my hand on Bleckner's beflabbed shoulder and turning him. "I have something I want to ask you."

He looked into my face like a stern old priest.

"The little girl," I continued, pointing to Sarah. "No need to have her out here, is there? She's seen so much already. I don't

know what your plans are for her, but please, you've got to spare
her from seeing this."

Bleckner's good humor fell away.

"The girl is insurance," Bleckner said. "Don't take me for a fool.
I like to think that I can trust you, Peter, but with your memory
loss—it's like we've only known each other for a few minutes,
really. I'm concerned that you seem to have forgotten entirely some
of the most crucial points on which you and I used to connect."

"Please," I tried. "I still connect with you."

"No," said Bleckner. "And in the future, don't question me in
front of the men." He turned and began to march toward Gunther
Hall, pushing the girl with him. (From their bored looks, I doubted
the men cared very much about who said what to Bleckner.)

"I'm sorry, but I have to insist," I said, catching up with him at
the door. I leaned in so we could speak confidentially.

"Who are *you* to insist?" he returned coldly.

"Look," I told him firmly. "You want a zombie in your gang?
That's fine. It doesn't have to be me. You can't threaten me, see? I
can't really feel pain, and I'm already dead. Just put the girl back
inside so she doesn't have to see me eat Sam's brain. What am I
gonna do? I'm unarmed, and you all have guns. I can't run either—
it's not physically possible for me."

"We saw you sort of jogging a little," Bleckner said.

"Oh, come fucking on," I told him. "That wasn't exactly a
sprint. You're telling me you're afraid I'm going to *get away?* I'm
surrounded by thirty men with guns. What are you afraid of?"

I stared Bleckner down as hard as I could.

"Clearly, you pose no threat to us," he said. "As you say."

"Well, then," I said, "unless you need to feel like a big man by
pulling my girlfriend's kid around, then let her go back inside the
building while I kill Sam."

"Fine," said Bleckner, and pushed the girl away. He stepped back
and stared at me hard. I think he was waiting to see if I was going
to do something—if this was a trick. Was I going to scream at the
girl to run, like in an action movie or something?

But I just stood there. So did the girl. She looked very sad.

"Fine," Bleckner said again. "Let's do this."

We walked over to the door, which the gang members had
crudely locked by jamming a wrench in the door and further tying
it with chains. It took a couple of minutes to "unlock."

The chain fell to the floor of the stone walkway with a loud
clatter, and Bleckner threw the door open wide. On the expen-
sively matted floor where liberal arts students once danced, a grim

compendium of refugees huddled—waiting to be killed, or worse. I think Bleckner relished the terror in their waiting faces.

As Bleckner watched, I took Sarah by the hand and pulled her to the doorway of Gunther Hall. Then I bent and whispered in her ear, then whacked her hard on the backside, as if to say "Get in there!" Sarah needed no further prompting. She ran straight past everyone and into her mother's arms. Vanessa, who was already holding her other daughter, embraced Sarah with a little cry like a wounded bird.

"We've come for you, Sam," Bleckner pronounced, spotting his target seated in a corner. Sam looked up at Bleckner, and then over at me. I put my hand on Bleckner's shoulder and nodded.

"That's him, all right," I said.

"Peter, don't do this," Vanessa cried. "This isn't the way to deal with Sam."

I did not respond.

Sam stood.

"Let's go," I told him.

Sam didn't look me in the face, but walked past me and exited the building.

"Why would you do this?" Vanessa shouted. "What does this accomplish, Peter?"

I turned away from her, and we closed the door on the hostages. Bleckner reattached the chain.

Sam marched dutifully toward the circle of men who waited, eyes straight ahead. I joined him presently.

"Peter, this is the man who killed you?" Bleckner announced more than asked.

"Yes," I told him, taking a position in the circle opposite Sam.

Bleckner stepped between us, like a referee. I looked at the sky, and wondered how much time was left. The sun seemed low. Too low. The western sky was already tinged with red. How long did I have until it qualified as "sunset"?

"Now," said Bleckner, as if settling in to deliver a long sermon. "These two men will settle things the way nature intended. The way real men do, in the *real* world."

Bleckner might have said more, but I don't remember. I wasn't listening. I was looking at Sam.

He looked horrible, like … I guess, like what he was—a condemned man. For a naturally chubby person, Sam's face had grown more gaunt than I would have thought possible. I looked hard at him, this man who had killed me. He wasn't much of a foe. He certainly didn't look like a killer. He looked sad and sallow.

There was no fear in his eyes, as I'd imagined there would be in a man waiting to be killed. Instead, there was only a grim emptiness. When Sam looked at me, he looked right through me, his shoulders slumped forward like a sullen teenager trying not to be noticed. He stared at the ground and at his feet.

And yet . . .

I could have sworn that a wry grin danced at the edges of his lips, fighting to become a full-fledged smile. I wondered what was playing in his mind. Was it the beginnings of the insane grin of a man unable to comprehend the implications of his own impending death? It sure didn't look like that. But neither was it the grin of a man with a secret that can save him. I was fairly sure there was no machine gun secreted in his pant leg.

No, it was closer to the grin of a man who has found the most profound irony in his life's last situation. It said that this was funny, because the opposite thing had been supposed to happen. Or that this had been supposed to happen, *but not in this way*. It said this was "The Cop and the Anthem." He had expected something *like* this, but *not* this, and not now . . .

Sam smiled throughout Bleckner's rantings. I found myself increasingly curious as to the source of his good humor.

I was roused from these wonderings by Bleckner's flabby hand upon my shoulder.

"All right, then," he said. "Peter, do you have anything to say before the men watch you exact justice?"

I looked up. The men, as Bleckner called them, looked only mildly interested in any of it. Murder and killing and zombies were nothing new to them. Whatever was about to transpire would be only one more in a long line of gory deaths they had seen in the past few months. Probably, Bleckner's idea to wrap a mundane, everyday murder in so much ceremony felt excessively formal to them—like carefully presenting a McDonald's hamburger on a sterling silver tray.

I stared hard at Sam—this crumpled, sad, yet furtively smiling man. And it was difficult, in that moment, not to smile a little bit myself.

Bleckner's preamble to our combat had been full of rhetoric, declaiming that far from being animalistic or base, violence was natural and authentic—especially violence between humans. All the great societies had known this, Bleckner declared, spouting off names of Greeks and Romans that I had long since forgotten (if I'd ever known them). Yet somehow, Bleckner seemed anxious about how to commence the proceedings.

"Do I just say 'go' or something?" he asked, unsure of himself. "Or maybe 'fight' would be good? What does that boxing announcer always say? 'Let's get it on!' That's it."

"Any of those, really," I told him.

"Ahh," he said, relieved in general, but a little annoyed that I hadn't picked one in particular. Bleckner stepped back from me and addressed the assembled gangsters.

"Well, then," he said. "Let's . . . get it on!"

Not great, but it would do.

A few of the gangsters cheered. One hooted. One, standing near Sam, said: "Yew gonna git eaten, boy. By a *damn zombie!* How you like them apples?"

Before I advanced on my opponent, I chanced a quick glance at the windows of Gunther Hall that faced the fighting pit. ("Fighting circle" was actually more like it. There was no indentation in the earth.) Much to my relief, the windows were entirely empty. Not a single face peered out to see what was about to transpire.

My smile became even harder to contain.

Then I was upon him.

Sam assumed no fighting stance, and at first, I feared this meant he might simply go limp and allow me to kill him as quickly as possible, which was not in my plans. But when I gripped him around the shoulders and attempted to throw him down, he began to fight back. He punched me in the face twice—clearly hurting his hand—then gripped me on each shoulder like a grappler.

I gripped Sam by his own shoulders and fought against him— albeit halfheartedly—by tugging and jostling. He wasn't strong— hunger and stress had taken their toll—but he was still more powerful than he looked. I pushed him around a little, eventually maneuvering him over to the edge of the fighting pit, where a marble Doric column had been overturned to serve as a boundary marker.

Sam started kicking my legs. I decided to use this. I let one of the kicks connect, and acted as though Sam had struck home. I fell to one knee and managed to pull Sam down with me. We toppled awkwardly, and then rolled.

Soon, I was on top of Sam. I began raining blows down on his ears and shoulders. Not as hard as I could, but enough that it seemed real. (Clearly, it seemed real to Sam, whose face was a picture of terror as he struggled endlessly against me.)

The men around us became further invested in the match. Some stood up and walked closer. One of them said: "Eat his brain, zombie!"

After landing several more blows, I pulled Sam closer and fell forward on him in an almost-amorous position. I put my mouth to the side of his head as though I was preparing to bite his ear off. Then I began to whisper.

"Hey," I said. His eyes rolled wildly, still consumed by fury and terror.

"Listen," I rasped in his ear, all the while flailing away. "I'm only gonna say this once. I'm gonna stand up and go after the provost. The moment I turn toward him, I want you to jump over that column and lay yourself down flat on the ground."

I pulled myself up off of Sam's ear and looked him straight in the face. He looked bewildered, as if he could not quite believe what was happening. I landed a theatrical blow to the side of his head, not really connecting, but kicking up a lot of dirt and gravel. I gave Sam a wink.

He managed a little nod back at me.

That was all I needed.

I jumped backward off of Sam, in an awkward dismount. Then I stood up fully. I paced back and forth, like a snake weaving as it prepares to strike again. Sam got up too, but only halfway— remaining in a sort of three-point crouch by the Doric column. The men around us were all cheering now. ("Yeah, zombie!" "Finish him!" "Eat that motherfucker!")

Never once looking away from Sam, I allowed my snakelike weave to drift over toward Bleckner. (He was applauding the violence, and saying "Yes! Yes!") Then, abruptly, I turned and faced him, and several things happened at once.

The first thing—which I only half-noted from the corner of my eye—was that Sam threw himself face-first over the fallen Doric column. This did not seem to alarm the gang members around him, as it was obviously not an attempt to escape. (If anything, his ducking behind the column likely appeared an insane, last-ditch attempt to hide from me.) It was clear, as he landed like a sack of potatoes on the other side of the expensive marble, that he wasn't going *anywhere.*

The next thing that happened was that I stepped in close to Bleckner. He smiled at me brightly and stopped applauding, instead, opening his arms to give me an encouraging pat on the back. He opened his mouth (I'm sure to say something like "Good goin', my boy. Very *authentic* of you!"). As he did, I gingerly opened the black vest that covered his white business shirt and snatched three of the grenades that hung inside, pulling out their pins in the same motion. "Whaaa—" was all the astonished Bleckner had time to say.

I turned and lobbed the grenades at the three largest clusters of gangsters, just as I had rehearsed in my mind. It made a triangle, with the fighting pit in the middle.

For an instant, the gangsters looked on, confused. One of them gently prodded a grenade that had landed at his toe. Then he realized what it was and screamed, "Oh, fuck!" I fell to the ground and covered my head with my hands.

"Don't just stand—" Bleckner cried, but he was cut off by three explosions in quick succession. The detonations were very loud. The ground seemed to jump beneath me with each blast. My mouth and nose were instantly clogged with dirt. There was a sound like a rain stick as airborne dirt and gravel fell back to the earth. Then I began to hear the screams.

I stood up cautiously, and found myself in a world gone gray and brown with dust. Men and parts of men were scattered all around, many of them emitting cries of horrible pain. I rubbed my dirt-encrusted eyes hard, trying to clear them. There was an automatic pistol on the ground a few feet from me. I picked it up and began killing gangsters with it.

A few of the men—likely those who had been at the far edges of the fighting pit—were largely unharmed by the blast, and were now fleeing into the forest. I let them go. The vast majority were dead. A few were only wounded or dazed. Of these, I began to make short work, stalking through the dusty camp, putting bullets into brains.

"Sam!" I called as I went about this grim task. "Sam, can you hear me?! Are you all right?"

I shot a staggering, blinded gangster in the back of the head.

"Yeah," a voice called tentatively from the dust. I had been more than a little disoriented by the blast, but as I turned in the direction of the voice, I saw that Sam was huddling on the far side of the overturned column. I shot a gangster through the forehead as he moved toward Sam, dropping him dead at Sam's feet.

"Sam, go open the door and let everyone out of Gunther Hall," I shouted, whirling around on my heels to check for more survivors (and to make sure they did *not* survive). Sam hurried to the door and undid the chains and wrench while I put down two more gang members who had staggered to their feet and found their guns. The dust had finally begun to clear properly, and I got a good look at the dimming blue sky. Sunset was practically here. We were going to make it!

I heard the creak of the door to Gunther Hall swinging wide.

"Peter!" Sam cried.

"Is everybody okay?" I called.

Then I felt something hard and cold pressed against the back of my head.

"Drop that gun," a familiar, sonorous voice cried.

It was Bleckner.

I obeyed.

Bleckner took a step back. I turned slowly to face him. A look of utter disgust and betrayal corrupted his face like a wound. Along with blood. Lots of blood. Bleckner's formerly white business shirt was now an obscene blotter of dirt and dark red splotches.

"Why, Pete?" was all he said.

Sam began to approach us, but Bleckner turned the gun on him and Sam halted in his tracks. The crowd of friendlies still stood by the door to Gunther Hall, and it would be easy for Bleckner to cover them in a single sweep of his weapon.

"Stop right there," Bleckner said.

"Look, it's time to give up," I said to Bleckner. "Your whole gang's dead."

He turned his gun back to me.

"Shut up, you ... zombie," he said, uttering the z-word like a most pernicious racial slur. "We could have had a wonderful, *real* world together. A place for real men. But you just ruined it!"

"Okay, seriously," I told him. "Look around. It's over."

"No, it's not," he said. Then, to my astonishment, he dropped the gun. (I thought perhaps I had misheard him.)

"I'll kill all of you," Bleckner said, his voice growing distant and maniacal. "I'll kill you *all.*"

Bleckner turned again toward Gunther Hall and the assembled friendlies. At first, this action did not alarm me, as Bleckner appeared to be unarmed. Then I saw him reach for his chest, as if scratching his armpit. I guessed what he meant to do a moment later, and took off toward him as quickly as my zombie-stumble would carry me.

By the time Bleckner had reached the crowd—most of whom had braced themselves, as if anticipating a fistfight—he had the grenade out of his vest and was holding it aloft. The pin had already been pulled.

I reached him and jumped on his back.

"Run!" I rasped to the onlookers as Bleckner and I fell forward.

We landed on the ground, atop one another. My first impulse was to try to wrest the grenade from Bleckner and throw it away, but in the fleeting instants that followed, it became clear that there would not be time. For all of his womanly fleshiness, Bleckner's grip on the little metal oval was as strong as any man's.

Instead of trying to free the thing, I used both of my arms to pull Bleckner's outstretched hand inward and toward us. Then I rolled over, and pinned the grenade between our bodies.

Then I waited.

They say that when you think you're going to die, your life flashes before your eyes. Zombies (who are not, strictly speaking, alive) don't seem to experience this. I would have welcomed the distraction a quick review of my life might have provided, but it did not occur. I had nothing to remove my thoughts from the realization that, in a matter of moments, I was going to explode. Yet—and I realize this might be a little hard to believe—my thoughts were not for myself.

As I lay there—holding the thrashing, gnashing provost to my breast—my only concerns were for those around me.

This was a failure. I had failed them. While being blown apart would, yes, probably mean a cessation of all consciousness for me, it would also mean the loss of my friends' only ticket out of Knox County and safe passage to the Green Zone.

I pictured the army helicopters landing on the hill, some sort of official-looking general guy getting out (all medals and epaulettes), and Sam and Vanessa trying in vain to explain to him that the Kernel really *had* been here, and had been exploded a second before the army had shown up.

I pictured Sam presenting the general with my smoking, half-destroyed Cedar Rapids Kernels baseball cap. Sam would smile up at him hopefully, and the stern general would do an about-face, order his troops back onto the helicopters, and they would fly away.

Yes, that was almost certainly what would happen.

But ... (There always seemed to be a "But.") Perhaps I *had* accomplished a few things. It was not "success" by any stretch of the definition, but I *had* helped the friendly humans defeat Bleckner's gang. My Kenton colleagues would once again have control of their hilltop. I hoped that with the two groups merging, they would find themselves stronger than either had been previously. Maybe they would even be strong enough to make a break for the Green Zone together—though that would be another story, one that I would not be around to see.

It is also worth noting that, in this instant of frozen, impending doom, I had no real anger left in my heart for Sam. He had protested his innocence to the last—even going so far as to blame another—but did I believe him? In the end, no. I didn't. I'd decided I'd never know for certain, but he had likely been the one.

The world going to zombie-hell, and his one friend (and possible love interest) was electing to make a final stand with a girlfriend rather than with him? Yeah, I understood it. It was an irrational, murderous, selfish lashing out, but I understood it. And I think I may have even forgiven him.

Anyhow, the grenade exploded, and everything went black.

It was serious blackness. Epic blackness. I saw nothing. I felt nothing. I heard screams, but they were muffled and distant.

There was only numbness.

I assumed I had been killed or was dying. Dying a zombie's death. Those were the only explanations that made sense now. It was so, so very black.

Perhaps I was now only a head. I remembered having read articles about scientists during the French Revolution trying to discern how long a head lived after being guillotined. I thought I remembered the results as having been inconclusive. (But if it was a few seconds for humans, then maybe it was a little longer for zombies.) I resolved to relax, and let the nothingness overtake me.

Instead, a hand overtook me.

Before I understood what was happening, I was extricated from a ball of gore that had once been a college provost. Tiny, strong hands gripped me by the scruff of the neck and pulled me up. A portion of Bleckner's neck fat—separated from the rest of his body by the grenade—had been covering my eyes like a fleshy blindfold, and it slid off and fell away as I was pulled upward.

I looked down and saw the remains of Bleckner's dead body. He had been pulverized. His chest and neck turned into mincemeat. The double chin had been blown away completely, revealing a skeletal jaw and chemically whitened teeth. His eyes were remarkably intact, and looked almost sentient. I nearly would have sworn they looked on as Sam pulled me up from the wreckage.

"Jesus, Pete," was all Sam said as he righted me. "Are you okay?"

"I think so . . . ," I began to say, but paused, unsure.

Sam helped me to my feet and stepped away. I stood awkwardly, and looked down to investigate my own body.

My chest, like Bleckner's, was a mess. My rib cage seemed to have held, but not the skin covering it. The damage got worse the farther up I looked. I reached up to touch my face and neck where I could not see, but there wasn't much to touch. I could run my fingers around the individual tendons in my neck. Scraps of burned flesh fell away. When I reached for my face, I felt muscle and bone, but little skin. I could still manage to speak, but my voice was now little more than a wheeze.

I looked over at Sam. He regarded me wide-eyed, clearly wondering if he should say anything.

"Am I ready for my close-up?" I asked.

That broke the ice, at least, and he smiled.

"Maybe for an anatomy film," he responded. "I can't believe that didn't kill you. But I guess your brain is okay, huh? The grenade just . . . really fucked up your front."

I shrugged.

"I've been a proper zombie all this time," I told him. "Maybe now I finally look like one. Scary and so forth."

The rest of the group approached me warily, including Vanessa and her daughters.

"Hey," I said. "You guys don't need to see this. Not the kids, at least."

As I finished uttering these words, my nose fell off, my own body seeking to emphasize my point.

"Shit—you saved us, Peter," Vanessa said. "That was incredibly brave."

"Yeah," said Sam. "That was really gutsy."

"Probably best not to mention guts right now," I told him. "My rib cage looks like organs trying to escape from a zoo."

Other members of the group stepped forward—some recoiling when they saw my state—and expressed their gratitude.

"You fucking saved us!" shouted Puckett. "Way to kick some ass, Mellor."

"No problem," I told him.

"Say 'thank you,' " Vanessa said to her daughters.

"Thank you," said Sarah, who regarded me cautiously from behind her mother's leg.

"You helped," I told her. "You told everyone to get away from the windows."

"Yeah," she said, averting her gaze from me.

I touched my forehead, but felt only skull.

"Has anybody seen my hat?" I asked. "I don't feel like the Kernel without it."

Everybody looked around.

A moment later, I overheard Kate, Vanessa's sister, talking to one of her daughters.

"Do you want *me* to do it?" she was asking. Apparently, one of her daughters had found the hat but was afraid to bring it over to me.

A tiny voice said, "Yes."

Kate stalked over, holding the hat.

"Here," she said, thrusting the hat into my hands. It was remarkably intact.

"Thank you," I said, placing it atop my skull. "Now I feel like me."

As if signaled by the safe return of my headwear to its rightful place, all at once we began to hear the din of approaching helicopters—a *chop-chop-chop* sound, like a distant factory press.

"Is that . . . ?" Vanessa wondered.

"Got to be," I said.

"Quickly," Sam shouted, "let's all get to the top of the hill!"

Exhausted and bedraggled, our group made one final, hasty ascent of the hill at Kenton College. We passed school buildings riddled with bullets, overturned and pillaged supply sheds, and at least three corpses. There were other, random things: A dead goat. (WTF, right?) A giant, bullet-riddled statue. A toilet—just a freestanding toilet, not connected to anything.

As we climbed the hill, Sam said: "Pete, I have to show you something before we leave. Something important. Vanessa should see it too."

"Show me what?" I asked.

"You'll see," he told me. "We just need to run by my house. It won't take ten minutes."

At the top of the hill, the trees opened into a giant clearing where most of the original college buildings stood. They were ancient structures with frowning, unperturbed gargoyles who had seen it all (a civil war, two world wars, and now a zombie uprising). When we emerged from the trees, the helicopters circling overhead came into view. There were three of them. One was huge—a military transport, big enough to carry trucks—with two enormous blades. The others were smaller. Escorts, but well armed by the looks of it.

As we assembled and pointed, they hovered tentatively.

"Stay where you are," I said to the group, and made a little "stay" motion with my hand. Then I walked forward into the empty vibrating grass, separating myself from the group. I took off my hat, held it up, and pointed at it.

For a moment, this changed nothing. (I wondered if I should give the finger again, as I had before. *That* had certainly elicited a reaction.) But then the largest helicopter began a gradual descent, carefully landing its enormous bulk between an administrative building and the college library.

Even when the enormous craft was settled on the ground, the giant blades continued to rotate. The sound was deafening. A metal door in the helicopter's side lowered on hydraulics, and soldiers with machine guns began to emerge.

I put my hat back on, and walked over to Sam.

"Give me a gun," I told him.

"What?" he said.

"Give me a gun," I repeated.

Sam obeyed, handing me an automatic pistol.

"Good," I told him. "The rest of you should probably drop your weapons. We want to look friendly, right?"

There was general agreement, and a casting aside of firearms took place.

"Why are *you* hanging on to a gun?" Sam asked.

"I expect this might require a little negotiation," I told him, and set off toward the soldiers emerging from the craft.

The soldiers, twenty or so, stayed close to the helicopter and held their weapons at the ready. I approached them slowly, with the pistol in my left hand, pointed down at the grass.

"Who do I—" I tried to say, but it was obvious that I would not be heard above the helicopter's enormous rotors.

With my free hand, I pointed to both of the giant blades, and made a slitting-my-throat gesture.

The soldiers just looked at me.

I crossed my arms like I was pissed off, and we just stood there.

After a few moments, one of the soldiers began signaling to the others in a complicated series of hand gestures. The final gesture was a point in my direction. Half of the soldiers sprang up and began approaching me, guns raised. One of them carried a giant net with heavy metal balls connected to it.

As the men drew close, I put up my right hand to say "stop," and with my left raised the automatic pistol to my temple. The soldiers continued to advance, but looked at one another.

To show them I was serious, I put the gun barrel in my mouth, cocked the trigger, and slowly fell to my knees.

The soldier in front lifted his right arm as if hailing me. The soldiers behind him stopped. I stared the lead soldier hard in the face. Then I pointed once again to each of the helicopter rotors.

He studied me cautiously.

I shrugged.

Regarding me warily—never taking his eyes from mine—the soldier reached into his helmet and pulled out an intercom receiver. He brought it to his mouth and spoke. A few moments later, the sound of dying machinery could be heard, and the two enormous helicopter blades ground to a halt. I could once again hear myself think.

I took the gun barrel out of my mouth and slowly stood.

"Was that so hard?" I asked the lead soldier in a quiet whistle.

There was no reply. The man seemed unused to jibes. They all did. (I noted, warily, that one of them still had his throwable net at the ready.) I returned the pistol to my temple.

"Whom do I have the honor of addressing?" I asked the soldier in my zombie-rasp. "I don't need your whole military title. I'm a first-name kind of guy."

"Staff Sergeant Roger," he responded.

"Your name is Roger—or are you 'rogering' something?" I asked. "Like: 'Roger that.'"

"It's my name," he said.

I noticed, though they were small, that Roger seemed to have more stripes stitched into his shoulder than the others.

"Nice to meet you, Roger," I told him. "Let's get down to business. I'm the Kernel, and you're here to take me back 'alive.' In exchange for me, you're airlifting a group of civilians to the Green Zone in Columbus. Have I got it right so far?"

"That's correct," the soldier said. Though his demeanor was still deadly serious, I noticed a flash of wonderment in his eyes each time I spoke. This man had likely seen as many zombies as anyone, but one who could address him and hold a pistol was still a marvel, even to a hardened military man.

I remembered the helicopter stuck in the legs of the water tower in Marengo, and what he'd said about my mythic status. I wondered, based on that, if Roger had volunteered to lead this mission, or if they'd drawn lots and he'd lost.

"Roger, you're very close to completing your objective here," I told him. "There's just one problem. I want you to give these people twenty minutes to collect their things from around the college, and to make sure everyone here gets on board. I also need to go away myself for a few minutes, but I *will* be right back."

Roger opened his mouth, but nothing came out.

"Here's your problem," I told him. "I'm a zombie. I mean, I see that guy over there with the net. And you can throw it if you want to, but the moment he does, I'm pulling this trigger. And then, boom, mission failed. Am I right?"

My tone had turned flippant, and Roger did not dignify it with a response.

"You can taze me," I continued. "You can shoot me with a tranquilizer dart. You can even try tear gas. Will it work? Hell, I don't know ... We're all making this up as we go along, aren't we? But what I'm telling you is that you're twenty minutes away from completing this mission. Twenty minutes from being the guy who brought in the Kernel. But you've got to decide: Do you trust me? If you do, then we all go get our stuff and get on the helicopters and boom, we're gone. If you try anything else—and I mean *anything* else—I shoot myself through the forehead right now, and you fail. Am I making myself clear? Is there anything about this you don't understand?"

He looked at me, then looked over at his men and flashed another hand signal. The men looked at one another—as if they could not quite believe it had been the right one—and slowly lowered their weapons. Even net-guy relaxed, letting the heavy metal balls attached to the webbing *clunk* against one another on the ground.

"If you're lying—" said Roger. I didn't let him finish the sentence.

"I'm *not* lying," I told him. "Now hold your fucking horses, and we'll be right back."

Vanessa and I followed Sam across the rapidly darkening campus. Here and there, residents readied themselves for the airlift. Puckett passed us pulling an overloaded suitcase with a keyboard sticking out of it. Dr. Bowles could be seen carefully pushing a long-retired emeritus—doddering in his wheelchair—across the quad toward the waiting helicopter.

We took a dirt trail the students had forced into the expensive college landscaping and cut between two low dormitories, into the neighborhood of modest houses behind, where professors lived. We passed the familiar Wiggum Street, where my home could be found, and eased our way east through empty yards. At the end of a block, we ran into a tiny square house with a red roof. Sam's place.

Sam motioned for us to wait on the front porch, then trudged around the side of the house. We heard a sound like a lawn mower struggling to start, followed by the steady hum of a generator. I let my hand rest idly on the butt of the gun.

Vanessa gave me a look as if to say *What? You still don't trust him?*

I shrugged and left my hand on the gun. Moments later, Sam returned. He registered my hand on my weapon but said nothing as he brushed past us.

"C'mon," Sam said, fumbling to unlock his door. "It doesn't have much juice left."

We followed him inside. I let Vanessa go first. Sam's tiny square house was almost as cluttered as mine, and smelled just as funny.

Sam conducted us up a dingy flight of stairs covered in vomit-green carpet. At the top, we turned down a narrow, cheaply paneled hallway. It terminated in a cluttered home-office. Sam kicked away piles of papers, books, and clothes, until the three of us could stand comfortably inside.

On a desk in one corner was a laptop with a nicotine-stained keyboard. Sam turned it on, and we waited for it to boot up.

"I knew it would be a bad scene if I ever had to show this to somebody," Sam said, as he entered passwords and opened files. "But Jesus Christ, I never thought I'd have to show it to *you*."

"What do you mean?" I asked him.

"Here, just watch," Sam said. He opened a file and it spawned a media player. Sam let it load for a few seconds, then hit the play button. The dark screen came alive, and I was confronted with myself. My pre-zombie, pre-winter-in-the-woods self. My hair was combed. My clothes were not full of holes. My skin was ruddy and red, as though I'd had a few drinks. I looked drained—not in a zombie way, but in a human way. My stare was empty, as though I saw into great cosmic distances. Of all of the horrible things I'd seen since waking up as a zombie, this battered, broken version of my living self was one of the most unnerving.

"Hello," I said in the video. My voice was strong and hale compared to the creaks I managed now, but utterly bereft of emotion or inflection.

"If you're watching this," I continued, "then there's been some question about the way that I died, or who was involved. So let me ... let me use this video to set everything straight. My name is Peter Mellor. I'm a professor at Kenton College. Sam tells me this video should be automatically dated by the computer, but in case there's any question ..." The video-me reached down and held up a copy of the *Columbus Dispatch*. The front page featured the words "moving cadavers" in no less than three headlines.

"This is the last newspaper that got out this far," the video-me said. "Anyhow, I'm making this to tell you that I took my own life, and nobody else was involved. Especially not Sam Horst. I cut my own brake lines so my car would crash somewhere at the bottom of the hill at Kenton College. I did this intentionally, so I wouldn't get afraid and change my mind halfway down. I did it *all myself*. Sam showed me where the brake lines were on my car, but that was it. Sam did *nothing else*. I cut the brakes."

Next to me, Vanessa put her hand on what was left of my shoulder. I started.

"Okay," the video-me said. "That should do it, right? Pretty clear?"

The video-me looked as though he thought the matter was concluded, but the bar on the media player showed that the presentation was not yet half finished.

"You want to say anything to Vanessa?" said a voice from offstage in the video. I realized it was Sam.

The video-me looked perturbed, and narrowed his eyes at the offstage video-Sam. There was a long, silent pause.

"C'mon, what if Vanessa has to see this?" video-Sam said. "It could happen. You never know."

The video-me sighed.

"I don't know ..." I said from the screen. "I guess I should say that I'm sorry. I did it like this so my death wouldn't hurt you. So it would appear to be an accident, and you wouldn't have to know. I love you, and I don't want you to blame yourself."

"And why are you doing this?" said offscreen Sam. "Tell Vanessa—or whoever—why you're doing this."

Video-me shot the unseen assistant another annoyed glance.

"I'm doing this because I'm a weak man," video-me said flatly. "I'm doing this because I know I'm not going to be able to cope with things—with the way the world is going these days. There are these zombies, eating people, and they're just horrible. I can't imagine anything more horrible. And it looks like soon there won't be food or laws or civilization anymore, either. I know that Vanessa is going to need me to be there for her, and I know I can't be. I'm not brave. I'm weak. I'm fat and a drunk. I can hardly take care of myself, much less, you know ... other people. I'm not going to be able to function in this new world. I don't want her to have to see me not functioning. I don't want her to count on me and have me let her down."

Emotion began to creep into the voice of the video-me. The eyes gleamed with a suggestion of tears.

"There's no way I can be there for her and her kids. I was barely holding it together before, you know? Just barely. And now, with these goddamn zombies ... I can't, I can't ... I'm just not built for this." The video-me abruptly stood up and walked offscreen.

"That's enough," video-me said from somewhere. "That's all I need to say. You can turn off the camera."

Sam powered down the laptop.

"I killed myself," I said, thinking how that was probably not a sentence that got said much. By anyone. Ever.

"Bingo," Sam responded.

"Wow," I said. "I guess I owe you an apology. Thanks for making this."

"Thank yourself," he said. "It was your idea. I didn't want to do it. Seemed morbid to me. Unnecessary."

Sam turned and began gathering up a few things from around his cluttered office.

"Why didn't you just tell me?" I asked him.

"Huh?" Sam said as he stuffed a filthy overcoat into a duffel bag.

"All those times before when we were together," I said to him. "You could have just told me 'You killed yourself,' or something. Instead, you only said that *you* didn't do it."

"I liked having you back," Sam said. "I didn't want you to remember that you didn't want to live. I didn't want you to get sad again. Maybe you'd even kill yourself again—become the first zombie to commit suicide."

"Huh," I said. "Well, don't worry. I don't want to do that."

"That's good," Sam said, giving up on the overcoat and shoving in a series of sweatshirts instead.

Behind me, I heard a noise like a small animal struggling to breathe. I turned to see an overwhelmed Vanessa leaning against the doorframe. She was whimpering and looking at her shoes.

"It's okay, Vanessa," I said, moving to her. She leaned at such a precarious angle, I was afraid she might fall.

"No, it's not," she said.

"Really," I told her. "It's fine. I don't want to kill myself anymore. I'm 100 percent better."

"But the old you did ... and he *did*," she said. "And *you* aren't who you were before. That was a different man. And that man— who I loved, and who I just watched on that computer screen— killed himself. And I don't know why he couldn't talk to me instead. Why he couldn't just man up and say what he was afraid of. I mean, I *understand* that he didn't feel like he could deal with ... *things* ... But it makes me so sad that—what? He thought it would be better for me to think he'd died in a car accident? That's horrible!"

"I'm—" I started.

"Don't, Peter," Vanessa said, cutting me off. "Don't say you're the same person, because you're not. Don't say you're sorry, either, because you can't be. You're not the man I fell in love with. You're not the man who went on walks with me. You're not the man who sat and graded papers with me. He was good and sweet and I loved him, and ... he killed himself. Because he didn't feel like he could talk to me."

Vanessa's last sentence was garbled and nearly lost. She began to sob.

"I wasn't going to say that I'm that man," I told her. "But I care about you. And I *do* have some memories and feelings. And I *am* a man. Sort of."

She waved her hand dismissively.

"He's right," Sam interjected from across the room. "This Peter isn't the old Peter ... but he is *a* Peter."

"What're you talking about?" Vanessa said, overcoming her urge to sob, at least for the moment.

"Well, what if Peter—the old Peter—had just hit his head and got amnesia, like we thought had happened at first?" Sam said, now filling a second bag of clothes. "Think about it . . . Would you still love that Peter-with-amnesia? Would you love him even if he'd forgotten your first kiss, and your favorite food, and the last secret you told him? Would you still love him?"

"I guess I would," Vanessa granted.

"Seems to me this is a bit like that," Sam said, continuing to stuff. "A Peter who lost his memory would be essentially the same man inside. And I think *this* Peter has tried to show you who he really is. He's risked himself to save you—and your kids and other people—several times. Hell, he's thrown his 'life' away to do it. He even tried to save *me*, and he thought I'd killed him.

"He's also fought the inclination to eat people—which, from what I understand, feels really fucking good. So . . . I dunno, Vanessa . . . You can stand there and say it's not the same man, and you'll be right on some level. But as for me, I prefer to concentrate on the part of Peter that's the same between this one and the old one. The part that's still here now."

I was beginning to feel more like a ghost than a zombie. I was there, but only in a leftover sense. But maybe leftover was better than nothing.

"Okay," said Vanessa, to Sam and then to me. "Okay."

"What?" I asked.

"I said, okay," she clarified.

"Okay?" I asked back. "Just like that?"

"Yeah," she said. "Just like that."

"I mean, I know I'm not the same man, even though I have some of his memories," I said in a raspy rush of words. "And I can't do some of the things he could. My dick doesn't work, for one. But I have good feelings for you, Vanessa. You know, maybe this time around, we're just friends. But what the fuck, right? That could be cool."

"Shhh," she said, putting up two fingers to stop my anatomy-chart lips. "That's fine. I'll take it, you know? I'll take you. Like this. The way you are. I'll take it."

"Oh," I said. "Good."

"If it's all settled then," Sam said, his packing, apparently, concluded, "I think we've got a helicopter to catch."

And he was right.

We did.

I held Vanessa's hand for most of the ride, but I also looked out the window.

The helicopter went up and up, and Knox County spread out below us and got smaller and smaller.

I thought about how all of it was there, right beneath us. Kenton College. The tiny towns. The zombies. The black turkey. The gangsters. The murder. The dead bodies. The death.

A few minutes into the ride, the sun dropped off the horizon completely. The sky went dark, and the ground—so very far beneath us—went even darker.

In such blackness, even the smallest lights stood out starkly, like stars in the night sky.

Epilogue
(Rest)

So.

That's the way it happened, more or less. Raises more questions than it answers, if you ask me. But who knows? Maybe you eggheads will be able to make sense of it. I hope something somewhere in there was useful.

You gentlemen have been great, by the way.

These tests have been more than reasonable. A few of them have even been fun. And my accommodations are certainly adequate—if perhaps a bit confining. But then, we're all doing the best we can with what resources we have, aren't we? And I *do* thank you for passing all my correspondence on to Vanessa and Sam. I hope I'll be able to see them again soon . . .

What do *I* think? Fuck, I don't know . . . Random chance sounds good. Like Sam said about the one person in one hundred thousand who gets HIV but doesn't *really* get HIV. It could all just be some statistical fluke. I was in the wrong place at the wrong time, so now I'm that one zombie who's just a little different from all the others.

I'll be honest with you, though. Sometimes I wonder if it's because I killed myself that I don't get to die. Seriously—like there's some sort of poetic justice to it. By killing myself, I hurt all these people—Vanessa, Sam, and I'm sure there are others—but by taking a coward's way out, I wasn't gonna be around to see the consequences of my actions.

Except I *was*.

So I dunno. Yeah. Sometimes I think about that. God or the Universe or whatever decided to use this zombie outbreak as an opportunity to show me what an absolute fuck I'd been. To really drive it home. Maybe to punish me for it, too. I don't know.

That's not much of a "science answer," though. Judging by your lab coats and all this equipment, I'm guessing you guys aren't here to listen to me wax theological.

Well . . . probably you aren't.

It's a . . .

Excuse me.

It's a funny thing . . . I walked around Knox County for months—day and night—and never needed to rest at all, except maybe to clear my head when I felt emotional. But all of this talking is suddenly making me tired. It's the darnedest thing. I'm really getting snoozy here.

First time I can remember feeling this way since I woke up there on the side of the road by Gant.

My head feels, like, thick, you know? It's really hard to focus.

"Talking tires out zombies." Write *that* down. There's your first science discovery.

Seriously though, can we have a break for just a little bit? Take five, or something?

I'd really appreciate it.

You just keep doing what you're doing, okay?

Great.

Just give me a second or two.

I'm going to lie back down.